FREE FALLING

"Helen, your harness is broken. We're dropping like lead weights," Rafe roared.

Eyes widening with alarm, she looked at her torn shoulder straps and reacted instinctively. Wrapping her legs around his waist and her arms around his shoulders, she buried her face in his neck.

He arranged Helen's body so the vee of her legs pressed flush against his arousal.

She bit his ear, hissing, "Don't even think of it."

He chuckled and countered by nipping at her neck. "Is this as good for you as it is for me?"

"Shut up!"

"I love it when you talk rough to me, baby."

"Aaaargh! You're going to kill us. Concentrate on what you're doing."

"If I concentrate any more, we're going to have space sex."

DESPERADO

SANDRA HILL

LOVE SPELL   NEW YORK CITY

LOVE SPELL®

November 2006

Published by

Dorchester Publishing Co., Inc.
200 Madison Avenue
New York, NY 10016

ISBN 0-505-52182-2

The name "Love Spell" and its logo are trademarks of Dorchester Publishing Co., Inc.

Printed in the United States of America.

Visit us on the web at www.dorchesterpub.com.

To my cousin, Robert Kobularcik, one of the most avid supporters of my books. As an unpublished writer, I confessed to him one day that I was writing romance novels. He hugged me with excitement and said, "I'm going to say a prayer for you tonight." The next week I sold my first novel.

To all men who aren't afraid to read women's fiction. They are the real romance heroes.

And a special thank you for the help from writers Kathleen Morgan and Lynn Raye Harris, as well as my good friend Bruce Heim, a handsome West Pointer and ex–Airborne Ranger, who served with the 101st in Vietnam.

Chapter One

"Hut, two, three, four . . . hut, two, three, four . . ."

Rafael Santiago peered up over the rim of his dark aviator sunglasses, watching the young trainees who marched like blooming idiots across the blistering tarmac in front of him.

"Eenie, meenie, minie, moe," their platoon sergeant called out in a raspy, Clint Eastwood–style voice.

Like robots, the soldiers echoed their leader's singsong "jody call" in time to their pounding footsteps.

"Catch a virgin by the toe . . ."

Oh, great! It's 1996, and I've landed in boot camp from hell—with a bunch of grunts calling out raunchy marching cadences.

Rafe put a hand to his throbbing head and wished he could be anywhere but in the middle of the California desert, on a hot August morning. *Hell, I think my hair's startin' to singe.*

"If she hollers, let her go . . ."

Geez! I'm thirty-four years old. I have a law degree. I should be soaking in a gold-plated Jacuzzi, instead of serving in the damn loony bin National Guards. I'm gonna kill Lorenzo for screwing around with my calendar.

"On the other hand . . . hell, no!"

Rafe's eyes widened with disbelief. He would have thought "Grody Jodies" went out with the Anita Hill hearings. *Didn't you military fruitcakes learn anything from Tailhook?* he thought with a rueful shake of his head. *Some feminist is gonna slap a sexual harassment suit on you*

7

quicker'n a hometown hooker's five-dollar trick.

But that was their problem, not his. Rafe had enough of his own. It was bad enough that he'd been forced to serve in the Guard these past twelve years to pay back college loans and to earn extra cash for bills. If he didn't get back to his law practice, his scatterbrained legal assistant, Lorenzo Duran, would have him representing every deadbeat on the West Coast, and he'd be even deeper in debt—if that was possible.

Rafe threw the backpack holding his gear over his shoulder and made his way across the airfield toward the C-141 Starlifter. The piercing sun beat down so unremittingly that even his toenails felt like they were sweating.

He'd arrived two days ago for the usual orientation in the special forces unit, but he still had twelve more agonizing days to go. He wondered idly if he'd survive. Or die of boredom.

Then he saw the tall redhead standing at the foot of the ramp to the training jet, her straight-as-an-arrow, slim body encased in puke camouflage—the standard green, brown, tan, and black BDU, or battle dress uniform—just like his. The female officer was checking off the soldiers' names on a clipboard as they boarded. She must be the replacement for Colonel Barrow, who'd suffered a heart attack the day before.

He recognized her immediately.

"Prissy" Prescott? My commanding officer for this ludicrous two-week military trek is Helen "Prissy" Prescott?

In that moment, Rafe knew his bad day was about to get worse.

As the woman turned her ramrod-stiff body toward the chanting soldiers, a sudden backdraft clearly outlined her curvy hips and long legs in their Army regulation pants, also camouflage chic. A few wisps of flaming hair escaped the tight bun anchored at the base of her neck like a badge of her no-nonsense personality. Then the dull gold of the oak leaf cluster embroidered on her collar caught his eye.

Gold oak leaf? A major? She must have spent the past

twelve years since their college graduation in the service—
a lifer. She clasped the clipboard against her body when
there was a lull in the embarking soldiers. Rafe's eyes
shifted lower to her chest. *And a very nice chest, it is, too,*
Rafe thought, glancing appreciatively at the full breasts
straining against the blouse—identical to his own shirt, but
immensely different.

Then he shook his head in self-disgust. *The sun must be
melting my brains if I'm getting turned on by Prissy Prescott.*

Major Prescott, he corrected himself as she narrowed her
glittering eyes at the sergeant who was calling out the offensive lyrics. Apparently, the slightly overweight, ruddy-
faced senior enlisted man didn't have the brains God gave
a Mexican goose. Failing to notice Helen, or being incredibly stupid, he chose to ignore her as he began to sing out
a new chant, "I don't know but I been told . . ."

The recruits repeated his words in loud rhythm. There
were no women in the company.

"Air Force babes are bought and sold."

Oh, boy. Rafe could hear Helen's gasp of outrage from
twenty feet away. He folded his arms across his chest, waiting for the inevitable fireworks. Helen Prescott hadn't been
nicknamed "Give 'Em Hell Helen" for nothing. And he
would bet his left nut that she hadn't changed much over
the years.

"I don't know but it's been said . . ."

Helen tucked the clipboard under her arm and straightened her shoulders, which only served to emphasize her
"endowments," Rafe thought idly, knowing full well how
she would hate that he had noticed. Then she stomped fu-
riously toward the group of soldiers who were marching in
place near the edge of the field. She even stomped rather
nicely, Rafe noted, her buttocks bouncing the slightest bit.

"Navy babes are wicked in bed."

Rafe turned his attention away from Helen and back to
the witless wonder. *Boy, could I recommend a good lawyer
for this schmuck. He's gonna need one, and soon.*

9

But the brain-dead sergeant had his back to Helen, who was about to tap him on the shoulder. Totally unaware that he was cutting his own throat, he sang out, "All I know is what I hear . . ."

Before the fool could open his mouth again, Helen finished for him in a clear, disciplined, carrying voice, "Court martials are somethin' to fear."

Rafe smiled. *Way to go, Prissy!*

The sergeant spun on his heels and his jaw dropped open in surprise. "Major Prescott, I didn't see you." He snapped a quick salute.

"Apparently." Helen returned the salute.

"I didn't know . . . Hell, I didn't know there were any women. I mean . . ." the flustered sergeant stuttered.

"AT-TEN-TION!" she yelled, real loud. Rafe was pretty sure they heard her five miles away.

Snapping leather, the flustered sergeant—who should have been the one to call "Attention" immediately—and his company obeyed without question. They stood rigid as boards, waiting for her next directive.

"The Army does not tolerate sexism, soldier," she barked at the red-faced NCO, "whether women are present or not."

"Yes, ma'am," the sergeant ground out.

"If you value those stripes, soldier, I would suggest you start singing a different tune."

"Yes, ma'am!"

She stared at him and his company for several long, drawn-out seconds, as if trying to decide what punishment to mete out. "Continue as you were," she ordered finally, granting a reprieve.

The sergeant let out a long breath of relief. Then he saluted, waited for her return salute, did a jerky about-face, and ordered his troop to march back toward the barracks. This time, there were no chants, just the sharp click of boot heels.

After they left, Rafe watched, transfixed, as Helen inhaled and exhaled several times, deeply, as if to collect herself. For one brief second, her shoulders slumped, and Rafe knew somehow that Helen hated her job. Then she raised her face to the sunlight, eyes closed, uncaring that she might add a few more freckles to those that dotted her straight nose and clear complexion.

Rafe felt a deep pulling sensation in his chest. He had forgotten how attractive Helen was—not beautiful, but compelling. He hated himself for remembering those painful college days they had shared. He hated feeling like a horny kid again, tripping over his too-big feet the first time an Anglo girl looked his way. Most of all, he hated the memory of his yearning for a young woman who had always been beyond the reach of the token Hispanic at an all-white, private military school.

Abruptly, Helen turned back toward the plane, breaking his unwelcome reverie. She walked with brisk, efficient steps. Totally in control now, her face was a mask of military resolve.

Rafe waited for Helen to recognize him as she approached, but she just cast him an assessing glance as she passed by, clearly finding him of no importance.

That irritated the hell out of him.

He'd spent his entire life fighting condescension and outright bias toward Mexican-American "greasers." He should be used to it by now. Not that there had been anything smacking of prejudice in Helen's dismissing glance. Actually, she'd treated him as if he didn't even exist. Somehow that was even worse.

Well, he'd show her.

She was already climbing the ramp to the aircraft by the time he caught up with her. With perfect timing, he waited until her hips were smack dab in front of his forehead, then asked in a silky smooth voice, low enough so the soldiers standing around couldn't overhear, "So, *Major* Prescott, do you still have your tattoo?"

Tattoo? Helen stopped halfway up the plane's ramp and cringed, clutching the rail tensely. No one had men-

11

tioned her tattoo in twelve years, ever since she graduated from Stonewall Military College. And that voice—oh, Lord—only one man in the world spoke with that sexy, Mexican-American twang.

Slowly, reluctantly, Helen turned and peered back over her shoulder. All she saw was a head of thick black hair and a pair of aviator sunglasses staring boldly, eye level, at her butt.

Aaaarrrgh! she groaned silently and fought for her usual calm composure. Then she pivoted and backtracked down the ramp. At thirty-four, Helen was rather sensitive about her hips and rear end, and the aerobics war to keep them from blossoming into Rubenesque proportions. No way was she going to wave them in the face of the lascivious, arrogant, bad-mouthed man who had been the torment of her life for four long undergraduate years at Stonewall.

"*Captain* Santiago," she snapped, noting the two black bars on his collar, "your remarks are ill-timed and inappropriate under any circumstances, but very, very foolish when addressed to a superior." She put a check mark after his name on the clipboard. "A warning," she explained sternly, raising her eyes.

Even though she was five-foot-eight, Helen had to look up at the lean, well-muscled soldier who grinned lazily back at her, not a bit intimidated by the threat in her voice or the note she had made on her clipboard. She couldn't make out the expression in his eyes behind the dark shades, but she could see the path they made as they appraised her from head to toe. And probably found her wanting, as he always had in the past.

Then, as if reading her mind, Rafe removed the glasses, and Helen almost staggered under the burning gaze of his pale, luminous blue eyes. Rafael Santiago threw off heat like a sexual inferno. If anything, his well-toned, dark-skinned body had improved with age. *Darn it!*

"So, Prissy, you didn't answer me. Do you still have the tattoo?"

Without thinking, Helen's palm shot to her right buttock

in horror. She could have kicked herself for the betraying action and the blush she could feel creeping up from her neck. She never blushed, or, at least, she hadn't in twelve long years. Time melted away suddenly, and Helen felt as if she were a gangly young girl again, flustered by the attention of a too-handsome, too-brash Mexican-American cadet.

She'd had a fierce crush on him all through college, although she'd made sure he never suspected. He'd dated flamboyant, easy women, and she'd been neither of those. The worst part was that, at eighteen, he'd turned her brain to mush. Now, two minutes in his company, and he was doing it again.

Helen knew by Rafe's raised right eyebrow that her embarrassment amused him, that needling her had been his goal. *Prissy! He has the nerve to call me Prissy! The man has not changed at all.* "My name is *Major* Prescott," she reminded him, "not that ridiculous . . . nickname."

The rat just smiled, displaying a disgusting set of white teeth, dazzling against the contrast of his dark Hispanic skin.

"So, *Major* Prescott, don't you want to know if I still have *my* matching tattoo?" he drawled with feigned innocence and planted a long-fingered, deeply tanned hand on his back pocket, and left it there, in challenge.

Helen had always intended to have the horrible butterfly removed from her buttock, but, in the end, she'd left it as a reminder of her one careless lapse in self-control. She looked up and glared at Rafe. The tattoo had been all his fault. They'd been seniors at Stonewall, and a group had gone to Tijuana at the end of finals week of their senior year. When a dozen of them, under the pressure of too little freedom and too many margaritas, had decided to get matching tattoos, Rafe had taunted and taunted her, in his usual fashion, until she'd agreed to join the crowd . . . to her everlasting humiliation.

She noticed the growing line of trainees and other personnel waiting to board the aircraft, behind Rafe, all of them listening with avid interest. What was wrong with her, allowing one of her men to carry on a personal conversation with her while on duty? It was strictly against the rules. And, if nothing else, Helen prided herself on attention to precise military protocol.

Bracing her shoulders, Helen belted out in her most authoritative voice, "Captain Santiago, get on this aircraft. *NOW!* There are a dozen paratroopers sitting up there in that sweltering tin can waiting for this parachute exercise to begin." Then she added in an icy undertone, "I don't know what you're doing here, Captain Santiago, but you can be sure you will be out of my company by the end of this day."

"National Guard, Special Forces," he answered flatly, walking by her to climb the steps. She forced herself not to move back, afraid he might accidentally, or not so accidentally, brush against her. He didn't, but his eyes twinkled knowingly as he explained, "I owed Uncle Sam a pigload of cash for seven years of college loans, and he decided the 'Nasty Guard' would be a good method of payback. Plus, I always need extra cash. This is my last tour of duty, but if you know a way to get me out now, I'd be eternally grateful."

"Why am I not surprised?" she muttered under her breath, knowing he'd never felt the loyalty to the military establishment that she had.

"I never took you for a 'Nasty Girl' type, though," he added, referring to the crude name given to women of the National Guard.

She arched a brow questioningly, which she regretted immediately when he responded, "Too much starch in your drawers."

Helen clenched her fists at her sides and counted to ten. "That's it, Captain. This goes on your permanent record." She made another check mark next to his name and was about to reprimand him further, but the smirk on his face stopped her cold. Just like in the old days, he was goading her into losing her temper. This time she disappointed him by turning away.

Then she had no more time to think about the jerk as she supervised the loading of the aircraft, trying to ignore the many eyes that seemed to rivet questioningly on her behind.

Oh, Lord. Helen just knew this was going to be the longest day of her life.

An hour later, the plane was airborne. Helen had given her unit—ten men and two women—instructions for their upcoming drop near the California/Nevada border, then checked all their equipment and jump gear. The soldiers appeared relaxed as they chatted softly among themselves, seated on the platform benches that lined both sides of the huge aircraft, but Helen knew they were pumped up with excitement. Regardless of all the precautions, there was always an element of danger, the possibility of injury or death, in any skydiving event.

Despite their usual full-time civilian status, all were experienced paratroopers who made at least one drop each quarter in order to stay on jump status and earn their incentive pay. Half of the soldiers were here today serving their annual two-week National Guard duty—so-called "Weekend Warriors"—but the others were making "pay drops."

Those in the special forces were hand-chosen for their particular expertise; they were doctors, lawyers, language or communications experts. Often they were used to help train troops in underdeveloped countries.

Even though he said he was in the National Guard, Helen figured Rafe was probably just a pay dropper the rest of the time—one of those occasional skydivers who made practice drops for the military to keep their skills up to date, for a fee. She instantly chastised herself for her lack of charity. Doing pay drops was not dishonorable—for the most part. Many of the men and women who did pay drops in the off-seasons were the same men and women called up to fight forest fires and other natural disasters. The backbone of the peacetime defense forces, they even went into emergency military action when necessary.

Helen looked over at Rafe sitting at the end of the bench on one side, near the tail. He sat several seat lengths apart from the others, further separated by a slight abutment—a loner, as he'd always been. His head rested back against the fuselage, his eyes were closed, and his skin was a mite greenish.

Tucking her clipboard under her arm, she maneuvered her way down the aisle and leaned over him. "Are you sick, soldier?"

His eyes opened lazily. "Why? Are you gonna rub my tummy?"

Helen recoiled, then made another mark after his name on the clipboard. "You're already in serious trouble, Captain. The next step is the stockade."

"Is it air-conditioned?"

She gritted her teeth. "Your conduct is arrogant and insubordinate. I've tolerated more than I should for old times' sake. Don't push me any further."

"Listen, Helen. I'm in a bad mood and I'm taking it out on you. Maybe we'd better not talk anymore."

The plane hit an air pocket and she swayed with the turbulence.

"Buckle your seat belts, ladies and gentlemen," the pilot droned over the loud speaker. "We've hit a temporary rough spot."

Reluctantly, Helen sank down on the seat next to Rafe and buckled up. He grinned at her like a mischievous child.

She made a clucking noise that sounded prissy even to her. "You haven't changed one bit."

"Neither have you." He smiled wickedly, his eyes making a bold assessment of her body.

"How so?" she asked, against her better judgment.

"You're as prissy as ever."

Seeing the look of consternation on her face, he leaned over and took the pen out of her hand, making a mark next to his name. "Just saving you the bother, babe," he explained.

Babe! She was about to rebuke him for addressing a superior officer in such an intimate manner when he made her protest impossible by asking, "Should you be talking to a lowly soldier like me? Isn't it against the rules or something?" He put special emphasis on the word "rules" as if they were something loathsome. As if he didn't know exactly what the rules said.

When Helen realized she'd played right into his hands, *again,* she forced herself to relax, to cut him a little slack. Rafe had always put her on the defensive, caused her to overreact, made her feel guilty for—well, practically everything—from the way she dressed to the patriotic values she revered.

"I asked you a question, Captain Santiago. Are you ill?"

"Do I look ill?"

"Yes."

"If I'm ill, do I get to go back to L.A.?"

"No."

He shrugged. "Then I'm not ill. Just a little hung over."

"Always looking for the easy way out, aren't you? Let me give you a little bit of advice, as an old friend."

He raised an eyebrow at her use of the word "friend," but she continued doggedly, "You're the same as you were back at Stonewall, and that kind of insolence won't cut it in today's Army."

Now it was Rafe's turn to stiffen. "Lady, you didn't know me then, and you don't know me now."

Helen felt her face flush with embarrassment. "You're right." But she couldn't allow his familiarity to go on. "Just don't call me those . . . names. I'm your commanding officer, in case you've forgotten."

His lips twitched with amusement. "Should I salute?"

"That would be a start."

"Whatever melts your butter." He sat up straight and gave her a short, smart salute.

"Well, that's more like it."

Sandra Hill

Then he ruined the effect by winking.

She ignored his wink, although it did strange things to the pattern of her breathing. Helen decided to change the subject, to start over on a fresh note. After all, she was the leader of this operation. Surely she could carry on a civil conversation with one of her men. "What have you been doing for the past twelve years?"

He hesitated. "Are we talking major and captain here? Or Helen and Rafe?"

With a quick glance, she saw that they were screened somewhat from the other soldiers by the protruding abutment. She studied him for a long moment. "Two old acquaintances," she conceded.

"I'm a lawyer."

"Oh, that's right. I remember reading something in the newspapers. 'Hotshot L.A. Lawyer Hired by Movie Mogul' or some such thing." Her voice carried a slight tone of contempt.

"You got it, sweetheart. That's me. Hotshot L.A. lawyer." He studied his fingernails casually, but Helen could tell that his teeth were gritted.

A woman sitting on the other side of Rafe, several seats away, leaned forward, craning her neck to watch them with interest. In truth, it was Rafe she was ogling like a delicious dessert. Heck, who wouldn't? He was a drop-dead gorgeous hunk. And, much as Helen disliked his values and lifestyle, in all honesty, she couldn't deny her attraction to him, as well. Even after all these years.

Meanwhile, his insolent eyes, fringed with lashes thick as black feather dusters, were visually caressing some intimate parts of her body. Trying to ignore the butterflies in her stomach, Helen hissed, "Stop looking at me like that. It smacks of sexual harassment."

"No, no, no! If there's one thing I know, it's the law. Sexual harassment is when I'm the ranking officer and I'm forcing my attentions on helpless little you. I'm just a *helpless* man here, admiring a good-looking woman who happens to be wearing a uniform. Don't read anything threatening into that. And, besides, you agreed this was a civilian conversation.''

"I didn't say I feel threatened,'' she said, pursing her lips with disgust, "but your insolence is intolerable under any circumstances, military or otherwise. And tasteless.''

"Stop acting like you're sucking a lemon all the time.''

Helen had to clench her fists tightly to keep from slapping the teasing smile off his handsome face. "You are truly the crudest, most arrogant man I've ever met.''

"Yep, that's me. Crude, arrogant, hotshot lawyer.'' He didn't look at all upset that Helen had such a low opinion of him.

"Well, at least, you achieved your goal, Mr. Hotshot Legal Eagle. All you ever wanted was to make a ton of money.''

"Right.'' His eyes flashed angrily as if he was about to argue with her. But then he deliberately banked their blue fires with a mask of unconcern. "Not everyone gets to be born with a silver spoon in his mouth, *like you.*''

Rafe's gaze riveted on the gold oak leaf cluster on her collar. Before Helen realized what he was about, he flicked one of them with the tips of his fingers, grazing her neck. Fortunately, they were screened from the other soldiers, because Helen felt branded by even that mere touch. His eyes held hers for a moment, hot and smoldering, and an unfamiliar heaviness pulled sensuously at her limbs.

She was going to have Rafe removed from her company the minute they hit the ground. She would never survive two weeks of close company with this prime example of walking testosterone.

"I see you went into the career military, like your daddy wanted you to,'' he said suddenly, jarring her back to harsh reality. "I thought you wanted to be an artist. Ah, well, Daddy's girl all the way, huh?''

"What's that supposed to mean?''

"It means, Prissy, that you still haven't learned to stand on your own two feet. You do what Daddy tells you to.''

"How do you know the military isn't what I want?''

He shrugged as if the conversation bored him suddenly. Then he noticed the ring on her left hand. Before she had a chance to protest, he took her hand in both of his and traced the large diamond with one forefinger. Alarmed at her racing pulse, she looked up guiltily to see if anyone was watching, but Rafe's back and the abutment still ensured their privacy.

"So, who's the lucky guy?" There was an odd note in his voice, almost like regret, which puzzled Helen. She decided it was probably sarcasm.

"Elliott Peterson. Colonel Elliott Peterson."

"Colonel. That figures."

Helen tried to pull away, but he turned her hand over and began to trace enticing little circles in the palm, holding her eyes the entire time. Helen yearned to close her eyes and yield to the sweet thrumming sensations spiraling from the sensitive skin of her hand to all the important nerve centers in her dormant body. At first, she didn't realize he was still talking to her. "What?"

"How long have you been engaged?"

"Three years."

His eyes widened, and he made a low snickering sound, shaking his head from side to side. "That figures, too."

Helen hated the way Rafe made her feel, all jumpy and achy inside. He always had. And he probably knew it. She yanked her hand out of his.

He laughed huskily.

"We haven't been able to coordinate our schedules," she said defensively.

He snorted rudely with disbelief. "So, do you and the colonel salute each other before you hit the sack? Hey, I'll bet you work hot sex around a schedule, don't you?"

Hot sex?

He hooted gleefully, slapping one hand on his knee. "Oh, Prissy, you are so transparent. You haven't the faintest idea what I mean by hot sex, do you?"

"Now I remember why I always hated you." She made another note on her clipboard. "You know that I can make the next two weeks very miserable for you, don't you?''

"I'm already miserable," he pointed out, continuing as if she hadn't even spoken. "I can just picture you and Colonel Sanders—"

"It's Colonel Peterson."

He waved his hand dismissively and went on. "Your tight-assed military dude probably says, 'Can I' and 'May I' and 'Please.' Probably pats you on the rump afterward for a job well done. And then falls dead asleep before he can do you again."

Do me? Helen bit her bottom lip to keep her jaw from dropping open. "There's nothing wrong with politeness."

"Hah!" Rafe chuckled softly as if suddenly enlightened. "I'll bet you even take that damn clipboard to bed with you."

She forced herself not to make another mark on the clipboard, knowing that was what he expected. "You're as bad as that sergeant who was yelling those gross jody calls earlier."

His head snapped back as if she'd slapped him. "I'm not like that jerk, Prissy. He was being a vulgar, sexist slob. I like women and I love sex. That's a natural part of life. And sometimes it's even crude. So what? Why don't you loosen up a little and live?"

Rafe's all-too-accurate assessment of her life cut deeply, but Helen would never admit that. She should get up and walk away before her carefully regulated emotions were exposed for a sham. She should never have stayed to talk with him. She should forget the ways in which his words had wounded her more than a dozen years ago, and still did today. But she stayed, yearning for answers. "Why do you always criticize me, Rafe? For four years at Stonewall, you made my life a nightmare. You—"

"I made your life a nightmare?" He cocked his head in surprise.

"Of course, you did. All that teasing—my old-fashioned values were out-of-date . . . the rules I followed were silly . . . I was Daddy's girl . . . my appearance was prudish and drab. Did you enjoy putting me down? I never did anything to hurt you.''

"Helen, Helen, Helen. I thought you were smarter than that.'' He made a clucking sound as if she were incredibly dense. "Talk about nightmares! Sweetheart, you made my heart skip a beat the first time I saw you at freshman registration. You were wearing a yellow sundress with tiny straps.'' He drew two lines from his shoulders to his chest to demonstrate. "Your hair was pulled back on each side with gold barrettes. And your perfume smelled flowery, like . . .'' His words trailed off as he realized how much he'd revealed with his words.

"You're making this up. I know you are.''

"Hah! Know this, babe—you were the center of every wet dream I had for four long years at Stonewall. And there were a lot of them.''

"How dare you! See what I mean about your vulgarity? Military insubordination aside, men don't say that to women they respect.''

"Maybe you've been running with the wrong men.'' He put a hand on her arm to stop her from releasing her seat belt and getting up, as she intended. In a softer tone, he added, "I did make fun of you a lot, Prissy. But it was because I wanted you so damn much. I thought you knew that.''

Her mouth parted on an exhale of amazement—not that she really believed him. He'd probably learned all his smooth lines in "Hotshot Lawyer 101.'' And the crude ones in "Sleazy Lawyer 102.''

"Didn't you ever wonder why I followed you around all the time?'' he persisted.

Helen was too dumbstruck to answer at first. It was true. He had seemed to be practically everywhere she was during their four years at Stonewall. "But you never asked me out.''

"Would you have gone?''

Her silence spoke volumes, and he waved his hand in a curt "So there!'' manner. Rafe's gaze held hers then, in challenge, and Helen detested the way he made her squirm.

Later, she would think about all he had said, but for now she sought desperately for some other subject, some way to rein in her roiling emotions and get back into her stoic military frame of mind. "I assume you're ready for this jump, Rafe. You have been keeping up on your skydiving practice, haven't you?"

He nodded, the twitch of mirth on his beautiful lips telling her he wasn't fooled by her change of subject.

"Did you serve in Desert Storm?"

"Nope. Got an emergency deferment."

Her upper lip curled with distaste.

"I did serve in the L.A. riots, though. Even though that's not normal special forces duty."

"What? Stealing televisions?" She rued her words at once, even before his eyes shot blue sparks at her.

"I shouldn't have said that. I'm sorry."

"I'm used to it. Once a greaser, always a greaser, right? A wetback in a suit is still a wetback." He looked away, dismissing her, but Helen saw the hurt in his revealing eyes.

"Rafe, I *am* sorry. I was reacting to you, not your heritage."

"Well, that makes me feel much better."

"You bring out the worst in me."

"Keep talking. You might draw blood soon."

She groaned. "I apologized. What more do you want from me?"

"Not a damn thing."

Intensely humiliated, Helen shifted and unhooked her seat belt. She was about to stand and walk away.

"Wait," Rafe said, halting her. He leaned so close that she could feel his warm breath against her neck. His gruff voice promised revenge for her insult. "I lied. I do want something from you," he whispered near her exposed ear. "If I had my way, we would go behind that curtain there and engage in a world-class wall-banger. I'd wrap your legs around my waist and bury myself inside you. And I'd be kissing you the entire time to muffle your screams. Be-

23

cause, believe me, babe, you would definitely scream.''

Stunned, Helen just gaped at him.

''Don't forget your clipboard,'' he reminded her with an infuriating grin.

She growled and came very, very close to bopping him with a left hook. And she could do it, too. Instead, she did what she should have done fifteen minutes earlier. She stood, her back rigid and her face scarlet with mortification, and walked away from the insufferable slimeball.

But the images he had painted in her mind lingered, just as he'd intended.

She should have been livid. She should have been offended.

Instead, she was tempted.

Chapter Two

Rafe watched stonily as one after another of the soldiers completed their passes out into space. Helen, the jump master, stood at the exit door, expertly overseeing the jumps. The special forces unit in the guard were among the few servicemen permitted to do HALO, or high altitude–low opening, jumps.

Because of the engine and wind noise, it was almost impossible to hear a verbal command. But that didn't matter because, in this type of exercise, it was the pilot who checked the wind drift and drop-zone location, and, when the time was right, the continual red light would change to green—a signal to go.

They'd already donned their nylon jumpsuits. Just before springing out into space, they hooked on their Kevlar helmets.

Helen avoided eye contact with him, and with good cause. He'd behaved like a bastard back there a little while ago. But, hell, she brought out the worst in him. He was thirty-four years old, but she made him feel all jittery and clumsy, like an adolescent with hormones oozing out his pores.

He'd reacted as he always had as a kid in the L.A. barrio—defensively. Hit before he got hit. Cut the enemy off at the knees before he cut off your balls.

But when did Helen become my enemy?

Maybe he should apologize.

Probably he wouldn't.

With a grimace, Rafe watched the female soldier in front,

an Ohio college professor and linguistics expert, listen to some final instructions from Helen, then step out into the blue sky. She drifted in a freefall for the recommended several seconds' delay before her parachute swooped open above her with a snap, changing shape like an enormous jellyfish.

The next jumper—a hotdog race car driver from Atlanta whose mechanical skills were renowned in the munitions field—gave a loud whoop before diving headfirst out into the open sky—a lumpout. Within seconds, he'd "fallen stable" into a high-speed delta position—straight legs, arms held back at an angle from the sides of the body. No flopping around for this experienced skydiver. Rafe thought he heard him yell, "Ooo-ee, baby!" as he went down.

Helen frowned with disapproval at the antics and made a mark in her logbook. The hotdog was on Helen's shit list.

It was Rafe's turn.

A familiar spiral of excitement began to unfurl in his gut, sort of like the beginning stages of sexual arousal. He'd always enjoyed the danger and exhilaration of skydiving. Did Helen feel the same? Damn, he had to stop thinking of her in that way, or these two weeks would be even more hellish than he already expected.

He approached the doorway, adjusted his harness straps, and was about to put on his helmet. Suddenly the plane pitched, hitting a particularly violent patch of turbulence. The aircraft seemed to veer slightly off course to the right, heading toward a canyon. The jump signal was now a steady red.

But then he noticed that the jerking motion of the plane had caused Helen to fall back against a sharp projection, catching her harness. When she righted herself, the back portion of her harness ripped on the cutting metal, the shoulder straps flapping in the wind. And she had veered dangerously close to the open exit.

"Helen!" he shouted in warning, even though he was only a few feet away. "Your harness!"

Her head snapped to the right to look at him, her brown

eyes wide with confusion. At the same time, he dropped his helmet and lurched forward to grab her by the waist and pull her back. Unfortunately, the plane made a sharp correction again, throwing them both off balance. And out the open doorway . . . free-falling through space. Luckily, Rafe had his arms wrapped tightly around Helen's waist.

Holy hell!

"You stupid ass! Let go of me," she shrieked, attempting to shove him away. They were falling fast. The pins flew out of the bun at her neck, and her long hair flew in his face, blinding him momentarily.

He spit out a clump of her hair that had landed in his open mouth. "Ouch!" Her knee had just hit him in the groin. "Wrap your legs around my waist," he shouted above the whooshing air and his pounding heartbeat.

"Not on your life, buster!"

They had about three minutes until landing—*if* their chutes opened properly, *if* he could hold onto Helen's squirming body, *if* he didn't have a heart attack. And he damn well couldn't waste time arguing with a stubborn, born-to-boss female.

"Helen, your harness is broken. We're dropping like lead weights," he roared. "You can't take a chance. No time."

Eyes widening with alarm, she looked at her torn shoulder straps and reacted instinctively. Wrapping her legs around his waist and her arms around his shoulders, she buried her face in his neck. Holding his breath, he arched his back and threw his arms out. Once their suspension lines were taut, the parachutes automatically unfurled above them in a cloud, slowing their descent.

Thank God!

He put his right palm under her buttocks and his left hand behind the nape of her neck, and smiled. The sexual high he always felt in skydiving blossomed into a full-blown erection. He wondered idly if a couple had ever done it while free-falling through space. Knowing some of the crazies who did skydiving stunts, he wouldn't be surprised.

He arranged Helen's body so the vee of her legs pressed flush against his arousal.

She bit his ear, hissing, "Don't even think it."

Rafe chuckled and countered by nipping her neck. "Is this as good for you as it is for me?"

"I'm going to kill you the second we hit the ground," she screeched. "I swear, if we survive this crazy maneuver of yours, you are dead meat."

Her hair was swirling around crazily like some picture he'd seen once of a Greek goddess with snakes coming out of her head. He didn't think he would share that information with her. "Now, now. It wasn't my fault, Prissy." He couldn't believe he was carrying on a conversation while he floated through the air, dovetailed to his commanding officer.

"Shut up!"

"I love it when you talk rough to me, baby."

"Aaaarrgh! You're going to kill us. Concentrate on what you're doing."

"If I concentrate any more, we're going to have space sex."

As he moved himself against her inadvertently, he heard a soft kittenish whimper deep in her throat. He would have ragged her about her involuntary reaction, but his breath was caught by a wave of desire. His hard-on felt like it could drill through concrete.

They passed the cliff on the edge of the plateau that should have been their destination. The fine hairs stood out all over his body as they swerved dangerously close to the sharp edges of rock near the outcropping. Maneuvering the cords on both chutes as he'd been trained, aided by a slight wind, he avoided disaster, and they approached the grassy canyon floor.

"Hold on tight. This is it," Rafe warned as the ground came up to meet them. He braced himself. With a loud thump, they fell to the hard earth and rolled, settling with Helen flat on her back, spread-eagled, and him on top of her, both of them covered by the parachutes.

For several long minutes, he lay, unmoving, trying to regain his breath. *Hot damn! This will be an experience to tell my grandkids about someday. Not that I ever intend to have any brats of my own, but . . . wow!* "Are you okay?" he finally asked, raising himself slightly on outstretched arms after flicking the fabric off their heads.

"No, I'm not okay, you imbecile. You are going to be court-martialed for this, soldier."

"Hey, I saved your life," he said with affront.

"Saved my life? Captain, you caused me to fall out of that freakin' airplane," she raged irrationally, her face turning a decided shade of purple.

"Tsk, tsk. Watch your language, *Major*."

"Oh . . . oh . . ." she stammered heatedly, no doubt searching for the right adjective to describe him. "You're going to be in the stockade for a year. I'm going to sue you for assault. I'm making it my personal mission to see that you pay for this debacle for the rest of your worthless life."

"Is that all?" he asked, grinning down at her. He'd just realized that a certain part of his body hadn't understood that the *uplifting* thrill of free-falling was over, and it was time for some *downlifting*.

Helen's mouth forced a delicious little "o" of surprise as she made the same discovery. Her windblown hair looked like she'd been pulled through a keyhole, backward, and freckles stood out like tobacco juice on her pale skin. But she was damned near irresistible, in Rafe's estimation.

He adjusted his hips against hers and whispered, "There's something I've always wanted to do, Helen. From the first time we met."

"That's all you ever think about," she choked out indignantly, but her thick lashes fluttered traitorously.

"Not *that*, Prissy," he said with a husky laugh, chucking her under the chin. "*This*." He lowered his face toward hers slowly, giving her the chance to protest, but hoping against hope that she wouldn't. "Just a kiss. That's all. Just one kiss."

"No," she said on a soft moan, but she was already raising her parted lips toward his.

At first, he merely brushed his lips across hers, but a spark of electricity ignited, so powerful his heart slammed against his chest walls and his skin tingled all over. "Sweet. So sweet," he murmured against her dewy lips.

Then he opened his mouth over hers. Kissing her deeply, he shifted and slanted until their lips fit together perfectly. If this was going to be the only kiss he ever got from Helen, he planned to make it memorable. A kiss for all time.

Helen knew she should push Rafe away. Kissing him was a big mistake. He was doing wicked, downright sinful things to her senses—nibbling at her bottom lip, easing his tongue into her mouth, teasing her with sensuous, mind-shattering strokes that had her yearning for more.

"Look!" a voice exclaimed. "Over there. *El hombre y la muchacha.*"

At the unexpected intrusion, Rafe tensed and stopped kissing her. They both listened alertly, unable to see anything yet.

"*Cuidado!*" another male voice cautioned, seeming to move closer, then swore, "*Ay, mierda!* I think it ees *El Ángel Bandido.*"

A chorus of muttered curses followed.

Helen started to push Rafe off her and demand an explanation, but he put a forefinger to her lips, signaling silence.

"*Sí,* you are right, Pablo. It does look like the Angel. Cover me while I move closer to check."

"*Bueno,* Ignacio. But does it not seem that *El Ángel* ees doing enough covering on his own . . . of *la señorita*? Heh, heh, heh."

Everyone chortled at the risqué joke.

"Who are they?" Helen whispered.

"I don't know. Maybe they'll go away if we ignore them," Rafe answered.

A sudden gasp echoed in the still air. "If he ees truly *El*

Ángel, do you think . . . Could this possibly be Elena?'' one of them asked.

"Elena?'' the others echoed incredulously.

"Son of a bitch! She mus' be Elena,'' one voice said.

"Do you think she's doing *el corcho tornillo* on him under that tent?'' another, younger voice asked.

"Sí," still another voice remarked hopefully. "She mus' be doing the corkscrew. Did you not hear *El Ángel* moaning and groaning with all the pleasuring she was giving him?''

"Maldito! Do you think she weel take us on next?'' the young voice squeaked out.

There was a resounding *"Sí"* from the other men.

"I ain't never had the corkscrew done on me,'' the young voice said wistfully.

"Hell, you ain't never had nothin' done on you, Pablo,'' an older voice remarked, and everyone laughed.

While this odd conversation took place in a matter of minutes, Rafe and Helen continued to lie stiffly in each other's arms, stunned by the amazing scene unfolding around them. The parachute still covered them up to their waists.

The only thing Helen could make out was that the discussion centered on some woman named Elena. She figured this Elena must be someone pretty special to evoke such awe.

Rafe slowly eased himself off her and sat up. His eyes were still misty with passion, and his lips were swollen from her kisses.

Oh, Lord.

Flicking the rest of the parachutes off their bodies, he stood in one fluid motion, pulling Helen up beside him. He proceeded to take off his cumbersome harness and jumpsuit, and she did likewise.

Three disreputable-looking men, dressed like old-time western bandits, sat on horses above them. Unshaven and filthy, the dark-skinned men raised guns from holsters at their sides, aiming them, unbelievably, at Helen and Rafe.

Helen flushed as she realized that they'd been watching

31

her writhing under Rafe's scorching kiss moments ago. But then she saw the danger of the lethal weapons staring them in the face. Relying on years of military training, Helen forced herself to calm down and assess the situation.

Okay, the make-believe bandits were clearly Mexican. Maybe they were friends of Rafe's playing a joke on him. Or her, if Rafe was in cahoots with them.

"What's up, guys? *Que es la problema?*" Rafe asked with steely calm, pushing Helen behind him protectively. "Lookin' for trouble?"

"Don't antagonize them," Helen advised, stepping around him. "Besides, I'm the officer in charge here."

He shot her a glare of utter disbelief. "Listen up, G.I. Barbie, don't tell me what to do. I've been facing these kinds of hoods all my life."

"They're not friends of yours?"

"Huh?"

Well, chalk that explanation off. Hmmm. If they're not friends of Rafe's, who could they be? Puzzled, Helen started to demand that the men lower their guns, but Rafe placed a restraining hand on her arm with gentle authority.

"I'll handle this," he whispered out of the side of his mouth in a poor Jimmy Cagney imitation.

"You will *not*," she protested. "Step back, Captain. That's an order."

He gave her a withering look and turned back to the pseudo-bandits who had gotten off their horses and were approaching, spurs jangling, guns cocked. The outlaws watched the argument between Rafe and Helen with bewilderment.

The leader, whom the men had addressed as Ignacio, wore a flat-brimmed, wide sombrero, a double-holstered gun belt at his waist, ammunition straps crisscrossed over his chest, and *calzonetas,* the fitted Mexican trousers that flared out when unbuttoned over riding boots. His sidekicks wore battered cowboy hats, woven serapes over their shoulders, gun belts, and calf-high leather boots. They were all covered with dust.

Ignacio stopped suddenly and leveled two long-barreled revolvers at them, one in each hand. His cohorts did the same with their own firearms. "Raise your hands, amigo. You, too, *señorita*."

Rafe began to step forward, snarling. "You scumballs better scram if you know what's good—"

A shot rang out, nipping the tip of Rafe's heavy leather boots. Rafe's eyes almost bugged out as he jumped back. He said a very foul word, then asked angrily, "Are you guys nuts?"

Geez! These creeps are putting on a good act, Helen thought, whoever they are.

"Raise your hands," the bandit repeated icily.

With the barrels of the pistols a mere ten feet away and the glaring ridge on the tip of Rafe's boot, they decided to comply.

"So," Ignacio gloated in a heavily accented voice, "The Angel finally gets his wings clipped." Then he frowned. "Why do you wear those strange clothes? And why ees Elena wearing men's trousers?"

Rafe and Helen glanced down, then back to the outlaws. They weren't the ones wearing odd clothing.

"And why do you and your woman dress alike?" the young man asked Rafe.

"Because we're G.I Joe and G.I Barbie, the military Bobbsey twins," Rafe growled. "Why the hell do you think we're dressed alike? A fashion statement?"

Even though he was holding a gun, the young man jerked backward at Rafe's little display of temper.

Ignacio shrugged, dismissing their garments as of little concern and moved on to more important matters. "Empty your pockets, both of you," the leader demanded, then added, "And take off the necklaces, too."

"What necklaces?" Rafe asked.

"No, no, no," Helen objected as understanding dawned. "Rules of military conduct state a soldier should never remove his dog tags."

The looney outlaw began to press both trigger fingers.

33

"Forget the friggin' military for once," Rafe exhorted, and she decided to comply.

They tossed their dog tags to the ground, along with Rafe's wallet and loose change, her packet of Kleenex, ring of keys, a Bic pen, and both of their survival vests.

Still holding one gun on them and lowering the other, Ignacio examined the loot and made grunting noises of disgust, the paper money and credit cards making absolutely no impression on him. The pen, keys, and Kleenex held no interest, either, but he handed the dog tags to his partners, who peered at them closely, tested the metal with their teeth, then put them on their own necks. Ignacio picked up the loose change, then kicked aside the wallet, which Rafe quickly pocketed.

Pablo examined Rafe's Ray-Ban's, made a disparaging remark about black spectacles, "mus' be fer blind people," and was about to throw them on the ground when Rafe cried out, "Hey, those shades cost me a hundred dollars."

"A hundred dollars?" Pablo exclaimed dubiously, but stuck them in his saddlebag, probably for some future profit.

Ignacio went to work on their survival vests. The bandits kept only the signaling mirrors, waterproof matches, compasses, and pocketknives. They scrapped the plastic-sealed food packets, unable to understand what they were or how to open them. Likewise, the items in the first-aid kits were discarded, though they kept the small containers. The trioxine fuel, water desalter, plastic spoons, insect headnets, fishing tackle, and snare wires were also kicked aside as useless. Ignacio's two pals donned the vests under their ponchos.

And finally, Pablo flipped the broken harness aside, but jammed Rafe's intact harness, along with the parachutes from the ground and the two, still-folded reserve chutes into his saddlebags. What he would do with those items, Helen had no idea.

"Thees ees all?" Ignacio questioned Rafe, motioning

with his gun barrel for him to raise his hands back up. "Where ees all the gold?"

"I don't have any gold."

"You spent it all?" Before Rafe could answer, he turned to Helen. "Give me the ring."

She followed the direction of his stare, realizing he wanted her engagement ring. She started to balk, but Rafe signaled her with a brisk shake of his head not to rile the strange "bandit."

Ignacio turned the diamond over several times, studying it. Then, apparently satisfied that the ring had some worth, he slid it halfway up his pinky finger and smiled broadly at them both. "It ees unfortunate that you carry no gold with you, but thees ees still our lucky day. You will bring us many gold coins when we collect the reward for your capture, *Señor Ángel*."

"What reward?" Rafe asked.

Ignacio's thick eyebrows rose in surprise. "You did not know? There ees a five-hundred-dollar reward for your capture—dead or alive."

"You must have me mixed up with some other guy."

"No, I would know the Angel anywhere. The most notorious desperado in all California."

"Des . . . desperado?" Rafe sputtered out, his arms still upraised.

Helen's arms began to ache from their awkward position. She just wished this stupid game, or dream, or whatever it was, would end. More than anything, she wanted to go home and soak in a hot bath and forgot she'd ever met Rafael Santiago.

Rafe took a deep breath to compose himself. "Listen, I know some people think lawyers are crooks," he said, scowling at Helen's snort of agreement, "but I'm not a bandit."

"No, no, no," Ignacio said, wagging his gun in Rafe's face. He smiled, displaying two chipped front teeth, probably from biting on bullets. "You cannot fool me. Everyone knows you been robbing banks and wealthy rancheros

35

ever since gold was discovered at Sutter's Fort two years ago.''

"Gold? Sutter's Fort? Two years ago?" Rafe looked at Helen, his brow furrowed. She shrugged, equally confused.

An odd expression swept Rafe's face then. He lowered one arm and hit the side of his head with the heel of his hand as if to clear his muddled brain. "Are you trying to say this is 1850?"

"*Sí*. Of course, amigo."

"Is this *Candid Camera*?" Rafe asked suddenly, turning to scan the trees surrounding the clearing. When Allen Funt failed to step forth, he narrowed his eyes. "Is this one of those movie sets, like a sequel to *The Three Amigos*?"

"A move-hee? What ees that?"

Rafe exhaled loudly with exasperation. "My name is Rafael Santiago. Captain Rafael Santiago. And this is Major Helen Prescott."

"Major? A woman *soldado*?" Ignacio burst out laughing and elbowed one of the other grinning bandits in the ribs. "Major? Heh heh heh! Do not try to deceive us, *señor*."

Helen lowered her hands and pointed to the oak leaf on her shoulder. "I am Major Helen Irving Prescott, and you men are under military arrest."

Ignacio made a rude kissing sound at Helen, commenting, *"Esa mujer está pendejada,"* at the same time twirling his forefinger in a circle near his head. Then he indicated with the barrel of his gun that Helen should raise her hands back up.

She decided not to argue.

"We know she ees the famous Elena," Ignacio told Rafe impatiently. "Do not think to keep her corkscrewing only to yourself."

"Corkscrewing?" Rafe and Helen asked.

Uncaring of the order to keep her arms raised, Helen lowered her hands and braced them on her hips, glaring at each of them.

"Esa senorita tiene figura de la primera," Ignacio re-

marked to Rafe. The bandit rolled his eyes, which roamed lewdly over her body.

Rafe grinned from ear to ear, then nodded in agreement.

"What did he say?" she asked.

Rafe still grinned—smirked actually. She barely resisted the temptation to whack him on the head.

"You don't want to know."

"Of course, I do."

"Helen, believe me—"

"Tell me, damn it."

Rafe breathed deeply, then told her, "Loosely translated, Ignacio said, 'That lady is built like a brick shithouse.' "

"Liar," she hissed.

"Trust me," Rafe said with a wink.

"Hah!"

"Los tetas esta que bonita," Ignacio continued, speaking to his companions while he gazed appreciatively at—oh, Lord—her breasts.

"Don't you want to know what he said now?" Rafe asked, obviously enjoying her discomfort.

"No. Yes."

Helen could see the gears grinding in Rafe's mind. But then his expression softened. "I shouldn't be teasing you like this, Prissy. You've really had enough harassment for one day, and there's nothing funny about it—whether from an Army sergeant or a bozo bandit. I've been pretty hard on you myself."

His gently spoken words touched Helen like a kiss. And she nodded her acceptance of his apology. In truth, she couldn't have spoken over the lump in her throat.

And she really didn't need Rafe to translate, anyway. One of Ignacio's sidekicks held two hands cupped in front of his chest, chortling at his leader's words.

Helen felt her face flame.

Ignacio spat out a big mouthful of Spanish words then, and Rafe answered him. Back and forth they conversed, their exchange tense. Ignacio's little band raised their guns higher.

Shaking his head incredulously, Rafe turned back to her. "You won't believe this. They think you—"

"Do not waste our time, *señor*," Ignacio interrupted him. "We know she ees Elena, your mistress. She ees famous throughout the West for her secret trick, *el corcho tornillo*. The *Americanos* call it the corkscrew. Men pay much gold for her services at Madame Rose's fancy house in Hangtown."

"Let me get this straight," Rafe said with an insufferable chuckle. "You're telling me this is 1850. You think I'm this dangerous Mexican desperado, the Angel. And you think Helen here, the prissiest prude in the West, is a prostitute with a specialty for corkscrewing? Helen the Hooker?"

"*Sí.*" They all nodded with silly smiles spreading across their filthy, whisker-stubbled faces. One of them even rubbed his groin in anticipation.

And Rafe, the brute, began to laugh uproariously.

Chapter Three

"Not on your life!" Rafe asserted as he took one gander at the two huge horses being led toward them from a string that followed behind the bandits.

"What's wrong?" Helen asked.

"I'm not in the mood for riding. I think I'll just walk."

She looked at him kind of funny, but he didn't care. One of the horses—a big black beast baring its yellow teeth—was sizing him up with eyes the size of bloodshot eggs. A regular Mr. Ed with an attitude. It was probably a stallion, he decided. Or a gelding. Oh, yeah, it must be a gelding, just waiting for some yahoo to pay for its lost manhood.

The animal threw up its head, made a loud neighing sound and stared him right in the eye as if to say, "Wait till I get you on my back, sucker."

"Uh uh," Rafe protested, starting to back away. "I don't think so." He'd been playing along with this funny business thus far, just to see how it would unfold. Time to bow out of the senseless charade now.

"Rafe, look out!" Helen shouted in warning, but it was too late. He bumped into Sancho, one of the bandits who'd snuck up behind him when his attention had shifted to the horses. "Ah ha!" Having the advantage of surprise, the short, older man wrestled Rafe to the ground, grunting and wheezing the whole time. "Stop yer damn squirmin'. Ow! *Bastante mierda!* You bit me, you *cabrón.*"

Meanwhile, Pablo, the younger outlaw, stopped Helen from rushing forth by pulling her arms behind her back. "You are in big trouble," Helen threatened, squirming un-

39

successfully against Pablo's tight hold on her.

Rafe tried to resist being restrained, using every street trick he could, but he was severely impaired because he was trying to watch out for Helen. But Rafe did get in one good punch to the dude's nose, causing a spurt of blood.

Even though he lacked agility and superior strength, Sancho finally won out by pressing Rafe onto his stomach in the dirt and sitting his 300 pounds heavily on Rafe's buttocks. Then he proceeded to tie Rafe's hands behind his back.

After the lardo stood up, Rafe struggled to a kneeling position.

Ignacio, the leader, chuckled, "Some *bandido* you are, *Señor Ángel*! Perhaps your reputation far exceeds your talent."

"Oh, damn! That hurts," Rafe groaned, climbing awkwardly to his feet, his wrists firmly secured behind him.

"Enough of thees!" Ignacio roared, waving one of his guns in the air. "We mus' get thees horses to Sacramento City and sell them before someone recognizes the brand."

"*Sí*. If not, we weel be the ones dangling from the lynch man's rope, not *Señor Ángel*," Pablo added.

Glancing to the side, Rafe saw Sancho grinning with self-satisfaction, despite the blood that continued to stream down to his chin. He must feel real good about having bested a much younger, more athletically fit man. *Me!*

Rafe used that opportunity to rush forward, head first, and butt the jerk in his flabby stomach. Sancho sank to the ground on his tail with a loud "Oomph!"

Rafe started to smile, but his pleasure was short-lived. Ignacio kicked him in the back, forcing him to the ground, face first in the dust, with his spurred boot pressed to his shoulder bones. Helen tried to come to his aid, but Pablo still held her hands behind her back.

"Do you give up now, you bastard?"

"Up yours!"

The bandit ground his boot harder, and Rafe stilled, deciding to choose his battles more wisely in the future. "I give up," he conceded. *For now.*

Finally, laughing maliciously, Ignacio allowed him to rise agonizingly to his feet. It was clear the leader of this band of misfits took great delight in Rafe's pain as he twirled his drooping mustache, probably contemplating some new torture. "Murietta weel surely let us join his gang now that we have caught his rival. He weel see that we are great *bandidos,* worthy of riding with him."

"Are you talking about Joaquin Murietta, the famous outlaw?" Rafe scoffed.

"*Ciertamente.* The greatest outlaw of them all." Ignacio sighed, then turned to his pals. "Perhaps, if we are stopped on the way to Sacramento City, we can blame *El Ángel* and his whore for stealing the horses."

"*Sí,* we could say they are the horse thieves and we are just bringing them to justice," Sancho added enthusiastically.

"And they would believe us because there ees a price on the head of *El Ángel Bandido,*" Pablo said, "and everyone knows Elena ees his woman."

"I'm not the Angel Bandit," Rafe said.

"I'm not Elena," Helen said at the same time.

"You're not Elena?" Ignacio's face sagged with disappointment. "*Es la verdad?*"

"No, my name is Helen Prescott—"

"Helen, Helena, Elena . . . there ees no difference!" Pablo exclaimed, throwing his hands in the air.

"And I'm not a whore," Helen asserted.

"Now that I cannot believe, *señorita.*" Ignacio stepped closer. "You travel with *El Ángel Bandido.* You have the red hair. You are Elena." He boldly scrutinized her body from head to toe and sneered, "Besides, a woman who wears trousers ees not a Sweet Betsy from Pike, as *Los Americanos* call their gentle women. No, you are a *puta,* for sure." He flicked the tip of one of his revolvers over her breast for emphasis.

Helen inhaled sharply with indignation. She probably would have clawed Ignacio's eyes out if Pablo wasn't still restraining her hands. Instead, Rafe could see she was about to spit on the stupid outlaw as she struggled against Pablo's restraining hold.

Chivalry had never been one of his strong suits, but Rafe couldn't let Helen suffer the consequences of antagonizing the brute. Who knew how he would retaliate.

So, he spit on Ignacio himself.

And turned the gorilla's fury on him.

BAM! Just like that, Ignacio shot at him, barely missing his ear.

Rafe threw himself to the ground to avoid a second shot, which luckily didn't come. Instead, Ignacio gave him another kick, this time in the thigh.

"Heh, heh, heh!" Ignacio chortled. "It weel give me much pleasure turning you over to *Los Americanos*. I hope they weel torture you before your death. And as for Elena ... Well, she weel give us much pleasure with the corkscrew before we sell her services to the men in Sacramento City. They are starved for a woman's company, those lonely prospectors, but a woman who can do the corkscrew ... Ah, we weel become very rich, *muy pronto*. Eh, Pablo? Eh, Sancho?"

"Sí," they both agreed, licking their lips with anticipation.

Helen sliced a haughty "just-try-it" look at the three fools, but, fortunately, she decided to remain quiet for one blessed moment. Rafe didn't think his body could take any more abuse right now.

Trying to get his bearings in this strange situation, Rafe moved his eyes warily from one to the other of the ragtag gang. Pablo and Sancho, the other links in this chain of idiots, weren't wrapped too tight—dumb, but not vicious. Ignacio, on the other hand, was a sicko, a sadistic S.O.B., Rafe decided. And he'd known way too many of those in his time—bastards who'd shoot first, with no real provocation, just for the fun of it. Yep, Ignacio was a man to watch closely.

"Tie her up, too," Ignacio ordered.

Pablo released Helen's hands for one brief second to cut

off a length of rope from the riata on his saddle.

"Why didn't you do something?" Helen said, tapping her foot impatiently.

Rafe couldn't believe his ears. She was actually criticizing him when he could barely stand, when his body was probably turning black and blue. "Like what?"

"Well, take their guns away, or something, before they tied you up. Oh, never mind. I'll do it myself."

"Give me a break!"

"Just watch," she boasted.

Pablo approached her with a determined glint in his eye. A length of rope dangled from one hand.

Rafe gaped incredulously as Helen assumed a karate self-defense position. If he didn't feel so weak, he would have laughed.

"I have to advise you, my hands are registered as lethal weapons," she announced menacingly to the dumbfounded trio.

Holy hell! Do real people say that with a straight face? Did she seriously think she could fight off three men, single-handedly, with her bare hands?

"No!" he barked out, then lowered his voice at the upraised eyebrows of the bandits. "Are you out of your mind?" he hissed. "They'll have you flat on your back with your legs spread in two seconds flat."

"Hah! I'll have you know I hold a fourth-degree black belt in karate. HIE-YAH!" She slashed the air with the edge of one hand and pivoted on her heel in a full circle, returning to a low karate crouch. "HIE-YAH!" She also let loose with some impressive grunting noises that probably meant something.

Pablo stood frozen in his tracks at her loud yell and what must seem a strange exercise to him. Hell, it looked pretty strange to Rafe, too.

Sancho, only a few feet away, stopped dabbing at his bloody nose with a dirty handkerchief, and his jaw dropped in amazement.

Even Ignacio stopped twirling his mustache and muttered, "*Carámba! La muchacha es loca.*" But he never lowered his gun, which was still trained on them both.

Helen balanced herself on one leg and held a pose that kind of resembled a crane, with her arms extended out at the sides, all the time making threatening, guttural noises.

"What are you doing now?" Rafe couldn't help asking.

"Finding my center of balance."

"Was it lost?"

"Stop bothering me. I'm gathering all my force fields together."

"Oh." Then he commented dryly, "That's really important now, is it?"

She ignored his sarcasm and performed a series of fancy forms that included flying side kicks, thrusts, punches, and various other Chuck Norris kinds of nonsense. Finally, she spun on her heel and once again took the self-defense position.

If his hands were free, he would have clapped.

"*Ay, mierda!*" Ignacio grumbled.

"I'll second that," Rafe said.

"Look at her arse when she bends over," Sancho remarked.

I'm looking. I'm looking.

"*Madre de Diós!* I think I am in love." Sancho sighed.

Yep.

"Ees that a dance she does before the corkscrew?" Pablo asked him in a voice filled with hope.

Rafe grinned. "Damned if I know."

Then he narrowed his eyes suspiciously. Most women would be screaming by now, but Helen wasn't exhibiting any fear at all. Instead, she was putting on a floor show. Hmmm. Maybe these slimeballs were friends of hers . . . military buddies.

Suddenly, he understood. "Ah ha! I know what this is."

"You do?" she asked, never taking her eyes off the young hooligan who was circling her with the rope.

"Oh, yeah, the lightbulb has finally gone on in my head. The gig is up, baby."

"Stop interfering with my concentration." She flashed him a quick glower of confusion, then clipped out, "What gig?"

Oh, she is good, but I'm not going to fall for her innocent act this time. "It's one of those lamebrained Army war game things. Throw a bunch of clueless grunts out in a field and pretend they're under attack from an enemy. Real gunfire. Danger. Teach them to survive. Well, I've had enough of this stupid shit. Call it off. *Now.*"

"You are delusional. What logical point would there be in the Army having 1800's Mexican outlaws as the mock enemy?"

"How the hell should I know? And who said the Army ever feels a need to be logical?"

Momentarily distracted, Helen didn't see Pablo make a lunge for her. In seconds, the young bandit wrestled her to the ground and bound her hands. She screeched like a banshee and issued some dire threats, but Pablo didn't appear fazed . . . until Helen shrieked and bucked him off, kneeing him in the nuts in the process.

"Oow! Oow!" Pablo cried in pain, rolling over on his back and drawing his knees up to his chest. "*Mi cojones! Mi cojones!*"

"Stop yer bawling, or I'll fix you so you can't ever do no balling again," Ignacio lashed out. He made a crude gesture at his genitals to explain his double meaning.

Pablo blanched and cupped his groin with both hands.

Clambering upright—a clumsy effort with her hands bound behind her—Helen shot Rafe a condemning glare. "That was your fault."

"Mine? What did I do?"

"I'm well-trained in self-defense. I could have gotten us out of this fix. You deliberately distracted me."

"I did not. Besides, I plan on getting us out of this fix myself, in my own good time, in *my* way." She made a very unflattering snort of disbelief.

Obviously, Helen considered him a total wimp. He gritted his teeth. She was really starting to irritate him.

"I'm the officer in charge here. You should obey me. Army regulations say you should—"

"Chill the hell out! You and your effin' Army are giving me a headache. Not to mention a stomachache. And a backache."

The eyes of the three bandits darted back and forth between them.

Affronted, Helen tossed her hair over her shoulders as best she could with her arms bound behind her and threw her shoulders back with stubborn pride. "I resent your continual ridicule of the military. Just because you . . ."

She continued to work up a good head of steam, rattling on in defense of good old Uncle Sam, but Rafe stopped listening. All his attention was riveted on her breasts, which strained against the fabric of her blouse with her arrogant stance.

Pablo's eyes were glued to the same enticing location.

Rafe wondered if her nipples were small and hard and—

"Stop that!" Helen demanded.

"Wh-what?" *Uh oh! Caught in the act.*

"Ogling."

"I don't ogle." *I wonder if that's one of those Wonder Bras, or if it's all Helen.*

"Yeah, right."

Suddenly, Helen's eyes latched onto his bound hands, then peered behind at her own restraints. "Oh, God, you wouldn't! Surely, even you wouldn't carry your depraved tastes this far."

He rolled his eyes. "Okay, what am I being accused of now?"

"Bondage."

"I beg your pardon," he choked out.

"This is one of those sexual fantasy things men dream about, right?"

Taken aback, he blinked at her. "You think this is a sex game?"

"Yep, and I'm not playing, you . . . you pervert. Oh, I knew you were sex crazed when you made those remarks on the plane about wall-banging, and when you kissed me on the ground, and—''

''Sex crazed! Sex crazed!'' he sputtered out. ''Puh-leeze!'' Then laughter bubbled up from his throat. ''I'm in a Stephen King nightmare with General Patton's clone. I just engaged in a two-man dive on one parachute. Every muscle in my body aches from being battered. And you think I want to jump your bones. Well, why didn't you ask, honey? Let me pull the whip and chains out of my pocket.''

''Whip?'' Pablo asked breathlessly.

''Chains?'' Sancho added. ''You use chains on Elena?''

''SHUT UP!''

Startled, Rafe and Helen both turned toward Ignacio.

''*Silencio!*'' Ignacio bellowed. ''*Diós mío!* You two are worse than cats in a fandango parlor.''

''Listen, guys, how about untying me now?'' Rafe suggested, trying to sound reasonable. Not that he was going to forget his treatment by them. Nope. He was going to clean a few clocks before this day was out. ''I'd like to get back to the base before dark and have a nice stiff Scotch on the rocks. Maybe even two.''

BAM! The loud report from Ignacio's gun was his only response.

Rafe looked down to see a crease in his left boot matching his right. This ape was definitely cruising with his lights on dim.

''Your continual chatter ees annoying me, *Señor Ángel*.'' Ignacio blew the smoke from the end of his pistol and replaced it in its holster.

''Well, golly gee. All you had to do was ask me to be quiet.''

''The next time I weel aim higher,'' Ignacio informed him coldly.

Rafe wasn't sure if he referred to his knees or his balls, but he wasn't taking any chances. He decided to shut up—for now.

Okay, I'll bide my time until the right moment. Then I'll show this bum a few dirty tricks I've learned over the years.

He might think he's got the upper hand here, but only till I'm ready. Wait till he sees what a real gang member can do.

But first things first, he decided, as Sancho began to lead the horses once again in their direction.

He was going to have to ride a horse.

Rafe tried to brave it out . . . until Mr. Ed attempted to take a bite out of his shoulder. "No dice! I am *not* getting on that horse. I'll walk first."

Helen shot him a glance of surprise. "Don't tell me. The hotshot L.A. lawyer is a shark in the courtroom, but he's afraid of a little ol' horse." Then she smiled. Actually, it was more like a smirk.

Rafe decided then that Helen wasn't as attractive as he'd always thought. In fact, her hair wasn't really fiery red; it was more like orange. And those freckles that stood out on her nose made her seem ridiculous, like an innocent kid who should be wearing pigtails. And her body wasn't all that great, either. Damn it, who cared if her breasts were round and high, like one of those Vargas models? Or if her legs were long and athletically muscled and would look terrific in a pair of black silk stockings. Or-

"You weel ride," Ignacio said, patting his holster, "even if I have to put a bullet in your ass and tie you to the saddle."

Helen didn't like the tone of Ignacio's voice. Oh, she knew he had to be a friend of Rafe's. What other explanation could there be for this perverse joke? But Ignacio carried the prank too far. It had seemed like he'd really kicked Rafe, and he could have hurt Rafe those times when he'd fired his gun.

The arrival of the horses interrupted her thoughts. She'd been riding since she was ten years old, and both animals looked like lively mounts. She'd enjoy a short ride if it weren't for the company, or this ludicrous scheme they were playing out.

"Saddle the horses," Ignacio ordered his cohorts as he waddled over to a shady tree. He was over six feet tall, but

48

he had a beer belly that stood out like the prow of a ship and a huge back end that went up and down in his tight trousers as he walked.

Pablo, the youngest of the bandits, and Sancho, the older man with a head of thick, curly gray hair, glared at their leader for assigning them the dirty work.

Suddenly, the absurdity of the whole situation struck Helen. "The Three Stooges of the Wild West!" she murmured. Her eyes connected with Rafe's, and they shared a smile.

Lord, he is gorgeous. What was it about Rafe that a mere smile could set butterflies fluttering in her stomach?

"What does that make us?" he asked drolly. "The Two Stooges of the Tame West?" He winked at her.

And the butterflies targeted another part of her body, much lower down. She was in big, big trouble if she didn't pull herself together right away. Forcing the wobble out of her voice, she said, "Really, Rafe, it's time to give up the joke. Couldn't you get any better actors than these?"

"You think I staged this comedy? Why?"

"Because you're brain dead. Because you enjoy teasing me. Because—"

"You don't suppose . . ." he proffered hesitantly ". . . you don't think we could have possibly landed in another time? 1850? I mean, look at those ancient Colt revolvers. And the saddles."

"What? Did you land on your head? Don't be ridiculous."

"Have you ever watched *Quantum Leap* on TV?"

"Oh, come on! Do you think you're some kind of Scott Bakula?"

"Now that you mention it, a few women have told me I resemble him." His lips twitched with a grin.

"Not on your best day!" she snapped. *Actually, you look a whole lot better.* "But, if you're Scott Bakula, what does that make me—that guy, Al, with the pocket computer?"

"Do you have a computer on you?" he asked expectantly.

"Give it up, Rafe. This is not *Quantum Leap*."

Time travel! It was an outlandish notion. Anyone could buy an ancient firearm if they had the money, she concluded. And the animals and the fine-tooled leather saddles were, no doubt, borrowed from some rancher or movie set in the area, one of Rafe's friends. Nope, Helen wasn't buying the time travel nonsense. No way!

A short time later, Rafe put on a false front of bravado, letting Sancho and Pablo help him onto the back of the black horse. He was, unfortunately, too unnerved by the skittering horse under him to try to escape when they released the ropes around his wrists and retied them in front so he could hold onto the reins.

As if I know what to do with reins! He clutched the saddle horn and eyed the rearing beast. Well, maybe not rearing, but definitely shifting.

Helen, on the other hand, looked perfectly calm and capable, sitting on the pinto. Not that he knew what a pinto was. The only pinto he'd ever heard of was a car.

Ignacio began to move out, followed by Helen and Rafe, then Sancho and Pablo in the rear, then a string of five other stolen horses they planned to sell in Sacramento City.

The only problem was that Rafe's horse didn't move.

"Giddyap," he urged his horse, and Helen giggled.

He was beginning to hate her.

"Giddyap? Why not yippee-kay-aye?"

"I was gonna try that next," he grumbled, meanwhile shaking his reins, using his knees to nudge the sides of the heaving horse—Mr. Ed was probably laughing, too—bouncing up and down on the saddle, then finally yelling, "Move, you son of a bitch!"

The horse glanced back at him over its shoulder, and he could have sworn it snickered. God, it looked just like F. Lee Bailey. He'd faced the legendary barrister in the courtroom once and he'd worn a condescending expression the entire time, just like this horse with an attitude.

"I think I should get some spurs," he concluded, "like

50

Ignacio and the others. What F. Lee Horse here needs is a good swift spur in the ass.''

"No, no, no," Helen said, moving her horse closer. "You have to be gentle. Whatever you do, don't kick the horse. Just nudge his flanks gently with your heels. Like this."

"And how do I make him stop?''

"Pull on the reins.''

"Oh, yeah. I get it now.''

The horse started to move, and Rafe was feeling really good . . . until Helen warned him to stop shaking the reins.

"That really riles a horse. Makes them bolt.''

He immediately stilled his bound wrists.

At one point, he decided to play along, as if this really was 1850, and asked Ignacio why they wasted time stealing horses when they could make a fortune prospecting for gold.

"It ees easier to rob those who do the work,'' he answered with a smug smile. "Besides, thees foolish *Americanos* waste their time searching for the mother lode. It does not exist. Soon, they will leave these hills, and only smart men, like me, will remain holding all the riches.''

Oh, yeah. You're one of the Einsteins of the Old West.

After that scintillating conversation, Rafe concentrated on his riding. Along the way, Helen constantly called his attention to the wild beauty of the shallow ravines and gullies, which merged into glorious fields of chaparral and wildflowers. They passed only a few people in the distance—shy foothill Indians at work in the fields, scruffy men in miners' duds riding mules, pioneers on the occasional wagon, moving slowly in the searing heat.

Sightseeing was not a top priority for Rafe; he was too busy holding on tight to F. Lee Horse.

"You're doing just great," Helen encouraged, "but try moving the horse with your inner thighs.''

"Oh, I get it. Like riding a woman," he observed with wide-eyed innocence. She looked too damn competent on her horse, while he stumbled along like the fourth stooge.

"Sometimes you gotta let a woman know who's in the *saddle*."

She honored him with one of those all-men-are-scum scowls, but didn't comment on his tasteless remark. Instead, she continued to offer advice. "Avoid bouncing up and down in the saddle, or else you'll end up with a sore bottom. And blisters."

Oh, yeah, blisters! Rafe thought four hours later when they dismounted and prepared to make camp for the night. He felt like his backside had been paddled with a wooden mallet, every muscle in his body screamed with pain, and he could swear he had a blister on his right cheek, just below his tattoo.

They released Helen's bindings, but not his. "She ees just a harmless woman, after all," Ignacio explained.

Idiot! There isn't a woman alive who's harmless.

Now would probably be a good time to escape, Rafe thought. Helen could untie his hands, and they'd be out of here. But he hesitated, still intrigued by the puzzling events. Maybe he'd wait a little longer to make his move. See what the hell was going on. Crack a few skulls.

Helen was expertly helping to unsaddle her horse—and his, as well. Her competence was beginning to rankle. She put a blade of grass in her mouth and startling whistling contentedly.

He hated whistling.

"Helen?"

"Hmmm?"

"Ah . . . Helen . . . honey . . . ?"

She looked up suspiciously.

"How would you feel about—?"

"Spit it out, Rafe. You were never shy before."

Yep, she is really starting to yank my chain. "How'd you like to look at my ass?"

Chapter Four

Helen stopped whistling and almost swallowed her blade of grass. "I beg your pardon," she choked out. Surely— *surely*—she'd heard wrong. Rafe couldn't possibly have asked her to look at his behind!

Even with his dark skin, Helen could see a slight pink tone of embarrassment flush Rafe's neck and face. But he lifted his chin arrogantly and demanded, "Look at my ass, damn it."

"No, thank you." She hoped her voice sounded cool and disinterested, not hot and very interested, like she was, unfortunately. With forced casualness, she put a new blade of grass in her mouth and began whistling again.

"Aaaaarrgh! Do it!" The pink flush on his face turned purple.

"No."

"Undo my zipper and pull my pants down," he said in a steely voice that, no doubt, caused his courtroom adversaries to quake in their Gucci boots. But not Helen. She just kept on whistling. No, she wouldn't let him intimidate her. She whistled louder.

"Quick. Before those yo-yo's come back and decide to mark another part of my body for a kick-boxing target."

Helen raised her eyes to see the three bandits making a campsite, keeping a watchful eye on them the entire time.

"C'mon."

Geez, talk about a lack of finesse. Helen felt somewhat disappointed. She'd expected Rafe to be a smoother, more persuasive lover. Heck, he probably didn't consider her worth the effort. Or else, he figured she was easy. Trying to remain calm, she stuck another blade of grass in her mouth and resumed whistling.

"I swear, the minute I get free, I'm gonna shake you till you swallow that weed. Then I'm gonna twist your tongue so you can't ever whistle again."

"Don't be so cranky."

"Cranky? Cranky?" he sputtered. "I'm dying here. Pull down my pants."

So that was it. "Do you have to pee?"

He said a really foul word.

"Well, *excuse* me!" He didn't have to relieve himself; so, it must be what she'd thought originally. The ape! As if he would die from unrequited lust!

"Helen," he warned.

"Shhh. I'm trying to think of a plan for us to escape. Should I untie you?"

"Later. It's too dangerous now while they hold all the weapons. First things first." He sucked in a huge breath, then hissed, "Look at my ass."

"Did aliens steal your brains? What in the world would make you think I want to engage in a quickie with you?"

He made a tsking noise of frustration. "Babe, when—rather *if*—I ever decide to make love with you, it's not going to be a quickie. It's going to be long and hard and noisy and—"

"Stop it! Stop it right now." Rafe had a knack for creating the most vivid, tantalizing, erotic fantasies in her head, and she wouldn't have it. She stamped her foot for emphasis, and her pinto shied away nervously.

"I have a blister," he blurted out.

"You have a . . . Oh!" Now it was her turn to blush. He hadn't been putting the make on her. He just needed her help with a blister. She wished the earth would open up and swallow her. "Why didn't you say so before?"

"Hurry! It's throbbing like hell, and Ignacio will probably find some way to make it hurt more if he finds out."

Acting hastily, Helen moved him behind the horse and

knelt. She feigned nonchalance as she undid the button of his fly and pulled down the zipper, but her fumbling fingers gave her away. That, and her barely quashed gasp as he grew hard at the slight brush of her fingertips.

"Oh . . . my . . . God!" Rafe gritted out. "Did you have to touch me?"

"Did you have to get *it* aroused?"

"Believe me, *it* has a mind of its own."

"But I didn't do anything."

"Helen, Helen, Helen. All you have to do is breathe, and I get turned on."

"You jerk. Undoing your pants wasn't my idea. Why do you twist every little thing into something sexual?"

"Sweetheart, your hand on my cock isn't any 'little thing.' Believe me, it's a great big thing."

"God, you are such a horny toad. You're hot for anything in skirts, aren't you?"

"You're not wearing skirts," he reminded her. "And I'll have you know, a woman opened my button-fly jeans with her teeth one time, and I wasn't half as turned on as I am now."

"Oh." His crude words pleased Helen in a cockeyed sort of way. Could a woman actually do that with her teeth? Giving herself a mental shake, she said, "Stop teasing me, and turn around. Or else I'll use my teeth to open that boil instead of your buttons, you randy goat. And I'll take a chunk of flesh with it, too." She gave his cheek a soft whack.

"Promises, promises." Chuckling, he did as she ordered, and Helen pulled the waistbands of both his slacks and his black silk boxer shorts down to his thighs. *Black silk? Oh, my heavens!* Yep, he had a blister the size of a silver dollar on the crease where his right buttock joined his thigh, directly below his butterfly tattoo.

She had to admit, it looked mighty good. The tattoo, not his well-delineated, hard-muscled tush. Lawyering must be a lot more strenuous than she'd thought, she concluded irrelevantly. He probably worked out chasing ambulances.

Without thinking, she placed a fingertip on the swollen center of the blister, and he flinched with pain.

"Damn, that hurts."

"Sorry," she murmured. "It'll have to be lanced and covered with an antiseptic ointment."

"Yeah, I'll bet these ding-a-lings carry medical supplies. Just break it and cover it with a Kleenex or something."

"I can't do that. It could get infected, especially in this heat. Besides, I have a tube of Neosporin I picked up after they dumped the survival vests. Although, during World War I, maggots were considered an accepted treatment for infected wounds—"

"You . . . are . . . not . . . putting . . . maggots . . . on . . . my . . . butt," he ground out, enunciating each word very cleary.

"*Ay, mierda!* I do not believe my eyes." Ignacio had crept up on them, and his eyes almost bugged out at the sight of her kneeling in front of Rafe's naked backside. "By all the saints! You two could not even wait till dark to do the corkscrew."

Sancho and Pablo scurried up to see what all the commotion was about.

"Can we watch?" Sancho asked in an overeager voice.

"I don't understand," Pablo interjected, tilting his head in several convoluted positions. "How do they do *it* with her—"

"That's about enough! You've all got your minds in the gutter." Helen stood and put both hands on her hips, glowering at the bandits. "Rafe has a blister, and I need to take care of it. Otherwise, he'll never be able to ride tomorrow. Untie him."

Ignacio started to protest, but she added, "Listen, there's no way Rafe could be this Angel Bandit guy. Did you see the way he rides a horse?"

Ignacio pondered her words, then nodded vigorously. "*Sí,* he rides like a *niña.* Heh, heh, heh."

"Do you people mind," Rafe protested. "I'm standing here with my bare butt to the wind."

The gang leader scowled contemptuously at Rafe.

"Are you going to untie him?" Helen persisted. "Even an imbecile can see he's no bandit."

"Is someone gonna pull up my freakin' pants?"

Ignoring Rafe, Ignacio told Helen, "But, *señorita*, he looks like *El Ángel Bandido*. And, if he escapes, we will lose the reward."

"My ass is gettin' a chill here, guys."

"Ah, what harm can he do?" Ignacio shrugged. "I have the gun. And he ees a weakling."

"That's what I've been trying to tell you."

"*Sí*, he ees as useless as a spare prick at a wedding. Heh, heh, heh," Ignacio quipped.

Helen glared at the vulgarity.

Rafe snarled at the insult.

Sancho chomped uninterestedly on a piece of jerky.

Pablo gaped with undue interest at Rafe's exposed buttocks.

"If I get pneumonia, someone's gonna pay." Rafe threw the words out flippantly, but Helen could see the spark of anger in his blue eyes at Ignacio's assessment of his prowess, not to mention his vulnerable nudity.

"*¡Maldito!* He ees a pain in the arse," Ignacio opined.

"Yeah, isn't he?" Helen replied sweetly.

Rafe shot her a look that said, "You'll pay, too."

Ignacio stepped to her side, about to untie Rafe's wrists, when he jumped back suddenly, shouting, "*¡Miré!* Look! Look there!" He pointed at Rafe's behind.

"*Sí!* It ees the angel's mark." Sancho and Pablo made exaggerated signs of the cross over their chests.

"Angel wings! He truly ees *El Ángel Bandido*," Ignacio said in awe. Then, "Thank you, sweet Jesus! The reward ees as good as ours."

"Those aren't angel wings," Helen corrected. "It's a butterfly." She traced the outline of the tattoo with her fingertips.

Rafe jerked and growled out to her in a low mutter, "Do you think you could stop touching me, Helen?"

"Oops," she said.

Rafe's eyes rolled in his head.

"So, you really are Elena," Ignacio whooped, directing his attention back to her. *"Muy bueno!"* He made an obscene gesture with his fat tongue.

Helen barely stopped herself from slugging him a good one. She restrained herself—for Rafe's benefit, of course. "Mr. Ignacio, are—"

"Villejo," he interrupted. "My name ees Ignacio Juan Rico Hector Villejo." His chest puffed out with pride.

"Yeah, well, Mr. Villejo, are you going to let me care for Rafe's injury, or not? The international rules of combat say that rudimentary medical treatment must be—"

"Chill out, Helen," Rafe said ungraciously.

Ignacio twirled his mustache speculatively for several moments, then agreed. "We weel untie The Angel for a short time so that you may minister to him." He laughed, as if at a private jest, adding, "Later, you may *minister* to me, too."

Pablo held the front waistband out from his loose trousers and glanced inside. "My balls are turnin' blue from all the kicks I got today. Do you think you could put some ointment on me, too?" he asked Helen.

"Get a life!"

"Huh?" Pablo blinked with confusion and squinted quizzically at Rafe.

"I think that means, 'Not now,' " Rafe translated. "Maybe later."

Pablo's doleful face brightened.

Helen's eyes sent icy daggers at Rafe.

"Maybe not," he added wisely.

"One wrong move and I weel take care of your blister, *Señor Ángel*," Ignacio threatened. "With a bullet in its center. Do you understand?"

Rafe nodded.

"Try to escape, and I weel shoot off your balls."

"Enough already!" Rafe grumbled as Sancho finally released his bindings. "I got the message. Loud and clear."

* * *

Helen was getting increasingly nervous about this whole outlaw scenario. At first, she had viewed them as bumbling idiots. Now, she was starting to get scared.

"Rafe, we have to talk," she whispered as soon as the bandits stepped away. She'd just put a gauze bandage over his boil after treating it. "Something weird is going on. I think . . . I think we really have traveled back in time."

"Huh?" Rafe said, assessing her like an escapee from an asylum. "You swallow that blade of grass? Maybe it was loco weed." He paused in the process of tucking in his shirt and zipping up his pants.

"Listen, this trail we followed today is very familiar to me. I hike in these hills all the time. This is *not* 1996."

"You hike?"

She made a clucking sound of disgust at his irrelevant question. "Focus, will you? We're heading toward Sacramento, but we should have passed several towns by now. And the area is entirely too thick with trees and wildlife. It hasn't looked this way in . . . well, one hundred fifty years."

Rafe's brow wrinkled, and he bit his bottom lip thoughtfully. "Actually, I've had some weird feelings, too." His eyes met hers and held. "Let's be honest here, Helen. Do you or do you not know these yahoos? Is this a military setup?"

"Of course not," she said indignantly. Then she asked, "As long as we're being honest, do you swear these men aren't friends of yours? Or someone you hired to play a prank?"

"You're obviously not playing with a full deck if you could think that. Why would I hire someone to shoot at me, kick me, tie me up, and force me to ride a monster horse till I get a blister on my butt? I mean, do you really think I'm having fun here?" Rafe braced his fists on his hips and glowered at her with exasperation.

"Then that must mean . . . Oh, Lord! Do you really think time travel is possible?"

"Maybe it's just a dream," he suggested.

"Would we both be having the same dream?"

"How the hell do I know? Nah, it's not a dream. If it were a dream, I know exactly *what* I'd be doing, and *who* would be doing it with me." He gave her a swift, smoldering once-over that needed no explanation.

"You are certifiable."

"Bet you wish you had your clipboard, don'tcha, babe?" He favored her with one of his devastating grins.

She inhaled to gather patience. "Could we concentrate on the subject here, Captain? Time travel, remember?"

"Are we back to this military rank crap again?" When she refused to answer, he forced a somber expression on his face. "Okay, if it's not a military maneuver, and it's not a dream, we must be dead."

"And this is . . . ?"

"Hell. Definitely hell."

"Shhh," she cautioned, pointing to Pablo, who glanced up from where he was stirring something in a kettle over the cook fire. Sancho had his back to them, tending to the other picketed horses. Ignacio sat with his back against a tree, one pistol laid over his lap. Although his sombrero tilted forward over his face, almost covering his slitted eyes, Helen was sure he was watching them closely. "I don't think they suspect anything about our coming from the future. But we'd better be careful."

"Let's move over toward the creek," Rafe suggested. "Maybe we'll find an opportunity to escape."

"Do you have a plan?"

He shook his head. "We have to keep our eyes open for the right opportunity. There's no way I can take on all three of them, and we'll never get away unless we take their guns and horses first."

"I agree. Timing is everything. The first rule of every good soldier."

He snorted rudely. "Rules be damned. We've got to make our own rules here." Before she could respond, he yelled over to Ignacio, "Hey, buddy, do you mind if I take a bath?"

Ignacio sat up straighter and Rafe heard the click of the safety being released on the revolver. "*Mierda!* You don't need no bath. Sit down where I can see you."

"Take it easy now. You can keep me in your gun sights. I just want to bathe. I have enough sweat on me to salt a ham."

"But the blister I just bandaged—" Helen started to say.

"You can redo it," he said impatiently. "C'mon."

Helen grabbed a small cake of soap from her pack, along with the ointment and gauze, following Rafe slowly toward the small stream. They both held their arms away from their bodies and moved in a nonthreatening manner so Ignacio wouldn't be tempted to shoot.

The bandit leader slitted his eyes suspiciously and stood, watching them intently, his guns now aimed at both of them.

"I'm just going to wash up a little, pal. No quick moves. No escaping. A bath, that's all. Okay?"

Ignacio nodded, sitting back down. Then he called out lewdly to Helen, "You want I should wash your *tetas* for you?"

She ignored him, turning to Rafe. "Don't you think . . ." Her words trailed off, and her jaw dropped.

The brute was already taking off his clothes, with total lack of modesty, of course. She got a real good rear view of Rafael Santiago in the buff. Her eyes traveled involuntarily from wide shoulders, down the muscled planes of his back, to a narrow waist and slim hips. Over his well-toned, hard buttocks. And long legs covered with soft-as-silk-looking dark hairs.

Helen liked what she saw. A whole lot.

He bent and took the bandage off his behind, placing it carefully on a rock.

Her mouth snapped shut. "What do you think you're doing?" Her voice had a shrill, panicky ring to it.

"Taking a bath," he informed her calmly. "We have to

61

bide our time. Act normal. Wait for the opening. Timing, Helen, remember?''

"Right," she said, nodding. *Maybe I'm the one who's certifiable.*

"Can you throw me the soap?" he called over his shoulder.

She pretended not to be looking. But she had to look when she tossed him the soap.

Which was a mistake. Spinning on his heels to face her, he reached out one arm and caught the bar with the ease of a seasoned pro.

And Helen got a 360-degree picture of the most gorgeous male this side of heaven.

She tried not to gape. In fact, she squeezed her eyes shut.

Rafe laughed.

She peeped.

Another mistake. Now she got a full frontal view of a man who had a knack for turning her knees to jelly and her brain to mindless, who-cares-if-he's-a-jerk mush.

And he knew it. But Rafe wasn't laughing anymore. Instead, he studied her as intently as she avoided studying him. Then, as if making a sudden decision, he spun around and walked out to the middle of the knee-deep creek. With a splash, he sat down, bringing the water up to his chest.

"Get back to work," Ignacio yelled at Pablo and Sancho, who'd stopped gathering firewood and preparing dinner to stare at her and Rafe. "Ain't you never seen a hombre scrub his hairy arse? Heh, heh, heh.''

"We were just waiting to see if Elena would join him," Pablo muttered, stomping back to the cook pot. Sancho shuffled off to gather more twigs.

"Hey, this is great." Rafe sighed loudly, beginning to soap his chest and neck, then his face and hair, ducking under the water repeatedly. "How 'bout joining me?"

Standing near the edge of the bank, Helen shook her head, although she was tempted. Her blouse stuck to her back and underarms. She felt sticky and incredibly hot. "Is it cool?"

"Very. C'mon, Prissy, live a little." He flicked a handful of water at her playfully.

She glanced back at the three bandits. They weren't paying much attention, for the moment. "Well, maybe I'll just wet my feet."

"Chicken."

She took off her boots and socks and rolled up her pant legs. Then she waded into the deliciously cool water. "Ooooh, that feels wonderful."

"Come closer and I'll show you something that feels even more wonderful." His eyes danced playfully.

"Behave."

"Relax, Prissy. There's no way we're gonna get those guns right now. We'll wait until nighttime when these goofballs fall asleep. Even if one of them guards us, he'll be less alert."

"Well, I suppose." She gave in hesitantly.

"Oh, look," Rafe said suddenly and pointed to the left. In that split second, his hand snaked out under the water, grabbed her ankle, and pulled her forward. She fell backward with a loud splash and went completely under the shallow water. When she came up sputtering, she lunged for him, but he swerved to the side, and this time she went under, face forward.

She was more careful this time when she emerged, slapping wet strands of hair off her face. "We don't have time for this foolishness," she chided, sloshing toward him where he sat, cross-legged, arms folded over his chest like a maharajah. She unbuttoned her filthy outer blouse and dropped it into the water. Underneath she wore a regulation green Army T-shirt.

"Would you like to see me float on my back?" Rafe asked, batting his eyelashes boyishly.

"Absolutely not!" she said, horrified.

"Oh, all right," he replied with deadpan innocence. "Besides, I'd rather check out your . . . ah . . . attributes." His eyes raked her body boldly.

Helen looked down and almost wept. Her wet T-shirt and

slacks were plastered to her body, revealing every nook and cranny from neck to ankle.

"Well, at least one question is answered here."

She refused to ask what question.

That didn't stop him. "You're not wearing one of those Wonder Bra things."

"Wo-wonder? Whatever are you talking about?"

"I was trying to figure out earlier today if you wear one of those 'push up–push out' bras . . . You know, the ones that make up for lacking assets."

"You wondered about my . . . my body parts?" she stammered.

"Yes. Purely in a scientific manner, of course."

She sat down in the water and glared at him.

"Okay, so I wasn't being scientific. But you gotta admit you've got some body under all those sexless military clothes."

"I think this conversation has gotten way out of hand. Drop it right now, soldier."

"It really is too bad you forgot to tuck a clipboard in your backpack. You could've given me a couple hundred more check marks by now." He shook his thick, black hair off his face and finger combed it back with both hands, presenting her with another marvelous view of his exposed chest and upraised, muscled arms.

Oh, my! She made a low gurgling noise in her throat.

He tossed the slippery soap at her with a laugh. "Wanna share?"

She caught it, then turned away when he stood up, a mere three feet from her, totally, gloriously nude. She refused to look when she heard him padding toward shore and then back again.

"You can look now, Prissy. I'm decent." He'd brought his shirt, slacks, boxers, and socks back with him, and sat in the water again with a huge splash. At her raised eyebrow, he informed her, "I'm doing laundry. I don't want to put these smelly clothes back on."

God, that sounded good.

"Why don't you take off your pants and throw me your blouse and socks? I'll wash them for you."

"Hah!"

"I won't peek. Honest." He made a big production out of making a cross through his chest hairs. She almost reached out to touch the dark curls, just to see if they were as silky as they looked.

"Rafe to Helen. Rafe to Helen," he mocked.

"Wh-what?"

"I said that I'll turn my back and keep guard against the tiresome trio. You can keep your T-shirt and panties on." He seemed really sincere. Then he spoiled the effect by adding, "You *are* wearing underwear, aren't you?"

"Get serious."

"Oh, I'm serious all right. But, no kidding, you don't need to worry about me, or those three," he promised, motioning his head toward the three men who were about thirty feet away. "I'll screen you with my body, and at the least movement from them, I'll throw your clothes back."

In the end, despite her better judgment, Helen took Rafe up on the offer. With an eye on the three bandits, Helen managed to bathe and wash her hair. True to his offer, Rafe washed both his clothes and hers, handing them back to her over his shoulder.

She had just bent over, prepared to insert one foot in a wet pant leg, when Ignacio came storming into the water, boots and all. Apparently he'd been watching them the entire time.

Rafe tried to stop him, but he slipped on the wet stones, scrambling to stay upright.

Pointing his gun at her back end, Ignacio raged, "*Dios mio!* What the hell ees that?"

"What?" she squeaked, holding her sopping slacks in front of her French-cut bikini pants.

"That mark on your ass," Ignacio growled. "You have the angel's mark on you, too."

"Of course she has my mark," Rafe declared, as if it

was the plainest thing in the world. "She's my wife . . . *mí esposa*."

"What?" Helen and Ignacio both said at the same time. Pablo and Sancho sidled up, too.

Ignacio's mean eyes narrowed. "I ain't never heard of *El Ángel Bandido* gettin' hitched."

"Well, the little woman and I got married this morning," Rafe lied baldly. "In fact, this trek to the mountains was supposed to be our honeymoon. No, no, don't feel the need to rush out and buy us a wedding gift." Beaming at her like a besotted dope, Rafe waded over and put a wet sleeve around her equally wet shoulder. Meanwhile, she still clutched her slacks to the front of her body. "Isn't that true, cupcake?"

She tried to wriggle out of his embrace.

"No, I do not believe you are married," Ignacio asserted, scratching his head with the barrel of one gun while trying to get a closer view of Helen's fanny.

"Just play along with me," Rafe whispered in her ear. "I know what I'm doing."

"Hah!"

"Really. Mexicans are almost always Roman Catholic," Rafe explained rapidly, shielding her surreptitiously with his body. "Very religious, and superstitious. Adultery is one of the biggest no-no's in the Church."

"Are you Catholic?"

"Sometimes. Put your pants on and stop arguing."

"Who's a Catholic? What adultery?" Ignacio looked dazed by the whole conversation.

"How can you be a sometimes Catholic?" Helen asked as she struggled to get into the wet pant legs.

Rafe waved her question aside as unimportant.

"Were you religious when you were a gang member?"

"No, I was more like a lost lamb. Get back on the subject!"

"And now you're not lost anymore?" She was truly perplexed by this apparent dichotomy in his character.

"Well, sometimes I still get lost," he said with a grin.

66

"Stop whispering," Ignacio ordered. "What were you saying to Elena?" he demanded to know of Rafe.

"Nothin'," Rafe lied. "I was just sticking my tongue in her ear. She likes that. A lot." He gave Ignacio one of those man-to-man looks.

Helen gasped with indignation.

Ignacio practically salivated.

"Ain't that true, sweetheart?" Rafe asked, daring her to disagree. She'd only got her one leg in the pants so far. He slapped one palm familiarly over her mostly bare right cheek.

She nodded, meanwhile grinding her heel into his instep.

He dropped his hand with a groan.

"Get out of the water," Ignacio ordered, waving his gun.

"They are married?" Sancho asked dolefully. "I knew it! Just my luck, there weel be no corkscrew today."

"No corkscrew! No corkscrew!" Pablo wailed. "You promised, Ignacio. You said, if I stopped bellyaching, I would get my turn tonight. You said—"

"Shut the hell up!" Ignacio roared, then turned angrily on Rafe. "Show me the marriage certificate."

"Sure thing," Rafe said. "It's in my backpack." Then he gave Ignacio a considering scrutiny. "You did remember to bring my backpack, didn't you? It was lying on the ground back where Sancho wrestled me in the dirt and tied my wrists."

When all three bandits looked at each other and realized that no one had picked up a pack, Rafe shrugged as if to say, hey, it wasn't his fault.

"You do not have proof of thees marriage?" Ignacio asked, clearly not buying Rafe's story. "Then Elena will do the corkscrew with us till you give us that proof."

"Oh, but I can give you proof," Rafe inserted glibly, "when we get to Sacramento tomorrow. The padre at the mission can verify the marriage. You know Father Fernando, don't you?"

Rafe's quickness with fabrication impressed Helen. It

was probably taught in freshman law classes, "Lying Through Your Teeth 101."

But she wasn't complaining. Anything to keep those grubby bandits away from her.

"And, besides, you wouldn't deny a bride and groom their wedding night together, would you?"

Little tingles of suspicion rippled through Helen. She looked closer at Rafe, whose roguish eyes gleamed with triumph. "What are you suggesting?"

"Now, precious, don't be shy. You and I are going to consummate our marriage tonight. You know that, darling." He put an arm around her shoulders again and squeezed her close.

Ignacio's beady eyes swept them both. "Consummation? Elena has not corkscrewed you yet? I know at least two dozen men who have dipped their wicks in her honey, and you are saying she denies you?"

"No, no, no," Rafe announced in a loud stage whisper, "Elena wants to pretend she's a virgin. It's a game we like to play." He winked at her.

"Aaaargh!" she snarled.

"Aaaahhh!" the bandits sighed in manly understanding.

"Can we watch?" Pablo asked.

"Sure," Rafe agreed.

Helen pulled out of his embrace and stuttered incoherently.

"Now, honey, he's just looking for a little *ménage à trois*." Rafe smiled broadly at the bandits then. "Don'tcha just love it when you stun the little woman speechless?"

Chapter Five

Rafe tried sending silent signals to Helen, hoping she would play along with his plan. He had told her they would make their move to escape after nightfall, but he was thinking now that he might be able to tackle Ignacio and wrest his pistols away from him since the three men had relaxed their vigilance.

He might not be able to ride a horse worth a damn, but one thing Rafe did know from his years in L.A. gangs was guns. If he could get a revolver, the rest would be easy street.

But first, Helen would have to cooperate.

And he saw immediately that cooperation was the last thing on her mind. In fact, as she jerked on her pants and zipped the fly, her brown eyes threw off sparks of fury. And a hint of hurt at his betrayal.

Guilt pricked his conscience.

He wanted to tell her that he hadn't meant to offend or embarrass her, but their captors stood nearby. He yearned to pull her into her arms and assure her that he'd never deliberately hurt her. And, hell, didn't she see how much he wanted to make love with her—had wanted to all these years—and that having an audience would be the last thing he'd countenance?

But there was no time for all those explanations now. He had to get her immediate cooperation in his plan. Maybe he could pretend he'd been joking, without the men hearing. Then, later, he'd explain to Helen what his intent had been all along.

"Gotcha!" he said through the side of his mouth, knowing the bandits wouldn't understand the word even if they did overhear.

"Gotcha? Gotcha? Is that all you can say?"

"Now, Helen, lighten up. Don't you have a sense of humor? Hah, hah, hah. Now's no time for a Prissy-hissy fit."

"Don't even talk to me. One more word and, I swear, I'll put a knot in your tongue."

"A kung fu knot?" he jibed.

"Drop dead."

Good Lord, she was so steamed she practically had smoke coming out of her ears. He cringed at the daunting task of smoothing her ruffled feathers.

Keeping an eye on the three bandits, who were watching them intently, Rafe reached out an arm for Helen. If he could get her closer, he would whisper a quick explanation in her ear.

She eyed his outstretched arm with loathing, then smiled enigmatically, seeming to change her mind.

He relaxed.

A *big* mistake.

In a mere instant, she took his hand, twisted around so her back pressed against his chest, bent, and flipped Rafe's body over her shoulder—all 200 pounds of him. He landed ignominiously with a huge splash on his back in the water. A sharp rock dug into his sore blister.

As he came up, shaking his hair back, he saw Helen swagger out of the water and do a flying side kick, yelling, "Hee-yah!" He figured "hee-yah" must mean something like, "Take that, bozo." Meanwhile, her foot connected with Pablo's poor battered groin, knocking the screeching young man to the ground.

About a million sparrows flew out of the trees at her shout and Pablo's scream. But Helen wasn't done yet.

"Eeeh!" she snarled out, real loud, spinning in a circle, and dealt a hand chop with the heel of her palm to Sancho's gaping jaw. Like a domino, he fell on the ground next to Pablo.

Then, she made some other grunting noises, like, "Uuut!" and "Oooot!" and "Hah!" while she danced around in a series of dramatic karate poses. Rafe was almost certain those noises translated roughly to, "Who's next?"

She was either a martial arts expert, or nuts.

Ignacio eyeballed her lethal antics with disbelief, but not fear. He just raised his pistol, pressing lightly on the trigger. "One step and I shoot, *puta*," he warned.

Panting from her exertions, Helen faced him, knees bent and hands raised in an attack position, as if she was actually considering another move.

"Don't, Helen," Rafe shouted behind her.

"Butt out," she replied without looking at him.

He decided not to persist, fearful that his advice would prod her to do the opposite. But, luckily, she appeared to recognize her weak position with Ignacio and dropped her hands.

Ignacio made a threatening growl but didn't move as Helen proceeded to glide by the numbskull, her chin raised with disdain. She seemed unafraid, except for the slight trembling of her hands, which she clasped together.

Rafe exhaled, never realizing he'd been holding his breath.

She stopped halfway back to the campfire and assumed another one of her karate poses. With one quick chop of her hand, she cut through a three-inch dead branch propped against a boulder. Then she made eye contact with each of them. "If any of you dares to try that corkscrew thing on me, this is what's going to happen to your precious private parts."

With those ominous words and several gasps in response from the bandits, Helen stomped off.

Rafe, for one, got the message. He was pretty sure the three *bandidos* did, too.

This is one ballsy babe. Rafe shook his head in admiration, unable to take his eyes off her departing back.

Helen's wet hair hugged her head, and her soggy clothes outlined her fine body as she stormed away from them all. Barefooted, she continued toward their blankets near the horses, her hips swaying with her wide strides. She sank down cross-legged on the ground and pulled a comb out of a saddlebag. While they all gawked at her, she idly combed out the long, red strands, as if she hadn't just felled three grown men.

God, she was like some Celtic warrior princess.

I think I'm in love.

But then Rafe glanced at the other men, and realized Pablo and Sancho were regarding her in the same way. Ignacio, though, glanced back and forth speculatively between Rafe and Helen.

"That woman ees *big* trouble," the ruffian proclaimed, turning to Rafe. "How do you stop from killing her?"

"Self-control," Rafe answered, unclenching his fists. He'd been apprehensive that the bandit might go after Helen, and he was prepared to fight for her. But it would have been a losing battle with Ignacio holding the firearms, and his two pals placed between him and Helen. No, the time wasn't right yet.

"The *puta* ees too fearless." Ignacio shrugged then. "Ah, well, after she corkscrews me five or six times, I weel sell her to a brothel in San Francisco. The cribs in the bay city weel take the fight out of her soon enough."

"How about me?" Pablo whined.

"And me?" Sancho added. "Don't we get corkscrewed, too?"

Ignacio nodded. "We all get our turns."

"You're not screwing Hel . . . my wife," Rafe lashed out. It was a rather foolish assertion in the face of Ignacio's revolvers, but they would touch her over his dead body.

"I weel do whatever I want with the whore," Ignacio declared icily. "Perhaps it weel be tonight. Then again, maybe I weel wait till after your death mañana. We shall see."

On that happy note, he forced Rafe to walk in front of him back to the campsite, where he hurriedly donned his damp clothing. Ignacio headed back to his tree, where he plopped to the ground, his gun in his lap, eying his captives with evil intent the entire time.

It took a long time for Rafe to get Helen to talk to him again. Throughout a meal of the most abominable, stringy rabbit stew and thick black coffee, she ignored him.

Throughout his detailed explanation of his motives in telling the bandits that he planned to make love with her and let them watch, she stared ahead stonily.

Throughout his clumsy efforts to reapply the bandage and ointment to his own aching ass, she tuned him out.

Even when he grudgingly praised her karate skills, she refused to budge.

The orange sunset gradually gave it up for another day. Flickering shadows began to blanket the secluded campsite.

Leaving their two captives alone for a brief moment, the three bandits began to lay out their bedrolls, but they kept a close eye on Rafe and Helen. Whispering furtively, they argued amongst themselves, presumably over which one got the first jab at Helen.

Rafe used that opportunity to approach Helen once again. His hands remained untied and, if he was going to make his move to escape, he wanted it to be tonight, after their captors fell asleep. But, first, he'd have to inform Helen of the plan. Timing was everything, as he'd told her before. And teamwork. So, he muttered an apology . . . sort of. "I'm sorry if you thought I really meant what I said," he blurted out ungraciously.

She raised her brown eyes, blinking with surprise. Although her hair was red, her eyelashes were dark brown and thick and incredibly sexy. Her full, sensuous lips opened, as if to speak, then clamped shut.

He hit his head with the heel of one hand to rid it of the unwelcome, consuming attraction.

Helen wasn't really mad at Rafe anymore. She'd accepted his explanation about the Mexicans' obsession with religion. For one thing, she'd had lots of experience in the military with recruits who harbored ridiculous, but deep-seated, superstitions, many of them grounded in religion. Some wouldn't go into combat without a certain blessed crucifix. There were pilots who were convinced they had to say three Hail Marys in a row—no more, no less—or their flight would be doomed.

Yes, these three nitwits might actually stay clear of her if they believed she was married to Rafe. But Rafe should have told her ahead of time about his plan. And he didn't have to be so crude when talking about their so-called marriage.

Marriage? A clear, erotic picture flashed in her mind of what marriage to a man like Rafe would be like. She recalled his words to her back on the plane; "I'd wrap your legs around my waist and bury myself inside you. And I'd be kissing you the entire time to muffle your screams. . . ."

Oh, my God! What's happening to me?

Rafe sank down beside her on the horse blanket that would serve as her bedroll, and she shifted away from his alluring body heat.

"Helen, I admire your bravery and your expertise in defending yourself, but don't you ever trust anyone besides yourself?"

"Huh? You mean, I should lean on a man, like some helpless little bimbo?" She batted her eyelashes at him, and he watched their fluttering with an odd fascination.

"No," he said, glancing away, then back again. "I meant that you seem to consider yourself the only one capable of taking charge or making intelligent decisions. Where's your Army team spirit? Not once today have you honestly considered me capable of handling this situation. You have a way of making a man feel, well, less than a man."

That criticism stopped Helen cold. She tried to think back. Had she really acted so superior? So condescending?

"You treat me like an imbecile," he continued. "I know I can't ride a horse—*yet*—but I can defend both of us.

74

Timing is everything in a fight. Give me some credit for waiting until the right moment to take care of these jerks. Hell, I spent the better part of my life on the L.A. streets with a knife in one hand and a gun in the other.''

His face was bleak for a split second before it closed over into an unreadable mask. ''And that's another thing. You never—not today, or anytime during the four years we were together at Stonewall—you never once asked me anything about my life. You made, and continue to make, judgments about me without knowing me. Oh, what's the use!'' He threw out his hands hopelessly.

''You are amazing. In the midst of the trouble we face now, you bring up ancient grievances. I can't believe you even remember me and the little contact we had twelve years ago.''

''Oh, I remember all right, babe. I remember every little thing.'' His blue eyes held hers ... beautiful eyes with long, ebony lashes. Unconsciously, he licked his firm upper lip, slowly, and she wished ... Oh, the things she wished didn't bear examination!

Rafe was a gorgeous, gorgeous man, and she was going to have to work very hard to stamp out her impossible attraction to the brute. ''And you've thought about these things all these years?'' she asked in astonishment.

He nodded. ''What was it that poet Langston Hughes said one time? Something about a dream deferred. It doesn't just wither up and blow away. Instead, like a raisin in the sun, it just festers and eventually explodes.''

A dream deferred? Oh, surely, he can't be referring to me as his dream. She immediately stifled that enticing thought. ''Rafael Santiago quoting poetry? Wonders never cease.''

He cast her a sheepish grin. ''Don't look so stunned. I'm amazed myself. One day in your company and I go off the deep end.'' He raked his fingers through his thick hair, no longer wet from his dunking in the stream. She had an unexpected, outrageous desire to touch the strands herself to test the texture.

"You're right, Helen," Rafe said, jarring her back to attention, "this isn't the time for this discussion. We have to talk about *today's* problems. I've been thinking—do you suppose that the Army gave us some kind of hallucinogenic drugs?"

"Would you get off your Army-bashing kick?"

"Hey, it wouldn't be the first time the military has done that kind of experiment."

"This nightmare we've landed in has absolutely nothing to do with the Army."

"What other explanation is there?" He was playing with the nap of the blanket as he spoke, his long, surprisingly graceful fingers stroking absently, first in one direction, then another.

What if . . . Oh, Lord!

He looked up abruptly and caught her watching his fingers with parted lips.

He knew.

She thought he'd laugh.

But he didn't. He stared at her questioningly, hungrily.

Helen closed her eyes against the sensual assault. Oh, he was a master at this game of seduction. She was a mere novice.

"Stop trying to rattle me," she snapped.

"I rattle you?" he asked with boyish pleasure, leaning back on his elbows and stretching out his long legs, crossing them at the ankle. He watched her the entire time.

"Back to our situation," she insisted, licking her lips nervously. The smooth line of his muscled thighs drew her eyes, and her pulse quickened. "I told you before. In my opinion, we've traveled back in time."

"Maybe it's UFOs," he said, ignoring her theory. "Yeah, maybe we're on another planet. But I never expected aliens to look like these three stooges."

"Stop joking. This is serious."

"Who's joking?

"Rafe, time travel is the only explanation. I know these mountains like the back of my hand. It's the same place, but different. I've studied the clothing on these three men, too. They're all handmade, and some of the fabrics are of a type no longer available. The guns are collectors' items, early models of Colt revolvers, I would guess. Worth a fortune.''

"A fortune, huh? Maybe we could take them back with us and send them to Sotheby's or some other auction house. I could really, *really* use the cash.''

"Is money that important to you?"

"Money is *very* important to me. In fact, you could say it's everything right now.''

How sad! She put that thought aside, for the present. "So, do you accept that this is time travel?"

"Hell, I don't know. I'll tell you this. If it is time travel, it wasn't caused by science. I think we sort of died, and God sent us here for a reason. You know, like Purgatory.''

She laughed. "*Sort of* died? Is that like being sort of pregnant?" She pressed the bridge of her nose with a thumb and forefinger, trying to solve the puzzle. When she looked back at him, she said, "Heck, your explanation is as good as any. Assuming we have time traveled at heavenly direction, how do you figure we're going to get back to the future? Sprout wings?"

He bit his bottom lip in concentration. "I haven't really thought about it, but I guess we'll have to go back to the site where we landed. I bet . . .'' His eyes brightened with sudden insight. ". . . I bet we need to parachute off that cliff where we almost hit.''

"Hmmm. Sounds logical. Does Pablo still have your harness and the parachutes?"

He thought a moment. "Yeah. I saw them when he started to set up camp.''

"Then we should be okay.''

They exchanged a hopeful smile.

She lifted her chin then. "Just remember, I'm still the officer in charge.''

"No, you're not. The ground rules changed the moment we landed in this time warp. You are Helen Prescott, and

77

I'm Rafael Santiago. Just two people trying to survive . . . together.''

She started to argue, then stopped herself. Perhaps she had been too rigid in the past. "Trust, right?" She held out a hand for a shake to seal the agreement.

"Right." He shook her hand solemnly, then ruined the businesslike nature of the gesture by turning her hand over in his, and kissing the palm.

She made a low hiss of protest.

"I couldn't help myself." He grinned boyishly and released her hand, which tingled with the imprint of his lips. She pressed it tightly with her other hand, but the tingle remained.

She fought for her usual emotionless poise. "All right. We've got to follow Army guidelines, view this as any other landing within enemy lines," she said, all business now.

"Huh?"

"You know. The Army survival manual. Live by your wits, but rely on basic skills."

Rafe groaned. "Here we go again."

She tried to recall the specific instructions. "Make decisions quickly. Improvise. Adapt. Remain cool, calm, and collected. Be patient. Hope for the best, prepare for the worst." She felt really good about remembering so much from the manual . . . until she looked at Rafe.

He was shaking with laughter. "You are a real piece of work, Prissy. Do you really believe all this crap?"

She stiffened. "Okay, Mr. Know-It-All, what's the plan?"

"First, we sleep together on this blanket tonight."

"Oh, Lord, we're back to that again." And the tingle on her palm raced up her arm, out to her breasts, and then, slam dunk, down to her groin.

"Trust, Helen. Remember?"

She eyed him suspiciously.

"We have to *pretend* we're married. No, don't look at me like that. I don't mean make love, or put on a show for these creeps. Although, if you *want* to make love, I'm willing.''

"Cut it out, Rafe."

"I'll try," he said with an exaggerated sigh. "Anyhow, what we need is time. Their belief that we're married will put them off for a little while. That, and your demonstration of how you'll karate chop their privates if they touch one hair on your . . . hmmm . . . you know, not your chinny-chin-chin."

She inhaled sharply at his vulgarity.

He didn't notice her reaction and went on. "We can make our move tonight, after they fall asleep. This is as good a place as any to ditch them."

"And head back to our landing site?"

"Uh, not right away," he said evasively.

"But, Rafe, we have to be careful. Don't forget that they believe you're the Angel Bandit, and there's a price on your head. Geez, in this primitive time period, the authorities might really hang you."

He waved her concerns aside. "I'll be careful, but I can't go back right away." He avoided looking at her directly.

"Why not? Spill it, Rafe. What exactly do you have in mind?"

"Oh, hell! You're not gonna like this—"

"Tell me," she demanded icily.

He held her eyes defiantly. Helen could bitch and moan all she wanted, but he'd be damned if he backed down from this one. It was too important. "If I have the dumb luck to land in 1850, I'd be a fool not to turn it into good luck, and . . ."

"And?"

Rafe hesitated, watching Helen's stubborn chin lift to the sky. He'd been avoiding this moment, but he couldn't put it off any longer. "And I'm headed for the goldfields. We've landed in the middle of the Gold Rush, for God's sake. I'm not going back to 1996 without a load of gold in my pockets."

She stood indignantly. "Money again? Everything

comes back to material goods for you, doesn't it? Is there anything more important to you than money?''

His eyes traveled over her body in a slow, smoldering sweep. "Well, there is one thing."

"Forget I asked." She glared at him. "What about me? What am I supposed to do while you gallivant off to prospect?"

He smiled optimistically. "You gallivant along with me. We'll be partners. We can share a claim. It'll be fun, Helen. Really. An adventure. We'll get rich together."

She rolled her eyes. "How long?"

"Just a few weeks. Maybe less."

"What if I refuse to go?"

"I'm taking my harness with me. You can do whatever you want." Actually, he cared a whole lot about what she decided, and he would never leave her behind, no matter what he'd just implied. He'd even force her to accompany him if she balked.

"You can't do this."

"Wanna bet?"

"What about all this teamwork baloney you just threw around?"

"We're still a team, baby. It's your choice whether you want to come with me or not." He crossed his fingers behind his back at his small lie.

"I don't believe this!" she exclaimed, then spun on her heel and started to walk toward the stream.

"Where are you going?" he asked worriedly. Knowing her, she might have a grenade in her back pocket and make him the target. "To bathe again?" he quipped with forced lightness in his voice.

"No, I'm going to brush my teeth. I've got a real bad taste in my mouth right now."

"Where'd you get a toothbrush? Did you bring it with you? How farsighted of you!" He was trying to change the subject and get her in a better mood.

"No, I'm going to make one with a shredded twig. Didn't you learn anything in survival class?"

"A twig?" Rafe muttered, his brow furrowed. Yeah, now that he thought about it, he remembered, but he wasn't exactly sure how it was done. "Hey, can you make me one, too?"

She said something incomprehensible through gritted teeth.

"I guess that means no."

This time, the words she sliced back at him were very comprehensible . . . and graphic . . . and not like Helen at all. Maybe it would take a little longer for her to adjust to his minor detour back to the future.

Rafe lay back on the blanket, very satisfied with the course he'd laid for them. His eyes drifted shut. It had been a long, tiring day, and he suddenly realized how much he craved sleep. Plus, he would need his wits later when they made their escape. Just a few winks.

He was jolted awake a short time later by a hand clamped on his arm, shaking him.

"Wha-at?" he said groggily.

Pablo peered down at him. And in the distance he heard the oddest noise, *"Glug, glug, glug, glug, glug . . ."*

"What is *that*?" Pablo asked, pointing to the stream.

Rafe watched as Helen raised a cupped hand of water to her mouth, swished the liquid around, *"Glug, glug, glug, glug, glug . . ."* then spit it out.

"Gargling," Rafe told the awestruck bandit. Son of a bitch! Even in a time-travel nightmare, she was concerned about every detail of dental hygiene. She would probably floss, too.

"Glug, glug, glug, glug, glug."

"Is she practicing one of her sexual tricks?" Pablo asked.

"Maybe," Rafe said with chuckle. "Yeah, I think she did mention a new trick she wanted to try."

"Gargling, it's called?"

"Yep," Rafe said and lay back down, smiling. His eyes closed once again. That would teach Helen to refuse to make him a toothbrush.

"Corkscrewing *and* gargling," he heard Pablo telling Sancho and Ignacio in the background before he dozed off again.

"Ooohm. Ooohm. Ooohm."

Rafe emerged from sleep once again, this time to the low chanting hum.

"Ooohm. Ooohm. Ooohm."

Rafe didn't want to open his eyes.

"Ooohm. Ooohm. Ooohm."

But the annoying chant just went on and on. Maybe it was an owl or some wild animal. Like a raccoon. Or a bear. *A bear!* He cracked one eyelid halfway.

Helen. Why was he not surprised?

"Ooohm. Ooohm. Ooohm."

She was sitting with her legs folded in one of those lotus positions that he recalled an old dancer girlfriend of his had used for meditation. Her back was erect, arms crossed over her chest, and she stared straight ahead.

"Ooohm. Ooohm. Ooohm."

"What the hell are you doing now?" he grumbled, coming to his feet.

"Meditating. *Ooohm.* Finding my center. *Ooohm.* I do this every morning and every night. *Ooohm.* You should try it. *Ooohm.* It cleanses the spirit. *Ooohm.*"

"I'd like to cleanse something," he walked away with a shake of his head. She really was a fruitcake.

After relieving himself in a bush, with a sleepy-eyed Pablo following him to keep guard, Rafe came back to the clearing.

Helen no longer sat in the lotus position. Instead, she was moving through her karate exercises, in slow motion. The deliberately decelerated, inadvertently sensual moves were like an erotic dance of seduction. She twisted her body like a ballerina, stretched her arms, spun and bent, all in one connected, smooth movement.

He felt himself grow hard.

The only sound in the dusky clearing was that of crickets,

and a faint breeze riffling the leaves, and breathing. Mostly his.

"What in God's name are you doing now?" he choked out.

"Forms," she answered without looking at him and continued her unconsciously sexual motions.

"Forms?" Pablo whispered and rushed off to his comrades. "She does corkscrews, gargling, *and* forms," he babbled excitedly to his friends. "Can we have her now, Ignacio? Can we?"

"No, no, no. We mus' wait till her husband ees dead . . . if he ees her husband. One more day," Ignacio interjected quickly. "We cannot risk the wrath of our Blessed Lord for taking another man's *esposa*. We are honorable men."

Honorable? Rafe thought. *Like snakes.*

"*Díos mío!* I cannot wait till we get to Sacramento City an' we can have her all to ourselves," Pablo said then, quickly overcoming his initial disappointment.

They all made salivating noises of appreciation and anticipation.

"After we get our reward money in Sacramento City, the sheriff weel hang *El Ángel Bandido*. *Sí*, we can wait one night," Ignacio told them. "Then Elena weel be all ours."

There were more drooling sounds.

But Rafe just smiled, watching Helen, because he knew something they didn't.

She is mine, mine, mine.

Chapter Six

Helen agreed to let Rafe share her blanket.

But then, she really had no choice. The bandits decided not to risk taking turns guarding them through the night, untied.

"Tie them up again," Ignacio ordered.

"Why?" Rafe asked. "You can trust us."

"Do you think we are *estupído*?" Ignacio countered.

Luckily, it was a rhetorical question.

After a lengthy argument, the bandits concluded that: one, Rafe really was the Angel Bandit, and therefore dangerous; and, two, Helen was a lunatic who attacked innocent men with weird hand and leg gyrations in the midst of fits.

Ignacio approached with a length of rope.

Helen had to give Rafe credit. He tried to wrest Ignacio's gun from him; however, just as he gained the weapon and had a stranglehold on the leader, Sancho came up from behind and walloped him over the head with a rock. Her efforts to waylay Pablo proved equally useless since he, too, held a revolver.

So much for Rafe's plan for them to escape during the night!

After the brief scuffle and Rafe's foul expletives over the goose egg rising on his crown, the outlaws tied them together, lying on their sides back to back. Rafe's arms were pulled backward around her waist and the wrists tied. Her arms were bound in a similar manner, back and around his body. In addition, the bandits secured one ankle each to a stake several yards away.

"Are you guys related to the Marquis de Sade?" she asked.

"What's a mark-key-sod?" Sancho inquired.

"Our arms and legs are going to be numb by morning," Rafe protested, ignoring Sancho's dumb query.

"Would you rather be tied belly to belly?" Ignacio chortled.

"Nude," Pablo added.

"Well . . ." Rafe said, considering.

"NO!" Helen said, absolutely.

"This is no way to spend a wedding night," Rafe grumbled.

"It's not our wedding night," Helen hissed, for his ears only.

"Abstinence ees good for the soul," Ignacio said. "Besides, you'd best be saying your confession tonight, *Señor Ángel*. By mañana, you may very well be a real angel. Heh, heh, heh."

They were all silent at that macabre reminder. Then Sancho conceded, with a sympathetic sigh, "*Ah, mierda!* Perhaps we should let *El Ángel Bandido* have his last night with Elena."

"And we could watch," Pablo suggested.

"You've got a real Peeping Tom fetish, Pablo," Helen declared. "Why don't you get a life?"

"What ees a fat-dish?" Pablo asked Rafe.

Rafe laughed.

Helen could feel it all the way down to his buns, which moved against hers. *Aaaarrgh!*

"The next man Elena corkscrews weel be me," Ignacio asserted.

"Aren't you afraid I'll tell God what you're doing to my wife?" Rafe tossed out to Ignacio. "After the hanging, I'll be going through those pearly gates. Then, I'll have easy access to the Lord's ear."

"Hah! You weel, no doubt, be in hell." But Ignacio

worried the edge of his big mustache between a thumb and forefinger. "Besides, I do not believe you are married."

Disregarding Ignacio's scoffing, Rafe went on with obvious relish, "I hear God has a special place in hell for adulterers. He gives Satan free rein to torture men who bang other men's wives. Hot irons. Eye pincers. Snakes."

Ignacio gasped at the word "snakes."

"Oh, yeah, snakes," Rafe said, picking up on Ignacio's fear of reptiles. "I hear St. Patrick sent all those leftover snakes from Ireland down *there* just so Lucifer could make up a pit for adulterers to sleep in. Yep, that's what my priest always said, 'Adulterers are snakes who should sleep with snakes for all eternity.' Hmmm. What'll He think of a man who corkscrews another man's wife? Think that counts as adultery?"

"She won't be your wife then. You weel be dead," Ignacio argued, but there was a slight note of doubt in his voice.

"Would you all stop talking about me like a piece of meat? I'm not making love with anyone tonight, and that's that."

Eventually, the three shuffled off, congratulating themselves on their prowess, and Helen and Rafe tried to find a comfortable position.

Unable to sleep, Helen finally said, "Rafe? Are you awake?"

"Yeah."

"Why do you keep goading me? It's really mean of you."

"Me? I just kept those guys from tying us together, naked, face to face. How is that mean?"

"It's the way you do it. There's always a sexual message in every reference you make to me."

"Well, it's like this, Prissy. A lot of sexual bells go off in my body every time I look at you."

"See. You're always teasing me."

"Who's teasing? Hey, even with only our backsides touching, I gotta tell you, my chimes are ringing."

"Oh, give me a break! I think you just get a kick out of being politically incorrect."

"Maybe. I'm a product of my environment, you're a product of yours. I don't know why you think it's mean of me, though. Don't you like knowing you're attractive to men . . . to me?"

Actually, she was liking it way too much. Despite the inappropriateness of some of his remarks. Despite his pushing the envelope of suggestiveness. But she'd never tell him that. "Ours is a professional relationship. There should be respect and distance and—"

"Distance? Hell, I can feel the seam of your panties with my butt. And you're talking distance?"

"It's impossible to talk to you. Let's change the subject."

He laughed. "To what?"

"Well, tell me what you've been doing all these years. You obviously went to law school. Where?"

"UCLA."

"And after that?"

"Public defenders' office for two years."

"Really?" She wasn't sure why that surprised her. Yes, she was. "You don't make much money there."

"Right. That's why I left."

A sudden thought occurred to her. She couldn't believe she hadn't asked before. "Are you married?"

He gave a short laugh. "No."

An unexplainable rush of pleasure washed over her. "Ever?"

"Never."

"Why?"

She felt his shoulders shrug. "I couldn't afford marriage."

"Oh." All kinds of possibilities arose in her mind. "Does that mean there was someone you would have liked to marry?"

He didn't answer right away. Eventually, he admitted,

"There was a girl once, a long time ago, but it never would have worked."

She wanted to know more. Was it a Mexican girl? Someone from his old neighborhood, or perhaps a fellow law student? And had he loved her? More important, did he still? She shouldn't care. She really shouldn't. But she did.

"Enough about me. When are you and Colonel Sanders gonna bite the bullet?"

Helen bristled at his deliberately misspeaking her fiancé's name, but this time she didn't rise to the bait. "Elliott and I will likely get married at Christmas," she said. Even Helen heard the lack of enthusiasm in her voice. Why did the image of her marriage to Elliott loom in the distance like a dark cloud, not the special bright event it should be? And had it always been so? Was that why she'd put off the date so many times?

Do I make Elliott's bells chime? Helen wondered. *I don't know.* She bit her bottom lip pensively. *Isn't that sad? I really don't know.*

"Will you stay in the military?" Rafe interrupted her disturbing reflections.

"Until I get pregnant, yes. I want to have lots of kids."

Rafe's body stiffened behind her.

"Being an only child, I've always dreamed of . . . Well, anyhow, Elliott and I plan on having at least three children. I'll quit the service then."

She expected Rafe to make a smart response, but he didn't. Instead, he informed her flatly, "I don't intend to ever have any kids."

"You don't? Never?"

"Never."

"You'll probably change your mind later . . . when you meet the right woman."

"I'll never change my mind—for any woman. And I've had a vasectomy to make sure."

"Oh, Rafe."

"Don't plan a pity party for me. It was my choice. Not everyone feels the need to overpopulate the world, or clone themselves all over the planet.''

"And that's the reason why you don't want children? Somehow, I don't see you being that altruistic.''

"There you go again, Prissy, making judgments about me.''

"You're right," she admitted meekly. Geez, when had she turned into such a judgmental prig?

Rafe chuckled softly, as if reading her thoughts. "Now, now, Prissy, don't be gettin' out the guitar and love beads. I never was much good at singing 'Kumbayah.' ''

Even she had to laugh at that picture.

"Nah, it's a lot simpler than that. I grew up the oldest of nine kids with a single parent—my mother. I know first-hand what it's *really* like to raise babies, and I've had enough of it.''

"But, Rafe, babies are God's gift to mankind. Little miracles.'' Helen couldn't imagine a life without children—her children. All her life, she'd dreamed of settling down in one place, surrounded by the love of a husband and family. Never lonely.

"Boy, are you in for a rude awakening. Once you get past the miracle, there's just a whole lot of piss and puke. To this day, I can recognize the smell of baby shit at fifty paces.''

"You are—''

"So crude," he finished for her. "Anyhow, the bottom line is, kids always have problems. And they're a constant money drain. I want to enjoy life sometime before I need a walker and dentures. Champagne, caviar, a Jacuzzi . . . Yeah, a Jacuzzi. A Rolex watch, a Lamborghini.''

"So, we're back to money again.''

"Yeah, I guess we are.''

"I know it's a cliché, but money can't buy happiness.''

"Bull! I never bought that crock. And I'd sure like to test the theory. Did you ever notice that the people denigrating the good life are usually the ones living high on the hog? Like you.''

"Me? It's true I never had to worry about money, but I

wouldn't categorize the way I've lived as the good life."

"Helen, I saw the fancy cars your father drove when he visited you at college. BMW one time, Mercedes another. You went on vacations to exotic places like St. Thomas or Italy. I vacationed at McDonald's in the L.A. barrio."

"I don't ever remember noticing my father's cars, or caring what kind of vehicles they were." She frowned. Wasn't it odd that something Rafe considered so important was totally irrelevant to her?

Rafe exhaled with disbelief.

"And the vacations always seemed so boring to me. My father usually combined them with military business, and I'd be left in a hotel room with room service and a book."

"Sounds good to me."

"Oh, Rafe! My mother died of cancer when I was eight. My only memories of her involve a sick bed." She coughed to clear her tight throat. "Dad was career military. He tried to be a good single parent, keeping me with him, but we moved from base to base, never more than two years in one place. Although we had a home in San Clemente, we rarely lived there. I was always so . . . alone."

"Alone? Since when is being alone a bad thing? When I was a kid, I yearned for quiet—one little tiny space to call my own. Hah! My family was—*is*—like an octopus. Tendrils everywhere. Pushing, pulling, screaming, crying, laughing, singing, talking. Not a minute's peace."

She bit her lip, trying to understand. "Don't you care for your family?"

"Of course. But they crush me. Suck all the life out of me. Everyone wants a piece of Rafe. And I'm damn tired of being responsible for everyone."

"And you think money will be the panacea?"

"I know it will."

A heavy sadness enveloped Helen. She wished she could see Rafe's face. "We're worlds apart," she concluded sadly. "We have nothing in common, nothing that connects us, at all."

A long, telling silence hung in the air before Rafe spoke

again. "Well, that's not quite true," he said playfully. "Could you move your hands up higher? Either that, or finish me off, because right now I'm feeling real *connected* to you."

To her horror, Helen realized that her bound wrists were resting on Rafe's crotch.

She yanked her hands upward, as best she could. "I didn't . . . Oh, God. You don't think I did that deliberately?"

"Hardly. Not Prissy Prescott."

His words hurt.

Then she discovered that his bound hands were lying familiarly over her upper stomach. She looked down, and through the light of the campfire, Helen could see the dark skin of his hands and the long fingers resting intimately where only a lover's should. For some reason, tears filled her eyes, and she wished . . . She wasn't sure what she wished.

But she didn't ask him to move his hands.

Needles of pain shot through Rafe's bound wrists, up to his numb shoulders. Day-old whiskers made his face itch. He licked his dry lips, and his tongue felt fuzzy and thick. He should have made himself a twig toothbrush last night, too.

Slowly, awareness crept over his aching bones. Something had awakened him in the predawn haze.

"Ooohm, ooohm, ooohm, ooohm. . . ."

"Damn! It's not even daylight yet. What the hell are you doing now?"

"Meditating. *Ooohm.* I told you I meditate every morning and evening. *Ooohm.* It's a ritual. *Ooohm.*"

"Even when you're hog-tied, cheek-to-cheek, with a man?"

"*Ooohm.* Meditating soothes me. *Ooohm.* My body is out of synch. *Ooohm.* Don't break my concentration. *Ooohm.* You're upsetting my rhythm. *Ooohm, ooohm, ooohm . . .*"

91

He gritted his teeth. Really, she was going to drive him bonkers if he didn't set a few ground rules. "I'll give you some rhythm, honey." He undulated his hips, back and forth, against her ass.

She gasped. *"Ooohm, ooohm, ooohm . . ."* Her chants resumed, but her voice wobbled.

Good! "Helen, sweetheart, how about concentrating on this."

"Ooohm, ooohm, ooohm . . ."

"Picture my tattoo pressed against your tattoo . . ."

"Ooohm, ooohm, ooohm."

". . . and we're naked."

"Oh-oohm." Her voice faltered again.

This was fun. Shaking up Prissy Prescott was a piece of cake. "My hands are suddenly free. I'm reaching behind me to touch your—"

"Well, I'm done meditating for today," she interrupted matter-of-factly.

He smiled to himself, then yelled out, "Hey, Sancho, time to get up and water some trees. How 'bout untying my hands?"

Helen ground her teeth at his indelicacy.

Dawn was creeping over the hill now, casting bright orange streamers of light through the misty sky. It was going to be another scorcher.

"Yo, Sancho! My teeth are floating here."

Sancho rolled over and opened his bleary eyes. Groaning, Sancho favored him with an ancient Mexican hand gesture.

"You know, Helen," Rafe remarked as Sancho took his good old time coming over to untie them, "I'm usually in a bad mood in the morning, before I have my first cup of coffee. But I'm feeling real good. Today, we're gonna get free from these bozos. And we're gonna become gold prospectors and find tons and tons of gold nuggets. You can be my *señorita,* and I'll be your desperado. Don'tcha just love it?"

Helen didn't say a word. She was probably giving him

an ancient Mexican hand gesture in her head.

Yep, this day was starting out real good. He'd shown Helen who called the shots here. From now on, she'd better think twice about annoying him. Life was good.

But a short time later, as he and Sancho emerged from the woods, Rafe wasn't too sure. His hands were still bound, and he'd been forced to suffer the ignominy of Sancho undoing his pants so he could relieve himself.

"Glug, glug, glug, glug, glug . . ."

He closed his eyes wearily.

"Glug, glug, glug, glug, glug . . ."

Opening his eyes, Rafe glanced disgustedly toward the stream where Helen was gargling like a fountain. Pablo stood guard over her with a raised revolver after having apparently released her ropes. A temporary reprieve, he suspected.

"Glug, glug, glug, glug, glug . . ."

Pablo was watching her with a rapt expression of ecstasy. "Oh, I can't wait till she gargles me," the dope kept muttering.

"How soon till the hanging, do you think, Ignacio?" Sancho asked as he packed up the camping gear, obviously willing the hours away until Rafe's demise so he could get his turn at being corkscrewed and gargled by Elena.

"Take off the Angel's pants," Ignacio ordered Sancho suddenly.

"Wha-at?" Rafe cried out.

"Your trousers, *señor*. I have decided I like them. We weel trade, for now. After the hanging, I weel take mine back, too."

Rafe sneered with distaste at Ignacio's filthy leather pants with their heavy embroidery and fancy fringe and bell-bottom legs that fit over the boots. "No, thanks."

"Elena says I would look good—*mucho macho*—in your trousers," Ignacio enlightened him coldly.

Rafe narrowed his eyes accusingly at Helen. "Mucho macho?" he mouthed.

She smirked. "Did you tell Pablo that gargling was a sexual trick?"

"Take off his damn trousers," Ignacio roared, pulling out his blasted pistol and aiming it at Sancho, who was balking at his order.

"Listen, Ignacio, your pants look about a size forty-four. I have a thirty-four-inch waist. Besides, I'm more a jeans kind of guy."

Ignacio raised his gun.

With Sancho's help, Rafe shucked his duds. Luckily, Ignacio couldn't fit them over his fat butt. So, a short time later, they rode off toward Sacramento City, but Rafe wouldn't forget what Helen had tried to do to him.

He slanted a sideways glance at Helen, who was looking very pleased with herself. Then she started to whistle. It sounded like fingernails grating over a chalkboard.

Maybe the day wasn't going to turn out quite the way he'd expected.

Helen took great pleasure in having turned the tables on Rafe. "Be careful you don't get a sunburn," she called out once when they stopped to water the horses. Pablo had given her his extra hat, but there was none for Rafe.

He shot her a you'll-get-yours look, and said sweetly, "Andrew Dice Clay was right. Women's tongues are good for only one thing."

"Pig!" she chided.

"Prude."

"Lech."

"Looney."

"Chauvinist."

"Femi-Nazi."

"Ambulance chaser."

"Nipples."

"Huh?" Helen looked down quickly, relieved to see that her chest was well-covered with her camouflage blouse. She raised her eyes to Rafe's laughing ones.

He winked. "Just wanted to see if you were paying attention."

By late afternoon, they were approaching Sacramento, and the closer they got, trivial personal squabbling faded in importance. The fantastic landscape convinced them both, like nothing had before, that time travel might really be possible.

"We should have passed Blue Valley Vineyard over there," she whispered.

"And have you noticed, not one airplane has gone over the entire day?" Rafe added. "Hell, this has got to be a major flight pattern direct to McClellan Air Force Base. In fact, Interstate 50 should follow just about the same route we are, and we haven't seen one single automobile."

He raised his face to the clear, cloudless skies. His thick, unruly hair lay sweatily against his neck and over his forehead, but he was unable to brush it back because his hands were tied in front of him to the saddle horn.

After two days of not shaving and all the dust of their travel, he looked as much like a Mexican desperado as their captors claimed him to be. And Helen had to admit that, after this second day in the saddle, Rafe was handling his horse just fine, like a true Mexican *bandido,* considering the deep pain he must be in as a new rider.

"How's your blister?" she asked.

"Fine, although my ass feels like it's growing callouses."

She clucked her disapproval at his language, but, even though Rafe continually ruffled her feathers, she couldn't deny her attraction to him. If her hands were free, she'd be tempted to wipe the perspiration from his whiskered face; however, since her karate exhibition, the bandits deemed her a danger, too.

They saw more people as they neared Sacramento—emigrants in wagons who had presumably traveled the overland trail across the plains, trappers coming down from the mountains, prospectors on horses or mules, traveling singly or in groups. Always, Ignacio kept their distance, making sure that she and Rafe couldn't make any contact with the passersby.

But even from that range, Helen could see that these were not actors in red flannel shirts and dusty homespun trousers. Huge beards covered their weathered faces, and they moved with the ease of men used to the saddle, not automobiles.

"We really have traveled back in time," Helen concluded.

"I know," Rafe agreed glumly. "I know."

Even when they passed through the primitive mining town of Placerville, Ignacio refused to allow them to stop for fear someone would come to their aid before he could collect his reward.

They did stop to water the horses at a ranch in the Sacramento Valley that sported an incongruously modern sign, "The Last Chance Ranch." As they rode up the lane, leading to the ranch house, several riders—presumably the owner and his hands—approached, eying them suspiciously. Ignacio and Sancho rode forward to talk to them.

Pablo stayed behind as guard. The three of them pulled their horses to a halt near a corral fence by the house and waited. Pablo had a cocked pistol hidden under a blanket over his saddle horn. He'd been given explicit orders from Ignacio to shoot if Rafe or Helen made the slightest move to call for help or ride away. As insurance, Ignacio warned that he'd personally put a bullet through Pablo's head if he disobeyed the command.

Helen was tired and dirty and extremely fearful of their fate. But her attention was nonetheless captured by the lady standing on the porch of the ranch house. "Look at that woman!" Helen exclaimed. "Doesn't she resemble that *Vogue* cover model, Selene?"

The tall, statuesque woman, with dark hair piled atop her head, studied them with unwarranted intensity, almost horror. Despite being very pregnant, she was absolutely gorgeous.

Rafe furrowed his brow, squinting in the bright sunlight.

"I met Sandra Selente—that's Selene's real name—at a cocktail party five years ago. She didn't look at all like this woman."

"That figures!"

"What?"

"That you'd be cavorting with the rich and famous."

"Cavorting? What the hell kind of word is that? And, I'll have you know, it was a barbecue. If it was for the rich and famous, I sure was out of place."

"Hah!"

"Hah!" he threw back.

Before they had a chance to move closer and speak to the woman, she slapped a hand to her chest in dismay. Then she spoke softly to a dark-skinned man beside her and rushed into the house.

They watered their horses under Ignacio's ever-vigilant eye. At one point, the owner—James Baptiste, they learned from Pablo—was arguing with Ignacio about his captives, telling him to release them. They heard Ignacio explain that Rafe was the notorious Angel Bandit, wanted for numerous robberies throughout California, and Helen was the prostitute Elena. Mr. Baptiste appeared dubious and walked up to their horses.

Helen saw Pablo raise his pistol under the blanket. He said in an undertone, "I weel shoot the gentleman if you misbehave."

The handsome Creole addressed Rafe first. "Ignacio says you're the Angel Bandit. Is that so?"

Rafe hesitated, then nodded.

Mr. Baptiste's lips thinned angrily. "You killed an acquaintance of mine in Sonora last year."

"I've never killed anyone," Rafe asserted, despite Ignacio's hiss of warning. Wisely, Rafe clamped his mouth shut, refusing to say more.

Mr. Baptiste turned to Elena. "And you? Are you an accomplice to this man?"

"Yes."

Throwing his hands out hopelessly, Mr. Baptiste walked

off then, muttering, "*Merde!* They all deserve each other."

"There will be other chances to escape," Rafe assured her a short time later when they moved on. She certainly hoped so.

As they proceeded on their grueling ride toward Sacramento, she and Rafe couldn't stop pondering their remarkable adventure. They both accepted that somehow, someway, they had landed in a time warp, and they discussed the repercussions of their situation.

"This is the damnedest thing that's ever happened to me." Rafe shook his head in confusion.

"And you think I bee-bop through the ages all the time?" Helen heard the shrewishness in her voice but was unable to control its stridency. Fear churned in her stomach, and Rafe's flippant attitude about the potential dangers they faced made it even worse.

"Rafe, aren't you worried about what will happen to us in Sacramento? I mean, they might really kill you if they believe you're this Angel Bandit guy."

"I have a plan, hon. Trust me." He winked.

"A plan?" She rolled her eyes, trying to imagine the leap of faith needed to trust this scoundrel. "And me . . . Well, what's going to happen to me? I sure as heck am *not* going to turn tricks in an 1850 mining town."

He grinned.

"It's not funny."

She saw him struggling to force a more serious expression on his face, but he couldn't stop grinning. The ass!

"The idea of you turning tricks just boggles the mind."

The fact that Rafe considered her so sexually unattractive that she couldn't even be a hooker in a female-starved mining town shouldn't bother her, but it did. She felt like crying. She was hot and tired and afraid and homesick. And she sat fighting back tears because a vulgar, arrogant creep judged her lacking in some way.

"You're more the kind of woman a man keeps to himself."

She jerked her head to attention.

"Sort of like a secret gift a guy hordes for himself."

She should tell him to stop. Right now. But her tongue stuck to the roof of her mouth.

"On the outside, you're all cool professional. Flame hair skinned back. Kissable lips pressed into a forbidding line. Sultry voice turned shrill. Smoldering eyes cool. Every sexy curve of your tempting body covered by sexless, drab clothing."

"Oh, my God," she whimpered, mesmerized by his wicked words.

"But your man—your lover—knows. *I know* . . ."

She gasped.

". . . that underneath, when you let your hair loose on the pillow and part your lips, your voice is a hot whisper of invitation. Your eyes mist with desire. And every move you make in those loose military clothes," he continued, inclining his head to indicate her garments, "well, I suspect that underneath there are five-foot-eight inches of pure ripe-to-be-turned-on woman, waiting to explode."

"You are the most outrageous, egotistical—"

"Yep," he went on, ignoring her tirade, "you were born to f—"

"No! Don't you dare utter that word!"

"What?" he asked with wide-eyed innocence. "I was going to say, You were born to fan a man's flame." He blinked at her with exaggerated confusion. "What did you think I was gonna say?"

Fan a man's flame? She glared at him warily. He'd done it again, disconcerted her, turned her knees to jelly and her brain to mush. The cad! "So, do I fan your flame?" she let slip before she had a chance to bite her tongue.

"Oh, baby," he said in a silky whisper. His eyes held hers, and the expression on his face turned solemn. "How can you even ask that question?"

"How can I ask? I'll tell you how. You're always taunting me, making fun of me. You make me feel . . . inade-quate."

His eyes shot up. "Are you serious? Man, oh, man,

maybe you should learn to listen to what people don't say sometimes, not what they do say. It might be a real education for you.''

''Stop talking in riddles.''

His eyes glittered angrily. ''You're my impossible dream. Don't you know that?''

''No, don't say that—''

Rafe immediately seemed to regret his impulsive words, but he went on angrily, ''I'll say it, all right. Damn it, you want to know the truth? Well, here it is. This is 1850, and thousands of men are rushing to California to find the pot at the end of the rainbow, their *El Dorado*. Well, you're my *El Dorado*, sweetheart, and always have been. The unreachable prize.''

''Oh, Rafe.'' This man, this infuriating man, had a way of making her blood boil with fury, then, in the next instant, making her heart melt with tenderness.

He gulped visibly and stared straight ahead, clearly upset that he'd revealed so much. Finally, he murmured, ''I'm sorry. I shouldn't have said that.''

''Rafe, you are driving me crazy with your Dr. Jekyll and Mr. Hyde moods. One minute you profess to care about me, and the next you stalk me, like a predator.''

His lips twitched with mirth.

''Can I ask you one thing, and get an honest answer?''
He shrugged. ''Depends.''

''If what you say is true, if I'm more important to you than gold, then let's go back to the landing site. I'm afraid to go into Sacramento. I have a bad feeling—''

He turned toward her. ''And if we go back . . . if I give up the quest for gold . . . Will I have you?''

His question stunned her, and she couldn't speak, at first. ''Of course not. I mean, I'm engaged . . . and, no, of course not.''

''Then we're not going back,'' he said. He was obviously not surprised by her answer. ''But let's get one thing clear. You have nothing to be afraid of if you come with me. In Sacramento or anywhere else. I promise you'll be safe. You might not ever . . . Well, you might not ever care for me, but you can at least give me the courtesy of your trust."

"Oh, Rafe."

"Stop saying, 'Oh, Rafe,' like I'm a pitiful little kid."

"Oh, Rafe."

He made a snarling sound, low in his throat, then informed her smoothly, "Before this trek is over, I'm going to teach you sixty-seven ways to say, 'Oh, Rafe,' and they're all going to be accompanied by a sigh or a moan. Guaranteed." And the heated look he cast her way was heavy with promise.

Oh, Rafe!

Helen realized, at that moment, that she was thinking of him as anything but a little boy, and that his promise held a tremendous, forbidden appeal.

Chapter Seven

They entered Sacramento City at dusk.

Having grown up in California, Rafe knew from his school studies that Sacramento City, as it was called then, had been the gateway to the northern mines during the Gold Rush, the staging place where most travelers stopped to rest and stock up for the grueling trek into the treasure-laden hills. But he'd never pictured it quite like this remarkable spectacle.

Truly, they'd landed smack dab in the middle of living, breathing history.

As they got closer, the roads and open stretches of land became thronged with teams of worn, weather-beaten emigrants coming over the mountains from the East or up from San Francisco. Most of the roads ran parallel to the coast, connecting the missions that had been built by the Franciscan padres in the previous century. When the exhausted Forty-Niners finally reached Sacramento City, they pitched their tents by the hundreds in thickets around the outskirts of the town.

Bug-eyed with amazement, Rafe felt like he'd stumbled onto an old *Gunsmoke* TV set. Any minute now, he expected to see Festus saunter out of a saloon, hitch up his trousers, spit a wide arc of tobacco juice, and say, "Dagnabbit, Marshal Dillon, let's go round up some cattle rustlers."

And James Arness would say, "Yep, but first I gotta go kiss Kitty good-bye. Don't forget to bring along Deputy Santiago, too."

Rafe smiled at the image—a boyhood dream realized.

But this was no dream, he reminded himself as his horse nickered softly in the furnacelike heat and tried to edge away from the crowded clearing.

"Easy, boy, easy," he crooned, nudging his horse with his knees. He was getting real good at judging F. Lee's moods and had learned he could control the fidgety horse with just the light pressure of his legs. Good thing, too, since his hands were still tied to the saddle horn. If it weren't for his sore muscles, Rafe would have felt pretty good about his improved riding skills. And the blister wasn't even bothering him anymore.

Ignacio led the way as their horses continued to weave through the tent city, being careful to avoid the briars and stumps of dead trees felled for firewood. Rafe followed, with Pablo and Sancho on either side of him. The stolen horses trailed behind them.

Ignacio had insisted that Helen ride with him on his horse once they neared the town, fearing the two captives would call for help or try to escape. Throwing a blanket over Helen's shoulder, the vicious outlaw had hidden his revolver pressed against her heart, warning, "One word from either of you, or one move to escape, *Señor Ángel,* and Elena ees one dead *puta.*"

Rafe had every intention of taking care of the bastard, and soon. It wouldn't be much longer before he made his move. Then the rotten creep would pay for every insult, threat, inconvenience, and bruise he'd delivered to either of them.

But for now, Rafe couldn't help gaping at the men who sat about the numerous campfires, talking enthusiastically. Others leaned against trees reading letters from home or smoking thin cigars. Some strummed guitars and fiddles, singing poignant songs. A few curried horses. Many were eating meager meals from tin plates in front of their sorry tents and drinking large amounts of what must be hard liquor from metal cups or straight from amber bottles.

And while Rafe was doing all his gaping, the scruffy,

sunburned, bearded prospectors, wearing the typical miner's garb of red flannel shirt; suspenders; baggy, snuff colored trousers; and high leather boots, gaped right back at him.

Actually, not at *him*. It was Helen who fascinated these googly-eyed men, most of whom were in their twenties.

Their passage was marked by a domino effect. The music gradually stopped. Voices stilled. And the raucous camp noises ground to a halt at first glimpse of that rare, and highly prized commodity in an 1850 mining town—a female. And an attractive one, at that. In Helen's wake, Rafe heard them murmur, with awe, "A woman!"

"She rides astride. Don't that beat all creation?"

"A woman! Hell's bells! And she carries herself like a high-falutin' lady."

"But she's with greasers. Can't be no lady, 'ceptin' mebbe a fancy lady."

Rafe bristled at the racist slur. He'd experienced more than his share of discrimination, but somehow he hadn't expected to find it here, too.

"A woman! Hot diggity damn!" new arrivals to the scene chanted to Helen's departing back.

"Would ya look at that red hair. Whooee! Bet she's a feisty one in the saddle. Ha, ha, ha!"

"Her legs look mighty fine grippin' that horse. I'd like her ta ride me the same way. Yessirree, I would."

"Lordy, Lordy, I ain't had me a good diddling in a coon's age."

"Me, neither," a whole bunch of the gold seekers concurred.

"Did you see her titty juttin' out against that shirt? Oh, damn, I bet the nipple's pink, and I do like me a pink nipple."

Luckily, Helen didn't hear the remarks that were made after she passed. Her attention was centered, like Rafe's, on the unusual historical view unfolding before them.

"Yep, redheads have brown ones, and they're big as grapes."

"How would you know, Zeke? You ain't never had a woman 'cept in a haystack with her skirts thrown over her head."

"Well, a man don't look at the mantel when he's pokin' the fire."

More laughter.

"Gawdamighty, do you think her woman hair is red, too?"

"You'll never find out, you sons of bitches," Rafe lashed out, finally fed up with the lewd observations. Whether Helen heard their comments or not, she was supposed to be his woman, and he couldn't allow the insults to go on.

The miners studied him for the first time, startled by his proprietary remark. Their eyes swept over his strange shirt and bound hands, questioningly.

Sancho and Pablo edged closer, their slitted eyes warning him to remain quiet. Their unholstered guns reinforced the message.

Rafe glanced forward to see Helen's reaction. Still unaware of the attention she was garnering or the suggestive utterances of the men, she pivoted her head from side to side, inhaling the fantastic sights from her vantage point in front of Ignacio.

Ignacio, however, noticed the dozens of prospectors who began to follow them on foot as they left the encampment and moved into the town itself, but he ignored their questions.

Pablo and Sancho were not so reticent.

"Who is she?" the miners asked.

"Elena," Pablo announced with a wide smile.

"*Elena?* Really?" the miners enthused.

"Elena . . . Elena . . . Elena . . ." The name rippled excitedly throughout the campsite, like an echo.

A beautiful white woman was one thing. A beautiful white whore would be quite another to these sex-starved young men, Rafe realized.

"And she belongs to us," Sancho told them, patting his pistol for emphasis.

"Will you sell her favors?" one grizzly trapper asked, scratching the groin of his buckskin breeches with anticipation.

"Maybe later," Sancho said generously.

"After she's corkscrewed us a few dozen times," Pablo stressed. "And done the 'gargle' and the 'forms' on us."

There was a communal sigh of, "Aaah, the corkscrew!" Then, they all inquired, at once, "The gargle? The forms?"

Pablo explained, with relish, the new sexual tricks Elena could do for her customers.

"I'll give ya fifty dollars fer one night," the trapper offered.

"A hundred," another yelled out.

"Two hundred, if there's an extry corkscrew."

"Five hundred, but she takes on the two of us," a pair of towhead twins, better suited to an Iowa farm setting, threw in, blushing profusely at the hoots of their friends.

"I'll buy her from you for five thousand dollars," a steely-eyed man with a French accent offered suddenly, throwing his cigar to the ground and stomping it with a polished leather boot. Rafe heard someone whisper that this was Pierre Lamoyne, who ran a brothel in San Francisco.

That last cash figure caught Ignacio's attention, and he halted his horse until they caught up. "She ees not for sale . . . *yet*," he told Lamoyne. "And your price ees much too low."

"Ten thousand, then," Lamoyne countered, stepping close to examine the merchandise.

Ignacio licked his lips greedily in consideration. "Perhaps—"

"Like hell!" Rafe shouted, and Helen jumped, seeming to come out of her trance. "She's my wife, and no one's touching her."

"I'll sell the *puta* if I want to," Ignacio asserted, tossing aside the blanket, exposing his gun pressed to Helen's heart.

Rafe's blood turned cold at the peril. Ignacio might pull the trigger on a whim. Rafe bit his tongue to force back more angry words. *Calm down. Take it easy. Wait for the moment. The opening. Don't panic.*

"His wife?" the miners asked. "*Who* is he?"

"*El Ángel Bandido,*" Pablo said.

"Ooooh," a number of the men said, and backed away.

"I'm *not* the Angel Bandit."

"Who said anything about selling me?" Helen wanted to know, suddenly alert. Fearlessly, she pushed Ignacio's pistol aside with her bound hands and twisted in the saddle to look back at the bandit. "Did you dare to tell these men that I'm for sale?"

When he just glared at her, she jabbed him in the stomach with an elbow. "You male chauvinist pig! When I get loose, I'm going to pull out your tongue and karate chop it off so you'll never be able to lie again."

Ignacio clamped his mouth shut real tight, but he pressed the gun back against her chest.

"I'm not the Angel Bandit," Rafe repeated.

"What's a shove-nest-pig?" the two farm boys asked.

"I wouldn't sell you," Pablo assured Helen ingratiatingly. "If I talk Ignacio out of selling you, will you gargle me tonight?"

"I do not gargle," Helen shrieked.

"Yes, you do," Rafe said. "Remember this morning . . ." His words faded off at the expression of outrage on her face.

Uh oh.

"I . . . do . . . not . . . gargle . . . *men,*" she said real slow, so he and all the men would get the message loud and clear.

Rafe did. He wasn't so sure about the others.

"Exactly how does a woman gargle a man?" one of the miners asked another.

"Damned if I know," his friend replied.

They both turned to Rafe.

"It's a Deep Throat kind of thing," he started to say, then stopped at Helen's hiss of fury. "I mean, I'm sure

107

Pablo is mistaken. There's no such thing as sex gargling.''

Pablo turned wounded eyes on Rafe. "But you told me—''

BAM!!! A pistol shot rang out.

Everyone gawked at Ignacio, who had aimed into the air.

"Enough! I am taking the Angel Bandit into Sacramento City to collect the reward. Perhaps we weel have a hanging tonight.'' He waited out the murmurs of enthusiasm at that gruesome prospect. "After that, *mis amigos* and I weel enjoy Elena's charms. All night long. Tomorrow, she weel be sold to the highest bidder. One night of corkscrewing at a time.''

A loud roar of approval met that announcement.

"I am *not* the Angel Bandit,'' Rafe repeated for what seemed like the hundredth time. "And anyone who lays a hand on Helen will answer to me.''

"Why does he say he's not the Angel Bandit?'' one man asked.

"I couldn't even ride a horse till yesterday,'' Rafe told him.

"That ees true,'' Sancho confirmed, bobbing his head up and down like one of those dashboard dolls.

"Perhaps he's not the Angel Bandit, then?'' the trapper said.

"But he has the angel brand on his arse,'' Pablo argued.

"He does?'' The miners frowned with confusion.

"*Sí.* Angel wings, right here,'' Sancho said, patting his own ample right cheek.

"Why are the Angel Bandit's eyes rolling up in his head?'' the trapper asked Ignacio. "Is he havin' a conniption?''

"It's not angel wings, you idiots. It's a butterfly,'' Rafe protested.

"Why would a man put a butterfly on his arse?'' the trapper asked.

"I'm a lawyer, not an outlaw,'' Rafe tried to explain. "I enforce the law. I don't break it.''

"A lawyer!'' several men exclaimed.

Then one commented, "Hell, lawyers are just as crooked as thieves."

"Did ya hear 'bout the two farmers who went to a lawyer, each claimin' to own a cow?" one man chimed in.

"Oh, hell, Harvey, not another one of yer infernal jokes!"

Harvey just went on. "While one farmer pulled on the head, and the other pulled on the tail, the cow was milked by the lawyer."

Everyone laughed some more.

But one young man tapped his unshaven jaw, eying Rafe with consideration. "I don't s'pose you could advise me on a legal matter?"

"Shut up, Hank. There ain't no way yer gonna divorce that two-bit Mexican whore you married. Even if you was drunk."

"Elena has the angel tattoo on her arse, too," Sancho contributed irrelevantly to the crazy, fifty-way conversation, and was rewarded by a loud "Aaaaaah" of delight from the crowd.

"Can we see?" several men asked Ignacio. They were practically drooling.

Ignacio nodded. "Before the bidding mañana, she will show you the angel mark."

Bidding?

"Have you all lost your minds?" Helen screamed. "My name is Helen Prescott, not Elena. I'm a major in the U.S. Army, and I demand to be taken to the nearest military installation. Furthermore, if anyone tries to look at my bare behind, or corkscrew me, or stick *something* down my throat, I swear I'll bite it off. And don't think I'm not serious."

"Elena is an officer in the Army?" the trapper said, scratching his head in puzzlement. "I di'n't know there wuz wimmen in the Army."

"*Caramba!*" Ignacio growled. "I have heard enough. She ees Elena, and he ees the Angel Bandit. And that ees that."

With a kick of his spurs, Ignacio propelled his horse forward into the town. Their horses followed him, and about three dozen men trailed behind, scurrying to keep up.

Over and over, the word passed that the Angel Bandit was about to be hanged, and Elena the Corkscrewer had arrived.

Helen's parade of fans increased by alarming proportions.

And Rafe decided he'd better do something soon to change the direction of this sideshow.

Face flaming, Helen stared straight ahead as they rode into the primitive 1850 town of Sacramento City. As dusk approached, she tried not to worry about the danger closing in on them: the dozens of lustful men following her, the threat of Rafe being lynched, the time travel itself. Instead, she concentrated on her surroundings, searching for a clue to help them escape.

The picturesque city was situated on the foggy, tree-lined bank of the brown Sacramento River, several hundred yards wide at its juncture with the American River. She'd been in the city many times before, but it had *never* looked like this.

Dozens of schooners and small boats formed a colorful panorama of masts along the levee on Front Street. Many of the vessels had signboards and figureheads on them, indicating they were being used as hotels or business establishments.

Pigs rooted about at the sides of the dusty street, sidestepping the busy inhabitants, little knowing they were the staple of the miners' diet. And cows driven up from Southern California hustled along to be butchered.

Trees from the original forest—oaks and sycamores with trunks as wide as six feet—still nestled throughout the busy town, which should have given it a cozy appearance. Instead, the hometown character was destroyed by the decadent nature of the buildings. Gambling "hells," saloons, and brothels occupied almost every canvas or ramshackle plank dwelling that lined the streets, barring a few exceptions, like general stores, restaurants, a daguerreotype shop, a newspaper office, billiard and ten-pin bowling halls, and presumably a sheriff's facility.

The canvas-sided dwellings, with their lanterns and candles, created an eerie atmosphere of shifting light and darkness. And everywhere Helen saw an abundance of crimson calico—as curtains, wall hangings, tablecloths, even tents. Some manufacturer from the East must have had a surplus stock of the bright fabric.

Helen glanced about in utter amazement. She couldn't believe she'd actually traveled back in time. She couldn't believe she had a horde of men following her, believing she was a hooker.

Maybe she had died after all. Maybe this was hell . . . although she didn't think she'd done anything *that* bad in her life to merit this punishment.

Helen shifted her eyes to see how Rafe was handling these new sights. He expertly guided his horse beside her and Ignacio, with Pablo and Sancho on either side of them.

Rafe didn't look at all like a man worried about his neck.

Or her distasteful fate.

"Well, this is a fine kettle of fish we're in now," she finally grumbled to Rafe. "I don't suppose you've got one of those *Quantum Leap* computers on you to zap us home."

"No, but stop worrying, babe. Remember what I said earlier about trust." He smiled, unfazed by their dilemma. She hated it when he smiled. Her stomach felt fluttery . . . queasy, actually. Yes, that was it, his smile made her sick in her stomach.

Hah! Who am I kidding? His smile would turn a nun to sin. And I'm no nun. Get a grip, girl. Stop gawking at him. Talk about boring, non–stomach fluttering things. "Can you believe this town, Rafe?" she said, motioning with her head toward the busy streets.

"No. I still have trouble accepting it, but time travel seems to be the only answer."

"*Silencio!* You are my prisoners," Ignacio snarled. "I

forbid you to talk about time to travel.''

Helen shot the buffoon a withering glare over her shoulder, then proceeded to ignore his command for silence. "But what can we do?" she asked Rafe.

"Do not answer her," Ignacio ordered Rafe.

Rafe, too, ignored the brute. "Remember how we agreed to be a team.''

"I never agreed—" Helen stopped talking suddenly when she noticed Rafe twisting his face in a funny manner, blinking his eyes rapidly, then mouthing some words at her silently.

Was he trying to signal her something? If so, why didn't he use military codes taught in officers' training? She knew the answer immediately. He'd probably forgotten, or never learned them in the first place. At the very least, he could have tapped out Morse code on his saddle horn.

"You got a bug up your nose?" Ignacio asked Rafe, observing his strange contortions.

"No," Rafe snapped, seeming at wit's end. "You told me not to talk; so, I was exercising my face muscles."

"Son of a bitch! I weel be glad when we are rid of you. I think you are becoming loco."

Suddenly, Rafe burst out in song, a rollicking fifties rendition of "Jim Dandy to the Rescue." Even with his hands tied to the saddle, he rolled his shoulders and bounced his butt in the saddle to the rhythmic beat. Several pigs stopped rooting and joined in with a chorus of oinks.

He glowered at the pigs, then started on that old Elvis song, "It's Now or Never." In the midst of his incredible, off-key song, Rafe suggested, holding her eyes intently, "Why don't you sing along, honey? You know the words, don't you?"

Helen couldn't have sung if her life depended on it. She was stunned by the phenomenon of Rafe bellowing out, over and over, "Jim Dandy to the *rescue* . . . It's *now* or never . . . Jim Dandy to the *rescue* . . . It's *now* or never . . ."

She narrowed her eyes. Finally, Helen nodded slightly,

and Rafe breathed a sigh of relief.

Before she had a chance to digest the fact that he had successfully sent her a message, Rafe began softly to hum the music to "Wind Beneath My Wings," her favorite song. Helen would have recognized the rhythm anywhere. At first, she was caught up in the beautiful lyrics. "Did you ever know that *I'm* your hero?" he sang softly, but horribly off-key. He must be tone deaf.

"Are you drunk?" she asked suspiciously.

He flashed her a look of irritation.

"Sunstroke?"

He continued to croon, "Did you ever know that *I'm* your hero?"

Huh? That isn't the way the song goes.

Helen's fuzzy brain puzzled over his odd behavior as he persisted in singing his own version of the popular song, all of the changes having to do with *his* being *her* hero. Was he trying to say that he was going to rescue her? Now?

"Why do you sing, *Señor Ángel?*" Pablo asked kindly. "Do you avoid thinking about the hanging? Don't worry. If you wish, I weel shoot you when the hangman pulls the rope so you weel feel no pain."

Rafe gave him a blistering once-over. "Don't do me any favors, pal."

"Perhaps he ees practicing for the heavenly choirs. Heh, heh, heh!" Ignacio joked, and some of the men who still followed laughed at his gallows humor.

Meanwhile, Helen was shaking her head rapidly from side to side, trying to signal Rafe not to take any chances. The last thing she wanted from him was some imbecile attempt at heroics.

"Now what?" Ignacio asked, staring at her head twitching. "Did the bug move from the Angel's nose to your ear?"

Well, that was as good an explanation as any. "Yes."

Rafe made a clucking sound of disgust, then bit his bottom lip in concentration. Finally, his eyes brightened. This time he belted out a rendition of "Band of Gold," except that in his version, it was "Hands of Gold."

Helen shook her head in dismay. She never was much good at charades. Okay, *hands,* he wanted her to focus on hands. With sudden insight, she glanced over at his bound hands and noticed for the first time that the ropes appeared somewhat loose. Her eyes shot up to his and he mouthed, "Finally."

Still, Helen frowned. *Hero. Rescue. Now. Hands.* Fear gripped her when she realized Rafe planned some foolish move. Even if he got his hands free, he was unarmed and wouldn't be able to challenge these three bandits with their lethal weapons.

"No!" she exclaimed, uncaring if the outlaws overheard. "It's too dangerous."

"I told you not to talk," Ignacio said, then furrowed his brow. "What ees too dangerous?"

Rafe crossed his eyes with mounting frustration at her words of resistance. Grimacing at her, he started another song, and she groaned, but still he carried on. This time he favored them with a Bobby Darin tune, "Mack the Knife." He tried not to emphasize the word knife in the song, but sang stanza after stanza of the old standby.

And Helen concluded that Rafe must have a knife. She squinted at him questioningly, and he tapped his booted foot lightly along F. Lee's flank.

He had a knife hidden in his Army boot. Well, of course, he would. Old gang habits died hard.

Helen studied Rafe closely, as if seeing him for the first time. No wonder he seemed unconcerned about their safety! No wonder he kept telling her to trust him!

She felt like such a fool, thinking him a defenseless wimp. He must have been laughing at her silly misconceptions, her karate attempts to defend them, her criticism of his cowardly failure to fight off the bandits.

She pressed her lips together, forcing back the lump in her throat, and Rafe apparently thought she still didn't understand. So, he started singing "Wind Beneath My Wings" again, promising in his weird, off-key version to be the wings behind her dreams.

And a slow tear slipped down Helen's cheek.

"See," Pablo told the crowd, "the Angel ees singing of angel wings to his wife."

Ignoring Pablo and the miners' "oooh" of understanding, Rafe tilted his head in bafflement at Helen's tearful response to his song. Then, he continued to sing softly, "Did you ever know that *I'm* your hero?"

And inside, Helen wept silent tears because she knew suddenly that she—strong, independent military woman that she was—had been waiting for a hero for a long, long time.

Chapter Eight

An ominous sign loomed up ahead, SHERIFF, SACRAMENTO CITY. The fact that the sign adorned a rickety plank structure, no more than ten feet by ten feet, covered with a canvas roof and the neverending supply of crimson calico, did nothing to dispel Helen's fears.

She glanced quickly at Rafe, who nodded significantly. Fortunately, he'd stopped his stupid singing once he figured she'd gotten his message. Rafe had a plan for their escape.

They were approaching a small alley, next to the City Hotel, when Rafe made his move. In a blink, he pretended to lose control of his horse and yanked on the reins so that F. Lee bumped Ignacio's mare. In the melee that followed, he pulled his hands from their loose ties and drew a deadly sharp switchblade from his boot.

"I don't believe it!" Helen exclaimed.

"Ay yay yay!" Pablo and Sancho said at the same time.

"What the hell—" Ignacio reached for his pistol.

But Rafe slid smoothly off his horse, grabbed Ignacio by the forearm from where he sat behind Helen on the saddle, and jerked him to the ground. Stunned, Helen could barely hold onto the saddle horn of the skittish horse.

"You bastard, I weel see you tortured before you hang." Ignacio stumbled to his feet, out of Rafe's grasp, and stretched both hands for Rafe's throat. He was so angry that spit dribbled from his thick lips and his eyes bulged like an enraged bull.

Rafe danced to the side and wrapped an arm around Ignacio's thick neck from behind, the blade pressing against

116

his throat. "One false move and I'll slit your stinking throat." He shoved the bandit's struggling body into the alley, away from the gaping crowd, which alternately cheered and threatened to come forward and capture "the Angel."

"Get the sheriff," Ignacio yelled above the chaos, and Sancho scooted off. Pablo, on the other hand, stood frozen with amazement, seemingly unable to decide whether to pee his pants or run for his life.

"A hanging weel be too good for you," Ignacio sneered. "Perhaps we weel make you watch as your *wife* ees raped first." The bandit's words were foolish in the extreme, considering his position.

Rafe pressed the knife tighter, drawing a thin line of Ignacio's blood.

Ignacio bellowed—a loud, bearlike sound—but he couldn't move with the blade against his throat. A steady, red stream oozed from the shallow cut toward the open neck of his shirt. He looked down and his eyes widened with panic. "Somebody do something. *El hombre es loco,*" he cried.

But the crowd was enjoying the spectacle too much. The exuberant men called out macabre bets right and left on the outcome of the struggle.

Easing herself awkwardly off her horse by holding onto the pommel with both hands, Helen approached.

"Get his guns," Rafe ordered tersely.

Even with her bound wrists, Helen was able to lift both revolvers from Ignacio's holster. She handed one Colt to Rafe, who reached out with the hand that had been wrapped around Ignacio's wide waist. With the gun pressed against the back of Ignacio's head, Rafe used the barrel to propel the bandit forward, face against the hotel wall, arms raised over his head. Only then did Rafe ease the knife away from the outlaw's neck.

"Hold out your hands," Rafe told Helen. Keeping one eye on Ignacio and the other on her extended arms, he cut the ropes tying her hands together. She flexed her wrists to

117

get the circulation going again.

"Unbuckle your gun belt and drop it to the ground," he commanded Ignacio. When the grumbling outlaw did as he was told, Rafe asked Helen, "Can you use a gun?"

"I'm a trained military officer. I can probably outshoot you."

"Yeah, yeah, yeah. Pick up the other pistol, Annie Oakley, and make sure this crowd doesn't come closer." He grinned at her, and Helen realized that he was enjoying this whole dangerous scenario. *Men!*

Tsking her criticism, Helen took the gun out of the belt, checked the barrel for ammunition, then took aim at the entrance to the alleyway, with both hands wrapped around the handle of the weapon. All the men took two steps backward, including Pablo, who gawked at her as if she was Madonna—and not the religious one. Great, now the blabbermouth would add gun moll to his list of her talents.

Rafe flashed her an appreciative smile. Even in the midst of peril, she felt that annoying flutter in her stomach at his killer smile.

"Maybe this really is a movie set—*Shoot-Out at the O.K. Alley,*" he quipped. Then his rascally eyes locked on the seat of Helen's pants, clearly delineated by the tight fabric of her slacks, which were tautened by her spread-legged, braced-for-firing position. "I know what I want to do when the action scene is over. How about you?"

Oh, God! The flutter fluttered some more.

Enough of this silliness! She glowered at Rafe, who was still grinning. "Grow up and stop kidding around. Besides, the only action you're going to see from me is a wave of the hand when I say bye-bye. You can pan gold till doomsday, but I'm going home."

"We'll see, *honey.*" He winked.

Criminey! Smiles and winks. I am losing ground here fast. Maybe this is one of those endorphin highs military men claim to get in the midst of combat.

Rafe turned back to Ignacio. "I'm going to step back a pace, but I still have my gun aimed at your head. When I move away, I want you to turn real slow and hand me your ammo belts.''

"I ain't givin' you nothin'," Ignacio protested, spinning to face him.

"Oh, I think you will," Rafe said. "Look there." Pointing to the City Hotel sign about twenty feet away, Rafe raised his gun, twirled it around his forefinger like a regular show-off gunslinger, then shot. Perfectly.

The miners stepped back another few steps, and a collective "aaaah" of approval swept through the crowd. Odds in the betting shifted in favor of Rafe.

"Someone forgot to dot the 'i,' " Rafe said with bald-faced arrogance. "Anyone have an 'i' they want dotted?"

Silence met his question.

Helen gaped at Rafe, who swiftly took her loaded weapon, handed her his to reload, and aimed once more at Ignacio, this time dead center on his forehead.

"You shoulda known, Ignacio, that the Angel could handle a gun," Pablo called out to his boss.

Ignacio shot his sidekick a scowl of incredulity, stuttering something about not needing advice from halfwits. But, wisely, Ignacio chose to lift his ammunition belts from his chest and drop them to the ground. "You weel pay for this, *Señor Ángel*. That I promise."

Rafe motioned to Helen. "Now, what do you say we head on out to the pass?" he drawled in a husky Gary Cooper rumble, already backing toward the other end of the alley. He held the gun and ammo belts in one hand, the raised revolver in the other.

Helen joined him, her gun raised as well.

They had backed up a short distance when a steely voice said behind them, "What the hell's goin' on here?"

Uh oh.

They turned to see a tall man wearing a shiny badge leveling a rifle at them. The lawman, who resembled John Wayne—*Good Lord, first Gary Cooper, now the Duke!*—was flanked by four other men, also wearing badges and carrying rifles. Sancho stood in the background, beaming with satisfaction. He gave a little wave to Helen.

"Lower your guns, nice and easy," the gruff-voiced sheriff demanded.

As they dropped their guns to the ground, Helen frowned at Rafe. "If you hadn't wasted time with your Clint Eastwood games, we would have been out of here."

"Do you ever stop nagging?" Rafe countered.

The Duke stepped closer. "Mind telling me what's goin' on here, folks?"

"He ees the Angel Bandit, and we have brought him here for the reward," Ignacio announced, rushing forward.

"And she ees Elena, the greatest corkscrewer in the West," Pablo added with pride, pointing to Helen, "and she belongs to us."

"We're gonna have us a hangin' tonight," some of the miners yelled, moving into the alley. "And tomorrow we're gonna bid on Miss Elena's favors."

Here we go again, Helen thought. "Any bright ideas now, hot stuff?"

"God, I'd like to duct-tape your mouth. And that condescending nose of yours, too."

"I'd like to see you try."

"Are you two married?" the Duke asked Rafe. "The little lady's got a mighty sharp tongue, jist like my wife."

Rafe shot Helen a "So there!" smirk, and she stuck out her tongue at him. She immediately regretted her immature reaction. Lord, when had she reverted to such childish behavior?

"Did you see what she did with her tongue? Did you?" Pablo enthused to the prospectors who now filled one end of the alleyway. "It mus' be another trick she ees practicing."

Helen put her hands over her ears to tune out the raunchy responses to Pablo's observation.

Rafe looked at her, a smile in his dancing eyes, and Helen threatened, "Don't you dare say anything."

The sheriff shook his head from side to side. "Yep, they gotta be married."

Ignacio pushed his way in front of the sheriff, whining, "When weel I get my money?"

"What money?"

"The reward for capturing *El Ángel Bandido*."

"This guy's not the Angel Bandit," the sheriff declared. "I jist got me a telegram from the marshall in San Francisco today. The slimy snake was caught this mornin' robbin' an Army paymaster near the bay."

"But . . . but . . ." Ignacio stuttered. "He mus' be. He looks jist like him."

"Mebbe." The sheriff shrugged. "But unless he has angel wings an' kin fly, there's no way he could get here from San Francisco in half a day."

"He *does* have angel wings," Pablo reported joyfully. "On his arse."

The sheriff looked at Pablo as if he'd flipped his lid. "I thought angel wings were supposed to be on the shoulders," he said with a guffaw. The other men joined in his derision.

"Show him yer arse," an embarrassed Pablo urged Rafe.

"Not on your life!" Rafe laughed.

"Elena has wings on her arse, too," Pablo continued, despite the hoots of ridicule.

Everyone's attention turned to her. She cringed as hot blood rushed to her face.

"It ees the truth," Pablo added, more weakly, his shoulders slumping with dejection.

Helen almost felt sorry for the fool. Almost. "For the hundredth time, I . . . am . . . not . . . Elena." She turned to the lawman then. "My name is Helen Prescott. I'm a major in the U.S. Arm—"

"Tell them," Pablo interrupted, calling on Ignacio and Sancho for corroboration. "Tell them she has the angel's mark on her arse."

Both men nodded vigorously.

"*Sí*, they *both* have matching angel wing tattoos on their arses," Ignacio elaborated. "That proves he ees the Angel, and she ees his woman, Elena."

"It's a butterfly," Rafe and Helen said at the same time.

"Gawdamighty!" the sheriff gnashed out with frustration. "I think ya all lost yer bloomin' minds."

"I want my reward," Ignacio asserted.

"There ain't gonna be no reward," the sheriff gritted out. "I already told ya that the Angel Bandit was captured this mornin' in San Francisco. Now, let's break up this crowd."

Ignacio's crafty face flushed purple with rage. Then he took in the new situation and changed direction. "Well, at least we still have Elena. She weel bring in *mucho dolares* at the bidding mañana."

"You're not touching my wife," Rafe snarled, linking the fingers of one of his hands with hers.

"You can't prove she's yer wife. She belongs to us," Ignacio shouted, pulling on her other arm.

Rafe clasped her hand tighter, glancing at the sheriff.

The Duke's eyes took in her trousers—clearly scandalous attire for that time—and he rolled his shoulders. "I'm not gettin' involved in any dispute over a whore. Settle it yerselves."

Helen seethed.

Rafe squeezed her hand.

Ignacio pulled harder on her other arm.

"Maybe you oughta check out the brands on those horses Ignacio and his gang brought into town tonight," Rafe suggested coolly to the departing lawmen.

The sheriff stopped suddenly and turned. His narrowed eyes cut to Ignacio, while his right hand began to raise a rifle. Apparently, harassing a whore amounted to no big offense, but horse theft was another matter entirely.

Ignacio released her arm, starting to back away. Helen saw Pablo and Sancho sidle toward the crowd of miners and disappear.

Raising his rifle higher, the sheriff growled, "I don't s'pose those horses have the Rancho Salerno brand on 'em?"

Ignacio made a low, gurgling squeak in his throat.

"C'mon, men, I think we got us a few horses ta inspect," ol' John Wayne said, his rifle now pressed directly into the fat belly of Ignacio, whose exit was blocked by the wall of miners. "How many horses they got?" the sheriff asked Rafe.

Rafe shrugged. "Ten, I think."

The sheriff nodded and motioned for Ignacio to move in front of him toward the alley entrance. The miners opened a path in their center for their passage, along with the four deputies.

Helen and Rafe stayed behind, realizing at the same moment that they were free. They shared a quick smile.

The miners seemed undecided about whether to follow the sheriff for that entertainment, or to stay and see what Rafe and Helen were going to do.

"Are you gonna be corkscrewin' t'night?" the trapper they'd met up with earlier called out to Helen, his attention shifting back and forth between her and the shrieking squeals of Ignacio out on the street behind him.

"No," Helen stated firmly.

"Well, not for anyone but her husband," Rafe added brightly as he buckled on Ignacio's holsters, inserted the discarded pistols, and crisscrossed the ammo belts over his chest.

"Not for anyone," Helen emphasized.

"We'll give you five hundred dollars in gold dust," one of the hayseed twins offered.

"Well . . ." Rafe said, tapping his chin pensively.

Helen could tell by the twinkle in his eyes that he was teasing, but she glared at him impatiently.

"Just kidding, guys. She's not for sale. Anytime. Anyplace. Anywhere."

Grumbling, the men began to walk away.

Rafe turned back to her then. "Happy now?"

A delayed reaction set in. Trembling, she could barely nod her head. "God, I am so tired and dirty and hot. I wish I could take a bath and sleep for two days. Then wake up in the twentieth century."

"Me, too." He reached out a hand and brushed a strand of hair off her cheek. The expression on his face was unreadable, but the whispery caress seemed to have significance. The gesture touched her deeply.

"How did I do as a hero?" he joked, but Helen saw a vulnerable, almost needful, emotion on his handsome face.

Her heart went out to him in a way she just couldn't explain. She should have answered in the same, light-hearted tone, but her innate honesty forced her to confess, "The best."

He smiled at her with such tenderness that Helen felt tears well in her eyes. Holding her gaze, Rafe leaned down and brushed his lips across hers—a brush of a kiss, so brief she almost missed it. But Helen's world tilted askew, and she knew from Rafe's sharp intake of breath that he was equally affected.

Without a word, they headed for the other end of the alley.

"So," Rafe said huskily, looping an arm over her shoulders as they walked, "we make quite a team, don't we?"

She prepared to make a prissy remark, to criticize him for the familiarity of his embrace, not to mention the kiss. Subordinate officers didn't kiss their superiors.

Instead, she laid her head on the cradle of his chest, nuzzling his warm neck, and murmured, "Yeah, we do."

For more than an hour, they strolled arm in arm, through the 1850 town of Sacramento, stopping every few steps to examine and comment on the extraordinary sights. With their escape from the bungling bandits and their impulsive kiss, their relationship had entered a new phase—tentative friendship and possibly something more precious. Rafe chose not to ponder the latter too closely . . . just yet.

Darkness now blanketed the town, but bright light from lanterns and candles filtered through the open doorways of the dilapidated structures and through the fabric of the canvas tents, making them glow like golden balloons. The nighttime businesses were putting out their welcome mats—saloons, brothels, and gambling halls—the seedy establishments that fed on the Gold Rush like parasites.

And they had plenty of comers. The main thoroughfare was alive with crowds of men, and a rare woman, mostly in their twenties, laughing, talking, cursing, gesticulating. Judging by their different languages and colorful attire, Rafe recognized the French, Irish, Italians, Australians, Chinese, Mexicans, native Californians of Spanish descent, and Blacks from the southern states.

"Talk about melting pots!" Helen commented. "I wonder how they all understand each other."

"There's a common language where gold is concerned." Rafe laughed. "Listen." Interspersed throughout all the conversations were buzzwords centered on the topic of the day—gold. Exciting words, like bonanza, Eldorado, placer, diggings, mother lode, rich vein, paydirt, big strike.

Helen nodded.

They crossed the dusty street and stopped in front of a big tent from which rich odors of food emanated. A homemade signboard in front proclaimed:

BIG JOHN'S RESTERANT
Sacramento Salmon and Boiled Taters, $3
Elk Steak and Boiled Taters, $5
Fried Pork, Beans and Boiled Taters, $2
Rhubarb Pie, $10.
Coffee, fifty cents.

"Well, one thing is clear," Rafe said. "Potatoes are plentiful and pie is scarce."

"There's another thing clear here, too," Helen added, biting her bottom lip worriedly. "Food is very expensive. Do you have any money?"

He pulled a wallet out of his back pocket. "Back at the landing site, Ignacio picked through my stuff but only kept the loose change. Credits cards and paper money are worthless here."

"What are we going to do?" Helen groaned. "I was so

125

worried about our getting free of those bandits that it never occurred to me that we have no way of surviving in these times.''

''Oh, I wouldn't say that. I can work as hard as any man to earn money. I could even open a law practice.'' Ignoring her scoffing look, he went on, ''But our immediate problem is food and lodging for the night. Tomorrow we can investigate the work situation.''

''Maybe we could borrow some money.''

It was his turn to scoff. ''Honey, I've seen the looks of disdain and the remarks about worthless greasers. No one's gonna lend me peanuts. And, unless you're willing to turn tricks, I suspect you're in the same boat.''

Helen blushed prettily. He liked that about her.

''Well, Mr. Know-It-All, what do you suggest?''

''Follow me,'' he said, heading inside the open-sided, unfloored tent where a mammoth Scotsman with a bald head and ginger-colored beard stood behind a counter. Several long plank tables and rough benches filled the entire space where the dining prospectors stopped eating and stared bug-eyed at the sight of a new woman in town, especially one in pants. The first thing Rafe planned to do when he got some cash was buy Helen a dress.

Slipping a thin gold chain and crucifix out of his boot, he reluctantly plunked them on the counter. He hated to part with the only piece of jewelry he ever wore, a high school graduation gift from his mother. At the time, when their only income had come from her housecleaning jobs, the extravagance had probably represented two weeks of scrubbing other people's toilets. Well, he had no choice. ''How much will you give me for this?'' he inquired of Big John, who was busy ogling Helen, like every other man within a mile radius.

''Huh?'' the burly restaurateur said, looking down for the first time at the glimmering item on his counter.

Helen picked up the chain and frowned. ''How come Ignacio took everything I had, and he didn't take this?''

''I always stick it in my shoe before a jump.''

"Oh, Rafe, you can't sell this," Helen cried when she turned it over, reading aloud the inscription on the back, TO RAFAEL, HAPPY GRADUATION, MAMA. Placing it back on the counter, she said, "It's an important memento."

"You can't eat mementoes," he pointed out, seconded by his stomach rumbling.

Meanwhile, Big John picked up the cross, examined it closely, tested the gold content with his teeth, then offered, "Two pork-and-beans dinners, and five dollars in gold dust."

"Two salmon dinners, coffee, two rhubarb pies—whatever the hell rhubarb is—and twenty dollars in gold dust," Rafe countered, seeing the two-foot, freshly baked fish lying on a plank table behind the owner.

Big John studied him warily, then agreed. "A deal. I could use me a little fancy fer Veroneesa over at Lily's Fandango Parlor."

"Isn't fandango the name of a dance?" Helen asked as they walked over to a far table, their tin plates piled high with food. He'd tucked the small poke of gold dust in his pocket. "Maybe we can go over there later and watch the dancing."

Rafe began to choke and almost dropped his plate. "Oh, Helen, your naïveté continues to amaze me. Yeah, fandango is the name of a dance, but, believe me, sweetheart, the men don't go there to tango, if you get my drift."

Her flaming face told him she did.

Big John brought their coffee over personally and sat down with them for a few moments. "Where ya from, folks?"

"My wife and I are from southern California, and we're headed for the northern goldfields."

"I'm not his—"

Rafe sliced her a glare and she heeded his warning.

"Well, we're not sure if we're going to prospect, or go home," Helen said sweetly. "We had the misfortune to run into a few bandits who brought us here, but now I'm trying

127

to talk my *darling husband* into the wisdom of giving up on the Gold Rush.''

"Seen the elephant, have ya?" Big John remarked to Rafe with a rueful laugh.

"Seen the elephant? What the hell does that mean?"

"Ya never heard the sayin'?" The big man raised his bushy ginger eyebrows in surprise. "It means ya got the gold bug. Well, no, actually it means more that a man gets hisself caught up in the excitement of the treasure hunt."

"But why an elephant?" Helen asked.

"The story goes, there wuz this farmer onct who allus wanted ta see an elephant but never had," Big John began his story with relish. Rafe saw men at surrounding tables listening closely to the tale, which they must have heard countless times before.

"Anyways, one day a circus come ta town, and the farmer loaded his wagon with eggs and vegetables and headed fer the market. Along the way he met up with the circus parade led by an elephant. His horses bucked and run away, and the wagon overturned. There wuz a godawful mess of broken eggs and bruised vegetables, but the farmer said, 'I don't give a damn. I have seen the elephant.' "

Helen's forehead creased with puzzlement. "And the point?"

"The point, sweet lady, is that I purely do agree with you 'bout the wisdom of gold diggin'. Mos' miners come back with nothin' more'n broken eggs and bruised vegetables, so ta speak."

"But," Rafe added, "you're also saying that seeing the elephant is worth it for the adventuresome man . . . or woman."

"Yep."

"Wisdom versus excitement," Helen asserted.

"Caution versus opportunity," Rafe amended.

"Ya both be right," Big John concluded, standing. "But my best piece of advice, *mi amigo,* is that, if yer gonna prospect, go far north. Mexicans ain't welcome in mos' mining camps these days." Rafe bristled. "Now, now, don't go gettin' yer blood up. I offer the advice kindly, jist so ya know what yer up agin.''

Rafe relaxed a bit. ''Thank you, then.''

''Ya heard 'bout the Foreign Miners Tax that the legislature passed a few months past, ain't ya?''

Rafe shook his head slowly.

''All the furriners that wants ta work a claim gots ta pay twenty dollars a month, iffen they'll even 'low you to file a claim a'tall. Mostly, furriners means you Mexicans and the Celestials, but really any man what comes from another country. Ya gots ta watch yer back, man.''

''I'm an American,'' Rafe grated out.

''Son, that don't make no nevermind. Any man with dark skin and an accent is a furriner here,'' Big John corrected. ''Hell, even the native Californeos who bin here forever are bein' called outsiders by the Yankees.''

A muscle twitched in Rafe's cheek.

''Now, young man, lower yer hackles. I dint say I agree. I'm jist tryin' ta save ya some aggravation.''

''Hey, no big deal! I've lived with this kind of crap all my life.'' Rafe raised his chin proudly, defensively.

Helen's heart went out to Rafe. Apparently, he would have to fight prejudice, even in these primitive times. And she, as a woman in the male-dominated military, knew how bigotry felt.

After Big John walked off, they consumed every morsel on their plates, even the rhubarb pie that Rafe, at first, turned his nose up at. Now they sat sipping their coffee.

The whole time they dined, Helen tried hard to ignore the gawking men and echoing whispers of ''Elena'' and ''corkscrew'' and ''gargling,'' and ''forms.'' Obviously, the miners still chose to believe she was the famous prostitute. Wishful thinking.

One of the men lit up a big smelly cigar and began to drag on it appreciatively. She coughed in revulsion as the offensive smoke drifted toward their table. Despite her exaggerated efforts to wave the smoke away, the man continued to puff enthusiastically.

She turned back to Rafe, who was studying her with a strange expression on his face. He hadn't shaved in days, and dark whiskers covered his jaw. His uncombed black hair was pushed back roughly off his forehead and behind his ears, down to his collar.

Helen watched, mesmerized, as his long fingers traced a path around the rim of his cup. The whole time, his pale blue eyes under their sinfully long lashes held hers in question.

"What?" she asked hesitantly. The smoldering look in his eyes bothered her a whole lot more than the overt remarks of the men surrounding them, or the blatant, erotic teasing he'd subjected her to for days. "Well, spit it out. What's the problem now?" she prodded.

"I want to kiss you all over."

Chapter Nine

A low strangling sound escaped her throat. "No!" she squeaked out.

His face fell. "Why not?"

"Why not? Why not?"

"Now, Helen, don't give me that commanding officer crap. I thought we agreed long ago that we're on equal footing here."

"Rafe, you just barely escaped hanging. I'm still dodging the corkscrewer rap." A waft of repugnant cigar smoke swept toward their table, and she shot a glare at the offending smoker behind her. Turning back to Rafe, she said, "I would sell my soul for a bath and a clean bed. Why would you all of a sudden *think* you want to kiss me?"

"There's no *thinking* about it, babe. Uh uh. I want to, *real bad*. And don't for one minute consider this a sudden inclination. I wanted to kiss you the first time I saw you sixteen years ago, and I've thought of nothing else since I saw you boarding that aircraft on Saturday."

"You're making this up just to disconcert me, and—"

"Do I disconcert you?" His lips turned up with satisfaction.

"Not in that way, you egomaniac. Besides, you did kiss me. In the middle of our skydive. And then again in the alley."

He hooted at her ready remembrance of those two brief kisses. "Those were appetizers. I'm looking for more, lots more. Plus, as I said, I want to kiss you *all over*. None of those five-second virgin pecks."

"I'm not listening to another word. I don't know why you get your kicks teasing me, but it's not funny at all."

She started to stand, but he reached across the table and nudged her back down to her bench.

"Do you see me smiling?" His voice was husky.

"Then why?"

"Well, it's like this, Helen," he said, taking her hand in his from across the table, despite her efforts to resist. He turned it over palm side up and began to create erotic patterns with a forefinger along the lines. "I want to make love to you so bad my teeth hurt," he admitted in a low, thick voice, his eyes holding her captive. "I don't know what's going to happen to us tomorrow, or even an hour from now. So, I'd kinda like to, well, seize the moment."

She blinked at him with utter amazement. "When did this conversation move from kisses to making love?"

"It's a natural progression for me," he said brashly, peering up at her through his ridiculously long lashes.

Speechless, Helen could only gape at Rafe.

Taking her silence for lack of enthusiasm, Rafe continued, "You wouldn't have to worry about getting pregnant. I already told you how I feel about kids and that I've had a vasectomy. No commitments, either. We'd end our relationship when we return to the future . . . if you wanted."

The insensitive jerk! She was fuming. And hurt. How could he think she would want such a casual, short-term affair? With anyone. "And what about my engagement?"

He clenched his teeth and his lips thinned at that reminder. "You never talk about your fiancé. Are you really in love with Elliott?" At least he'd used his name this time. "Do you really expect you'll still marry?"

She glanced down at her ringless finger and realized that she'd failed to retrieve her engagement ring from Ignacio. How could she have not missed the symbol of her impending marriage? It was a telling lapse on her part. "In all honesty, no."

"No what?"

"No, I'm not in love with Elliott. I care about him, but

I'm not 'in love' with him. And, no, I won't be marrying him now."

The smile spreading across Rafe's face was so beautiful, she gasped. Battling for self-control, she told him, "Elliott and I were headed for a breakup long ago. That's probably why we've been engaged so long. But that doesn't mean I'd want to . . . to . . ."

"Make love with me?" His lips were parted sensually, and he looked as if he might lean across the table and kiss her.

She tried to wrest her hand out of his grasp. He held on tighter and laced his fingers with hers.

"C'mon, Helen, live a little. Stop thinking about what's logical and correct. Do what feels right."

It was the most outrageous suggestion anyone had ever made to Helen in all her life, even if he was being bluntly honest with her. "I've got to admit, you stun me—"

"Stun is good."

She gave her head a rueful shake. "—but the answer is—"

He pressed his fingertips against her lips. "I promise you this, babe, you wouldn't regret it."

"I'm already regretting listening to you."

"I'd make it last so-o-o long."

She laughed. "Your humility is endearing."

"You'd be so hot, you'd beg me to quench your fire."

"Hah! You couldn't even ignite a spark in me."

He flashed her a knowing grin. Surely, he didn't suspect the flames of desire that licked through her already?

"I'd teach you to come, over and over and over, till your tongue curls," he promised.

Helen knew he was just trying to shock her, but she bit on her tongue just to make sure it stayed right where it should, uncurled.

"I'd take your screams in my mouth, and you'd take mine in yours."

Screams?

"It might only be for the brief time we're together, but

133

it would be the best time of both our lives. That's not bragging, honey, it's a fact.''

He pulled her hand up to his lips and kissed her wrist.

She thought her pulse would jump through the skin.

He smiled coaxingly. "So, Helen, will you make love with me?"

She should have said no, instantly. *Oh, Lord, I am so tempted.*

She should have slapped his face. *He looks so vulnerable. How can a man making an obscene suggestion appear vulnerable?*

Molten need pooled between her legs, and suddenly she felt dizzy.

It must be a delayed reaction to the events of the past few hours, she told herself. She stood shakily, inhaled deeply, and almost choked on a huge draft of cigar smoke.

And then she fainted.

Groggily, Helen swam up from the bottom of a deep pool. The wetness of the water cooled her heated face and droplets ran down her neck. She opened her eyes slowly to the sun and saw, instead, a canvas roof. And Rafe!

She tried to sit up, but he forced her back down to the cot where she was lying. Dipping a cloth into a bucket of water, he leaned over her and gently wiped her brow. The expression of concern on his face would have touched her if she wasn't so worried herself.

"Thank God," he said when her eyes opened. "Are you okay?"

She nodded sluggishly.

"Boy, I've known women to swoon over the prospect of making love with me, but outright fainting? Damn, that's a first for me. Do you faint when you come, too?"

She swatted his hand with the wet cloth aside and scanned her surroundings. Big John stood behind Rafe, wringing his hands. "It weren't my fish what made 'er swoon. No sirree, I don't serve bad fish."

Behind him in the flap that separated the makeshift sleeping area from the restaurant stood a half dozen curious miners. "Mebbe she's breedin'," one of them said.

Rafe stiffened. "Are you?" he asked accusingly.

"What?"

"Pregnant?"

"No!"

His shoulders relaxed and he turned away, ordering, "All of you men, out of here! Now!"

Grumbling, they obeyed, even Big John, who was still muttering, "Don't be blamin' me. I serve fresh fish."

Rafe sat down on the cot next to her. "Are you sure you're not knocked up?"

Her hot face felt even hotter. "I'm absolutely sure. It was the cigar smoke that made me faint. I can't stand cigars."

"Maybe we'd better find a doctor to double-check."

Fighting back wooziness, she forced herself to a sitting position. "Give it up, Rafe. I'm not pregnant. It's impossible."

Maybe you need a few lessons in the facts of life, Helen. Men and women make love. Babies result."

"Aaaargh! I didn't make love."

"You didn't? Ever?"

"Of course, I've made love, you idiot. Just not . . . lately." She immediately regretted her disclosure when a smug grin spread over his face.

"Define lately."

"No." She stood and tried to brush the wrinkles from her pants and blouse. It was a hopeless endeavor.

"A month?" he persisted, rising to his feet.

She refused to answer and began walking to the doorway.

"Two months?"

She made a tsking sound of disgust.

"Three months?"

Her head jerked up sharply in reflex.

"Well, I'll be damned," he whooped. "You haven't made love with a man in three months. Not even with your

135

Kentucky Fried Colonel.'' He threw an arm over her shoulder and pulled her close. ''We're gonna be so good together.''

They were still arguing, ''Yes, we are,'' ''No, we're not,'' when they hit the street and the harsh reminder that this was 1850 California, and they didn't have enough money for a bath, let alone a hotel room to make love.

But the harshest reminder came when they glanced across the street to an open lot where a large crowd had gathered.

''Oh, my God!'' Rafe said and pressed her face into his chest. But not before she saw Ignacio hanging by the neck from a tree limb. Dead.

Helen gagged and made no protest when Rafe led her quickly in the opposite direction with an arm still wrapped around her shoulder. The furious miners were congratulating themselves.

''Damned greasers! We oughta string 'em all up.''

''Horse thieves and Mexicans . . . They're all the same.''

''Dang it all, I never did meet me an honest tamale eater.''

''Let's go get a drink. Lynchin' sure does work up a thirst in a law-abidin' man.''

A short time later, they stood in the same dark alley where they'd escaped the bandits. Braced against the wall with both hands in his pockets, Rafe brooded, trying to decide on their next move. Helen was rinsing her mouth with water from a bucket at the back door of the hotel.

''Ignacio was a vicious man, but I never would have wished this on him,'' she said when she returned to his side.

''Me, neither. I should've known, though. Pablo told me about a man who'd had his head shaved and ears cut off, and was given a hundred lashes just for stealing a poke of gold dust.''

She stared at him, aghast. ''Well, don't blame yourself.''

136

"I'm the one who told the sheriff about the stolen horses."

"Stop the blame game, Rafe."

He shrugged. "At least Pablo and Sancho have escaped. Helen, we've got to get out of town as soon as possible, too, before the miners change their minds about us."

She nodded. "We'll go back to the landing site."

"No."

Even in the dim light from the half-open doorway of the hotel, he could see the flare of her nostrils. "It's too dangerous to stay here," she insisted.

"I'm not going back till I have gold," he said obstinately. "Lots of it."

"I'll give you money if that's all that's keeping you here," she pleaded. "I have a trust fund from my mother. Would . . . would twenty thousand be enough?"

Hurt and rage washed over him in a blinding tidal wave. "I don't want your money," he lashed out.

"Why not? What difference does it make how you get it?"

He bristled with indignation at the insult. Did she think he had no pride at all? "It makes a hell of a lot of difference. I earn my own way. I always have. What do you take me for? Some kind of gigolo?"

"No! A gigolo gives sexual favors for money, and—"

"And I'd give those to you for free," he finished for her with a tight smile. "So, it must be that I'm just a low-class, ignorant, ethic-less, Mexican greaser out for a quick buck."

"Oh, get off it, Rafe. It has nothing to do with your nationality."

He sliced her a look of disbelief. "I'm staying here till I earn enough gold to go back to the future a rich man. Frankly, I've lost my appetite for making love with you. So, do whatever the hell you want." Rafe stomped away.

"Where are you going?" Helen asked as she caught up with him.

"To a gambling hall."

That drew her up short. "Should we be mingling in public? People might still think you're the Angel Bandit.''

"That's a chance I'll have to take."

"I suppose you want to gamble so you can make enough money for gold-digging supplies."

"Yeah, but in case you haven't noticed, sweetheart, we don't have enough money even for a place to sleep. Only the twenty dollars in gold dust that Big John gave me. And look at the sign on the City Hotel. Five dollars a night, not including bath and breakfast. Per person."

She gave him a considering appraisal. "Are you any good at gambling?"

He grinned. "Yeah."

She shook her head with exasperation at his inflated ego. "Do you cheat?"

He flinched. "I can't believe even you would say something so offensive."

"Lord, you're right." Ducking her head in shame, she apologized.

"Are you with me on the gambling, or not?"

She studied him for a really long time, during which he held his breath. "For now," she said finally.

He exhaled slowly with relief. "You won't regret it, Helen." He patted her hand reassuringly.

She slapped his hand away. "I already regret it. And, believe me, I'm going to make you regret forcing me into this position. You'll wish you'd never met me."

He doubted that very much.

Sacramento City pulsed with life. And if gambling was its heartbeat, then gold surely was its pumping blood.

The first gambling "casino" they entered was a huge round tent. Numerous lanterns hung from the ceilings, casting an eerie glow. The small string orchestra that played to one side could hardly be heard over the raucous noise of shouting miners crowded around at least fifteen tables. Frazzled waiters darted between the tables serving drinks to grubby prospectors betting their hard-earned fortunes on games of chance, like lansquenet, monte, faro, poker, or roulette. More gold and silver than she'd ever seen in her life lay in piles on the tables.

"C'mon. C'mon. Who'll buck the tiger?" she heard more than one banker call out.

Still others cajoled, "Jack and deuce. Make your bets, gentlemen. All down? All down?"

Or, "One hundred against the house. Who'll be a winner tonight?"

At the bar, cut-glass bowls were filled with peppermints, lemon drops, and the blasted cigars, and bartenders with wide thumbs took pinches of gold dust from the customers in exchange for what appeared to be whiskey, wine, ale, and liquors.

The babble of voices, slap of cards, jubilant shouts and doleful groans, music, clinking of glasses and bottles, all provided a backdrop to the smells. And they were overwhelming. Body odor, perfume, whiskey, cigarettes, stale liquor, and Chinese punk, which lay smoldering in miniature jars for the convenience of those needing to light up.

"Oh, boy!" Rafe exclaimed.

"What?" she said, then gasped as she noticed the direction of his gaze.

The circular canvas walls were covered with paintings, no doubt completed by some down-and-out artist turned prospector. The murals all depicted women. Nude women in erotic poses.

"Great! The Playboy Club of the old West!" Rafe laughed.

"Maybe you can pick up a bunny later," she proposed sarcastically. Only a few women, clearly prostitutes in sleazy, low-cut gowns, were there. Some dealt cards at the gambling tables; others acted as "come-on" girls or lures for the bar; still others worked the crowd for their own personal gain.

"Honey, I'm not that horny. These bunnies bark."

She was about to chastise him for his crudity, but saw that he was smirking expectantly, just waiting for her to rise to his bait. She clamped her mouth shut.

"Besides, I have you, babe," he crooned softly in her ear.

She elbowed him in the ribs. "Behave."

As they moved through the crowd of about two hundred, Helen saw some of the men glancing from her to the paintings, probably picturing her in similar positions. She shifted uncomfortably.

"Let me guess. You want to go somewhere else."

"Can we?"

Surprisingly, he agreed. "It's too crowded in here anyway, and smoky. We can't have you fainting all over the place."

The next tent, The Plains, also was adorned with oil paintings, but these were of scenes of the overland trail to California: Independence Rock, the Sweetwater Valley, Fort Laramie, the Wind River Mountains, the Sierra Nevada Pass.

Rafe decided that tent was too crowded, as well.

They strolled through J and K streets near the levee where most of the saloons and gambling places were located. As they made their way through the labyrinth of half light and moving shadows, musical instruments sounded from practically every quarter—flutes, French horns, violins, fiddles, trumpets. And because the establishments were jammed so close together, all the musical sounds blended into a chaotic symphony.

In the distance, she heard the occasional report of a gun firing and the sound of male baritones singing ballads, like "Old Dan Tucker" and "Sweet Betsy from Pike."

From one of the tents, a brassy woman's voice said, "How do you want it, cowboy?" followed by a gruff male reply, "French." Three other men were lined up outside, waiting their turns.

Helen blushed and pretended not to hear, even when Rafe chuckled.

Next, they tried The Humboldt, The Mansion, The Diana, and Lee's Exchange. Eventually, they settled on a small tent at the end of K Street. It had only three tables and a board over two barrels that served as a makeshift bar. Whiskey was the only beverage served. A dark-haired *señorita* in an off-the-shoulder camisole and a colorful full skirt leaned against the tent pole talking to a handsome Spanish vaquero. A thin brown cigarillo dangled from her loose lips.

At one of the tables, chuck-a-luck—a simple dice game—was being played. At another, it was monte. At the third, poker.

"Which one are you going to try?" she asked in an undertone.

"Monte. It's the fairest game. Least chance of cheating."

They stood for a half hour, watching the action, before a young miner threw in his cards, having lost what seemed a fortune to Helen.

To her discomfort, she recognized the banker—the slimy Frenchman who had wanted to purchase her earlier that day for a brothel in San Francisco. His cold snake eyes watched her and Rafe with calculating interest.

Rafe squeezed her hand when she shivered with apprehension.

"Well, *Monsieur Ángel,* care to try your luck?" the gambler said with oily condescension. "My name is Pierre Lamoyne."

"Sure," Rafe said, sitting down on the stool, "and the name is Rafael Santiago. Mr. Santiago to you."

Lamoyne's elegant nose turned up at the affront. In the background, Helen heard someone remark snidely, "These greasers jist don't know their place."

"And this is my wife, Helen." Rafe reached over his shoulder and pulled her up tight against his back, placing her hand on his shoulder. "For luck," he said aloud to the other men, but for her ears only, he murmured, "Stick close, baby. I'm not feeling warm, fuzzy vibes here."

That was an understatement.

"Enchanté, ma chérie!" Lamoyne said in response to Helen's introduction, inclining his head toward her with respect. Then he ruined the aristocratic effect by remarking

to Rafe, "Your wife? *Non,* she is *certainment* a . . . um . . . *une fille de joie.*"

"What did he say?" she asked, leaning down near Rafe's ear.

Rafe told her, "He thinks you're a pavement princess, babe. A hooker." When her fingers clawed into his shoulder, he cautioned, "Take it easy, hon."

"Where is your ante, *monsieur?*" Lamoyne barked, suddenly impatient.

Rafe pulled out his meager pouch of gold dust and ignored Lamoyne's snort of disdain.

"Five dollars a hand," Lamoyne announced.

"Two," Rafe corrected.

"*Alors,* perhaps you and your *wife* should go down the street where the stakes are lower and the company less discriminating."

"Perhaps," Rafe said smoothly and started to rise.

"Two dollars then," Lamoyne capitulated ungraciously.

After an hour in which Rafe won some hands and lost others, Helen was disgusted to see that his pile remained pretty much the same as when he'd started. Lamoyne looked equally disgusted.

"Enough of these penny-ante games. Let us increase the odds here, *monsieur.*" The gambler laid a pile of nuggets in the center of the table. "Five hundred dollars."

Reluctantly, Rafe shook his head. "Can't do. I don't have that much."

The sleazeball twirled his mustache with sly satisfaction, his crafty eyes connecting with Helen. "Ah, but you are wrong, my friend. You have something of equal value to wager."

Rafe's body under her hand grew rock stiff. "She's not for sale."

The gambler shrugged and started to pull his pile of nuggets back.

Rafe raised a halting hand. "Perhaps we can make a deal." He reached in his pocket and pulled out a pair of sunglasses. "Ray-Bans. Worth a hundred dollars," he said and put them on to demonstrate. "They protect your eyes from sunlight."

"I thought Pablo took those."

"He did, but he gave them back to me today . . . said they were useless."

Lamoyne checked out the sunglasses when Rafe laid them on the table. With a grunt of derision, he picked them up and tried them on. The *señorita* made a cooing sound of appreciation at his appearance, and the vain little fop preened.

"So, do you want them?" Rafe pushed.

With heightened color, Lamoyne snarled, "*Oui,* fifty dollars."

Next Rafe took off his camouflage shirt, leaving on his tight-fitting green T-shirt.

"You can't do that," Helen admonished. "It's against Army regulations."

He cut her a telling glare that said clearly, "Get real!" The shirt brought another fifty.

"How about black silk boxer shorts?" Rafe offered.

Helen burst out laughing. "You are crazy."

"Well, I can't think of anything else. I don't want to give up my boots."

"Boxer shorts?" Lamoyne asked.

"Men's underpants."

Lamoyne balked. "Why would a gentleman want another man's filthy undergarments?"

"These are silk," Rafe informed him. "And clean. I washed them last night, didn't I, Helen?" Without waiting for her answer, Rafe leaned over and unlaced his boots. Then he stood and began to undo his pants. "Look the other way, honey," he told the *señorita,* but he winked at Helen and told her, "You can look, though."

By the time Helen peeked back, Rafe's boxers were lying outrageously in the middle of the table, and he was zipping up his pants over bare skin. Helen forced herself to stop thinking about all that bare skin under his pants.

After examining the shorts—joined by the other card

143

players and the *señorita*—Lamoyne agreed to another fifty dollars.

"That's only a hundred and fifty dollars," Rafe muttered.

"How about my underwear?" Helen blurted out, and everyone in the room turned to gawk at her. Including Rafe, whose gawk quickly changed to an ear-to-ear smile.

"I mean, if you can give up stuff, so can I," she said in a weak voice. After a few quick words from Rafe, she went to a back room, partitioned by only a red calico curtain, and removed her bra and panties. Rafe stood guard on the other side of the drape.

Face flaming, she returned and placed the white lace bra and French-cut briefs on the table, along with her camouflage blouse.

Rafe sat back down, then glanced back over his shoulder, taking his first gander at her. His eyes locked on her breasts, naked under the thin T-shirt. Licking his lips, he whispered huskily, "Maybe this isn't such a good idea, after all."

To her embarrassment, her nipples hardened under his appreciative scrutiny.

Rafe's sharp inhalation of breath only made them tighten more. She folded her arms over her chest and demanded of Lamoyne, "Well, do you want them or not? We can always go elsewhere if you're not interested."

The gambler picked them up, one at a time, examining them closely, especially the filmy cups of her bra.

"Jay-sus," one Irishman exclaimed, "you could prob'ly sell that over at Lola's for a thousand dollars."

Rafe sat in front of her, barely stifling a snicker. She cuffed him on the shoulder.

Finally, Lamoyne grumbled, "It's a bet."

And fifteen minutes later, Rafe and Helen left the tent posthaste with their belongings, as well as $520 in gold nuggets and dust.

"Let's get away from here," Rafe said, pulling on her hand. "I don't trust Lamoyne. He'll be after us in a flash."

"I know." She rushed to keep up with him.

Rafe looked at her and groaned.

"What?"

"Your breasts are jiggling in that T-shirt. I think I'm about to co—"

"Don't say it," she snapped. "I'll put my blouse on as soon as it's safe to stop."

He mumbled something about never stopping.

But he did stop soon after that in front of the City Hotel. "Did you say something earlier about being willing to sell your soul for a bath and a bed?"

"Oooh, yes!" she said on a long sigh. "I can't wait."

"Me neither, baby. Me neither," he agreed, taking her hand and leading her through the front door.

Something in Rafe's smooth-as-butter voice set off alarm bells in Helen's head, and she halted, pulling him back sharply. "I'm not selling anything here, Rafe. Especially not a corkscrew."

A warm laugh escaped his lips before he wagged a finger chidingly. "Tsk, tsk, Prissy. That's not what I meant."

"Oh." She felt heat rise from her chest to her hairline.

"Although I do think I deserve a reward for being a winner."

She narrowed her eyes. "Like what?"

"Oh, well, I don't know. Let's see." He tapped the edge of his bristled jaw with a forefinger consideringly, then brightened. "How about a kiss?"

"A kiss? That's what you want? That's all?"

"Yup."

"Just one?"

He hesitated. "For now."

"Oh, all right."

He dazzled her with a wicked look of triumph then, and the promise in his pale eyes nearly scorched her already hot skin.

She almost reneged on the deal, especially when he added, "But I'll take my reward later, after we bathe, because . . ."

He was already pulling her along into the hotel when she prompted, ''Because?''

''Because when I collect my kiss, I want it to last a *real* long time.''

Chapter Ten

Helen sat cross-legged on the homemade, three-quarter-sized bed that took up most of the small room they'd rented in the City Hotel for the night. The two-story building with its projecting balcony was a former sawmill built by the famous Captain Sutter—primitive by modern standards—but they were lucky to get a separate room. The majority of the guests slept dorm-style in tiny cubicles or in double-decker bunks, sharing a bathtub and even—God forbid!—a communal toothbrush and razor.

The only other furniture in the second-floor room was an oak washstand, hardly visible in the shadowy light thrown by a lone lantern. Wooden pegs on the wall held their meager supply of clothing. Crimson calico lined the walls.

Despite the crude accommodations, Helen felt gloriously clean, though slightly sunburned. She'd just bathed and donned a scratchy cotton nightgown, which Rafe had purchased while she was in the tub. His consideration in paying extra cash from their small hoard for clean water and a locked door to the "bathroom" would endear him to her forever.

He was down there now, taking his own bath, but he'd made her promise not only to bar the door from the inside but to brace a slat under the handle for extra insurance, and to keep one of the pistols handy. The gambler Lamoyne might still come after them, or the sheriff could have second thoughts.

Combing her wet hair, Helen felt hopeful for the first time in days. A bright moon shone through the one grimy window, and Helen figured it must be well past midnight.

"Helen, open up." Rafe's whispered voice came from the hallway, accompanied by a sharp knock. "Hurry! I just saw Lamoyne out on the street, and he didn't look like he was coming over to say 'Howdy.' "

Briskly, she removed the wooden slat and slid the bar. Rafe walked in, barefooted, carrying his dirty clothing and boots in one arm, and a raised revolver in the other. Without even glancing at her, he dropped everything to the floor and locked the door, double-checking the strength of the bar and wooden brace. Next, he examined the open window to make sure no one could enter that way, either. Luckily, there was no roof or balcony nearby to give access to their room.

Only then did he turn to Helen. "What? Why are you looking at me like that?"

Rafe was wearing only his camouflage slacks, slung low on his hips, exposing his navel. Beads of water still rolled off his slicked-back, wet hair and down his neck to bead on his chest. He had even shaved.

Helen swallowed and a knot of tension coiled in her stomach. She tried to avert her gaze from the wide expanse of shoulders, the muscled planes of biceps and ridged abdomen, the flat male nipples. She really did try—but his body was so beautiful.

"I like to look at you, too, Helen," he rasped out.

Her eyes widened, locking with his. He smiled knowingly at her, but not in a mocking way.

He moved closer, an easy job in the close confines of the tiny room. The hungry, predatory gleam in his eyes alarmed, and excited her.

Helen backed up a bit, hitting the wall next to the bed with a bang. The comb she still held in her hand dropped to the floor. "What . . . what are you doing?"

"Collecting my reward," he said huskily, reaching out to brush a loose strand of damp hair behind her ear.

She gasped at the intense pleasure created by just that whisk of his fingertips across her face. "What reward?"

He grinned, then licked his upper lip with his tongue. He made a low, savage sound deep in his throat and stepped even closer. An animal moving in for the kill. "My kiss. Don't you remember, Helen? You promised me a kiss."

A kiss? That's all he wants? A kiss? Helen's jumbled brain tried to assimilate the softly murmured words. She felt the heat of his bare chest, only inches away. She smelled the strong odor of lye soap, and clean male skin . . . Rafe's own scent. Her breasts filled and tautened into aching points. A delicious shudder rippled through her body, and she clenched her fists at her sides to keep from opening her arms in welcome. She'd never been aroused so swiftly or so fiercely by a man in all her life.

"A kiss. That's all. One kiss," she insisted, forcing a cool tone to her voice, praying for control.

"One kiss," he agreed with an enigmatic chuckle. "For now."

His lips were so near. She closed her eyes.

"Why did you moan?" His warm breath fanned her lips.

She hadn't realized she'd moaned. She would have to be more careful. "Because I want this to be over as quickly as possible. Just do it so I can go to sleep," she snapped, scrunching her closed eyelids even tighter. *I'll never sleep tonight. Never.*

"Liar," he hissed, placing two fingers on the wildly beating pulse in her neck. "And don't give me any of this I-am-a-martyr-and-you-are-the-satyr bit. This is going to be a mutual kiss, a willing give-and-take. We're talking long, hot, slow, wet—"

Her eyes flew open. "I never agreed—"

But it was too late. His lips were already covering hers. Soft. Brushing back and forth till she opened for him. Slanting. Seeking the right fit.

She didn't know who moaned then, him or her. It didn't matter. She wanted his kiss. She wanted his kiss desperately.

He put both hands on either side of her face, and his firm lips took possession of her mouth.

Willingly, she wrapped her arms around his shoulders. With one hand behind his nape, she pulled him closer. His lower body sought out the cradle of her hips, and she knew, without a doubt, that he was as aroused as she was.

With his tongue buried in her mouth, he inserted a determined thigh between her legs, separating them. Expertly, he undulated his arousal against her arousal.

She tried to keen out her spiraling pleasure, but his tongue, slipping in and out of her mouth, stopped her cries.

All the time, he continued to kiss her, ravenously, never coming up for air, probably fearing that the minute they broke contact, the kiss would end. Their agreement would end.

With a growl of frustration, Rafe put both hands on her buttocks and lifted her, pulling up the hem of her nightgown, adjusting her bare legs around his waist. She locked her ankles and tightened her thighs against his hips. Her shoulders rested against the wall.

He cupped her bare bottom with his hands, then began to move against her in earnest—rhythmic thrusts against her parted center. She wanted him so much. She couldn't seem to get enough.

Through the fog of his bone-melting passion, Rafe became aware that Helen was kissing him back, with abandon. Licking his lips, nibbling, sucking, inserting her tongue into his mouth, grinding her lips against his.

Tears were streaming down her face and incoherent pleas came out as whimpers into his own mouth.

He turned and lowered her to the bed, following on top of her. His lips never left hers. He wasn't taking any chances.

"Please," Helen pleaded against his lips, then broke contact, jerking her head to the side. Her chest was heaving and she panted, writhing from side to side.

"Hold on, babe, hold on," he promised, running a hand up her leg to her inner thigh. At the first touch of her wetness, he almost came. "Oh, sweetheart, you feel so good."

She raised her hips up off the bed and parted her bent

legs more. He could feel the muscles in her arms and legs grow rigid.

"Relax, sweetheart. Just relax."

"Relax?" she choked out incredulously.

He smiled. "Do you want me to touch you again?"

"No!" Then, more weakly, "Yes."

His thumb strummed her slickness.

She distended and pulsed.

He could barely breathe.

"O-o-oh, Rafe."

"I told you I would teach you how to say, 'Oh, Rafe!' "

"Shut up," she ground out with a laugh.

"I want to look at you."

"Not now," she asserted, holding his hand in place with one of hers. The other hand reached down and caressed the length of his erection through the fabric of his slacks.

He saw stars.

With a guttural, animal sound of surrender, he placed himself against her, arousal against arousal. Bracing himself on straightened arms, he simulated the act of love—a hard rhythm, up and down.

And she met his every thrust with an opposing thrust, a sweet, tantalizing counterpoint.

"Oh, God, oh, Rafe, oh my, oh-h-h-h," she screamed exultantly, arching high off the bed, knees bent and bracketing him, feet planted on the bed linens.

He came against her in a searing gush of pleasure, so powerful his body shuddered for several long minutes afterward. Decreasing spasms continued to ripple through him. He'd never had such a satisfying orgasm, even when inside a woman.

He let himself rest on her, heavily, for several moments, trying to get his heart pumping back to normal again. When he finally raised himself on his elbows, he saw that Helen was trembling, too, gazing up at him with awe.

He shared the feeling.

And this was just the beginning. What would it be like when they really made love? When he was imbedded inside

151

her welcoming folds? When she climaxed around his erection?

He stifled a groan.

Grazing a thumb across her kiss-swollen lips, he said in a hoarse voice he barely recognized, "That was some kiss, babe."

She nodded. "This is probably par for you, but I never—"

He pressed his fingertips against her lips to halt her next words. "No, it's not par for me. Believe me, what just happened to us was different . . . special."

"Rafe, don't say things you think I want to hear. It happened. That's all. I don't expect anything from you."

He gritted his teeth. For some reason, he wanted her to expect things from him. And he wanted her to admit it was special for her, too. "I want to look at you," he said huskily, and began to tug on the hem of her gown.

She covered his hand with hers, stopping the hem at mid-thigh. "I don't know if this is such a good idea," she replied nervously.

"Don't go shy on me now, honey."

He pushed the rest of her gown over her head and flicked it off the bed. "Well, I'll be damned!" he exclaimed, surveying her body. "I was right. You *do* have Vargas breasts."

She tried to cross her arms over her chest and close her legs with belated modesty. Before she had a chance to curb her tongue, she blurted out, "What are Vargas breasts?"

He pulled her arms apart and over her head, holding them by the wrists with one hand. With the other hand, he cupped one breast, testing its weight. "Champagne breasts. Round and full. Puffy aureoles. Pebbly, pink nipples," he explained thickly. "Vargas was an artist who painted nude pinups like that for *Esquire* years ago."

"Pinups? Pinups?" she sputtered, her face burning with mortification as she squirmed to get free from his grip. But not too hard, he noted.

"I love your freckles," he added. "I love that they're

152

all over, even in your secret places.''

She moaned.

''And I love it when you moan for me.''

She moaned again.

He moved his hand lower, pausing over her flat stomach. ''So smooth. You're skin is *so* smooth.''

''Except for my scar.''

''What scar?''

''Just above my belly button. You can't miss it. I had a port wine birthmark removed when I was ten years old.'' She glanced down, and then jerking her hands out of his grasp, sat up. ''My God, the scar is missing. That's incredible.''

He shrugged and reached for her again.

She ignored his open arms and stood, moving closer to the lantern, examining her stomach for the missing scar, then studying her right knee. She was momentarily unaware of her nudity, which he was enjoying immensely. ''My knee surgery scar is missing, too. I tore up the cartilage in a skydiving jump five years ago and decided to have the shredded cartilage removed by laser surgery.''

''Hmmm. That's odd,'' Rafe said, but his smoldering eyes said he had something else on his mind. ''I mean, it's odd that we would retain our tattoos, but not other body scars.'' He jiggled his eyebrows at her. ''C'mere and let me check out your other bodily anomalies.''

She laughed. ''I'll give you anamolies.'' Then she thought of something. ''Maybe it has something to do with scientific anachronisms.''

''Say that again.''

''You know, it was possible to have tattoos in the nineteenth century, but cosmetic operations didn't come into vogue until World War I. And a swollen knee joint wouldn't have been cause for surgery. So, we only carried back with us those medical marvels that were possible in this time.''

She moved back toward the bed. ''Don't you have any scars, Rafe? Didn't you ever have any surgery?''

"Well, actually . . ." he said, folding his arms behind his head. He was really, really enjoying the play of light and shadow on Helen's sexy buns and magnificent breasts. "The only surgery I've ever had, if you could call it that, was the vasecto—"

The blood drained from his head as he bolted to his feet, rushing over to the lantern. Even before he looked, he knew what he would find. *No vasectomy scar.*

"No!" he exclaimed, then turned to her hopefully. "Please tell me you have an IUD or birth-control implant."

She shook her head slowly, apparently not understanding his dilemma.

Damn! He felt all his hopes for this night, in fact the remainder of this time-travel adventure, go up in smoke.

"What?" she asked, looking pointedly away from his genitals.

"My vasectomy scar is gone."

Helen stared at Rafe, trying to understand the horror in his voice.

"And I only have three damn condoms in my wallet."

"Well, why is that such a big deal?"

"Why is that such a big deal? Why is that such a big deal?" He mimicked, moving away from her, pressing his palms against the wall. "Because that means we can't make love, that's why. And believe me, babe, to me that is a *very . . . big . . . deal.*"

"But if you have three condoms . . ." she said hesitantly. "I mean, three condoms is surely enough."

He cast her a frown of utter disbelief. "Babe, three times wouldn't be nearly enough for me. Once I have you, I won't be able to stop at three times."

"In one night?" Her mouth dropped open, and she hastily clamped it shut.

He laughed mirthlessly. "Oh, Prissy! You are so naive." With a groan, he turned and pounded his forehead against the wall in frustration.

"Oh, Rafe," she said behind him.

"Hush up, Helen. What I don't need now is your sym-

154

pathy. What I need is your hot sex.''

A long silence followed his words.

Eventually, he turned around and saw that she'd already donned the damn nightgown again.

She peeked up at him, her face pink with embarrassment. In a low voice, she homed in irrelevantly on only one part of what he'd said. ''My sex is *not* hot.''

He started to laugh then. It was a good thing, too, because otherwise, he might have cried.

Helen awakened at dawn, as she always did. Her internal alarm clock apparently still operated, even in time-travel mode. Lying on her side, facing the window, she saw a bright orange sun rising on the horizon, portending another blazing day.

Rafe slept soundly behind her. Even with the rolled blanket that separated them, at his insistence, Helen was intensely aware of the man. His heat, his scent, his masculinity.

She couldn't imagine what had happened to her carefully controlled defenses last night, but she couldn't stop thinking about the night's events, either. How it felt to be kissed by Rafe's lips. How she had opened herself for his touch. She tried to remember ever feeling that way with Elliott, or any other man. She couldn't.

Sliding herself quietly off the bed, Helen looked down at Rafe. He slept on his stomach, arms thrown over his head with total abandon, boxer-clad legs spread slightly, face to the side. The long, luxuriant lashes of his closed lids fanned his face. He breathed softly through parted lips.

Helen's heart grew and grew with a strong, new emotion. She was drawn to him, always had been. She couldn't deny that. But why? Logically, there should be more things about him to repel her than attract. His maverick personality. His lack of patriotism. His greed. His crudity and constant teasing.

Oh, he was handsome, no doubt about that, but she was

surrounded by men everyday, many of them much better looking.

Intelligence? Hmmm. She'd always been drawn to a man with intelligence, and Rafe clearly fit that criterion. His reputation as a top-notch lawyer hadn't come easy.

Sexual chemistry? Yes, there was that. To the nth degree.

But, no, it was something else—perhaps the vulnerability that she always sensed in him over his ethnic background. His extreme sensitivity probably resulted from a lifetime of hurts she couldn't fathom. And the needful, yearning expression in his eyes when he watched her sometimes in an unguarded moment . . . Well, what woman wouldn't be flattered?

Helen shook her head in confusion, not sure she wanted to understand this thread that connected them. He was a dangerous man, dangerous to her well-planned military life, her well-planned future, her very well-being. Taboo. Off-limits. Not to be considered.

Still, Helen had something she needed to do for Rafe this morning, before he awakened. Dressing quickly, she took a few gold coins from the sack, strapped a holster and gun around her hips, and slipped out the door, locking it behind her.

Down on the empty street, she looked about, trying to locate Lily's Fandango Parlor.

"Oooohm. Oooohm. Oooohm. Oooohm."

Rafe awakened reluctantly from the best sleep he'd had in days.

Oh, no! Not again. He buried his head under a pillow, trying to wipe out the sound.

"Oooohm . . . Oh, you're awake . . . *Oooohm* . . . Good . . . Oooohm . . . Give me a minute. . . . *Oooohm* . . . I only have two more sets to go. . . . *Oooohm* . . . I brought you coffee and a cinnamon bun. . . . *Oooohm"*

His eyes shot open. *Where did she get coffee? Unless she'd gone out. She wouldn't! Would she?*

He sat up, holding the pillow in his hand.

Helen sat all twisted into a pretzel at the bottom of the bed, facing the window, fully dressed in camouflage pants and green T-shirt, wearing his gun belt. A quick glance at the door showed the wooden brace was not in the same place he'd put it last night.

Yep, Helen had gone out this morning while he'd slept. The realization hit him in the gut like a sickening sucker punch.

"Oooohm. Ooooohm. Oooohm. Oooohm."

Angrily, he pitched the pillow.

"Oooohm. Ooooohm. Ooooh—"

The pillow hit her smack in her chanting mouth. *Good!*

"Why did you do that? I wasn't done," she protested.

"Oh, you're done all right." He stood abruptly.

She dodged out of his path and headed for the washstand, which was all of two feet away. Ignoring his grumbling, Helen took a handful of water from the china bowl and began to gargle, spitting into a brass bowl on the floor.

Gargle, spit. Gargle, spit. Gargle, spit. *"Glug . . . glug . . . glug . . . glug . . . glug . . . glug . . ."*

He felt like fingernails were scraping across his eyeballs.

"Do you think we could buy a toothbrush and toothpowder today?" she asked blithely. *"Glug . . . glug . . . glug . . . glug . . . glug . . . glug . . ."*

Rafe crossed his eyes. His frayed nerves would surely break with one more "glug."

"Glug . . . glug . . . gl—"

He grabbed her by the forearms and shook her, which was a big mistake. Her unconfined breasts moved under the T-shirt, drawing his eyes like an X-rated magnet.

He dropped his hands and turned away, fighting for composure. When he felt sure he could speak above a croak, he demanded, "Where did you go this morning?"

"Lily's Fandango Parlor."

That was the last thing he'd expected. He jerked about and stared at her in astonishment. She was peering into a small, wavy mirror over the washstand, cleaning her teeth with a twig, oblivious to his outrage.

"What did you say?"

She put the twig down and faced him, a secretive, pleased look on her face. She'd pulled her hair back off her face into a ponytail, tied at the nape with a piece of lace from her gown. She would have looked like a little girl if it weren't for her lush, kiss-swollen lips.

He gulped.

"I went to Lily's. And you were right, it is a brothel."

Oh, brother!

"Did you know that those women get fifty dollars for something called 'Hair of the Dog'?"

He put both hands on his hips and grinned, despite his being upset.

Her eyes followed his hands to his hips, then dropped lower. Her head flew up like a rocket and her face turned beet red.

He was very pleased. So was a certain part of his body.

She made a slight coughing sound, then continued. "You should have seen the outfit one of the girls was wearing— pure Victoria's Secret. Anyhow, it was really hard to find Lily's because it didn't have a sign outside, and I had to go to Big John's and wake him up to give me directions. He's the one who gave me the coffee and cinnamon bun. So, you should be really grateful for all the trouble I went to."

"Grateful? Grateful? Do you have any idea how dangerous it was to leave this room? And why the hell did you go to Lily's?"

Smiling, she reached into her back pocket, which only accentuated the outline of what had to be the most perfect breasts in all creation. He was afraid he might lose it right there on the spot.

"Well? Aren't you going to take it? It's a gift for you."

"What?" he blinked, feeling like a blundering idiot.

She held her open palm out in front of him, offering him his gold crucifix and chain. His heart stopped, then started beating so fast he thought it might explode. Chug chug

chug chug . . . He was pretty sure tears were welling in his eyes.

As if understanding, Helen pulled his hand forward, opened the tight fist, and placed her ''gift'' in his hand.

''Oh, God,'' he whispered. Then, ''Why?''

She shrugged and went to the other side of the room, packing their few extra garments into her backpack. ''I could tell how much it meant to you, and you were willing to give it up for us. It was the least I could do.''

He forced the lump back in his throat as he put the chain around his neck. Other than his mother, no one had ever done such an unselfish thing for him. If he'd had trouble getting Helen out of his system in the past, how would he ever forget her now? Even if he survived this time-travel fiasco, he would never be the same. Never.

''Did you take some gold to pay for it?'' he asked finally.

She nodded, her back turned to him.

''How much did she charge?'' Rafe hoped it wasn't too much. They were going to need a hell of a lot of gold to outfit themselves for the mining camps.

She didn't answer.

''Helen?''

''Well, actually,'' she said, turning slowly, her face pink with a becoming blush, ''Lily wouldn't take any gold.''

He tilted his head in question. ''She didn't charge you?''

''Oh, she charged me all right.''

Rafe noticed her arms folded over her chest then, and suddenly he understood. With a hoot of laughter, he guessed, ''Your bra, right?''

''Yes. Can you believe it? Apparently word spread about your card game last night. And my bra was a hot commodity. Also . . . Oh, never mind.''

''What?'' he prodded.

Her face grew pinker and she fidgeted uncomfortably.

''Spill it,'' he demanded.

''I sold her my panties for an extra fifty dollars,'' she admitted. ''And I don't want to hear one single snicker, do you hear?''

He gaped at her. Then a horrifying thought occurred to him. How in God's name was he going to travel with her for days, maybe weeks, knowing she was wearing no underwear? With the memory of her scorching kisses still branded on his lips? With the picture of her naked body impressed forever in his libido? With three lousy condoms in his wallet?

Maybe he had died and gone to hell, after all.

Chapter Eleven

After leaving the hotel, they argued back and forth about their next course of action. Rafe decided that arguing was the second best thing he and Helen did together.

"Of course, we're going back to the landing site," she declared.

"Over my dead body," he asserted, repeating his intention to join the Gold Rush.

The only thing they agreed upon was the need to leave Sacramento as soon as possible.

"I thought you'd accepted the fact that we're headed north to the mining camps," he finally snapped. "Besides, there's a reason why we have to head north, if you'd only listen for a min—"

"What would make you think that I'd agreed to go north?" Then she gasped as something suddenly seemed to occur to her. The color drained from her face, and her fingertips fluttered to her mouth reflexively in dismay. "Oh, no! How could you?"

He frowned with confusion, especially when Helen backed away from him.

"That's what last night was all about, wasn't it?" she accused in a wounded shriek. "You seduced me deliberately. Manipulated me."

"Huh?"

"You are the same old Rafe. No ethics. Any end justifies the means."

At first, he didn't understand. When he did, he lifted his chin angrily. What a low opinion she had of him!

"And I was so easy. Lord, you must have been laughing inside. Prissy Helen. She's so hard up. Give her a quick tickle and she'll follow like a sheep."

"Yeah, that's right." Was she really that dense? Even a blind person could see how much he wanted her. But he'd be damned if he'd explain himself to her. And tickle? Hah! He'd like to show her a tickle. Forcing himself to remain calm, he commented, "Frankly, your nagging *is* beginning to sound exactly like the bleating of a sheep." Then, he walked stiffly away.

She rushed to catch up. "Don't walk away from me, you jerk. I'm talking to you."

Stopping abruptly, he faced her. "No, Helen, you're not talking. You're lecturing. Well, I've had it up to my eyeballs with your stupid assumptions and low opinions of me. Find someone else to be your whipping boy." He pointed to the dozen miners who followed her like horny hound dogs after a bitch in heat. It was barely seven A.M., and already she had an entourage.

"Is she yer intended?" one man asked Rafe.

"Oh, yeah, I intend—"

"Shut up, Rafe," she snarled.

"Hey, lady, I'll give ya a hundred dollars if you'll let me sniff yer skin," another guy yelled.

Helen gave the poor dimwit a look that would blister paint, and he shuffled off with his tail between his legs. Rafe laughed and strode away from her, too.

She followed him to where he stood in front of the newspaper office of the *Sacramento Transcript*. Her fan club skidded to a halt behind her. Really, this ménage à mob was becoming a bore.

Rafe turned on the salivating miners and drew one of his pistols from its holster. "Get lost, guys. You're annoying my wife." He shot a bullet in the air for emphasis.

The miners jumped with surprise.

"Is the lass really yer wife?" one red-haired man with a heavy Irish brogue asked, completely unfazed by the gunshot.

"Yes, I'm his wife. So, go away."

That got Rafe's attention—Helen agreeing to be his wife. He wondered if her eyes were rolling with horror at such an admission, and couldn't resist checking.

Nope, her eyes stared straight ahead, murderously. And he was the target.

"Are you still here? I thought you'd left town already. Hiked on back to the landing site and Colonel Sanders."

"Stop being sarcastic."

"Stop talking. I'm in a bad mood, and you're giving me a headache."

"Ooooh, I'd like to . . . to . . . to . . ."

"Lost for words, Prissy?"

She gritted out, "You're not going to abandon me, Rafe."

Her voice droned on shrewishly, but Rafe tuned her out. ". . . and I know what you're up to here." She was still babbling on . . . *blah, blah, blah* . . . unaware that he wasn't listening. "You figure if you start an argument with me, that gives you an excuse to just walk off with no regrets."

"Listen to yourself sometime, Helen. First, you claim I seduced you so you'd follow me. Now you say I'm deliberately trying to get rid of you. Make up your mind."

"Well . . . well, you're not leaving me here alone, I'll tell you that."

"Alone?" he scoffed. "Look around you. There's about a hundred men willing to take my place. And every one of them would like to get in a good 'tickle.' "

"Stop being an ass."

"Stop being a shrew."

"I'm sick of your teasing. I'm sick of your sexual advances. I'm sick of your crudity. I'm—"

"So, Helen, why don't you tell me how you really feel." Lord, if he wasn't half-hard for the woman all the time, if his heart didn't ache sometimes when he looked at her, well, her waspish nature sure would turn him off.

"I swear, when we get back, you are going to be court-martialed for insubordination. More than anything, *Captain*,

I am sick of your total lack of regard for military conduct.''

"And I'm sick of your trying to pull rank every other minute. This is the nineteenth century, and you are *not* in the Army anymore, babe. The only rules here are those between a man and woman. Did you hear me? Male and female.''

"Oh, here we go again with the sex stuff!"

"You bet your sweet ass. Damn it, why don't you be honest with yourself, Prissy? The only reason you're so mad at me is 'cause we didn't do the deed last night. Frustration, that's what this is all about, pure and simple.''

Bright red color blossomed on her cheeks. Then she swung her arm in a wide arc, slugging him in the stomach. "I'm going to kill you. I swear I am. You lowdown, egotistical, male chauvinist horse's patoot.''

He saw her attack coming and managed to step back slightly. The punch hardly hurt at all, but he winced, anyhow, just to make her feel guilty. "What do military rules say about an officer striking a soldier? Or using language unbecoming to an officer? Sounds like court-martial grounds to me. Hey, maybe we could get court-martialed together.''

Through the storm of Helen's rage and his quick rejoinders, he realized they still had an audience.

"The two wee angles mus' be havin' a lovers' quarrel," the Irishman was explaining to the miners around him.

"Is it true she's Elena?" one man asked.

Several others gave resounding shouts of "Yes."

"Mebbe she and her husban' will go thar separate ways since they don't hardly seem ta be gettin' along. Mebbe she'll set up her own corkscrew tent here in Sacramenty. Mebbe she'll—"

Helen grunted with disgust, muttering, "E-nough!" Spinning on her heel, she whistled loudly between her teeth to gain their silence.

Rafe's headache bloomed into a class two ear ringer.

"I'm going to say this just once, real slow. So, listen

carefully, you thick-headed fools. I . . . am . . . Helen . . . Prescott. Major . . . Helen . . . Prescott. I am not now, nor have I ever been, a prostitute. I have no idea what a corkscrew is. So, I can't say for sure if I've ever done it, but I'm pretty sure I haven't. I am not interested in finding another man. The one I have now is more than I can handle.''

Rafe tried to put an arm on her shoulder, and she shrugged him off.

"Yer not a whore?" the Irishman asked. Barely pausing, he added, "Well then, when you get tired of the greaser, will ya marry me?"

Several men protested, chiming in with their matrimonial offers.

Chuckling, Rafe turned back to the broadsheet pasted on the outside of the newspaper office. A headline on the paper displayed outside the tent-office announced the discovery of "pound diggings," or paydirt that yielded a pound of gold a day, at Devil's Bar on the North Fork of the American River.

Hmmm. Maybe he'd head there. He could ask for directions once he got to the general store.

But, no, there was another, even more interesting article about hundreds of miners scurrying north, lured by rumors of a lake of gold. *A lake of gold?* Sounded good to him. Even better than the pound diggings.

"Rafe! Are you listening to me?"

He turned back to Helen, who stood with hands on hips, having succeeded in getting the grumbling miners to drift off. She tapped a foot impatiently, waiting for his response. His eyes shot to the front of her camouflage blouse, which she'd left unbuttoned over her T-shirt. He saw right off that her foot tapping had set her bare breasts to jiggling.

Helen was right. He was developing a one-track mind. He should be ashamed of himself.

Instead, he was enjoying himself immensely.

"What now?" He pretended to be still annoyed with her.

"I said that I just thought of something. Where are the harness and parachutes?"

"That's what I tried to tell you earlier, Helen. Remember, way back before you started spouting off about tickling, I tried to tell you there was another reason why we had to head north. The parachutes and harness were on Pablo's horse, and I found out last night, when you were taking a bath, that Pablo rode out of town. And he was traveling north."

"What? Why didn't you tell me before?" Her face was red with chagrin. Between her continual anger, and her sunburn, she was starting to resemble a beet.

"Helen, Helen, Helen, remember how you attacked me the minute I entered our hotel room? I plum forgot."

"You're plum nuts. How could you have let him go?"

"Don't start on me, Prissy."

Her face fell. "Now what are we going to do?"

"Well, I guess we'll have to go prospecting," he offered, real quick. "The guy who was in line to take a bath last night told me that Pablo has a brother at Rich Bar. That's one of the northernmost diggings."

Frowning, she considered all that he'd told her.

"And check out this newspaper article about a lake of gold being discovered in that region. See, it's fate. God must want us to become gold diggers."

"A lake of gold? God? Fate?" she sputtered out. "I'll show you fate." She swung her arm in a wide arc, about to punch him in the stomach. Again.

He ducked aside with a laugh. "Really, Helen, you've got a vicious side to you."

She clenched her fists at her sides and appeared to be counting to ten. When she was done, she tried a patient tone. "This is serious, Rafe. Whether we go digging for gold or not, we need those parachutes to get back to the future."

"You're right, Helen. Tell you what. We'll go search for Pablo. But, once we recover the parachutes, you have to agree to go prospecting with me afterward, *before* we go home.''

Her eyes narrowed and she studied him suspiciously.

"Is it a deal?" he asked.

"For how long?"

"Probably only a few weeks."

"Do you promise? On your honor? We'll go back then?"

"I promise," he swore.

She extended her arm and shook hands with him. "A deal."

He held onto her hand when she was about to pull away. Pulling her closer, he whispered, "How about another deal? How about if, on our last night here in the past, you and I break in those three condoms?"

"Is that all you can think about?" She yanked her hand out of his grasp with disgust.

"Actually, yes."

She cut him one of those you-are-a-maggot, I-am-superior smirks.

"Think about it, Helen. If I had *that* to look forward to, it'd probably take me half as long to finish here. I'd probably work twenty hours a day with you as my incentive. I'd probably settle for a lot less gold than—"

"At least you're being honest about your motives now. None of those flowery words or I'm-dying-for-you-baby lines. Any woman would do for your purposes."

"You really believe that I deliberately set out to seduce you? That it's not you, and only you, that I wanted last night?"

She nodded emphatically.

He shook his head. "You don't have much confidence in your own sexual attraction, do you, babe?" But maybe that was for the best. If she knew how much he wanted her, she'd be the one manipulating him. He'd be back at that landing site faster than he could get his pants unzipped.

"Maybe I just don't trust you, Rafe, and never have."

That hurt, and he lashed out, "Well, fine. I'll stay away

from you. But you'd better not try to seduce me, either."

"Get a life!" She started to walk away from him, headed toward the mercantile.

He hurried to catch up. "You wanted me last night," he reminded her.

"I was suffering from intellectual exhaustion."

Rafe bit his bottom lip, making a mental list of about fifty ways to exhaust her intellectually over the next week or so. Fifty ways to prime her pump. He smiled with anticipation. Not that he was going to make love with her. Uh uh, not with three lousy condoms. Except for their last night together in this time warp. Then—man, oh, man— she'd better beware.

Helen stomped on ahead of him, oblivious to his devious plans. Knowing she would be annoyed, he took particular delight in studying her rear end, which bounced rather nicely. Despite her rigid demeanor, she had a real hot-cha-cha kind of walk. Yep, next to her breasts, he was definitely partial to her ass.

"Hey, Helen," he called out to her departing back. "I hear there's a Chinaman down by the levee who does real good tattoos. What say we have matching tattoos put on our other cheeks, as a remembrance of this journey?"

Her step faltered.

He didn't like being ignored. No, he did not. "Maybe halos to match our angel wings," he suggested as he caught up with her. "Or clouds. Yeah, clouds that move when the butt muscles flex. They would be nice."

She slanted him a scowl of exasperation. It was obvious she exercised restraint, trying not to react to his baiting.

He didn't like restraint, either. "Betcha miss your clipboard real bad, don'tcha, honey?"

She made a hissing sound of pure malice.

Checkmate! He'd obviously won that round.

But, just in case, he decided to watch his back for the next hour . . . or year.

* * *

Helen stood near the counter of Collis Huntington's general store, waiting while Rafe handed over more and more of their precious gold nuggets and dust. He watched the storekeeper carefully to make sure his thumb didn't tip the scales.

She shifted uncomfortably in the long, green calico dress Rafe had bought for her, insisting she drew too much attention in her slacks. The short-sleeved gown had a scooped neck and hung down to her ankles, but she wore her slacks under the dress for ease in riding.

"I must look ridiculous," she grumbled, glancing at her heavy military boots peeking out from under the gown.

"Yeah," Rafe agreed brightly.

The rat! "I think you deliberately picked out the ugliest dress in the store," she muttered, while the storekeeper weighed out their gold.

"You noticed, huh?" He grinned at her, then chucked her under the chin. "Helen, you'd look good in a sack."

"This is a sack."

"Exactly." His smile would melt butter.

"That'll be three hundred and fifty dollars," Mr. Huntington announced finally.

She and Rafe both blanched, although the total wasn't a real surprise, considering the exorbitant prices listed on a wooden board on the wall: sugar, $2 a pound; flour, $1 a pound; shirts, $30; socks, $2; wool blankets, $30; rum, $20 a quart; apples, $1 each.

The problem was that they still had to purchase two horses and saddles for their trip into the goldfields.

"That leaves us only one hundred and seventy dollars. Will that be enough for the horses?" Helen asked.

Rafe turned to the storekeeper, who nodded. "Should be able to get yerself two good animals and saddles fer 'bout a hundred dollars or so." He directed them over to the horse market at the bottom of K Street.

They made arrangements to leave their supplies at the store while they went horse shopping. Just before they exited, Rafe said, "Don't say I never give you anything."

She stared at the small tablet and pencil he shoved into her hands. "What's this?"

"A present." He chuckled. "Sort of a substitute clipboard."

She tried to cuff him on the shoulder but he ducked out of the way, laughing.

"Oh, I forgot something. Wait right here." He ducked back into the store and sought out Mr. Huntington, who was dumping miniature cucumbers into a large barrel of brine. At first, the merchant's eyebrows rose in question.

Rafe was talking earnestly, gesticulating with his hands. Once, he pointed at his groin. Finally, the storekeeper shook his head vigorously and Rafe shrugged with resignation.

When Rafe opened the door to return to her side, she heard Mr. Huntington hooting with laughter as he shared the joke with a group of miners milling about the store. Only one word stood out in his conversation. *Condoms.*

"You didn't?" she accused Rafe as heat suffused her face and neck. "Oh, don't tell me you tried to buy condoms in a nineteenth-century store."

"Okay, I won't tell you."

"Did you?"

"Hey, it was worth a shot."

"I told you we aren't going to make love."

He flashed her a look that said, loud and clear, "Wanna bet?"

"Ooooh, you are the most insufferable, crude, womanizing—"

"Who says I'm a womanizer?" he asked with affront.

"I can read you like a book."

"Really? Hmmm. I don't suppose you like to read in bed?"

"Aaargh!"

"Actually, I'm a serial monogamy kind of guy," he continued blithely. "By the way, how many lovers have you had?"

Her chin dropped at his unexpected question. He was

always disarming her like that. "Hundreds," she lied.

"Good," he said. "I won't have to teach you any old tricks. Just the new ones."

"Oh, oh, oh . . ."

"You say that a lot, Helen. Is it a speech impediment?"

"Ooooh, you make me so mad. I feel like I'm hanging from a cliff by my fingernails here, and I'm not getting a whole lot of help from you."

"Try Jell-O."

At first, she didn't understand. When she realized he was suggesting that she strengthen her fingernails, she seethed. "Don't talk to me, you slob. For the rest of this trip to hell, I don't want to hear another word from you. I'll go to the goldfields with you; I have no choice. But I refuse to talk to you ever again."

"Well, now, this should be interesting. Actually, I always was better at body language, babe." He smiled sweetly.

She pressed her lips tightly together. Then she noticed the large horse trough on the edge of the street. It was filled with muddy water. Dead bugs and scum floated on top.

"On second thought, I've changed my mind. I will talk to you."

"You will?"

"Yep, 'cause I've got a message for you, *babe*." With one quick karate move, she swung out her right leg, hitting him behind the knees. His legs began to buckle.

"What the hell—"

Helen used his momentary surprise to shove him with a side hip thrust and an elbow against the side of the shoulder. Losing his balance, Rafe landed smack dab in the middle of the trough.

When he came up sputtering, she smiled at him. "How's that for body language, lover boy?"

Chapter Twelve

"Put me down," she shrieked.

"What, you don't like *my* body language?" Rafe inquired as he adjusted her squirming body over his shoulder and strode angrily toward the horse market. "How about this?" He deliberately settled a wide palm over her behind and gave it a few good rubs and a whack before holding it there.

She screeched and howled, flailed out her arms, but to no avail. Once, she almost booted him in the crotch.

In retaliation, the wretch nipped at her right buttock with his teeth. Even through the fabric of the dress and slacks, she felt the sting. "Try that again and I'll put a permanent bite mark around your tattoo."

Gritting her teeth, she pressed her hot face against the wet flannel of his red shirt near the lower back. She could see that his miner's pants were sopping, too, and his leather shoes squished with each step. Even his suspenders dripped. *Good!*

Once they got to the busy horse market, which was situated in the middle of a grove of oak trees at the bottom of K Street, Rafe turned with her still draped ignominiously over his shoulder.

Her continual screams to be put down were drowned out by the cacophony of braying mules, neighing horses, and a half dozen auctioneers selling their animals around the clearing. Helen craned her neck from her upside-down position behind Rafe's back, but all she could see were the blue-and-white canvas tents of the auctioneers and an open-sided livery stable. The smell of fresh hay and manure permeated the air.

Rafe walked beyond the horse market and up a small rise with a screen of bushes, then dropped her. Before she had a chance to spring to her feet and claw his face, he followed her down to the ground, pinning her with his heavy body, soaking her with his wet clothes. His slicked-back hair drizzled onto her face, and her gown blotted up the extra water from his clothes.

She tried to push him off, but he threaded his fingers through hers, forcing both hands to the ground above her shoulders. Digging in her heels for leverage, with bent knees, she bucked against him, but only managed to shift his body so his hips were more firmly wedged against hers.

Closing her eyes briefly, she stopped struggling and took several deep, calming breaths. When she finally lifted her lashes, she expected to see him gloating, or grinning.

Instead, he stared down at her somberly, bracing himself on straightened arms, his hands still linked with hers. His lips were parted and he panted from their exertions. Blue eyes that had been angry only moments before swept her face with an expression Helen could only describe as wistful.

Her heart skipped a beat. Fighting for sanity in an insane situation, Helen complained, "You shouldn't have carried me through the streets like that. It was humiliating."

He nodded. "You're right, but you shouldn't have pushed me in the horse trough. *That* was humiliating."

"You deserved it, you brute, for trying to buy condoms."

"I'm a brute for wanting to protect you?" He tilted his head quizzically.

"That's not the point. Mr. Huntington and all these goofball miners will think you and I . . . that . . . I mean . . ." Her face turned hot. In fact, she was feeling real hot, all over.

"Make love?" he finished for her. "Helen, we're supposed to be married. I'm supposed to be a bandit. You're supposed to be a whore. Of course, they think we make love."

"Oh, you twist everything I say," she snapped and tried to look away, but his compelling eyes held hers.

"You're not making sense."

No kidding! Suddenly, the air resonated with tension, and Helen was acutely aware of the sun, the singing birds, and Rafe. She felt sensuous and sensitized and sensational, lying under him. No wonder she wasn't making sense. "You shouldn't have tried to buy condoms because you're not going to need condoms."

"Why is that?" he asked huskily as he released her hands and cupped her face.

Her arms remained frozen to the ground in a posture of surrender. "Because . . . because . . ." Oh, Lord! His face was lowering to hers, his breath fanning her face. His mesmerizing eyes were half-shuttered and smoky with desire. *Oh, my!* "Because I found out you were using me. Because we're not going to make love. Remember?"

"Honey, we're making love right now." He sighed against her lips.

"We are?" she choked out, and couldn't believe she opened for him, helping him shape her lips to his gently coaxing kiss. She touched the tip of her tongue against his and boldly invaded his mouth, seeking his taste, his heat, his wet hunger.

This wasn't her—not Major Helen Prescott, a model of propriety and stern emotional control. No, this was a dream woman, a wanton, who was plunging her tongue into a man's mouth, making those vulgar sounds, demanding . . . Oh, my goodness! What was happening to her?

With a low, male sound, Rafe met her arousal with his own.

Her breasts swelled, the tips hardening. At the same time, her lower muscles constricted, then melted into a needful, quivering pool.

She moaned.

He hissed through clenched teeth.

With a jerk, he dragged his mouth from hers, burying his face in her neck. "Oh, God, oh, God . . ." he muttered, as if in pain. His chest heaved against hers with each soughing breath he took.

She understood completely. Grabbing his hair in both hands, she pulled his head up so she could see his face. "Rafe, let's go back to the hotel." Her voice was so hoarse with passion, the words came out as a sultry whisper. "We can stay here another night. Please."

He studied her for a long moment, his blue eyes throwing off sparks. "Why?"

She hadn't expected that question. The answer was obvious, wasn't it? "Because I want you," she admitted, glancing to the side, unable to face him after her too-honest response.

He tipped her chin up, urging her to meet his eyes. "Do you love me?"

"Huh? No. Of course, not. Don't be ridiculous." *Maybe. Oh, my God! Maybe I do.* "I mean, why would you ask such a thing?" She thought briefly, then added, "Do you love me?"

"No," he said flatly, but he didn't seem too sure, either.

Blood roared in her ears and her heart expanded in her chest until she could barely breathe. "Don't make this complicated. I want to make love with you, Rafe. That's all."

"That's not enough."

She made a small mewling sound of distress, and he kissed the side of her mouth . . . softly, soothing. "Shhh, it's all right, honey. Don't worry."

"We're not going to make love, are we?"

He shook his head sadly. "Not now, babe."

"Why?" she cried out, appalled at her pleading tone, but unable to accept his words.

"It's too dangerous to stay in Sacramento. But, even so, there are other reasons why—"

"Oh, don't bring up those stupid condoms again. I don't care about that."

"But I do," he said with grim finality.

"Well, what difference does it make if we use those three damn condoms now, or the night we go back?"

"Oh, sweetheart, I know myself. If I have you one time, or three, I won't be able to stop. You're my Achilles' heel. But I care too much to make babies irresponsibly," he said, laying a flat palm over her stomach for emphasis.

Helen had a sweet image then of her growing big with Rafe's child. Would it be a rascal of a boy with black hair and brown eyes? Or a darling redheaded pixie with Rafe's mischievous blue eyes? The mental picture was so beautiful and poignant that tears welled in her eyes.

"Why are you weeping, Helen? Don't cry. Please."

"I'm not crying," she lied, wiping at her eyes. "Let me ask you this. You're a gambler—why not take a chance in our making love? Let the chips fall where they may?"

"Uh-uh," he said, shaking his head vehemently. "That's Russian roulette, and I don't take chances with contraception. No babies! No way!"

Helen felt a sense of shattering inside as all her unconscious hopes were crushed. When had she begun to form illusions about a life with Rafe after returning to the future? Had she carried unconscious feelings for him all these years?

No babies.

They had no future together, that was certain. While she yearned for the day she would have children, a warm home, a large family, Rafe wanted none of those things. Her maternal instincts were so strong she'd almost married a man without loving him—Elliott. Perhaps she still would.

No babies.

She shouldn't care.

She did.

". . . so you don't need to be distressed." Rafe had been talking in a soft murmur, stroking away her tears while she was lost in her painful thoughts.

"What did you say?"

"I said that you don't need to be upset. I can bring you

just as much satisfaction with my hands, and mouth, if you want.''

At first, his meaning didn't register. When it did, she gasped and shoved his surprised body off her and to the side. ''You big baboon! You blathering idiot! You . . . you . . .'' She stood and towered over him. ''Do you really think that's what I want from you?'' Without waiting for an answer, she stomped through the bushes and down the rise to the horse market.

For a moment, Rafe just stared after her.

That had been a crude, cruel suggestion he'd just made to Helen. But deliberate. He'd known she would be affronted. A tongue job or a finger flutter wouldn't be Helen's idea of making love. Hell, it wasn't what he wanted from her either.

But he was coiled tighter than a Slinky, and tempted beyond his normal restraint. He doubted he would have been able to hold out against Helen's pleas to make love to her. He'd felt like an out-of-control train racing down the tracks, all cylinders firing, bound to crash. And the only way he could think to stop the train was to turn Helen off.

But he'd wanted her so bad. Still did.

''And another thing . . .''

''Huh?'' Rafe looked up to see that Helen had returned. She rested her hands on her hips, belligerently. Her red hair billowed out from under the cowboy hat Pablo had given her. Her normally creamy complexion was mottled with rage, and freckles. The ugly, green, flower-sprigged dress he'd bought her earlier hung loosely over her frame, and her military trousers and boots peeked out, incongruously, from the antique gown.

She should have looked silly.

God, she was beautiful.

He rose to his feet to face her.

She jammed a forefinger in his chest.

He backed up slightly, laughing.

''And another thing,'' she started again, giving his chest another jab. ''You'd better stay away from me from now

177

on. No more seducing me. No flashing that sexy smile. No—''

''Sexy smile?''

She gave him one of those you-are-a-toad looks and continued with her litany of orders. ''No more suggestive remarks. No sweet talk. No more singing 'Wind Beneath My Wings.' No touching, at all. Definitely no touching.''

''Because?'' he prodded.

''Because I'm warning you, Rafe, now that I've decided I want you—though God knows why, I must have lost my mind—I'm probably going to have you.''

He laughed, despite himself. *She wants me.*

''Unlike you, though, I have scruples. So, I'm giving you fair notice. I want babies, and I wouldn't mind having yours, even—''

''Oh, my God!'' *She wants my baby.*

''—even if you are a louse.'' She peered at him closer. ''Why are you turning green? Oh, I see. You think I want to marry you. Don't worry. I wouldn't deliberately get pregnant. I'm not trying to trap you.''

''I never said you were trying to trap—''

''You made me give up my plans to marry Elliott just to have a baby.''

''What? I did?''

''I'm drawing a line in the sand here, mister.''

''Are you saying this is war?'' His lips twitched with suppressed amusement.

''In a manner of speaking. You pushed and pushed and pushed till you got me turned on. Well, I'm not a faucet to be turned on and off at will.''

''Prissy, don't challenge me. Ask me to back off, but don't issue ultimatums. I'll have to fight back, and I fight dirty.''

''I've had too many years in the military to be afraid of a battle. Maybe I know how to fight dirty, too. Furthermore, you can stick those condoms on your ears for all I care. Consider yourself forewarned. Kiss me again, and I'll corkscrew or gargle you or whatever it takes to make you forget you don't like babies.''

He grinned. He couldn't help himself.

She gave his chest one final poke with her forefinger and walked away again.

And for the first time in ages, Rafe wished he didn't hate babies.

Rafe's warm, fuzzy feelings for Helen didn't last long.

At first, he was in a good mood, having been fortunate enough to buy F. Lee Horse from its original owner, Señor Salerno, at the outdoor auction, along with a beautiful gray mare for Helen, all within their budget, and with fifty dollars to spare.

And, despite all his misgivings, he couldn't deny being flattered that Helen wanted to make love with him. It wouldn't happen, of course, until their last night in the past, but it was nice to know he still had the old sexual appeal. Even so, every once in a while, she gave him one of those little Mona Lisa smiles—the kind that said I-know-something-you-don't—and he wondered if he was taking her threat too lightly.

But he had other worries now. Señor Salerno had pulled him aside to give him a bit of friendly advice. The Angel Bandit had escaped the jail in San Francisco, and because of their similarity in appearance, he advised Rafe to hotfoot it out of town, or else join Ignacio in that great gold mine in the sky.

He and Helen decided to head due north to Marysville, about eighty miles from Sacramento. They could have sidetracked slightly to the west and hit the colorful Grizzly Flats, or Hangtown, or Murderer's Bar, but those were busy towns with a reputation for hating Mexicans. At the least rumor that he was the Angel Bandit, he'd be wearing a rope necktie.

Once they put some distance between themselves and Southern California, the Angel Bandit's territory, they wouldn't have to be so careful. In the meantime, they rode their horses hard, avoiding the main road, which was heavily trafficked by dozens of mule teams and wagons carrying supplies, as well as hundreds of prospective miners and budding entrepreneurs, on foot and horse and mule.

He and Helen stopped only when absolutely necessary to water the animals, or relieve themselves.

That was when Helen started whistling.

And whistling.

And whistling some more.

Hey, he didn't mind a little whistling now and then. It was a visible sign that Helen felt chipper, more cooperative about their gold-seeking adventure. But after a while, with the blistering heat—it must have been 115 degrees—the incessant dust of the well-traveled road, his sore butt, and F. Lee's gas—geez, he hadn't known a horse could fart—he was not in a good mood.

To top it off, F. Lee stepped on his sunglasses. A hundred dollars down the drain!

That was the first three hours. Then Helen resumed her blasted *ooohm-ooohm-ooohm* meditating.

How could a guy go from thinking he was "in love" to thinking he was "in loathing" in such a short time?

Ooohm. Ooohm. Ooohm. Ooohm.

"Who ever heard of meditating on a horse?" he grumbled.

She laughed, a bubbly kind of laugh, and that irritated him, too. He couldn't stand perky women.

"I never heard of it, either, but, actually, the rocking of the horse is conducive to rhythmic chanting. Don't you think?" Flashing him another one of those Mona Lisa smirks, she inquired sweetly, "Cranky, are we?" Without waiting for an answer, she continued with her hippie humming. *Ooohm. Ooohm. Ooohm. Ooohm.*"

He heard a grinding sort of noise—probably the sound of his own gnashing teeth.

Nah, on closer inspection, he realized F. Lee was farting again.

Maybe he wasn't cut out to be a prospector after all.

*   *   *

The day wore on, and Rafe decided that riding a horse was a world-class bore. *Give me first-class accommodations on a jet with a magazine and a Scotch on the rocks. Or a nice smooth-riding BMW with Aerosmith on the CD and the air conditioner blasting.* Not that he traveled first class, or had a BMW. But someday he would. That was his dream.

Occasionally, between whistles and *ooohms,* Helen pulled out the notebook he'd given her, interrupting his daydreams. She managed somehow to guide her horse with her thighs while she braced the notebook on the saddle horn to write. Which, of course, started him on daydreams of a different sort.

Betcha she has really muscular thighs. Betcha they clutch a guy when she's ridin' him. Betcha she could control the pace of lovemaking with her thighs alone. Betcha I better get my mind on other things or I'm gonna embarrass myself.

"What'd I do now?" he asked the third time she pulled out the notebook, figuring she must be giving him more check marks.

"I'm making a list."

"To report my transgressions?" he teased.

She swept him with a condescending glance. "*That* list is in my head. This list is of things to do before we return to the landing site. Plus, I have a breakdown of our income and expenses thus far, with a projection of how much we need to earn. In crude spreadsheet form, of course."

"Of course." *Hell, I'm traveling with a human calculator.* He snorted with disgust.

"What? You don't like lists? Or planning?"

"There's such a thing as too much order."

"Do you think so?" she asked, seeming genuinely puzzled. "I really wish I had my Franklin Planner with me. I could organize this venture much better with a daily itinerary."

Screw your itinerary. "I prefer spontaneity."

"Spontaneity breeds chaos."

"Huh?"

"By the way, exactly how much gold did you say you need to take care of your money problems?"

"I didn't say."

"How can I plan how many days we need to stay unless you tell me? I can make a chart for our daily input of gold and output of expenses, cross-referenced with the price of gold today, compared to the market value in 1996.

"Hell!"

"You swear too much." She tapped her pencil impatiently on her pad. "Well?" she prodded.

"A hundred thousand or so," he mumbled.

"Wh-what? You're joking, right?"

"I wish I were, babe. I wish I were." He rode ahead then, not wanting to discuss the matter further. The amount gave him a shock, too, every time Lorenzo ran it up on his adding machine.

Later, he saw a group of Indians up ahead near a riverbank and decided to stop for a break. It was well past noon and he was hungry. Besides, that should stop her whistling and *ooohm*ing and list making for awhile.

"Do you think they're friendly?"

"No, I think they'll probably scalp us, after they stop picking those flowers," he snapped.

The dozen or so Indians, wearing grass skirt garments down to their thighs, really were picking flowers, or rather they passed large conical baskets back and forth under a bunch of wildflowers and shook the seeds into similar baskets on their backs.

While Helen went into the bushes to relieve herself, he watered the horses, then walked over to the wary "redskins." They looked as if they would run at the first sign of a tomahawk.

None of them seemed to understand English, but finally one old Indian sitting under a tree nodded and said, *"Sí,"* when Rafe tossed out, *"Habla Español?"*

Rafe threw out a bunch of questions in Spanish, and the

toothless man said he hadn't seen anyone answering Pablo's description, and told Rafe it would take another day for them to get to Marysville.

Curious about the shy Indians—mostly women and children—who kept darting inquisitive peeks his way, Rafe asked, "What are they doing?"

"My people gather the flower seeds. The women crush the seeds, then mix them with ground acorns and grasshoppers for bread making," the old man said in stumbling Spanish. " 'Tis our way, taught by our ancestors." He handed Rafe a slice to sample.

Grasshoppers? Yech!

Helen ambled out of the bushes then, hips swinging with an exaggerated sway—something she'd been doing since issuing her challenge. Rafe noticed immediately that she wore only a T-shirt over her sweat-dampened skin, having ditched her camouflage shirt and gown.

"What the hell?" He stood menacingly. "Put the gown back on, Helen, or I will."

"It's too hot to wear all those clothes," she said defensively, dancing off to the side to avoid his grabbing her. "Besides, no one can see me the way we're traveling off the beaten track."

The old Indian watched them expressionlessly. He was probably thinking, *Crazy palefaces!*

Damn it, Helen knew he obsessed over her breasts, and the T-shirt called attention to them. He could see that she took great pleasure in his discomfort, especially when she smiled seductively and then deliberately tucked the shirt into her slacks, real tight.

"I guess I'd better rub the horses down before we eat," she said. But first she rolled her head on her neck, presumably to get the kinks out, then put her hands on the small of her back and arched outward. A Vargas model couldn't have done it better.

At the sight of her perfect breasts outlined by the damp fabric, every drop of blood in his body rushed to the lightning rod between his legs. And Helen knew perfectly well what she did to him. This was all part of the new game she'd decided to play.

Well, he'd always considered himself a worthy adversary in any fight. And he wasn't about to wimp out now.

"Helen," he said, stifling a grin.

"What?" She batted her eyelashes innocently.

Hah! She was as innocent as Eve in the Garden of Eden.

"How would you like a slice of Indian bread, honey?"

"Well, gee, I don't know."

"Lots of protein."

"Okay." She reached for the bread and began to eat, at first slowly, then with relish. "Yum. This is really good."

My point, sweetheart.

Chapter Thirteen

Later that day, they met up with a man sitting next to a stream, talking to his horse. He appeared to be lost.

Rafe introduced himself as Rafael Santiago and Helen as his wife, explaining that they were heading for the northern mines to prospect for gold.

The young man—no more than twenty or so—identified himself as an author from New York, Henry Phillips. He'd been hired after graduation from Harvard College by publisher George Putnam, a friend of his father's, to write a book on the Gold Rush. Henry wore rust-colored corduroy-type pants and a purple flannel shirt in great contrast to his curly auburn hair and florid complexion.

He rode a horse, but had a mule trailing behind him, loaded not with the usual mining gear, but, instead, with dozens of journals and sketchbooks, a barometer, a compass, a spyglass, one place setting of silverware, and a pewter table service. He sheepishly admitted that his mother had insisted on the latter refinements. In addition, he carried a special case for playing cards, like most miners did, known as "The California Prayer Book."

"Let him travel with us for a while," Helen coaxed Rafe. "He seems harmless."

"More like inept," Rafe grumbled, rubbing his butt.

"Do you have another blister?" she asked with concern.

"No, Helen, I don't have another blister. I have a sore ass. And, yes, he can travel with us. Maybe it will give you something to do besides whistle and *ooohm*."

"Aren't you just the bluebird of happiness today?" she

commented, but she was pleased with his mood. It meant her ploy was working.

Back at Sacramento, when he'd kissed her witless, then declined to make love until *he* was ready, she'd come up with a plan. What if she was the aggressor? What if she constantly made suggestive remarks? What if she deliberately provoked him with her body, which seemed to hold a fascination for him? What if she acted as if she'd like nothing better than to hop in the sack and make mad love all day long?

It was a gamble, but one that seemed to be paying off. Any moment now, she expected Rafe to throw in the towel and declare that they were returning to the landing site and his one night of making love. Really, men like Rafe were ruled by their passions, not disciplined logic. Soon he would give in.

To be perfectly honest, she was anticipating that one night, too. Rafe had a way of making her breathless with just a look or a smile. And, when he touched her, even in passing, her heart raced and blood rushed to the spot. Yes, she was sure she would enjoy their one-night fling . . . immensely.

In the meantime, she was going to do everything in her power to make him miserable. And Henry could act as the buffer between the two of them, especially this first night when otherwise they would have been camping out in their tent, alone.

Rafe lay in his tent with his arms folded behind his neck, waiting for Helen to call it a day. She was outside teaching Henry how to meditate. For heaven's sake, it sounded like they were *ooohm*ing themselves into a trance. Every bird from here to Monterey had flown off shrieking long ago.

Not that Henry cared any more than he did about her transcendental nonsense. Nah, the cow-eyed jerk, who had a full-blown crush on Rafe's "wife," saw an opportunity when it hit him head on. He probably would have stood on his hands and done the polka if Helen had asked him.

First, Henry had taken to whistling in tandem with Helen as they'd ridden along. Even F. Lee snorted with disgust. Later, the horse, which must be very intelligent, rolled his eyes up at Rafe, as if pleading, "Can't you shut the two kooks up?"

At dinner that night, Henry showed Helen how to make Indian johnnycakes on a shovel—*a shovel!*—over the open fire. Helen oohed and ahed as he made a hole in the middle of a pile of meal, dumped in warm water and a pinch of salt, then spooned the soft dough onto the flat shovel, putting it in the coals. You would have thought the kid had invented sliced bread.

"I can make tortillas," Rafe said.

Helen and Henry gawked at him as if he'd said he could piss and blow smoke at the same time. He said something about needing to check on F. Lee and stomped off to feel sorry for himself.

Thinking back, Rafe had to concede that Henry had passed along a lot of interesting information as they rode, including the fact that he'd met up with Pablo, who'd been riding hard, alone, to Marysville. He'd even noticed "the unusual silk material"—their parachute—that Helen had described for him. In fact, he'd related that Pablo was using it for a tent, of all things. Apparently, he kept getting caught in the odd strings.

Pablo had tried to rob him, Henry told them, but the bandit had dropped his gun at the critical moment and shot himself in the foot. About par for Pablo, Rafe figured. With any luck, they'd catch up with the goofball bandit tomorrow when they reached Marysville.

Henry had also shared his notebooks and sketches with them, giving a nineteenth-century perspective on the history lessons Rafe and Helen already knew. Millard Fillmore had become president in July, replacing Zachary Taylor, who'd died in office. California was not yet a state, but would be soon. Federal census takers sent into the hills were estimating that more than 100,000 males, most of them in their twenties, had flooded into California over the past two years, lured by dreams of gold.

And the exciting news to those lonely men, according to Henry, was the French government's recent decision to ship off hundreds of its incarcerated prostitutes to the California wilderness. A red-faced Henry apologized to Helen as he relayed that racy information.

Finally, Henry showed off his sketches, which were quite good. The crowded San Francisco Bay with its abandoned ships. A fiesta on a native Californian's rancho. The teeming streets of Sacramento City.

"Look," Helen exclaimed then, drawing Rafe's attention to one of Henry's rough sketches. "It's those foothill Indians we saw earlier today gathering flower seeds."

"Yes, they were unique," Henry agreed, pleased at their interest in his work. "I even wrote down the receipt for that unusual bread they make with ground flower seeds, acorns, and grasshoppers." He searched through his notes to find the recipe.

And Helen turned outraged eyes on Rafe. "Grasshoppers? You gave me bread with grasshoppers in it?"

He shrugged. "Protein, Helen. You're always yammering about protein and proper diet and yoga. All that granola crap."

"Did *you* eat any?" she had asked.

"Are you kidding? I get my protein in a Big Mac, thank you very much."

He smiled now. He should feel guilty, but he didn't. Hell, she probably ate bugs all the time on her Army survival missions.

Yawning widely, he stretched and felt his eyes drooping with sleep. This horse riding and adventure stuff was tiring. He'd give it up in a flash if he wasn't so damn poor. Just last week, he'd been forced to tell his sister Jacinta that she would have to go to grad school at a state university, instead of Loyola, because he just couldn't afford the private tuition. And his mother's roof leaked. And Miguel, his sister Luisa's kid, needed braces. And Lorenzo wanted a raise.

And there was this really, really nice BMW he'd been eying for years.

"Move over," Helen said waspishly.

He hadn't realized she'd entered the tent and removed her boots and gown, leaving only her slacks and T-shirt. That damn T-shirt was going to be the death of him yet.

"And stop muttering about BMWs."

His mouth curved upward in the dark as he made room for her under the blanket. As hot as California was during the day, it got cool at night here in the mountains.

She slid in, as far from him as possible, facing away.

He chuckled.

"And don't you dare touch me, you louse," she warned.

How had she known he was about to reach for her? He must be losing his smoothness.

"I'm not going to forget about the grasshoppers."

"Did you write it on your list?"

She proceeded to tell him then exactly how many of his transgressions had made it to her list. On and on she went shrewishly until his sleepy brain could take no more. She'd been teasing him constantly since she'd turned the sexual tables on him in Sacramento. She probably didn't really want to make love with him. It was a bluff. A defensive ploy.

If so, it was working, damn it.

Pulling her back against him with a jerk, Rafe ignored her squeal of protest and whispered in her ear, "How do you feel about oral sex, Helen?"

"Wh-what?" she gasped and slapped at one of his hands, which was about to fondle her breast. Then she quickly grabbed for his other hand, which already rubbed her flat tummy.

"Hey, it's the natural solution. No babies that way." He grinned to himself at her suddenly stiff body. Not that he seriously considered oral sex a solution. Sex play of that nature was mere foreplay to whet his appetite for the real thing.

"I'd rather wait until we're really alone and can go all the way," she lied.

She was as transparent as Saran Wrap. Why hadn't he seen through her charade earlier? "Are you sure? About the oral sex, I mean?" he inquired sweetly. "I've noticed that you seem tense, even with all that guru-schmuru inner-sanctum yodeling, and I'll bet—*I'll just bet*—I could find your real center and—"

"Oh, go to sleep," she snapped. And she held fast to both his wrists at waist level to keep them from moving to forbidden territory.

Rafe adjusted his hips against her rear, though. If nothing else, he planned to have some super dreams tonight.

It was already dark by the time they reached Marysville the next day. Henry told them that the little town at the junction of the Feather and Yuba rivers was named for Mary Murphy, a survivor of the ill-fated Donner expedition four years before. Of course, the town flourished now with the Gold Rush.

Every muscle in Rafe's body ached. He smelled his own sweat. The mother of all headaches was doing a jig behind his eyes. And he had a hard-on with a mind of its own.

Helen, on the other hand, looked cool, calm, and invigorated by their grueling eighty-mile trek from Sacramento City. She and Henry had been whistling and *ooohm*ing for four straight hours. And she and the bumbling kid had something else in common. They both liked to brush their teeth and gargle three times a day. Henry had practically salivated over the Franklin Planner Helen described for him.

Rafe felt like puking.

Thank God, Henry went off to find a cousin who owned a house in Marysville, promising to connect with them the following day.

Rafe and Helen dismounted near a livery stable. He started to say something, then forgot what he was about to say. Helen was stretching languidly, making a purring sound of pleasure.

Does she purr after she climaxes?

She'd refused to put her gown back on this morning when the sun came up like a fireball. He hadn't been able to argue with her logic about the blistering heat, but Henry had gaped at her T-shirt the entire day like a teenager at his first porno flick. Rafe noted dryly to himself that it surely took coordination on Henry's part to gape and whistle and *ooohm* all at the same time.

"Put on your gown," he ordered now in a testy voice, "before every male with a lick of testosterone gets a whiff of eau-de-female."

She bent over to tie her shoelace, thus giving him a fine view of her well-rounded behind. "Does that include you?" she challenged over her shoulder.

"In spades."

He leaned against the wall of the stable and crossed his ankles lazily. His eyes roved over her body, from raised eyebrows to dust-covered boots. "Don't push me too far, Helen," he advised silkily. "You might get a helluva lot more than you can handle."

After parking the two horses at the livery stable and Helen at a hotel, thus using up a sizable portion of their remaining gold, Rafe did the thing men who are royally pissed have been doing for ages. He headed for the nearest saloon.

By now, Helen, settled into their minuscule hotel room, had probably moved from whistling and *ooohm*ing to gargling and forms. After two days of watching her breasts move with every beat of her horse, he didn't think he could stand forms, too. Her breasts didn't exactly jiggle, he corrected himself. They swayed. And that was even worse. After a while, he'd found himself swaying on his own horse to the same rhythm.

Sometime soon, he intended to spend about two hours worshiping those perfect Vargas breasts of hers.

He would look at them. For a long time. Weigh them with his hands, molding them and reshaping them to fit his palms. He would resist kissing them or touching them with his lips for a long, long time. Only when he had brought the nipples to hard, aching points by rolling them and flicking them with his fingertips, only when she begged him to suckle her, only when she purred ... Well, that's when he'd take her in his mouth. Hard, at first, then soft. Wet. Oh, yeah, wet. Then—

"What's yer poison, mister?"

Rafe blinked at the surly bartender standing before him, then shook his head hard to rid it of his fantasies. *The woman is driving me absolutely bonkers.* "A whiskey. No, make it a double."

The bartender bypassed the fine labeled bottle on the shelf behind him and reached for the keg on the floor. Probably rotgut.

"No way, buddy. I'll have that," he insisted, pointing.

"Mebbe you should take yer bizness somewheres else, *greaser.*"

The insult ricocheted through him like a lightning bolt. He did not need this grief tonight. "Give me the damn whiskey."

The bartender straightened and cast his eyes over to the corner where a wiry, mustached man in a black suit and blue brocaded vest stood eying him with disdain—probably the owner. Finally, the fancy dude nodded.

Turning back, the bartender pinched out two huge thumbfuls of Rafe's gold dust and poured the good booze reluctantly into a tin cup, sliding it forward. "Take it over there," he ordered, pointing toward a corner on the far side. "We don't 'low no Mexs at the bar."

Rafe stiffened and reached for the guns at his sides.

"I wouldn't do that, *señor,*" the bartender said. Rafe peered over his shoulder to see two nineteenth-century bouncers cruising his way.

Weighing his chances, Rafe moved to the back of the room. But he didn't like it one bit.

He joined a group of about two dozen men, mostly Mexicans but some Chileans, Hawaiians, and native Californians, too. They leaned against the wall, sat at rough tables playing monte, or spoke with a few of the Spanish prostitutes who'd dared to sashay over from the other part of the saloon. Apparently "foreigners" were allowed on the other side only if they were whores.

A band played raucously on a raised stage at the far end of the room—a fiddler screeching in competition with two guitar players and a trumpeter. Some of the miners were harmonizing in a drunken rendition of "Hangtown Girls."

> *Hangtown gals are plump and rosy,*
> *Hair in ringlets, mighty cozy,*
> *Painted cheeks and jossy bonnets—*
> *Touch 'em and they'll sting like hornets.*

The miners immediately launched into another version, this one even more boisterous:

> *Hangtown gals are curious creatures,*
> *Think they'll marry pious preachers,*
> *Heads thrown back to show their features—*
> *Hah hah hah! Hangtown gals.*

Rafe raised an eyebrow at the Mexican vaquero standing next to him. He told him, in Spanish, that Hangtown girls were scarce and snooty. Then, with a smirk, he added something vulgar in English.

Looking once again at the band, which was trying to make a louder noise than the singers, Rafe noticed a sign announcing that Felicia Mantero would be performing an operatic aria that night.

He asked the same man if he'd seen anyone matching Pablo's description. The guy mumbled "No," but his friend said that Pablo and some fellow named Sancho had left town in a hurry that morning. "They said something about a hanging and stolen horses."

193

Rafe groaned with dismay. "Any idea where they were going?"

"North, I think. Maybe Rich Bar. I dunno, really."

Great! More horseback riding. Well, I'm gonna stop and do some prospecting this time. Until we catch up with Pablo—

Taking a huge swallow of the burning liquid, Rafe stared up at the stage to see the owner motion for the band to stop playing and the men to quiet for a moment. "Uh . . . I have an announcement to make," the nervous man in the blue brocade vest tried to shout over the crowd, which appeared angry about something. "It is my misfortune to . . . uh . . . have to tell you . . . that, well, Felicia will be unable to sing tonight. It 'pears she's indisposed."

Bellows of outrage greeted his words before they were barely out of his mouth.

"We coulda gone to the Palace, you worm."

"I doan think he ever had Felicia. It were a come-on."

"Yeah, let's string the bastard up by his toes."

"I ain't dancin' with no more men gussied up like ladies. The las' time I got Buford fer a partner,'n he belched the whole time."

"How 'bout one of them Mex gals? Singin' and screwin' comes natural to them."

"We want Felicia. We want Felicia. We want Felicia . . ." The drunken sots began to chant and stamp their heavy boots on the dirt floor.

The wily owner scrambled off the stage and out through the rear. The band started up again, more raucous than before.

Rafe let his shoulders rest against the wooden support of the canvas wall. He closed his eyes against the stench of several hundred unwashed bodies, the ear-splitting din of music and gambling and now shouting, and the heart-squeezing pain of the racial bias he felt closing in around him.

"You got some money, *señor*? Calina can show you a good time if you got gold."

He opened his eyes slowly to see a young Spanish tart waiting expectantly for his answer, hands braced on her slim hips. She stood so close he could smell her cloying rose perfume. Her eyelashes were loaded with black goop, her lips painted crimson, and her flimsy camisole blouse hung so far off one shoulder that half her breast was exposed.

She was about fourteen.

"*Chica,* go home to your *madre,*" he scolded her in mixed Spanish. "You should be playing with dolls, not men."

"*Bebé,*" she shot back at him, in broken English, "I ain' got no *madre* no more, and *mi padre* sold me to a gringo sailor for fifty pesos when I was twelve. Hell, eet ain' such a bad life. I eat good. I sleep on a soft bed. All I have to do ees close my eyes and hold my nose for ten minutes."

"Yeah? How many times a night do you have to close your eyes and hold your nose?"

She shrugged. "Fifteen or twenty."

"Shit!" He wasn't going to make any progress trying to turn this girl around.

"So, do you have the money to play with Calina tonight?" She pressed up closer and allowed the blouse to slip down lower so he could see the whole of one immature breast pressed against his shirt front. One of her hands snaked up around his neck and tried to pull him down for a kiss.

Before he could push her away with revulsion, he heard a sharp hiss. He gazed over Calina's head.

Helen.

Oh, great! Now the you-know-what is going to hit the fan. What was she doing here? He'd told her to stay in the room.

Her newly washed red hair was tied at the nape with a strip of lace, but soft curls spilled out around her cheeks and over her shoulders. Her face, with its sprinkling of freckles, glowed fresh and lightly tanned. She wore her military boots and the ugly green gown, which hung loosely on her, but she was lovelier to him than any woman. And more precious.

He felt like a vise was closing around his heart, and he could barely breathe. Looking down, he realized it was actually Calina who had wrapped herself around his body tighter than a Cuban cigar. *Damn!* While he tried to extricate himself from her stranglehold, Rafe attempted to get Helen's attention. Several men had approached and were saying something to her, but she gave them the cold shoulder.

Glancing back at Rafe one more time, Helen's brown eyes grew huge with hurt and began to well with tears. But only for a moment. Anger instantly took over. She lifted her chin, spun on her heel, and prepared to rush out.

But the rambunctious miners blocked her way. "Hey, boys, lookee here. We got us a new singer. We doan need no Felicia. No sirree. Jist take a gander at this l'il redheaded filly." They passed her toward the stage, ignoring her shrill objections.

Rafe moved to go after her, but somehow the Mexican *señorita* had twined one leg around his calf and he tripped, almost taking both of them to the filthy ground. By the time he finally got himself loose from her clinging hands and legs, Helen was being shoved up onto the stage with demands that she sing.

"I can't sing," she rebelled. "Will you men just listen to me? I'm not a singer."

"What *can* ya do, honey?"

Much laughter followed that question.

"She 'pears a mite like that Elena gal, don't she?" one man speculated.

"Ya mean the one that corkscrews?" another responded.

And that held a lot more appeal to this crowd than singing.

"Singin' or corkscrewin'? What's it gonna be, darlin'? Let's get on with it," snarled a mountain man, about six-foot-five with half his face covered with slash marks. He'd probably tangled with a grizzly bear at one time.

Rafe noticed that one of Helen's short sleeves was torn, and her eyes darted wildly through the crowd, imploringly, searching for him. He tried to force his way forward toward the tightening crowd, to no avail, and the two bouncers he'd met up with earlier stood in front of him. One of them barked, "Weren't ya told before? No greasers on this side of the room. Out!"

Rafe backed up.

Since she obviously wasn't going to sing, the men now demanded that Helen dance—a prelude to her corkscrewing the entire damn lot of them.

Rafe rapidly assessed the situation and decided he had no choice but to leave through the front door.

Helen stared at his departing back and couldn't believe her eyes. He was actually abandoning her to this mob. Well, what had she expected? Just a few moments ago, she'd come into this hellhole to give him some important news, only to see him making out with some Mexican bimbo.

She bit her bottom lip to stop its trembling and refused to allow the tears in her eyes to overflow. With more courage than she felt, she tried to outshout the obnoxious men. "Would you all just shut up for one minute and listen to me?"

The music slowly petered to a stop, and the shouting died down to a low rumble. The only sounds were the clinking of coins at the gambling tables.

"My name is Helen Prescott. I don't sing and I don't corkscrew. You ought to be ashamed—"

She heard a rustling movement behind her and saw Rafe crawling under the tent flap. *Thank goodness!*

"What's that greaser doin' up there? Someone oughta put 'im in his place."

"Yeah, let's show 'im what we do to them what tries to mix with their betters."

"He's my husband, you blockheads," Helen yelled.

"Her husband?" exclaimed the huge mountain of a man with a clawed face. He spit a wad of tobacco on the floor, splattering the boots of all the miners around him. No one seemed to mind. "What kind a white woman marries a dirty Mex?"

Rafe had stepped up beside her and linked his hand with hers. He gave her a quick squeeze of encouragement.

"Can we both scoot out of the tent the way you came in?" she whispered.

He shook his head, watching the crowd warily. "No time. They'd be on us in a flash."

"Can you shoot our way out of here?"

Again, he shook his head. "Too many of them. No, we have to divert them."

"How?"

She saw several men in the front pull out their revolvers, and the man who appeared to be the owner stood nearby wringing his hands. "Damn, they're gonna tear my tent apart any minute now," he whined.

Helen sliced the weasel a look of contempt. No concern for their safety. Just his private property.

"Can you dance?" Rafe asked suddenly.

"Wh-what? Now? You must be drunk."

"Not nearly enough, sweetheart," he said, and asked the band to play a Mexican tune she didn't recognize. The band was rotten, but the song carried a sultry Spanish beat.

He began to circle her body in a slow, seductive rhythm. Hips swaying, fingers snapping, he eyed her like a virile predator, ready to pounce.

She backed up slightly.

Their audience hooted with laughter, considering it a well-planned act.

Rafe held her eyes and motioned with the crooked fingers of both hands, beckoning her closer.

She stood frozen. *She couldn't. She just couldn't.*

Rafe held open his arms for her.

"I can't do this," she protested weakly, even as she stepped reluctantly into his embrace. "Really. I'm not a good dancer."

"Honey, these men could care diddly-squat about the

198

quality of your dancing. Besides, the kind of dancing we're going to do will bring the house down.''

He pulled her brusquely into his arms and looped her arms around his neck. He placed both of his hands firmly on either side of her waist.

She eyed him suspiciously. ''And what kind of dancing would that be?''

''The lambada.''

He drew her close. Very close. Breasts pressed against his chest. Her stomach rested against his groin. Catching the slow rhythm, Rafe began to sway, then undulate his hips with hers.

The crowd stilled.

''Arriba!'' one of the Mexican musicians called out and made a loud trilling noise with his tongue. She had no time to think about that, though. It was Rafe she was worried about.

''What kind of dance did you say?'' she choked out.

''The lambada. The forbidden dance.''

''Wh-what's that? I never heard of it.''

''It's just like . . .'' Rafe smiled. ''. . . dirty dancing.''

Chapter Fourteen

"Just pretend we're making love."

"I beg your pardon," she said in a suffocated whisper.

"The lambada . . . It's like making love without penetration. Relax and let your body speak for you."

Making love without penetration? Oh, my!

They were swaying from side to side, slowly. Hmmm. She'd never had much time for dancing, but this was really kind of nice. *Sway and turn. Sway and turn.*

"I think I've got the hang of it," she said.

"Good. Now for some real lambada."

"What? Ooomph. Stop that."

He bent her over backward so that her upper body was flung over his arm and her breasts were arched up in a provocative pose. She had no choice but to clutch his upper arms or risk falling to the floor.

The crowd went wild with cheers of encouragement.

"Arriba!" the Mexican guitarist yelled out, as he had earlier, following it with the yipping noise.

"What . . . are . . . you . . . doing?" she asked Rafe in a strangled voice.

"Dipping. Geez, Louise! Haven't you ever dipped before, Helen?" The jerk was laughing at her.

"Undip me. Right now," she demanded.

He grinned and yanked her upright without missing a beat of the dance rhythm. Once they straightened and were back in the traditional slow-dance posture again, she protested, "Rafe, let's just get out of here. It's obvious that I'm no good at dancing."

"I don't hear anyone complaining."

In fact, the prospectors were stamping their feet and clapping, enjoying the spectacle immensely. And the Mexican musician kept repeating that stupid *"Arriba!"* yell. Helen felt like she'd fallen into a bad movie script.

"Besides, we can't leave yet," Rafe told her hurriedly, in between two more deep dips. "I met Henry and his cousin outside. They agreed to get our stuff from the hotel and bring the horses. They'll signal with two whistles out back when they're ready."

"Oh, Lord!"

Still in the normal slow-dance position, Rafe boldly placed both palms on Helen's buttocks and was guiding her backward and forward against him, teaching her the "dirtier" movements of the dance.

Her mouth dropped open in astonishment. "Get your hands off my bottom, you brute."

"I told you it was dirty." His mouth lifted with humor. "C'mon, Helen, loosen up. Close your eyes. Pretend it's just you and me. Put your body into it."

Before she had a chance to react, he flung her away from him, holding onto one hand, then twirled her under his arm for six rotations, all in cadence to the music. John Travolta couldn't have done it better. She emerged dizzily from her spin to find herself clasped in such a tight embrace she'd probably have groove marks on her stomach from the zipper of his fly.

Belly to belly, he rotated their hips, as one, in an erotic circle. Even their breathing came in unison now. It really *was* like making love.

And Helen began to forget the cheering miners, and the coins and gold nuggets being thrown to the stage, even the nineteenth-century setting. There was only Rafe and her and the music. And the forbidden dance.

A savage sexual energy flared between them as they learned the rhythm of each other's bodies. He no longer had to show her the moves. She initiated her own. When he held her close, she felt the thud of his heartbeat against

201

hers. When his hungry, pale blue eyes held hers, she couldn't look away. She saw the pulse leap at the base of his neck, and she thrilled that she could affect him so.

"Helen."

Just that soft-spoken word caused a tingling ripple through her oversensitized body.

He inserted a foot between her gown-covered legs and flashed her a challenge.

Brazenly, she took up his silent dare and rode against his thigh in the undulating Latin tempo.

His gasp of pleasure was her reward.

Finally, he turned her, spoon fashion, with his chest to her back. With his left arm wrapped around her waist and his right hand holding her right hand upward, he rolled their hips together in a sweet, scandalous circle, imitating the sex act.

Her knees almost gave out.

He made a low, gurgling sound of male desperation and nipped her shoulder playfully, propelling her in a dancing walk toward the back of the tent. Kissing the side of her neck, he then shoved her rudely to the floor.

"Wh-what?"

"Now!" he clipped out, and she realized, through her sensual haze, that Henry was whistling on the other side of the tent.

Jolted back to reality and the danger at hand, she lifted the canvas and was about to crawl under when she heard an uproar behind her. Rafe had both pistols leveled at the crowd, which was about to rush up onto the stage.

"Go!" he shouted. "I'll be right behind you."

She bit her bottom lip indecisively, but obeyed. Henry hurried her to the horses being held by his cousin and helped her mount, murmuring several words of caution. For several long seconds that seemed like years, they waited. Then there was a gunshot, which caused all three of them to jump with alarm.

Almost immediately, Rafe emerged, unscathed. "I shot in the air," he explained quickly as he vaulted onto his horse. He nodded to Henry's cousin, then reached down to shake Henry's hand. "I can't thank you enough, *mi amigo*," he said thickly.

"Me, too," Helen said tearfully. She blew Henry a kiss as she and Rafe turned their horses and galloped off, out of town in a northerly direction. She glanced back and saw that the angry miners were already swarming from the back and around the sides of the tent. Henry and his cousin melted into the shadows.

When they emerged on the outskirts of town, Rafe slowed his horse for a moment and rode next to her horse. Panting slightly, he gazed at her, a fiery expression on his face. There was anger in his glittering eyes and tight jaw—probably because she'd come to the saloon against his orders—but there was something else, too.

Without warning, he reached over and wrapped one hand around the nape of her neck, pulling her closer. Then he kissed her hard, bruising her lips and sending a shiver of fierce longing through her body, which still hummed from their forbidden dance. The kiss lasted only a moment, but the message was clear.

Tonight.

She had to be sure. "What?" she whispered, touching her fingertips to her lips.

His eyes sparkled with amusement. "Tonight is payback time, *mi cara.*"

Nudging his horse with his thighs, he moved forward again. She did likewise.

"I thought you were going to wait until our last night," she argued weakly.

"I changed my mind." He smiled mischievously. "But we have to find a safe place to stop first. I don't think those drunk miners will follow us, but we can't take a chance."

She nodded, equally concerned about the danger. "Rafe, the reason I came to the saloon was because some men were talking in the hall of the hotel, outside our room. They'd heard rumors that the Angel Bandit was in town.

They planned to search for him—*you*—to get the reward. I thought there was danger.''

He listened closely. "Then there was all the more reason for us to leave Marysville. Besides, I learned tonight that Pablo joined up with Sancho. They've moved farther north.''

She sighed. "Do you think our troubles will ever end?''

He slanted her a devilish look. "Honey, one of those troubles is going to end tonight.''

"We'll talk about this when we stop.''

"No, we won't, Helen. The time for talking, and teasing, and constant hard-ons is over.''

"Constant har . . . Oh, you're always trying to shock me.''

He shook his head vigorously. "No, I'm not. I'm preparing you. And while you're *preparing*, think about this. I'm picturing your widespread legs on that horse. With each rhythmic roll of the horse's gait, you can feel the saddle pressing against your soft hairs . . . and open folds . . . and swelling—''

"Stop it! Just stop it!'' she gasped out.

"And I want you to imagine that it's me under you.''

She tried to shut out his enticing words, to no avail.

"Are you wet already, Helen? Don't lie to me. I know you were just as aroused as I was by our dance. Do you still feel the . . . throb?''

"Why are you talking like this?'' she cried out. "I deal with men everyday. Do you think vulgar language is something new to me? I don't expect it from you, though.''

"Vulgar? My talking about our making love is vulgar? Helen, if I were saying these things to some stranger, it would be insulting. Harassment, even. But this is you and me. A man and a woman. If it's not to your taste, fine, but don't paint it as perverted, or intimidating. Can you honestly say that my words don't excite you at all?''

She groaned. "Do you enjoy torturing me?''

"This is foreplay, sweetheart. The most delicious torture there is. By the time we stop an hour or so from now, I want you so turned on and hot, you'll blister my skin at fifty paces."

I could probably do that right now.

He clucked to his horse and moved into a slow gallop. Her horse soon caught up. They rode for about a half hour without talking before he slowed.

"How're you doing?" he asked.

"Fine. I'm not that tired, and my horse can probably go another—"

"Helen, Helen, Helen. That's not what I meant." He reached over and ran a palm fleetingly over her thigh.

A shot of electricity ran from her toes to her groin to her brain. She put a hand over her mouth to stifle her telling moan.

He laughed. "Babe, we are going to be so good together."

"I don't like it when you talk like this."

"Why?" he asked, cocking his head with surprise.

She lifted her chin and turned her face away from him, afraid she would reveal too much, even in the dark.

"Prissy, is your loose gown rubbing against your breasts?"

Her heart skipped a beat, and she refused to answer.

"Are your nipples hard? Do you want to be suckled? Do you like it hard or soft? Wet or dry? Whatever you wish, I'll do. Everything. No holds barred."

Her breath stopped. Every nerve ending in her body was listening to his insolent, erotic words, and increasing in sensitivity.

"I knew a woman once who could come just by having a man play with her breasts. Do you think you could do that?"

She tried to shut out his words.

"Helen," he murmured in a cracked voice, betraying his out-of-control state, too. "Do you know what I'd really like?"

"No, don't tell me."

He grinned at her vehemence. "I'd like you to drop your

reins for a moment and look at me. Then, while you're holding eye contact, I'd like you to lift your own breasts. And touch the tips. Just for a second. That's all.''

Helen was shocked. This time, she really was.

The most shocking thing of all was that she was tempted.

Helen kicked her horse into a gallop before she actually embarrassed herself, and Rafe, by complying.

One time he caught up with her and asked, ''I don't suppose you'd consider riding naked?''

''Get real!'' she snapped.

After another hour, they veered off the road and up a steep mountain. Thunder had been rumbling in the distance for some time, and they needed to set up camp before the storm broke. Finally, they came to a wide overhanging outcrop of rock.

''This is the kind of place that often has some caves,'' Rafe conjectured aloud. ''Stay here while I explore.'' He returned shortly and motioned for her to follow. ''It's perfect. Just enough room for us and the horses.''

While Rafe went out to gather firewood, Helen began rubbing down the horses at the back of the small, low-ceilinged cave. With the dampness of the ''room'' and the breeze from the coming storm, a definite chill hung on the air. *Or is it my fear of what's to come?* In any case, a large fire would be welcome.

She started the kindling in a space close to the cave opening so the smoke could escape. Meanwhile, Rafe went in and out five more times, carrying armloads of broken limbs, which he stacked to the side. By the last trip, he was soaking wet from the pounding rain.

''Helen, see if you can find soap in one of the saddlebags.''

She looked up from the fire she was feeding with pieces of kindling. On an indrawn breath, she asked, ''What are you *doing*?''

Rafe already had his boots and socks off, along with his soaking shirt. Water ran down his face and chest from his hair. He was about to unzip his pants.

He chuckled, apparently understanding her alarm. "Unlike you, I didn't get to bathe tonight at the hotel. I'm going to wash in the rain."

"Oh." She found the soap and handed it to him. Oh, Lord, he was already down to his black boxers. The light from the fire highlighted his sleek body, wide shoulders, hard abs, flat stomach and narrow hips, beautifully long legs, and narrow feet.

"Want to join me?" he asked huskily, intensely aware of her scrutiny. And not at all self-conscious of his near-nudity.

Shaking her head, she kept her eyes averted, disconcerted by her reaction to him. *I'm thirty-four years old and getting flustered by a man. I'm an Army major, for heaven's sake, surrounded by men. Why should this one affect me so?*

She heard him step out of his shorts and pad toward the cave entrance. Just before he went out, he said, "I'll be right back." A heavy pause ensued during which she refused to look up, and he added, "Have the blankets ready for us, Helen. I need you . . . real bad."

She did look up then, but all she saw was the back of his nude body moving out into the driving rain.

Rafe was gone for a long while, and every few moments, as she built the fire higher and higher, Helen glanced over to the blankets piled in the corner. She knew that Rafe was giving her time, that if she actually made a bed for them, it would be her answer. He was throwing the choice in her lap as to whether they made love or not.

Should I? The mere question flicked a switch in her already overly aroused body. She wanted to. Yes, she definitely wanted to.

What about Elliott? Helen immediately discarded her engagement as a deterrent. No matter what happened—or didn't happen—with Rafe, Helen was not going to marry Elliott. She knew now that she didn't love him, even though he was a good man. She couldn't stop dreaming of marriage and a stable home and children, but they would mean nothing in a loveless marriage.

Sandra Hill

Control? I have no control over Rafe, or over myself when he gets too close. Helen didn't like feeling so helpless. She'd built a life for herself based on logic over emotion. If she allowed herself to unravel this one time—this one night—would she be able to put herself back in order again? Probably not. Still ... What would it be like to really lose control with a man? With Rafe? She closed her eyes for a second at the overwhelming tide of want that flooded her at that alluring possibility.

I don't even like him. Well, that wasn't quite true. The more she got to know Rafe, the more she realized she didn't know.

Love. That was the big element here, Helen concluded. What if she fell in love with Rafe? What if she already loved him? Now, that was a dangerous prospect. They had no future. They were too different—their ideals, their backgrounds, their dreams.

He doesn't want children.

A one-night fling, that's all it would be. Would that be enough? Of course not. But what was the alternative? Not knowing. Never experiencing. Taking no risks.

With a tinkling laugh of surrender, Helen rose and shook out the blankets, laying them near the fire. Later, she would move the saddles closer for pillows.

Pensively, she began to undo the buttons down the front of her gown, from neck to stomach.

"Helen." Her name came off Rafe's tongue in a rasp, like a dark, smoky plea.

She glanced up and saw him leaning against the cave entrance, watching her with a feral expression on his face.

"Don't stop." He folded his arms across his chest, waiting. His rampart erection gave visual evidence of his desire for her. His skin was dark everywhere, a reminder of his Hispanic heritage. Without the modern trappings of his clothing, he looked just like the wild, desperate bandit he was accused of being. A desperado.

Rafe's heart was beating like a jackhammer. Hot breath burned his lungs. This was the moment he'd been awaiting for so long. His dream. "Don't stop," he repeated in a voice much harsher than he'd intended.

Helen stood frozen, like a frightened deer, her brown eyes wide. Did she view him as the hunter? A threat?

Calm down, calm down, he told himself, taking deep breaths. *Put on the brakes. You'll scare her with your raging hunger.*

"Will you strip for me, Helen?" he asked gently. "Real slow."

She nodded hesitantly and undid another button. Eight more to go.

"Make it last, baby. Make me want you *so bad.*"

Another button. This one at chest level. The fabric of her green gown parted, giving a glimpse of creamy white skin and a scattering of freckles.

He felt as if he would explode if he didn't touch her soon. Instead, he clenched his fists. "How do you feel?"

"Wanton." Another button.

Wanton?

The inside curve of her breasts was exposed. A shudder ran through him.

She waited.

"Feel your skin. Is it hot?"

Refusing to break eye contact with him, she popped another button, then pressed the fingertips of both hands against her bare abdomen. "Scorching."

He gave out a short laugh of delight. Helen was losing her shyness. *Good.*

She undid two more buttons hastily and peered up at him questioningly.

"Do you know what I want, Helen?"

She smiled ruefully. "Oh, yes."

He smiled back. "Not *just* that, babe. No, I want more . . . much more."

She raised an eyebrow.

"Honey, I want to do things to you that no man has ever done. I want to make you feel things you've never felt before."

"I already feel things I've never felt before," she confessed. "I'm not a virgin, Rafe, but I feel like . . ." She fought for words. "I feel like . . . well . . . this is the first time."

Strangely, he did, too.

She shrugged out of her gown, letting it drop to her hips. His body went still, and his mind went blank.

Her hands dropped to her sides. Although her face flamed, she held his eyes in challenge, daring him to find her flaws.

There were none.

She was a goddess with her fiery hair. Her skin was creamy smooth—not porcelain, or even deep tan, like so many women he'd known, but the peach-tinted hue of a pure redhead. Her slender neck led down to the most magnificent breasts he'd ever seen. Vargas breasts. Perfect globes of ivory capped with puffy aureoles and pebble tips of a raspberry tint. Champagne breasts, as he'd told her one time.

And that wasn't all. She had a narrow waist that flared out to curvy hips. Her flat stomach framed an indented navel that he longed to explore with his tongue. Her gown hid the rest, but he could wait. This was enough for now. Almost too much.

He started toward her. He couldn't wait.

She held up a halting hand. "Do you remember . . . do you remember what you asked me to do earlier?"

He frowned. Hell, he couldn't remember his own name, let alone something he might have asked her to do before. "When?"

"Tonight. Earlier tonight." She raised her hands slowly. And he remembered. *Hot damn!*

She placed both palms under her breasts and lifted them a little, creating a more voluptuous cleavage. Then she moved her hands upward, past her breasts, and . . . *oh, my God!* . . . she licked first one forefinger, then the other. And touched her own nipples.

She closed her eyes and moaned.

He closed his eyes and moaned.

In three quick strides, he was in front of her, pulling her into his arms. She almost collapsed, grabbing for his shoulders.

His mouth covered hers ravenously, forcing her lips open with his thrusting tongue.

She returned the kiss with equal hunger, drawing him deeper.

He wanted to be gentle, but he forgot how. She deserved a masterful lover. He was out of control.

His brain said, *Time for a speed bump.* His brain-dead body said, *Shut up. We're off to Indianapolis.*

His hands swept over her back, from shoulder to buttocks. Pressing. Kneading. Exploring.

Her fingers gripped his shoulders, convulsively.

Slow down.

He plunged his tongue into her mouth again, then withdrew.

Slow down.

Her foolish tongue followed his into his mouth.

Slow down.

He stroked in, and she followed back.

Slow down.

Her mouth, his tongue. His mouth, her tongue. The deep, incredible kiss never ended. It became one fluid motion of sliding intimacy. A joining.

Slow down, or this will be over before it begins.

Finally, his brain got through to his other organ. Either that, or his arteries were clogged with testosterone.

He leaned away slightly. Cupping her face with both hands, he braced his forehead against hers, panting for breath.

Helen's hands still clutched and unclutched his shoulders, spasmodically, until she calmed down. Only her heaving chest and a small whimper betrayed her continuing turmoil. If he was in a testosterone tailspin, she was surely in hormone heaven.

When he was able to speak above a croak, Rafe brushed

his lips against hers. "Lady, you know how to make a man lose control."

"Me?" she asked skeptically. "I'm the one out of control."

"You are?" He grinned. "Good."

"I don't want to wait anymore."

"I don't either, baby." He inhaled deeply. "But we will." He took both her hands in his, kissing each of the fingertips, then held her arms out from her sides. He stepped back to get a better view, then groaned. "I knew three times wouldn't be enough."

"Enough for what?" she squeaked as he undid her last three buttons and whisked the gown off her hips to billow at her feet.

"To satisfy this wild need I have for you." He skimmed the knuckles of one hand over her red curls for emphasis.

She sighed.

The soft silk, and her sigh, beckoned him to do more, but he exercised restraint. It wasn't easy. "Lie down," he choked out and stumbled over to his pile of wet clothing. Eventually, despite his clumsiness, he found his wallet and took out the three foil-wrapped packets.

When he returned to the blanket, Rafe tossed the three condoms to the side and feasted for a moment on the sight of Helen waiting for him. She lay on her back, her arms thrown over her head in abandon, her nude body—her gloriously nude, beautiful body—waiting for him. To make love.

I'm going to make love with Helen. After all these years and all the dreams, I'm going to make love with Helen.

Helen felt as if she was standing outside her own body. This writhing creature couldn't be her. This was a woman with no modesty, no inhibitions. Her skin glowed with arousal. Her bruised lips parted. Her breasts ached with a sweet yearning to be laved. Hot liquid pooled at her center, inviting. No, this must be a fantasy.

But Rafe wasn't an illusion. No, the man standing above her, gazing at her like the answer to his dreams, was flesh and bone and pure turned-on male. She saw his desire for her. Not just in his erection, but in the fire of his blue eyes, his heaving chest, and his fists, which kept clenching and unclenching.

I have the power to do this to him. She was delighted. She didn't understand any of the sexual force that wrapped itself about them, but, for once in her life, she didn't care about explanations.

Reaching up her arms, she drew him down to her. She reveled in the delicious agony of his crisp chest hairs abrading her sensitized breasts, the nip of his teeth again the curve of her shoulder, the intrusion of his thigh between her legs. She wanted to isolate each sensation, to savor each nuance, but everything was happening too quickly. One caress blended into another. Pleasures like none she'd ever experienced before slingshotted all over her body, wherever he touched.

It was too much, and not nearly enough.

"I want you so much," he whispered as he brushed her hair off her face and took one earlobe between his teeth, tugging.

"Then take me," she started to say, but his tongue was doing erotic things to the inner whorls of her ear. The wet tip traced its path, then plunged in as far as it could go. Over and over, he repeated the pattern. *Ear sex,* Helen thought, and would have giggled if her body weren't responding to the carnal rhythm. *Oh, my!* Without thinking, she parted her legs and moved against his thigh. "I want . . ." she mewled.

"I know, sweetheart. Soon," Rafe promised and propped himself on one elbow, admiring her body.

She turned her face away, suddenly ill-at-ease, having him see how much she craved his sex. He tipped her chin back, forcing her to look at him. "Don't turn away, Helen. Show me what excites you."

"Everything excites me, you fool."

He grinned. "Really? Like this?" His fingertips traced a circular pattern around one breast, getting closer and closer to the peak. When he finally strummed it back and forth with a thumb, she bowed her back and keened with want.

"What?"

"It's . . . not . . . enough," she ground out.

A glint of understanding flashed in his eyes and he lowered his head. He laved the nipple with his tongue till it was wet, then began to suckle in earnest. Soft at first, then harder, and faster. Her breasts swelled and throbbed with every excruciating draw of his mouth. And each pull on her nipple brought an echoing thrum between her legs.

He lifted his head once to study the breast he'd been ministering to and she hissed, "Don't you dare stop."

With a husky male sound of satisfaction, he answered, "Not on your life!" and attended to the other breast, flicking it with his tongue, grazing it with his teeth, then suckling deep.

"Oh . . . oh . . . oh, yes!"

Meanwhile, his hand moved lower, over her flat stomach. His fingers parted her, exploring her slickness, finding the swollen treasure. She screamed when he touched her there.

He jerked back. "Did I hurt you?"

"No." She felt mortified at the extent of her arousal.

"Then what?"

"I want you too much," she admitted.

His smile was boyishly triumphant as he reached for one of the condoms. "Oh, Helen, you could never want me too much. And, believe me, it's not half as much as I want you."

Fumbling with the packet, his nervous fingers didn't seem to work properly. In the end, he ripped it open with his teeth and smoothed it on with one hand. Rolling over between her legs, he apologized, "I'm sorry. I can't wait longer."

"Sorry?" she gasped at the first feel of his hardness against her. "Any longer and I'm going to go up in smoke."

He tried to laugh but it came out strangled. Placing both palms under her buttocks, he arched her and began to ease inside her tightness. To her shame, he'd barely entered when her body convulsed around him in wave after wave of an involuntary climax.

She started to cry.

"Shhh," he said, "I love the way you come. Don't be embarrassed."

"Too soon," she choked out.

"Do you think so?" Supporting himself on extended arms, he pressed himself deeper and deeper until he was fully imbedded.

She stopped crying and blinked up at him. *Incredible!*

He filled her, impaled her, then seemed to grow even wider as her inner folds shifted to conform to his size. He was gritting his teeth with restraint. Veins stood out on his muscled arms. He seemed to have trouble breathing.

The first time he pulled almost all the way out, then slammed back in, she thought her eyes must be bouncing in her head with the violent pleasure that rocked her.

The second time, she was ready. She wasn't going to be shocked this time. She braced her feet on the ground and elevated her hips to meet his stroke.

A futile effort. Despite her resistance, skyrockets exploded in that fluttering heart of hers, setting her afire. By now, her eyes were probably circling behind her eyelids like one of those slot machines with fruit. Cherries and pineapples and oranges and . . .

"Don't fight it," Rafe coaxed.

She tried to tell him she was trying, but there was fruit salad dancing in her head.

She lost count of Rafe's strokes. Her head rolled from side to side in the throes of mindless passion. She thrashed and pleaded. She thought she might have touched her own pulsing breasts one time, or maybe she'd guided his hands to her. She wasn't sure.

Rafe was in no better condition. His eyes were closed, the dark lashes forming perfect black fans against his flushed skin. Harsh breaths escaped his parted lips. Rearing his shoulders and neck back, he strained toward fulfillment.

And each time he thrust into her, his pubic bone pressed that engorged knot of arousal in her wet folds, bringing her higher and higher toward a keening, spiraling cataclysm of sensation.

She spread her legs wider and arched like a bow, then surrendered to the waves of ecstasy that shook her body. Every nerve ending in her body exploded into a splintering orgasm. Spasm after spasm grasped Rafe's hardness.

With a masculine growl, Rafe, too, gave in to his climax. Pumping hard, he gave one last thrust, then jerked inside her with reflexive tremors.

They both must have passed out for a few seconds because, when Helen came to, Rafe lay heavily on her. Their hearts beat a rapid counterpoint against each other, gradually slowing down to a normal rate.

Finally, Rafe raised his head. She feared he might laugh, or make a flip remark about how good they were together. Maybe even say something about her clipboard.

Instead, he gazed at her seriously, in wonder.

"I think I love you," he said, his voice breaking with emotion. "God help me, but I think I love you."

Chapter Fifteen

Rafe looked down at Helen, her big brown eyes gazing up at him, doelike, with shock. "Rafe, I don't know what—"

"Shhh," he said, pressing his fingers to her lips. He was already regretting his hasty confession. "I just wanted you to know how special this was to me. I'm not asking you to reciprocate, so don't get yourself bent out of shape. Hell, it was probably just a line."

He replaced his fingertips with his mouth and brushed his lips across hers. God, he loved kissing her.

She bit his bottom lip.

"Ouch!"'' he exclaimed. Sitting up, he swiped the back of his hand across his mouth, checking for blood. There wasn't any, but there could have been. "Why'd you do that?"

"Was it?" She scrambled to her knees and shoved him in the chest angrily.

He nearly fell into the fire, especially since his eyes were riveted on her swaying breasts. "Are you nuts? Was it *what*?"

"A line? Was it a line?"

He started to smile.

"Don't you dare smirk." She stood, somehow managing to wrap one of the blankets protectively around her naked body in the process. It was a feminine knack he'd never been able to figure out. All women had it. Probably could be traced back to Roman toga days. Yeah, he could see it now. A goddess screwing a centurion until his forehead vine withered, then feeling the need to cover herself modestly with a sheet afterward.

"I wasn't smirking," he declared with a smirk, lying back down on the remaining blanket. Resting his head on arms folded under his neck, he watched as she moved to the woodpile, sulking. He *really* liked watching Helen move. He wondered if her nipples were still hard.

And those red curls of her . . . Damn, everything had happened so quickly, he hadn't had time to really explore *there*. But he had lots of time now. A sudden thought occurred to him. *Did I say "explore."* Oh, yeah, Marco Polo, eat your heart out. He planned to explore every latitude and longitude of her hemispheres. North Pole. South Pole. The Equator.

"You are so disgusting," she said, glaring at him as if she could read his mind. With a snarl, she picked up a small log and threw it onto the dying fire. Sparks flew everywhere. One almost hit him in a delicate spot—real close to *his* Equator. He glanced over to see if she'd noticed.

She had, and she didn't appear too concerned, either.

Women! Go figure!

"No, Helen, it wasn't a line," he conceded, deciding he'd teased her enough. "I've never said those words before . . . to any woman." *And you can be sure I won't be so careless again.*

"You haven't?"

He looked up. Oh, great! The doe eyes again. "Listen, forget I ever said it. Pretend that—"

"Forget? Forget?" she shrieked. "Women don't forget things like that."

Right! "Then don't blow it up all out of proportion. It's not like I'm proposing marriage or anything. Picket fences and babies weren't my style before, and they aren't now."

Helen flinched. "I never said I wanted to marry you," she said in a small voice, raising her chin haughtily.

Damn, he couldn't seem to say the right thing. And now he'd managed to insult her, too. But his loose tongue was on a roll. "Good. Because marriage is a nonnegotiable item."

The look she gave him could have peeled bark off a redwood. "Is that lawyer talk, or—"

"Helen, let's start over." Rafe sat up and raked the fingers of both hands through his hair. "This is ridic—"

"Or is it scared-to-the-bone-of-commitment man talk?"

"Damn straight."

"Which one?"

"Both."

"Hah! Cluck-cluck."

"Are you saying I'm a chicken?"

She swept him with a telling assessment that lingered on his lower anatomy. "You do everything but cock-a-doodle-do."

A grin crept over his lips, but he stopped it abruptly when he saw her drop down into a cross-legged position. *Oh, no!* "What?" he asked suspiciously.

"I'm going to meditate."

She's going to ooohm? *Now? I knew things were going too smoothly.* He groaned. "Ah, Helen, c'mon back over here. No meditating now. Let's make love again. I'm a bumbling idiot, but I'll make it up to you."

"I'm too upset. I need to think—to find my center."

"Baby, I've been to your center and it's just fine. Take my word for it."

Her face turned a delicious shade of pink but she refused to rise to his bait this time. Instead, she launched into a full-fledged chant. *"Ooohm, ooohm, ooohm, ooohm. . . ."*

"At least you could take off that blanket," he grumbled. "If you're gonna give me a headache, I should be compensated with a little peek at your nipples."

"Ooohm, ooohm, ooohm, ooohm. . . ." Even though she was facing him across the fire, she stared straight ahead, her eyes blank.

That really irritated him. He didn't like the fact that she could go from red-hot sex to cool indifference in such a short time. Especially when his body was still in a fever.

Okay, two could play this game.

"Ooohm, ooohm, ooohm, ooohm. . . ."

He shifted himself into that hippie-dippie lotus position, which wasn't too easy. His knees cracked and his legs didn't want to fold like a pretzel. At last, after a few swear words and some straining thigh muscles, he succeeded and faced her over the flames.

She was gaping at him in astonishment, her concentration broken. *Good!*

"What are you doing?"

"Meditating. Finding my center." He looked down, then back at her. "It's still there," he informed her with a wink.

She tsked prissily and resumed her *ooohm*ing. He joined in, much to her chagrin.

"Aaahm, aaahm, aaahm, aaahm, . . ." he hummed, deliberately misspeaking her refrains, just to annoy her.

"Ooohm, ooohm, ooohm, ooohm, . . ." she said, but he could tell he'd succeeded. She was annoyed.

"Aaahm, aaahm, aaahm, aaahm, . . ." he continued for a really long, boring time. About a minute. "This is so-o-o soothing, Helen," he lied. "We should do this more often."

"Ooohm, ooohm, ooohm, ooohm. . . ." She was staring through him, as if she was in a trance.

He couldn't have that. He decided to go for variety in the tempo. When she *ooohm*ed, he interjected an *aaahm*. *"Oooohm, aaahm, ooohm, aaahm, ooohm, aaahm . . ."*

"Would you stop that?" she snapped.

"Why? Am I breaking your karma?"

"No. You just sound stupid." Then she tuned him out again, turning on her zombie face. *"Ooohm, ooohm, ooohm . . ."*

He was tired of meditating. He wanted to explore. "How 'bout we do forms now? Naked forms. Yeah, I think I could manage those."

She didn't even break an *ooohm*. In fact, she pretended she hadn't heard him. Maybe she hadn't. Maybe he needed a bigger shock to her senses.

"So, Prissy, did I ever tell you I can make my tongue have an erection?"

He heard her sharp intake of air before her jaw dropped in amazement. No more *ooohm*s now.

"You are pathetic."

"Yeah." He grinned.

"You lie."

He jiggled his eyebrows. "Do you think so?" He crooked a finger at her. "Why don't you rhumba on over here and find out?"

Her lips twitched. Then he heard a slight giggle, followed by a spontaneous laugh.

Hallelujah!

She pulled the blanket tighter around her body and stood, walking awkwardly over to his side of the fire. He forced his hands to his sides, even though he really wanted to pull her down on top of him.

"Well?" she said, glaring down at him.

"Well what?"

"Well, show me, you fool."

"What? You expect me to have an instant tongue hard-on without any foreplay?" he said, snickering.

She pointed to his erection. "*It* doesn't seem to have any trouble rising to the occasion."

"*It* has no class. My tongue is a more refined instrument. It needs . . . Well, maybe if you dropped that toga, it would—"

"Toga?" she asked, raising an eyebrow.

"Blanket. Shroud. Tent. Whatever."

Before he had a chance to blink, she let the folds fall open to the ground and kicked them aside.

And Rafe's tongue did, indeed, seem to grow three sizes and appear to have a mind of its own. He was speechless.

Helen got tremendous satisfaction out of turning Rafe speechless. She looked down as he sputtered for breath, his eyes wide with appreciation of her nude body. Gee, she wished she had her clipboard now. She'd like to take notes on fifty ways to turn Rafe speechless, starting with female nudity.

God help me, but I think I love you, she mimicked Rafe in her head. Then, *It was probably just a line.* The jerk couldn't fool her. He loved her, all right.

She guessed she'd just have to teach him a lesson.

Stepping over his body, she used the instep of each foot to frame his hips. "Say it," she ordered.

"Tongue hard-on."

"Not *that.*" She could tell he enjoyed verbal sparring with her. The lout! She touched his erection with her big toe.

He shot up off the blanket about four feet. "Holy hell!"

She was pretty sure the tremor going through his body was from extreme pleasure. She'd never dreamed she could be so bold or uninhibited or excited. Or in love.

Openly amused, she pushed him back down with a foot braced on his chest. This was fun, being the aggressor. "Say it."

"No." He was grinning again.

"Yes," she insisted, using the pad of her foot to circle one of his nipples. His heart just about jumped out of his chest.

"Maybe I changed my mind."

"Men! Don't you know *those* words can't be taken back?"

"Says who?"

"It's an unwritten rule. Now say it, damn it." She drew her foot lower.

"Helen," he warned. His teeth were making a funny, grinding kind of noise. Could be he was trying to exercise restraint. Good thing someone was. She'd lost hers about three miles back in Marysville. Probably with the first dip.

Before he could guess her next move—heck, *she* didn't know what her next move was going to be—she dropped to her knees and sat on his upper thighs, *real high.* His arousal pressed against her stomach.

After Rafe's eyes rolled around their sockets a few spins,

he gasped out, "Son of a bitch! Are you trying to kill me?"

"Just a little," she murmured, leaning forward. Her breasts grazed his chest hairs, then swelled and began to thrum with a sweet ache. She wanted to tease him, the way he always teased her, but she felt woozy and disoriented, as if she were drunk.

When she was so close his warm breath fanned her lips, she asked, "So, how's your tongue, honey?"

"I swallowed it." He smiled against her lips.

And it felt so-o-o good. A smile-kiss. She liked it. So she smiled back against his lips.

He grabbed her by the waist, compelling her back up to a sitting position. God, he was so handsome, with his dark skin and flashing eyes and firm lips that begged to be kissed. She leaned forward again to do just that when he held her back. "What are you trying to do?" he ground out.

She blinked with confusion. "I don't know. I forget. Oh, I remember. I want you to say the words. Again." She licked her lips to see if they were as puffy as they felt. Rafe's eyes followed the path of her tongue with avid interest.

"Convince me," he rasped out.

"How?" She tilted her head questioningly.

"Touch me."

She brushed her fingertips over his flat male nipples. "Like that?" she asked. She could tell by his loud inhale that he liked it a whole lot. Then she replaced her fingertips with her mouth and suckled him the way he had her.

He responded with a thundering heartbeat and clenched fists at his sides. No words.

"And this?" She moved lower and took him in her hand for a brief second, stroking lightly.

"Definitely," he choked out.

The only sounds in the cave then were the background rain, the crackling fire, the shifting horses, and Rafe's ragged breathing. She relished the feel of his hot skin under her hands, the male scent of him, aroused and wanting her.

With her hands and mouth and her skin abrading his skin, she worshipped his body from beautiful toes to creased forehead. And all the time, he whispered sweet, hot words of encouragement, some of them in Spanish. Some of them so explicit she blushed, all over.

When she raised her eyes to his face, it was vulnerable and open. She realized with sudden insight that she could hurt this man deeply. Thank God, she only wanted to bring him pleasure.

"My turn," he growled, arranging her on her stomach.

"I want to see you," she protested.

"Shhh. Later. First, I want to explore." She heard devilment in his voice when he said the word "explore." She raised her head to peer at him over her shoulder, but he drew her hair back, exposing her neck, and nipped gently with his teeth, forcing her face back into the blanket. "My turn, my way, sweetheart. Slow and easy."

Slow and easy? Oh, yeah! At this point, my hormones are already programmed for fast and furious.

First, he kissed her ear, doing those wonderful things with his tongue—which he hadn't swallowed, after all—that he'd done to her earlier. The wet, fluttery motions that simulated the sex act made her feel like sinking right into the blanket.

"Do you like that?"

"Yes."

"And this?"

"God, yes."

There wasn't an inch of her body that he didn't examine with his rough palms and warm lips. He spent a lot of time on the curve of her spine. "I always thought the small of a woman's back was the most erotic turn-on . . . until I saw your breasts," he told her. And she had to agree that he'd revealed a new erogenous zone for her.

He traced her butterfly tattoo and pressed his lips to it. "It's my mark on you," he said with hoarse possessiveness.

Then he showed her another erogenous zone—the back

GET UP TO
4 FREE BOOKS!

You can have the best romance delivered to your door for less than what you'd pay in a bookstore or online. Sign up for one of our book clubs today, and we'll send you **FREE* BOOKS** just for trying it out...**with no obligation to buy, ever!**

HISTORICAL ROMANCE BOOK CLUB

Travel from the Scottish Highlands to the American West, the decadent ballrooms of Regency England to Viking ships. Your shipments will include authors such as CONNIE MASON, SANDRA HILL, CASSIE EDWARDS, JENNIFER ASHLEY, LEIGH GREENWOOD, and many, many more.

LOVE SPELL BOOK CLUB

Bring a little magic into your life with the romances of Love Spell—fun contemporaries, paranormals, time-travels, futuristics, and more. Your shipments will include authors such as LYNSAY SANDS, CJ BARRY, COLLEEN THOMPSON, NINA BANGS, MARJORIE LIU and more.

As a book club member you also receive the following special benefits:

- **30% OFF all orders through our website & telecenter!**
- **Exclusive access to special discounts!**
- **Convenient home delivery and 10 day examination period to return any books you don't want to keep.**

There is no minimum number of books to buy, and you may cancel membership at any time. See back to sign up!

*Please include $2.00 for shipping and handling.

YES! ☐

Sign me up for the **Historical Romance Book Club** and send my TWO FREE BOOKS! If I choose to stay in the club, I will pay only $8.50* each month, a savings of $5.48!

YES! ☐

Sign me up for the **Love Spell Book Club** and send my TWO FREE BOOKS! If I choose to stay in the club, I will pay only $8.50* each month, a savings of $5.48!

NAME: _____

ADDRESS: _____

_____

TELEPHONE: _____

E-MAIL: _____

☐ **I WANT TO PAY BY CREDIT CARD.**

☐ VISA   ☐ MasterCard   ☐ DISCOVER

ACCOUNT #: _____

EXPIRATION DATE: _____

SIGNATURE: _____

Send this card along with $2.00 shipping & handling for each club you wish to join, to:

**Romance Book Clubs
20 Academy Street
Norwalk, CT 06850-4032**

Or fax (must include credit card information!) to: 610.995.9274. You can also sign up online at www.dorchesterpub.com.

JOIN NOW!

of her knees. By then, she was a quivering mass of flesh. She whimpered for release, but he just laughed, holding her down with a hand on her back. When he skimmed the crease at the back of her knees, a current of electric pleasure shot through her legs, up, up, up. When his tongue repeated the caress, something wild and frighteningly intense broke free inside her.

At the first spasm of her approaching climax, he turned her on her back and took a breast into his mouth. He drew on the aching tip with a rhythm that matched the waves ebbing between her legs, undulating outward. She tried to scream, but her throat closed. Increasing the strength of his suckling, Rafe whisked a hand over her stomach, skittering over the damp curls, then touched her.

She saw stars.

When she tried to close her legs, he kept them open with one knee, exposing her to his tantalizing fingertips.

"No more, no more, no more," she sobbed, and pounded against his chest.

"Easy, easy," he coaxed every time her thighs tensed against the onslaught. "Stop fighting me. Relax."

"Relax?" she squeaked in disbelief, trying to hold his wrist in place. He withheld his hands until she obeyed. Then he embarked on the exercise again.

Over and over. Raging arousal. To the edge. Then halt. Relax. Start again.

When she finally reached her peak and shattered, she heard the high-pitched squeal but could barely connect it with herself, this flailing, arching, brazen woman pleading for forbidden delights she'd never dreamed existed.

At the height of her orgasm, Rafe demanded in a strangled voice, "Look at me."

She unshuttered her heavy lids and saw him poised on his knees between her widespread legs. Her knees were bent, buttocks resting on his thighs. Even as shudders racked her in waves, he placed both hands on her hips, lifting her higher and wider.

"No," she said, realizing his intent.

"Let me . . ." Lowering his head, he nuzzled her hair from side to side with his mouth, then used his tongue against the molten slickness, turning her to liquid fire.

Another agonizingly intense climax began to build.

She thrashed. She bucked. She fought the cataclysm.

He no longer entreated her to relax. He was making low, masculine sounds of heightening excitement.

Then he adjusted their positions, and slammed into her, filling her. Her body welcomed him with shifting ripples and fierce clasps.

She screamed.

He roared.

"So hot!" he gasped out. "So good!"

"Oh . . . Oh!"

"I wanted to be gentle."

"Don't . . . you . . . dare."

He almost pulled out and gazed at her through eyes that seemed misty, teary-eyed. "Tell me what you want."

"You," she whispered.

He plunged into her so hard and deep he drove her off the blanket. She wrapped her legs around his waist and cried into his ear, "I'm losing control."

He chuckled. "That's the point."

"I'm afraid."

"I'm with you. Together."

So she held on and matched him stroke for stroke, letting him lead the way on a journey she'd never taken before. Beyond sex and biology to a joining of flesh with spirit.

He rolled onto his back, still in her, and let her set the pace for a while. Slower. Deeper. He touched her breasts while she rode him, and she felt herself melt around him, anointing him with her pleasure.

"You're wonderful . . . wonderful . . . wonderful. I never dreamed . . ."

"Say it," she pleaded.

He hesitated. She could tell he didn't want to. But he did. For her. "I love you."

She closed her eyes and surrendered to the overwhelming spirals.

He turned her on her back again and pressed her knees to her chest. "Hold on tight, babe. This is the last stretch." Braced on muscle-strained arms, he thrust into her with shorter, harder strokes. "Now!" he shouted, and she felt him expand, then come inside her.

Her heart raced, her ears rang, and every nerve ending in her body shook. Finally, finally, finally . . . Her inner folds broke into wave after wave of convulsions, trapping Rafe's manhood with her orgasm.

He howled—a raw, male sound of pure satisfaction.

And she blacked out for an instant with utter, unadulterated ecstasy.

It was several moments before she became aware of her surroundings again. Rafe lay heavily on top of her, probably paralyzed. Her back was pressed to the dirt floor, five feet from their blanket. When she lifted one eyelid, she saw a horse's hoof mere inches away from her cheek. She looked up to see F. Lee staring down his aristocratic nose at the two of them, probably thinking, "Dumb homo sapiens!"

Rafe lifted his head, gulping for breath. "I think I'm hyperventilating." He kissed her lightly and smiled. "Damn, I was good."

She returned his smile, correcting, "Damn, *we* were good."

"Ri-i-ight!" He froze then, as if stunned.

"What?"

"Did you just lick my tattoo?"

"I beg your pardon."

She glanced up and Rafe peered over his shoulder. F. Lee's tongue took another wide swipe across Rafe's right buttock.

"Oh, my God!" Rafe exclaimed as he began to assimilate their new location in the cave. "How did we get here?"

She shrugged. "You were the 'driver.' "

Rafe hooted. "Oh, no! You're not going to lay that one on me." Wrapping an arm around her shoulder, he pulled her closer. "If I ever call you Prissy again, just karate chop my tongue."

She cuddled against his chest. "When it has an erection?" she asked sweetly.

He made a choking noise. "You're never going to let me forget that, are you?"

"Never."

"Let's see if we can find a pepperoni pizza and a Coors in one of those saddlebags," he said. "I'm starved." His legs almost gave way under him as he stood. He grinned sheepishly at his weakness and held out a hand to pull her up.

His thick hair was mussed. His blue eyes scanned her body with lazy possessiveness. His lips were slack in passion's aftermath. There were bruises and bite marks on his dark skin. In essence, he looked like a man who'd just engaged in sex, and had a real good time.

She loved him.

"Why do you have tears in your eyes, *mi amor*?" he asked, drawing her upright and into his embrace.

Cupping his face in her hands, she whispered, "Say it again."

He sighed deeply with understanding. He was obviously uncomfortable.

She cringed with hurt and tried to pull out of his arms.

He held her fast. "Don't you dare start misinterpreting everything I say or do. This is all new to me, and—"

"And you think it's same old–same old to me?" she said on a sob.

"Helen," he said with exaggerated patience, "you're wine, and I'm beer. You're granola, and I'm Froot Loops. You're apples, and I'm jalapeño peppers. You're broiled chicken, and I'm chili dogs. You're—"

"You're looking for excuses, Rafe," she snapped. "Besides, I make a mean Mexi hot dog."

"You do?" He smiled wearily. "You didn't let me finish. The most important thing is that you are babies, and I'm . . . well, I'm not.''

Yes, there was *that* important stumbling block always in their path. Her shoulders slumped.

"Now, let me finish before you stiffen up on me. I'm just trying to say that we're different, and neither of us is thinking beyond this incredible chemistry we have, and that's okay, but—"

"Stop beating around the bush, Rafe.'' She braced herself for the rejection that was undoubtedly coming.

"I love you,'' he said, gazing at her through hazy eyes that were confused and vulnerable and wonderful, wonderful, wonderful. "Bottom line . . . I love you,'' he confessed in a whisper.

Her heart expanded in her chest almost to bursting, and a big tear slid down her cheek. "You'll probably try to take those words back tomorrow,'' she charged, trying to smile, but failing.

"Probably,'' he conceded, kissing the tear off her chin.

Another tear soon followed.

"I love you, too. Honest to God, I really do,'' she said bleakly.

"And that's why you're giving my chest hairs a bath?'' he bantered as one tear after another ran down her face.

She nodded, then shivered. "What's going to happen to us?''

He walked her over to the fire and wrapped one of the blankets around her toga-style. "We'll work it out somehow, I promise. Didn't I tell you I was going to be your hero?''

"Please, you're not going to sing again?''

"No, first I'm going to feed you. To build up your strength,'' he said as he arranged several logs on the fire. "Then . . .'' He flashed a mischievous grin at her.

"Then?'' she prompted.

"Then we're gonna play Marco Polo.'' He winked.

She giggled and burst out laughing.

"I get to go first, of course.''

"Of course," she said dryly. "Will I need a compass?"

He chuckled. "Nah, just follow my anchor."

"Hmmm," she said, swiping the last of the dampness off her cheeks. "Maybe I could be the figurehead on the prow of the ship. You know, one of those waist-high buxom babe things."

"That's the spirit, darlin'. And I could swab your decks."

"Well, I don't know. Would that occur before or after I raise your flag?"

"You've played this game before," he accused boyishly.

They exchanged a warm smile across the fire. He was pulling food items from one of the saddlebags.

She knew Rafe had changed the subject in an effort to make her feel better. He was probably as confused and scared as she was.

Maybe things would work out, after all.

Chapter Sixteen

"Time for the last dance, sweetheart."

Helen felt so warm and sleepy. She cuddled closer under the furry blanket and refused to open her eyes.

"Wake up, little Suzy," the furry blanket said. "One more for the road."

Helen chuckled in her sleep. *What a dream!* There she was on a Hollywood set, waltzing around with Fred Astaire, whose fuzzy sweater rubbed sensuously against her chest. No, it was Patrick Swayze, and they were dirty dancing in the Catskills. Maybe he wasn't wearing a sweater, at all, and he was calling her Suzy, like that old song title.

But why did Patrick have dark hair and blue, blue eyes? And, boy, could he dip!

She slept some more, drifting from dream place to dream place. Now she was a little girl and her daddy was giving her a puppy. "Thank you, Daddy."

"I'm not your Daddy," her daddy said.

Poor man! It had always pained her father to refuse her a pet throughout her childhood, but they moved constantly from base to base.

"What a cute puppy! How affectionate!" she giggled. The darling, frisky pet was licking her belly.

She thought the darling, frisky pet grumbled, "I am not a dog," as she yawned widely. Or maybe it was, "I'll show you cute."

Before she gave up her dreams for deep sleep again, she thought, *That's the nice thing about dreams. Blankets can dance and puppies talk.*

231

Moments later, she entered a new dream. This time, she was holding a baby in her arms. "Oh, sweet baby!" she cooed.

"Now we're getting somewhere," the baby growled in a deep voice. It must be a boy baby.

Helen looked down at the black-haired infant, and tears filled her eyes. A child to love! She would never be lonely again. Her dream come true. She ran her fingers through its surprisingly thick hair and cradled it closer. The infant's mouth clamped over her breast, rooting.

Whoa! This baby has some suction power. And teeth. Teeth?

Her eyes shot open. "Oh, baby!" she exclaimed.

"You called?" Rafe grinned and slid himself up her body. Lying on top of her, with elbows braced on either side of her head, he began to lower his mouth to hers.

She realized that her breasts were full and taut, pressed against his chest. Her legs parted and rubbed sensuously against his furry thighs. The fire had died down to embers, and dawn light filtered through the cave opening. Obviously, this "dream" had been going on for some time.

"What have you been up to, Rafe?" she chided with mock seriousness.

"Exploring." He nipped at her bottom lip. "You wouldn't wake up. So, I started without you."

"Oh. Did I miss anything special?"

"Probably. I guess I'd better start all over again, huh?" And he did.

"I don't suppose you swabbed the decks yet?"

"No, but I did raise the flag." He ground himself against her to demonstrate.

"Some flag!" she remarked dryly.

"Some prow!" he countered, rubbing his crisp chest hairs across her breasts.

"Man the gunwales, matie."

"Anchors aweigh."

"Is that a whale on the starboard?"

"No, it's a tongue hard-on."

"You fool!"

"Just call me Captain Hook."

"Who said you get to be captain?"

"Well, I'm steering *this* boat right now."

"Can I steer later?" she asked sweetly, cupping his "hook" in both hands.

"Aye-aye, Tinkerbell," he choked out.

They stopped clowning around then, and this time their lovemaking took on a slow, poignant character. Helen understood without Rafe saying the words that he fully intended that this third time would be the last until they were back in modern civilization with birth control protection.

So, he cherished her body with gentle caresses and lingering kisses. And kept murmuring, "Last time, last time, last time . . ."

She basked in his expert ministrations, stifling her contrary thoughts, "In your dreams, in your dreams, in your dreams . . ."

A few hours later, Rafe was outside saddling the horses.

They'd already eaten breakfast—a hearty meal of fatty bacon, undercooked beans, stale bread, and God-awful coffee. A Sunday brunch at the Beverly Wilshire couldn't have tasted better.

Helen was still inside the cave, gargling and meditating, no doubt, but Rafe didn't care today. Nope, he was feeling mellow, and he couldn't stop smiling. Hell, he even caught himself whistling one time until F. Lee gave him one of those "don't-you-dare" looks. Translated, "If you whistle, I get gas." Rafe stopped whistling.

When Helen came out finally, carrying a saddlebag with their provisions, she was smiling, too. And he stopped smiling.

She'd combed her unruly red hair back into a ponytail, tied with a strip of cloth. She wore the ugly green gown over her camouflage pants because they'd both agreed that they couldn't continue to avoid the mining camps on the way north. Her fresh scrubbed face gazed up at him adoringly as she walked closer, marred only by the whisker burns on her cheeks and the puffiness of her lips. He saw a dark bruise on her neck and another on the soft inner skin of her upper arm. There were lots more under the concealing dress—he knew because he'd examined every delicious one of them earlier—and just as many on his own body.

His heart skipped a beat, then seemed to swell inside his chest with love for this woman. She was so beautiful.

He loved her. And she loved him. A miracle.

But one thing became alarmingly clear in that instant when she smiled at him. There was no way Helen had accepted his decision not to make love again.

She dropped the saddlebag at his feet and raised her lips to give him a fleeting kiss. "Good morning," she whispered throatily, and walked over to her horse, hips swaying. She started whistling right off.

Helen was a woman on a mission. And he was the target.

He cringed. "Helen, we have to set some new ground rules."

"Oh," she said, already in the saddle. "I thought you didn't like rules."

"I don't, but sometimes they're necessary. Like now."

"You have a hickey on your neck."

He counted to five, silently, for patience. "Helen, I have five hickeys, and one of them in a place that would shock you."

"Really? Did I do it, or did you?"

"Do what? Give myself a love bite *there*?"

She grinned.

"Stop changing the subject. This is serious. Last night was wonderful. Incredible. But it can't happen again until we get back to the future. It just can't."

"And?"

"And I need your cooperation."

"I think I've been cooperative," she said suggestively.

"Helen, please. Help me here. This is going to be hard enough as it is, without you tempting me."

"Do I tempt you?"

"All the time. That's why we have to set some rules."

"Like?"

"No sex."

"Define sex."

He gave out a loud whoosh of exasperation. "No intercourse. No naked bodies. No sleeping together." He was getting aroused already, just thinking about what they wouldn't be doing.

She frowned, then smiled brightly. "I can handle that. There are *other* ways, you know."

He busied himself tying the extra saddlebag on his horse, trying not to imagine those *other* ways. He fought for the words that would convince Helen of his determination. Damn, he was a lawyer. Words shouldn't be hard for him, but they were when the adversary facing him knew how to make his tongue get hard.

"Helen, there aren't going to be *other* ways, either. I know myself. It wouldn't stop there."

"Can't you control your sexual drive with women?"

"I've got real good control, babe. With other women. Not with you."

He ignored her smile of satisfaction and tried to explain. "It's like St. Augustine said, abstinence works, moderation doesn't. In other words, a hard-on has no brain."

"St. Augustine said *that*?"

"Not in those words exactly," he said, grinning. "But he was right. Don't start the horse to galloping unless you plan to take a ride."

She laughed. "I can't believe you know the works of St. Augustine."

"Hey, I told you—my mother was a dictator. Other kids got Doctor Seuss for bedtime stories. We got the lives of the saints."

She tapped her chin thoughtfully. "Wasn't St. Augustine the guy famous for saying, 'Lord, make me pure and chaste—but not quite yet?' "

"So?"

"No wonder he's your favorite saint!" she hooted. "But

235

back to your birth control problems . . . I don't see why you couldn't . . . well, you could always, uh . . .''

"You want me to 'leave before the gospel?' Good old coitus interruptus?''

She nodded. Her face was scarlet with humiliation.

"No."

"Why not?"

"Number one, I'd probably forget—you have a way of turning my brain to mush—or I'd say 'to hell with it' at the last minute—that's also related to your turning my brain to mush. But, most important, the method's not foolproof.''

She pulled a face at him for his firm refusal. "Okay, so you're saying no actual sex and no *other* sex and no sharing the same blanket. Any other rules?''

"No touching.''

Her eyes widened with shock. "At all?"

"It's gotta be that way, babe. And no kissing, either.''

She cast him one of those wounded looks, one women use to make men feel guilty.

He did.

Laughter bubbled out from her lips then and continued until tears streamed down her face. Wiping them away, she nudged her horse into a slow canter, moving down the hill away from him. When he caught up with her at the bottom, she was still laughing.

"What's so funny?''

"You. Oh, Rafe, I can't believe you think that we won't make love again for weeks, maybe longer. It's impossible.''

"Not if you cooperate.''

She lifted an eyebrow in disbelief.

"I'm stronger than you think.''

"We'll see.'' Her mouth turned up in a Cheshire cat smile.

"So, do you agree to the rules?''

"Sure,'' she said, blinking with exaggerated innocence.

She lied, and Rafe damn well knew it. *St. Augustine, you'd better send down some heavy-duty ammunition. I'm a man in deep, deep trouble.*

* * *

Four days later, they made their way down the final stretch to Rich Bar, the northernmost town on the Feather River, a mining camp that had been established earlier that year on rumors of a lake of gold.

Helen's nerves were strained almost to the breaking point. Rafe had proven formidable in his efforts to resist making love with her. Among other things, he forced her to sleep on the other side of the fire every agonizing night, darn him.

It hadn't been easy for Rafe, either. Several times, the howling of wolves had awakened Helen in the middle of the night. She would open her eyes to find Rafe staring hungrily at her across the fire, white-lipped with restraint.

But it was the grueling travel that took its greatest toll on them both. Neither had anticipated the rough terrain as they climbed higher and higher into the mountains on their route north.

Riding hard each day, they passed through such colorful camps as Rough and Ready, Lousy Level, Helltown, Gouge Eye, Dead Man's Bar, Whiskey Flat, and Slumgullion Gulch. They recognized a similarity in them all: Gaming houses and brothels popped up like mushrooms after a rain in every mining town, all with canvas tents, rough plank buildings, and the everlasting crimson calico.

The miners who endured the backbreaking labor of panning gold under the hot sun all day long could be seen using the same pans over a campfire at night. And often the *entrée du jour* was rattlesnake, or "bush fish," as the delicacy was called, with a side of those neverending beans.

They camped by late afternoon each day so that Rafe could pan for gold in the many streams they passed—streams that were crowded almost hip to hip with gold-hungry prospectors. Thus far, Rafe had managed to accumulate a small bag of gold dust, worth about fifty dollars. Not much, but encouraging.

More than once, they'd been forced to seek other camping sites because of mutterings about a dirty Mex trying to steal the gold that rightly belonged to true-blooded Americans. On a few occasions, Helen had wanted to take a stand and fight off the bigots, but Rafe insisted they pick their battles wisely, not ones in which they were so outnumbered.

"Besides, I'm used to it, babe," he said over and over.

Helen wanted desperately to fight for him, to wipe away all the hurts he'd suffered over the years—still suffered.

For now, she could only think about the dangerously narrow trail they were traveling. They were proceeding down the five-mile trail to Rich Bar—a narrow path along a steep incline with a dangerous precipice on one side. One misstep of their horses, and they would fall hundreds of feet down the almost perpendicular cliff into a dun-colored canyon.

Rafe kept throwing out encouraging words behind her. "Just a little bit longer, honey. Don't give up. You'll be okay."

She couldn't even turn to glare at him. Not that she was able to answer anyway, her jaw was clenched so tightly.

"Just stare straight ahead," Rafe advised. "Don't look to the side."

So Helen concentrated on the tiny valley ahead of them, only eight hundred or so yards in length, and a mere thirty yards wide. The Feather River, *Las Plumas,* meandered along at its base, hemmed in by lofty mountains of beautiful fir trees.

Finally, they reached the bottom of the trail, which emerged at the edge of the small town. A gloomy atmosphere pervaded the dismal camp. Little sunshine ever reached this deep recess in the tall mountains.

Miners right and left put down their tools and gaped. She wasn't sure if it was shock at the sight of two new travelers, or that rare commodity—a woman.

Helen was shaking so badly she couldn't dismount. Rafe came up quickly and pulled her off the horse and into his arms.

"Damn, Helen, I'm sorry. I never would have come if

I'd known it would be this dangerous.'' He was holding her tightly, one hand at the nape of her neck, pressing her face against his heaving chest, the other hand making wide sweeps across her back. ''Stop shaking, honey, please. It's okay now.''

It was the first time in four days that Rafe had embraced her, and she clung to him with embarrassing fervor. Even when her shivering ceased, she wrapped her arms around his waist, relishing the feel of his warm body.

She drew away slightly. ''I love you, Rafe.''

''I know, honey. I love you, too.''

''But right now, I hate you, too.''

He grimaced. ''I don't blame you, I guess.''

''And do you know what the worst part is?''

''What?''

''We have to go back up that blasted trail to go home.''

A week later, they were still stuck in Rich Bar, and Rafe was not a happy camper. ''I hate beans. I hate red calico. I hate fleas and lice. I hate the song, 'Sweet Betsy from Pike.' I hate chewing tobacco. I hate celibacy,'' were just a few of his complaints.

She wasn't feeling too jolly herself, for numerous reasons.

No Pablo. Apparently, he hadn't arrived yet, although his brother Carlos worked as a bartender at the Indiana House.

No gold prospecting. Rich Bar had a law against claims for foreigners, and Rafe, being of Mexican heritage, was considered a foreigner. But they couldn't leave Rich Bar for other diggings until Pablo arrived and they retrieved the precious harness and parachutes.

No sex. This had become a particularly tense subject since they were pretending to be married and, therefore, had to share a bed at the Empire Hotel. Rafe claimed his jaw hurt from grinding his teeth all the time, and Helen had taken to *ooohm*ing almost twenty-four hours a day.

No money. Their meager supply of gold, earned in Sacramento and replenished slightly with Rafe's prospecting along the way, was fast dwindling with the exorbitant prices for lodging and food. Rafe had been forced to take a job dealing monte in a local gambling hall when his efforts to set up a law office failed because no one would hire a Mexican attorney.

She was considering taking a job as a "waitress" at the Lucky Dollar Saloon, which pretty much amounted to letting a bunch of lecherous men ogle her in a revealing gown while she handed out overpriced drinks. That was why she'd asked Rafe to come now to the Indiana House for dinner.

She studied him across the table, fiddling with his tin cup of coffee. He wore the usual miner's garb of red flannel shirt with suspenders and homespun trousers. He'd shaved just before they left the hotel—God, she liked to watch him shave—and his smooth skin only accented the dark circles of worry under his eyes and the bleak dullness in his eyes.

She reached out a hand and covered his on the table.

"No touching, remember?" he said huskily, raising his chin to look at her. At the same time, he turned his hand and twined his fingers with hers. Their gazes held, and the pulse in her wrist beat strongly against his.

"Rafe, Jack Fulton asked me to work in the Lucky Dollar. The pay would be . . . well, phenomenal."

He tugged his hand out of their clasp. "Doing what? Corkscrewing?"

She recoiled. "Waitressing."

"No."

"But, Rafe, we can use the money, and—"

"No." He glared at her icily.

Helen knew Rafe's pride was at stake. He wanted to be able to care for her himself. But pride could only go so far.

"Maybe we should leave Rich Bar for a while and go somewhere else where I can file a claim. We could leave word with Carlos to tell his brother how desperately we need the parachutes."

"You know that's not a good solution."

"You're not working for a damned whorehouse." His face was flushed with anger.

"It's not a whorehouse. It's a bar, and there's nothing wrong with being a waitress."

"Get real! It may be a bar, but what the hell do you think Rosalinda and Irene do there?"

Rosalinda was married to Carlos. She and Irene were among the half-dozen females in the entire town of five hundred men.

"They're hookers, sweetie," Rafe continued more softly, "and Jack plans the same for you, too. If not now, eventually."

Helen blushed. She'd suspected as much. "Then let's go back to the landing site. I could probably make a parachute with some canvas material and lightweight rope."

"Are you nuts? No way am I jumping off a cliff with a homemade parachute. And neither are you."

She tapped her fingertips on the tabletop, deep in thought. "Rafe, have you ever considered that we might not be able to return to the future? What would we do if we couldn't go home?"

He pondered her question seriously for several seconds, then smiled. "We'd hit the sack so fast they'd think a tornado had hit town. We'd make love every which way, and then some. We'd set a new world record for multiple orgasms. We'd probably come up for air in about a week, then go down again."

She propped her elbows on the table and braced her chin in her cupped hands. "What about birth control?"

He shrugged helplessly. "The way I feel, I know I wouldn't be able to keep my hands off you. We'd probably have babies coming out of our ears. A dozen, at least." He shuddered. "It boggles the mind."

She smiled widely, not as appalled at the prospect as he. "Forget Pablo and the parachutes. Let's stay."

His face went white. "Don't even kid about that."

"Who said I was kidding?"

He took her hand again and lifted it to his lips, nipping

241

at the knuckles with his teeth before pressing a light kiss over them. "Behave, Helen. You promised."

"I did?" Geez, just that playful touch of his lips on her skin set all kinds of indecent thoughts racing through her mind. She tugged on his hand and reciprocated the gesture, giving his knuckles a little bite and a kiss, adding a quick lick of her tongue.

He exhaled sharply.

She inhaled sharply.

A dangerous game, and they both knew it.

Rafe started to lean across the table, his lips coming closer and closer to hers.

"Well, don't you two jist beat all—" a booming female voice interrupted them with fortunate timing—"making lovey-dovey all the time. Tarnation! How long did you say you bin married?"

A strapping young woman of almost six feet, big-boned and dressed like the miners right down to her heavy boots, dragged a chair up to their table and straddled it from the back. Mary Stanfield, known only as "The Indiana Girl" because her father owned the hotel in which they were eating, smiled at them companionably. She had become a good friend to them this past week, delighting in their horror over the five-mile trek down the mountain. Last spring, she'd walked down that same dangerous trail carrying a fifty-pound sack of flour on her back.

"What kin I do fer you folks?" she said, chortling as Rafe and Helen jerked their hands apart. "We got Hangtown fries on the menu today."

"What are Hangtown fries?" Helen asked, putting her hands on her lap under the table. They still trembled from Rafe's kiss. She saw Rafe do the same thing, then wink.

"You ne'er heard of Hangtown fries? Land's sake! Where you been? They's a mix of fried-up eggs and bacon and oysters. Mighty fine eatin' ta fill a hollow stummick, iffen I do say so myself."

"Oysters!" she exclaimed.

"No, I don't think Helen and I need any oysters," Rafe

added drolly. "I'll just have the usual. Venison steak and coffee."

"We're out of taters."

"That's okay. Just give me some extra bread."

"Is there any trout?" Helen asked.

"There's allus trout. If there's one thing the Feather gives us, 'ceptin' chilblains, it's a good supply of fish. Lordy, sometimes I smell them scaly critters in my sleep."

"I'll have the trout then. And coffee, too."

After delivering their food, and a special treat of blueberry cobbler, Mary sat down with them again. "You folks thought anymore 'bout my suggestion that you link up with Zeb on his claim?"

Helen glanced over at the corner where Zebediah Franklin sat, snoring drunkenly, as usual. Apparently, the old man had a promising claim high up in the mountains that he'd abandoned after his wife died six months before.

"You know we can't leave Rich Bar until Pablo arrives," Helen reminded Mary. They'd told her that the young bandit had an important possession of theirs without giving her too many details about their past.

Mary shrugged.

"Besides," Rafe added, "Zeb's claim is probably taken over by someone else by now."

"There ain't too many men willing ta work that high in the mountains. It's a mighty lonely spot, I hear."

"So, you're saying that the spot is so remote and dangerous that even a Mexican could file a claim without pure-blooded Americans having any objections?" Rafe remarked caustically.

"Don't go takin' that wrathy tone with me," Mary snapped. "I ain't got nuthin' ta do with them furriner rules."

"I'm sick of rules," Rafe muttered.

"Me, too." Helen flashed a secret smile at Rafe.

He groaned.

"I got some more of them dime novels," Mary told Helen. "Yank brought 'em over yestiddy from his store on Smith's Bar."

Gunfire rang out down the street, but that wasn't unusual. Guns were always being fired. This time, though, a woman's screams accompanied the repeated firing, and men started running down the street, past the Indiana House, toward the outskirts of town. One of the miners yelled in, "Some Mex greaser jist killed Frank Bollings and his partner, Hiram Flagg. They's gonna be a lynchin', fer sure."

More gunfire followed.

Rafe and Helen exchanged wary looks, then rose to rush after Mary and the excited miners. Helen thought about her earlier teasing with Rafe, how she'd hinted that staying in the past might not be such a bad idea. She changed her mind now.

Rafe put an arm around her shoulder, pulling her close. "Maybe we should go home. Maybe I'd be willing to jump off a cliff with a homemade parachute, after all. Maybe it's time to leave this hellhole of the past."

Unfortunately, they soon learned that it was too late.

Chapter Seventeen

A high-pitched scream rang in the air, and went on and on and on.

Mary rushed along with them down the crowded street, drawn by the wrenching cry. Even Zeb had awakened from his drunken stupor to lope behind them, remarking woozily, between belches, "Mebbe it's the haints come ta punish us fer our fornicatin' ways."

"Shut up, you old fool," Mary called back. "You ain't done no more fornicatin' than I have in a good spell. If there's any punishin' ta be ladled out, it'll come from the Good Lord's pitcher and it'll be fer all the corn likker you bin suckin' up."

"Hell's bells! Do you allus have ta talk so gol-durned loud, Mary? My stummick feels like the bottom of a milk churn."

"If you weren't so rip-snortin' corned all the time—"

"Oh, my God!" Helen shrieked, stopping short. She couldn't believe the horror unfolding before her.

Rosalinda, the Mexican prostitute from The Lucky Dollar, was being held back by two men, one of them her boss, Jack Fulton, and the other, Curtis Bancroft, owner of the Empire Hotel. The wild-eyed young woman was covered with blood, although she appeared to have no wounds. She was alternately screaming and crying, then throwing out insults to the angry prospectors. *"Ay, Diós mío!* You bastards! You killed my husband. Damn you all to hell. Oh, Carlos! *Mi esposo!"*

On the ground lay her husband, Carlos, Pablo's brother.

Blood poured from a fatal bullet wound delivered to his chest. Beside him on the ground were two white men, presumably Hiram Flagg and Frank Bollings, their faces and necks and chests covered with multiple stab wounds.

Rosalinda held a bloody knife in her hand.

In the background, near the canvas-roofed hovel where Carlos and Rosalinda had lived, stood a dry-eyed Mexican boy of about eight, holding a wailing, near-naked infant in his small arms.

"Que pasa? What's going on here?'' Rafe said, pushing men aside to step forward. He addressed Rosalinda, who was still restrained by the two men.

Her crazed eyes fixed on Rafe, recognizing a potential lifeline in this mob of bloodthirsty men calling for a lynching. She spewed out a fiery explanation in Spanish, at one point spitting on the two white men at her feet. This caused the miners to edge closer with raised fists. Rafe questioned her in her native tongue, gesticulating with his hands.

Finally, Rafe told the crowd, "She says these two men broke into her home and tried to rape her.''

"Ya cain't rape a whore. Ever'one knows that,'' one man shouted.

Rafe ignored that ludicrous remark. "She says the men were drunk. She was in bed with her husband. Her two children were sleeping on a pallet on the floor when the men barged in.''

Mr. Bancroft spoke up then. "That's no excuse for killing two men.''

The miners heartily agreed, chanting, "Lynch the harlot.''

"I'd like to remind you, Mr. Bancroft, that there are three dead men here. Not two,'' Rafe said coldly.

Mr. Bancroft's face flushed red and his lips thinned into a surly frown. He did not like being corrected by Rafe. Could it be because he was a Mexican?

"When Carlos asked the men to leave, they refused,'' Rafe continued to translate. "Carlos declined to leave his home with his two children so these men could rape his *unwilling* wife. That's when they shot him without warning or provocation."

His words prompted many shouts from the crowd.

"That's her word."

"Who sez a whore is ever unwillin'?"

"He wuz jist a dirty Mex. A furriner. Ain't like he wuz a real American. The Jezebel had no call ta stab Hiram and Frank. They wuz good fellers. Good American fellers."

Helen had met Hiram and Frank. In her opinion, the two men had been lowlifes. Mary made a clucking sound of disgust next to her, obviously sharing her opinion.

"Who are you ta be speakin' fer Rosalinda?" Mr. Stanfield, Mary's father, spoke up. He was a good-hearted, honest man, but clearly a product of his primitive time and place.

Rafe raised his chin defiantly. "I'm her lawyer. Surely, even a Mexican has a right to a trial in this country. I thought that was the *American* way."

Some of the miners didn't like the challenge at all, and their grumbling threats grew louder.

"Perhaps we should string him up, too," one red-faced New Englander said in a thick Boston accent. "In fact, let's get rid of all these greasers in town. They're always stealing our gold and our women. Maybe we need to teach them all a lesson."

"Now, now, we'll have none of that," Mr. Bancroft said, trying to be a voice of sanity in an insane situation. "Let's take Rosalinda back to the Empire. Since we got no jail, we'll lock her in one of my hotel rooms. Tomorrow we'll call a miners' meeting, and select a jury ta decide the case. By the law."

"You kin be her lawyer, if you want," Mr. Stanfield added, sizing Rafe up with disdain. "And, yes, we got our laws. Even here." He surveyed the mob. "Ain't that right, fellers?"

The disgruntled mob soon disbanded, following the keening woman and her captors to her "jail." Mary went with them to help secure the woman in her "cell." After a wagon came to cart off the three bodies for burial, Rafe and Helen stood, alone, staring at each other with dismay.

Well, not quite alone. The little Mexican boy stood frozen near the hut, shifting from foot to foot under the heavy burden of the baby he held precariously on one hip. The infant's cries had faded to a long string of unending whimpers.

Helen went over and hunkered down in front of them. "Can I help?" she asked softly, reaching for the baby.

He clutched the infant even tighter, causing the baby to start screaming again. All the time, his huge black eyes stared at her as if she were the enemy. The only sign of emotion in the boy was the trembling of his lower lip.

Helen patted the baby's filthy head and tried to calm its sobs, to no avail. "Shhh," she crooned, "everything will be all right. That's it, darling." The baby's gaunt face reddened and it screamed even louder.

"Hell!" Rafe muttered and walked over to them, dragging his feet reluctantly. He shot out a string of words in Spanish to the boy, who immediately handed the baby over to him.

"What did you say to him?" Helen asked.

"I told him to hand over the kid or I'd kick his ass."

"Oh, you did not!"

Rafe said something foul under his breath about not being able to escape babies, even in a nightmare.

"What's wrong?" Helen asked worriedly fifteen minutes later when the baby persisted in crying, even when Rafe cradled it against his shoulder and patted its back in an expert fashion.

"Follow me," he said, ducking his head to enter the little makeshift house.

It was only a ten-by-ten-foot structure with a dirt floor, a homemade rope bed, a rough table with two chairs, and a Mexican rag rug on the ground. They must have cooked outdoors because there was no stove or fireplace.

"See if you can find some soap and water and a clean cloth to diaper the baby," he ordered Helen. He told the boy, who hesitantly disclosed that his name was Hector, to prepare a sugar teat until they could take the infant to be nursed by his mother at the Empire.

Rafe laid the baby gently on the bed and undid the soiled cloth tied on either side of its tiny hips. It was a girl. With a grunt of disgust, he tossed the stinking rags to the corner. The baby's cries died down to soft hiccoughs as she stared up at Rafe, who was alternately blowing on her grubby, sunken stomach and crooning soft Spanish words. "Hush now, *niña*. Hush now."

Helen handed Rafe a tin basin with a scrap of cotton fabric and a pottery bowl of soft, pungent soap. Little by little, Rafe washed the still whimpering child from dark silky hair to perfect toes.

He inhaled sharply when he was done. "Get a load of this."

The little girl's sallow skin was covered with flea and mosquito bites, and her bottom was raw with diaper rash.

"And she's sick, too. The color of her skin isn't right."

"What do you think it is?"

He shook his head hopelessly. "I don't know. Maybe jaundice. Maybe worse. Her ribs are practically sticking out."

On Rafe's advice, Helen rushed back to their hotel room to get her ointment. She asked around for a doctor, but learned there was none residing in the town. Returning shortly, she stopped in the doorway, frozen with disbelief. Her heart expanded almost to breaking and her eyes burned at the sight before her.

Rafe sat on the bed with his back propped against the headboard, softly singing a Spanish lullaby. The baby was cradled in one arm against his chest, sucking rhythmically on the hunk of sugar-coated cloth he held at its pursed lips. Hector cuddled against his other side, fast asleep, with a skinny arm thrown over Rafe's waist, holding on for dear life. In sleep, tears made white tracks down his grungy face.

Rafe looked up, noticing her for the first time, and their eyes locked for a long moment.

"It doesn't mean a thing," he said finally. His face was blank, but his voice was raspy.

"How can you . . . I just don't understand you, Rafe. I mean, how can a man who is so good with children not want any of his own?" she cried out.

"If I'm good with kids, it's because I've been surrounded by them all my life. I had no choice," he said bitterly. "But I'll be damned if I make the same choice for my own future."

Hot air choked Helen's lungs. She could think of no words to convince him he was wrong.

The baby girl sighed, and the makeshift teat fell out of her darling angel-bow mouth. Then, reflexively, her tiny fist closed over Rafe's finger, clutching. Her lips settled into sleepy exhaustion, her sunken chest wheezing up and down.

Rafe gazed down at the infant and his lips curved with tenderness as he traced a knuckle along her downy cheek. He seemed to catch himself immediately. Glaring at Helen, he repeated, "It doesn't mean a thing."

But Helen was hopeful for the first time in days. And she couldn't love Rafe more than she did at that moment.

The baby died the next night.

They hanged Rosalinda four days later.

Helen sat at the Indiana House with Mary afterward, shaking from the ordeal. "How could they? Oh, it was horrible!"

"I told you not ta go," Mary said gruffly, patting her on the shoulder. They were sitting in Mary's small sitting room off the main dining area. "Besides, Rosalinda wuz a no-good slut. She din't deserve yer pity."

"That's not the point," Helen said. "Over the past few days, you and I have gotten to know Rosalinda well. You're right. She was a coarse, immoral, totally unlikable person. I couldn't believe how unfeeling she was when her baby died."

"Yep. All she said wuz, 'She's better off dead.' The woman was lower'n a snake's belly."

Helen nodded. "Even so, I can't fathom a society that would hang a woman—or a man—on so little evidence. That 'trial' yesterday before the Miners' Committee was nothing but a kangaroo court."

Mary shrugged. "I mus' say that yer man's lawyerin' wuz mighty fancy. I could see how puffed up with pride you wuz fer him."

"He did do a good job, didn't he?" Helen beamed. "It's not his fault that the jury was predisposed to convict any Mexican who killed an American. All they were interested in was rushing off to the nearest saloon to celebrate."

"Now, let me give you a bit of caution, honey," Mary said sternly. "I wouldn't be talkin' thataway. Folks're already fired up at yer husband fer interferin' with the trial. And the feelin's toward Mexicans is running high. Don't be rilin' 'em up no more. It's over, and you gotta be thinkin' 'bout yer own future."

Helen swallowed hard and looked toward the doorway. Rafe should be back soon. A short time ago, he and Zeb had gone with the boy to his old house to pick up any personal belongings that were left. The ramshackle hovel had been taken over almost immediately by four miners, even before the jury's verdict.

"What will happen to Hector now?"

"Well, I don't rightly know." Mary scratched her head. "He's become real attached ta Zeb, fer some reason. Guess he kinda looks on 'im as a gran'pappy. Zeb lost two sons and a daughter ta the cholera years ago, an' he's been so consarned lonely since his Effie died. Well, who knows! The good Lord do work in mysterious ways sometimes."

"Perhaps Pablo will take Hector when he comes," Helen offered. "After all, he is the boy's uncle."

"Mebbe," Mary said dubiously.

Hector had been staying with Rafe and Helen and Zeb the last few days, all crowded into the one hotel room. She couldn't exactly recall how Zeb and Hector had become part of their group. It just seemed to happen.

The boy hadn't seen his mother die that morning, but he

couldn't help but be aware of what was happening. He never cried, and he rarely talked, although they'd learned that he spoke fluent English, having grown up in brothels patronized by mostly American men. His only show of emotion was the way he clung tenaciously to Zeb—his only anchor in this crazy world.

Helen's gloomy thoughts were broken then as Rafe showed up, with Zeb and Hector following close behind. And Helen realized that, like Hector, Rafe wasn't showing much emotion, either, these days.

He'd become attached to the baby—Maria had been her name—and Helen knew that her death had affected him deeply. But he never wept or talked about it, not even when he'd dug her tiny grave on a rocky hillside outside town.

Immersing himself in Rosalinda's case throughout the day, and dealing monte at night, had been his way of handling his grief. All to no avail. Rosalinda was dead, and their supply of money was virtually depleted.

She stood and walked over to him. Although he remained stiff and unresponsive, she wrapped her arms around his waist and hugged him tight. Only when he relaxed a bit and mumbled something about her cutting off his circulation did she let him loose. He smiled grimly at her attempt to comfort him and palmed her bottom, rubbing intimately.

"Ra-afe!"

"Just checking to see if it was still there."

At least his humor was back, even if it was at her expense.

Mary chuckled and Hector giggled, the first sound of amusement she'd heard from him. Zeb added sagely, "A man should pinch his wife's arse at least onct a day ta show 'er who's boss. That's what my pappy allus said."

Mary guffawed, leaning down to give Zeb a whack on the back.

The old man cringed. "Tarnation, girl, you got the boomiest voice in the whole valley. Even worse than that feller of yers . . . What's his name? Hank?"

"Not Hank. Yank. And he's not my feller."

"Hah! He follers you around like a randy bull. Givin' you those yellow dime novels to get yer juices risin'. Yep, I'd say he's yer feller all right. Jist waitin' fer the right moment ta corner ya, he is."

They all laughed then, forgetting for the moment the somber situation they were in.

That evening, very late, Helen sat up waiting for Rafe to finish his shift at the gambling hall. She tried to read one of Mary's dime novels, *The Maiden and the Knave,* by lantern light, but was too distracted by her many worries.

Zeb and Hector slept soundly on the floor, wrapped in the extra blankets Rafe had brought from the house.

Helen needed to talk to Rafe about their future. So many things were happening to them so quickly. Maybe now he'd agree to go back to the landing site. But what about Pablo? And the parachutes? Exhaustion soon overtook her, and she decided to lie down, just for a minute.

It was already daylight when she awakened to a loud pounding on the door. The first thing she did was look to her left in the bed.

No Rafe.

Oh, my God! He never came back from work. Something must have happened. Oh, my God!

"It's that Indiana Girl," Zeb said, sitting up groggily on his floor pallet.

"Helen, open up. It's me, Mary."

Helen opened the door. "What? What's happened?"

"It's yer husband. He's been hurt. Now, don't get yerself all in a fret. He ain't dead."

Dead? That thought had never occurred to Helen. Helen dressed and hurried over to the Indiana House with Mary. Despite her admonitions to stay behind, Zeb and Hector followed after them.

Along the way, Mary informed her, "We found him in the back of The Lucky Dollar. He wuz beaten up mighty bad, but don't you be worryin' none. Papa and me strapped up those cracked ribs and cleaned up the blood from—"

253

"Blood?" Helen squeaked out.

Mary waved her hand with unconcern. "Mostly jist from a wallop to the nose. He has a few loose teeth, but he din't lose none. Lots of bruises, though."

Well, that's reassuring. "Who did this?" Helen asked icily.

"I don't rightly know, and I don't think yer husband does, either. Too dark las' night."

"But why?"

"To teach 'im a lesson, and cuz he's a Mexican, I s'pose. Mos' addlepated men don't need much reason fer a fight."

Helen seethed with indignation. The slimy bigots!

"You know you two have got ta leave Rich Bar, don't you? Tain't safe fer you here."

Helen nodded. Maybe this would be the push that would convince Rafe they should try to go home.

"Course, you got to head north fer a bit," Mary added, as if reading her mind.

Helen shivered with foreboding, sensing she would not like Mary's next words.

She didn't.

"Some men come up from Sacramento City yestiddy, and they claim yer husband is some outlaw—the Angel Bandit, I think—and yer some soiled dove by the name of Elena." She eyed Helen suspiciously. "I don't s'pose you know anythin' 'bout that?"

Helen's chin dropped before she started to howl with laughter, probably hysteria. She was still laughing when she and Mary, arms linked, entered the room where Rafe had been taken.

"Great! I'm dying, and she's laughing," Rafe slurred, his eyelids fluttering in an effort to fight sleep, or unconsciousness.

Helen looked at Mr. Stanfield, who sat near the bed. "We gave him a few dollops of whiskey ta kill the pain," he explained sheepishly.

"A few dollops!" Mary whooped. " 'Pears ta me you dumped the whole durn jug down his gullet."

Helen moved closer to the bed, and her laughter died.

Mr. Stanfield had removed all Rafe's clothes, except for his boxers. To her horror, she saw that most of Rafe's body, from forehead to calves, was covered with cuts or bruises or swellings. Tight strips of linen had been wrapped around his ribs.

Rafe moaned.

In that instant, Helen made a decision. It was the only decision she could make, of course. She had to get Rafe somewhere to recuperate, where he would be safe until the time was right to return to the future.

"Zeb," she said, turning to the old man standing behind her in the doorway, twisting his hat in his hands. Tears misted his eyes, witness to the affection he'd come to feel for Rafe these past few days.

"Yessum?" Zeb answered, stepping forward.

"Is your offer still open for Rafe and me to work your claim with you up in the mountains?"

Zeb's rheumy eyes brightened with sudden hope. "Thanks be ta God! It surely is."

"Then it looks like we're all going to be gold prospectors together for a while. Partners."

"God sent you two ta save me," Zeb declared vehemently. "I jist knew Effie would have a talk with the good Lord, and He sent you, sure as shootin'."

Helen smiled at his whimsical words.

Hector tugged on Zeb's hand, and both of them looked at Helen.

Helen hesitated for only a moment. "Heck, why not! Yes, Hector can come with us, too."

In a spirit of camaraderie, they turned to the bed, where Rafe was snoring lightly. At least, they thought he was snoring until he cracked one eye open and tried to grin through his split lip. He held out a hand for Helen, and she sat down next to him on the bed, barely stifling a cry over his pitiful condition.

"Am I still a handsome devil?" he teased. He looked like a battered Rocky after the worst of his fights.

"Oh, yeah."

He crooked the fingers of one hand at her, motioning her closer. When her face was near his, he whispered, almost knocking her over with the fumes from his whiskey breath, "Did Zeb tell you the name of his claim?"

She shook her head slowly, wary of the gleam in Rafe's eyes.

"Angel Valley," he informed her with a laugh that came out more like a choke. "It must be fate."

She pressed a soft kiss on his cheek and brushed a strand of hair off his forehead. It was matted with blood.

"Helen, my tongue feels funny."

"It's probably numb from the booze."

"Nope," he said, attempting to shake his head but groaning with the painful effort. "I think my tongue's having a hard-on."

Helen laughed through her tears. "You're delirious."

"No, I'm not," Rafe argued. "Come and lie down with me, Helen. I want you to check my tongue."

She pulled her hand out of his and eased herself off the bed. "Behave, Rafe."

"We're all partners now, aren't we?" Rafe asked with a little sweep of his hand that encompassed her and Zeb and Hector.

"Yes," she agreed.

His eyes were serious then. "Are you my partner, Helen?"

She knew the question had meanings beyond the mere words, but she didn't need time to consider. "Yes."

Chapter Eighteen

Higher and higher they climbed, for four long days, into the thickly wooded Sierra Nevada mountains.

As the bird flies, it should have taken them only one day, but there wasn't any road up the pine-scented, sometimes impenetrable terrain. The higher they climbed, the cooler and thinner the air became. No wonder the number of prospectors dwindled to almost zero as they moved farther from civilization.

"Don't you be worryin' none," Zeb kept reassuring them. "You'll see, it's the bes' spot in all Californey. A real paradise, Angel Valley is."

Helen *was* impressed with the splendor of their surroundings. Pine trees rose to monumental heights. In the safety of age-old solitude, deer stood surprisingly near, watching their progress with limpid eyes before bounding off.

But what a crew we are! Helen thought with a rueful shake of her head.

First, an aging prospecter cussing out his stubborn mule, and spitting. *Spitting!* Zeb had given up boozing, but he persisted with his equally deplorable habit—tobacco chewing. *Yeech!*

Second, an eight-year-old Mexican boy whose brooding silence melted away layer by layer the farther they traveled from Rich Bar. Hector's constant, youthful chattering amazed them all. You'd never know the resilient boy had just lost both parents and a little sister. The child took great delight in every little animal—the tiny lizards who peered up from mossy rocks, the pastel-colored butterflies flitting

257

amongst the numerous wildflowers, and the saucy squirrels nibbling on sweet acorns.

Third, a battered, infuriating, gorgeous L.A. lawyer who rode his F. Lee horse stoically up the punishing incline. One eye was swollen almost completely shut. His bottom lip was split and seeping blood. At each rest stop, Helen checked his ribs and drew the bandages tighter. But, as they traveled, his tight jaw and occasional blue language were his only concessions to what must be unbearable torture for his beaten body.

And finally, her—a presumably sane, level-headed military officer skipping off into the wilderness with a stranger, who could be Freddy Krueger for all they knew, and an even more dangerous male who melted her heart with the smallest glance.

She smiled. A little while ago, they'd started to travel downhill, and the riding was easier.

"There it is! There it is!" Zeb shouted and kicked his mule to spur it down the remainder of the sloping path. Hector galloped quickly after him on his pony.

"Oh, my God!" Helen and Rafe exclaimed at the same time.

It *was* paradise, just as Zeb had boasted. She and Rafe exchanged a look of incredulity.

Zeb's crude cabin nestled at the bottom of a tiny valley, surrounded on four sides by the verdant blue fir trees of the Sierra Nevada. The cabin was surrounded by colorful flowers and bushes that Effie had transplanted from the woods. A small garden, overrun with weeds, held prominence behind the home.

On the far right, melted snow from the high summits rippled down through the mountain channels to cascade into a small, picturesque lagoon. The blue pool then meandered off into a stream that bisected the valley about twenty feet from the home.

Another, smaller dwelling—a rock-and-sod hut—was built right into the side of the mountain, with only rocks visible in the front and a plank and canvas roof. It was probably the original cabin, but now served as a makeshift barn.

Rafe nudged his horse slowly forward. Helen moved up alongside him.

"This is the homestead me and Effie built fer ourselves ten years ago," Zeb said in a wistful voice, walking up to them. His mule and Hector's pony grazed on the soft grass near the creek bank. Hector was already running about, examining everything with boyish eagerness. "It was a new beginning fer us after our children passed on. I know it ain't much right now, but we allus dreamed of buildin' a bigger place,'specially onct the Gold Rush commenced." He peeked up at them, obviously seeking approval.

"It's wonderful, Zeb. You and Effie must have been very happy here."

His eyes welled up and he put a big red handkerchief to his nose to honk loudly.

Helen slid her right leg over the back of the horse and stepped to the ground. Every muscle in her body revolted and she could only imagine how Rafe must feel. She turned to him. "You'd better dismount and let me check your ribs again."

When he didn't answer but continued to press his lips together, Helen moved closer, little alarm bells going off in her head. Rafe's dark complexion appeared grayish white, and his eyes glazed over. When she touched his forearm in concern, a feverish heat emanated from his skin.

"I can't move," he gritted out and slumped forward.

"He must be in shock," she cried to Zeb.

After she and Zeb somehow managed to get Rafe off the horse and into the cabin, he collapsed, unconscious, onto the dusty bedstead built into one wall. It was not a promising introduction to their new life in Angel Valley.

A month later, Rafe lay on his back in the cozy bed, a homemade quilt drawn up to his waist. Zeb and Hector were out at the stream, trying some nighttime fishing. At dusk, he and Zeb had finished their nineteenth straight

Sandra Hill

twelve-hour day of back-breaking gold prospecting. Thus far, they'd only accumulated a grand total of three hundred dollars in gold dust—about one-twenty-fifth of its 1996 value.

But Rafe was still hopeful.

He was supposedly still recuperating—thus his early retiring to bed—but he was really relishing their bucolic surroundings, a real switch for a city boy who usually only heard police sirens and honking horns from his L.A. home. Closing his eyes, he listened to the night sounds—a breeze whispering through the trees, crickets chirping, coyotes and wolves howling, the occasional hoot of an owl or scream of a wildcat, deer rutting, and always the bubbling stream.

With an odd contentment, he opened his eyes and inhaled deeply, savoring the smells of pine and wood smoke and Helen. Mostly, he was watching Helen as she moved about the lantern-lit cabin, tidying up from their evening meal— baked mountain quail with mushroom stuffing, wild endive garnished with vinegar dressing, fresh bread, and even a dried-apple tart for dessert. She'd adapted well to their primitive surroundings.

He, on the other hand, felt the usual raging fever boiling just under the surface of his skin. Oh, it wasn't from his injuries; he'd recovered from the beating within a week of their arrival at Angel Valley. This fever had bloomed out of control since the day they'd arrived at Zeb's cabin and Helen had put aside her nineteenth-century gown for the sake of practicality, donning camouflage pants, tight green Army T-shirt, *and no bra*.

Her perfect Vargas breasts drew his eyes like a honing device. All the time.

They swayed as she bent over the fireplace to check the contents of the iron kettle.

They jutted out, perfectly still, as she stood at the stream giving him constant advice on how better to pan for gold. Even her nagging and the icy cold water up to his thighs didn't tamp down his need for her.

They pressed into his back like branding irons in the

middle of the night. Because Zeb and Hector believed they were married, they slept on makeshift pallets near the fire. He and Helen shared the big bed, which was entirely too small for both of them and his nonstop arousal.

They were a visual reminder of the night they'd spent in the cave and their perfect lovemaking. He wanted desperately to be inside her again, to hear her whisper that she loved him, to take her shout of his name into his mouth at her climax.

But he had no condoms, no sure-fire methods of birth control, and he could not, *would not,* take the chance of impregnating Helen.

"I'm going to go brush my teeth," Helen informed him. *Good! Maybe the grating sound of her gargling will get rid of this hard-on.* He stared at her, unblinking. "Maybe you should meditate out there, too, honey." *Yep, gargling and ooohms should put a damper on my dipper.* "Maybe I'll join you. Remember when I meditated with you back at the cave." *Naked.*

A pink blush spread across her face and down her neck. Probably spread over her breasts. And lower. *I'm losin' it here, St. Augustine. Are you sure this celibacy stuff is the best route? Maybe just a little foolin' around would be okay? Maybe if we didn't take our clothes off, we could kiss, and fondle, and—*

"Oh, well, it's probably too late for meditating tonight," Helen interjected blithely. He could have fried an egg on her face.

Thank you, Auggie.

Zeb came in while Helen was still outside gargling. Within seconds, he heard a different gargling sound and realized that Hector had joined Helen. *Gawd!*

"Uh, Rafe . . . uhm . . . there's somethin' I bin meanin' ta say," Zeb stuttered, shucking down to his long underwear and spreading several blankets down on the plank floor by the fireplace.

"Yeah?" he prompted suspiciously.

"You see, I couldn't help noticing how tense you been

lately. And I know a man's got his drives—''

"Drives?" Rafe sputtered out.

"Yessirree," Zeb said, nodding his shaggy gray head. "A man's juices don't never stop flowin' when he's yer age. Anyways, I jist wanted you ta know . . . Uh, gol-durnit, Hector falls fast asleep onct his head hits this here pallet. And me, well, I'm a heavy sleeper. Tarnation, son, what I'm tryin' ta say is, you don't need ta worry none about me hearin' the bed ropes squeakin' through the night. Jist go to it."

Rafe started to laugh, and his chest was still shaking when Helen slipped in beside him a short time later.

"What's so funny?" she asked, making a point of keeping her distance from him in the bed. Her nightly ritual always started out the same—prissy to the point of ridiculous—but by morning she'd be climbing all over him like grapevines on an arbor. And his arbor couldn't stand much more. She always defended herself by saying she wasn't aware of what she did in her sleep, but sometimes he had his doubts.

He moved closer and whispered close to her ear. "Zeb had a man-to-man talk with me tonight."

"Oh?" she whispered back, her fresh breath fluttering against his lips.

Shock waves moved in reaction down to his personal seismograph. It was registering about ten-point-five on his Richter hard-on scale.

"Zeb said that a man's got his 'drives,' and when the juices are flowing, a man and his wife should just 'go to it.' ''

Her mouth curved into a smile.

Blood roared in his ears, and his "scale" went up another notch or two. *If a smile can do that, she'd damn well better not touch me.*

"What about a woman's drives? Did Zeb mention those, too?" She shimmied a little closer, not touching, but near enough that he could feel her body heat. And he could imagine all the rest.

"Do you have drives?" he groaned, closing his eyes against her allure.

She didn't answer, so eventually he turned on his side toward her and cracked open one eye. She was gazing at him with such longing he felt his defenses crumbling. *Help!*

"Rafe, I want you so bad. Let's make love." She moved against him, one hand caressing his face, a leg thrown over his hip. Before he could see past the stars splintering behind his eyelids, she began to plant soft kisses on his bare chest.

With a growl of surrender, he flipped her on her back and rolled on top of her tempting body, between her legs. The nightgown and his boxers were no barrier at all to the consuming passion that melded them together. He ground himself against her center and felt her dampness. He almost climaxed then.

A soft cry filtered through the night air, then died. At first, he thought he or Helen might have moaned. But it was Hector whimpering in his sleep. His cry sounded just like a baby's, a signal Rafe had heard over and over throughout the thin walls of his childhood homes in the L.A. projects. A call to responsibility, and distasteful duties, and neverending problems. *Babies.*

With a jerk, he lifted himself off Helen and stood beside the bed. Drawing on his pants, he stared resolutely down at her, his trembling hands clenched into fists at his sides.

"Where are you going?"

"For an icy swim," he said, panting. "If I don't come back, you'll know I've swum all the way to the Pacific Ocean, and I'm still rock hard and wanting you."

"Oh, Rafe."

"Save the 'Oh, Rafe's' for later, babe. There's gonna come a day of reckoning when I collect for every damn one of these days of abstinence. But not now."

"But what if our time never comes?" she murmured under her breath just before he went out the door. But he heard her.

You wouldn't do that to me, would you, God? Yo, St. Augustine?

Rafe heard no God or St. Augustine giving him heavenly reassurance.

He was on his own.

The next morning, Helen and Hector sat at the rough oak table in the center of the cabin. She was peeling carrots she'd managed to salvage from Effie's long-neglected garden out back. The vegetables and some wild onions would taste delicious cooked in the juices of the huge trout—at least eighteen inches long—that she planned to bake later that day.

The boy was bent over a piece of paper from her tablet, diligently writing out the letters of the alphabet. His tongue peeked out between his lips as he concentrated. Although the eight-year-old could speak fluent English and his native Spanish, he'd never been taught to read or write. At Zeb and Rafe's urging, she'd initiated two-hour daily lessons for Hector. She enjoyed the chore immensely.

In fact, she was surprised at the satisfaction she derived from homemaking, too. Normally, Helen would have been offended at being relegated to caring for the tiny home and the cooking chores—a woman's job—when she was more than capable of performing a man's job just as well. But she loved every minute of her domestic duties.

She cared for the log cabin as if it were a castle. The only furniture in the single room—about twenty feet square—was the massive built-in bedstead, which she'd come to think of as her torture chamber, and the oak table with matching benches. Off to the side were two homemade chairs—upended stumps with cut-off branches serving as tripod legs, and Effie's prized, armless rocking chair.

A cooking fireplace took up one wall. The only light came from the open doorway and two most unusual windows. There was no glass, but Zeb had cut out two windows in facing walls and filled them with colored bottles and glass jars, the area between their necks being filled in with clay. When she'd asked Zeb where he'd got so many pieces of glassware, he told her they'd previously held brandied fruit and pickles and liquor. It had been his wife's idea, he'd added, and the result was a stained-glass effect when the sun shone brightly.

Effie's touch was evident in other areas of the primitive dwelling, as well: Her hand-stitched crimson calico curtains—*was there any other color?* Helen wondered; exquisite quilts; a few pieces of china displayed on a wooden shelf Zeb had built for that purpose; rag rugs thrown over the rough puncheon floor.

Helen looked over and saw that Hector had been watching her closely. "I don't ever want to leave here," he said fiercely. "This is my home now."

"Of course it is, honey," she said, patting his hand.

"You and Mr. Rafe are gonna leave sometime, though," he accused.

"Yes," she conceded, "but we won't abandon you."

"When you go, I'm gonna stay with Mr. Zeb. He sez I kin call him Granpap." His voice quivered with tears of uncertainty.

"We'll see, but it's nothing for you to worry about now." She corrected his work, then scooted him out the door. He and Zeb were going hunting for rabbits that afternoon.

She checked the sourdough in a crock near the fireplace. Mary had given her a starter batch, and every day she added a little flour, sugar, and water to keep it working. With care, it would last forever. She also picked an arrangement of Effie's wildflowers and put them in an empty whiskey bottle. The flowers and the colored light from the "bottle windows" created a warm, homey atmosphere for the cabin.

Afterward, she ambled toward the stream, planning to help Rafe with the gold digging. He was standing thigh-deep in the icy water to the far left of the little valley, working alone. Zeb and Hector must have already left. Usually, a claim was worked by three adult men who could wash out eighty to a hundred pails of dirt a day, but they had to pace themselves here, knowing there were other chores to be done about the cabin.

Many of the miners used more sophisticated methods of prospecting—long toms, or cradles, or sluice boxes—but they required at least a half-dozen men to share the labor. Simple panning—adding water to a pan of dug-up gravel and swirling it around so the water and lighter materials spilled over the top and the heavier masses, like gold, sunk to bottom—was a centuries-old method of prospecting that still worked for the one- or two-man gold-digging operation.

An unusually warm October sun beat down on Rafe's bare back, which glistened with sweat. Occasionally he stopped swinging a pick against the outcropping of rock and he stood, arching his shoulders.

Helen picked up a shovel and pan that Zeb had discarded nearby and scanned the area. She stepped into the frigid stream, boots and all, with her shovel and pan held up high.

"What do you think you're doing?" Rafe asked, just noticing her.

"I'm going to help you."

"No, you're not. Don't come any closer," he warned. "Oh, no, oh, please, don't do anything to get that T-shirt wet."

"Honestly, you have a one-track mind. In the middle of muscle-deadening work, you can still think about—" Her right boot slipped on a moss-covered rock, and her feet went out from under her. She landed flat on her back in the shallow water.

She expected Rafe to be howling with laughter when she came up spluttering for air, flinging her wet hair back over her shoulders. But he was gawking, transfixed, at her sodden chest.

Looking down, she saw her breasts clearly outlined by the clinging fabric right down to the nipples, which had hardened in the cold stream. "Now, Rafe," she said, backing away.

"Son of a bitch!" he exclaimed, throwing his pan and pickax up onto a boulder. "Even St. Augustine was never given this much temptation, I'll bet." He made a flying leap for her, and they both landed in the stream. The snow-cooled waters did nothing to stem his ardor or her fast-matching arousal.

Like a madman pushed beyond his limits, Rafe kissed her lips and neck. His hands roamed frantically over her breasts, across her back, cupping her buttocks. "Touch me ... Oh, please ... Oh, yes, like that," he pleaded, then almost screamed when she did.

They rolled in the water, splashing, falling under, coming up laughing and kissing and trying to speak but only able to come out with disjointed words. When Rafe's mouth closed over Helen's breast, T-shirt and all, she keened and pounded on his back with her fists. "Damn you! Damn you for making me want you this much."

He stood, pulling her to him, grinding himself against her to show how much he wanted her. She wrapped her legs around his waist and licked at his ears while he walked up the bank, hissing out wicked words of retribution he planned to enact on her. Instead of dropping down to the grassy bank with her, as she'd expected, however, he stopped abruptly.

"What?" she asked, drawing her head back to look at him. He was still carrying her with her legs wrapped around his waist.

"Shhhh. Don't move." Backing away, he moved into the water and set her on her feet, drawing her over and onto the wide boulder on the other bank. Only then did she follow his gaze to the cabin, where a loud ruckus took place. A huge grizzly bear appeared in the doorway, their trout dinner in its mouth.

"I don't suppose you brought a gun out here with you," he asked.

She shook her head. "It's in the cabin."

Rafe looked at the pickax in his hand. A lot of good it would do against a thousand-pound beast.

The bear appeared again, and this time it was covered with flour and feathers from Effie's goose-down pillows. Molasses dribbled from its snout.

For more than an hour, they sat perched on the rock

watching helplessly as Big Ben trashed the inside of the cabin. They could only hope he found enough to satisfy his hunger and didn't come seeking human fare. Or that Zeb and Hector wouldn't come back onto this dangerous scene.

Finally, the animal loped out, stood on its hind legs, and let out a mighty roar, eying them across the too-short distance. The grizzly seemed to be considering whether to attack them when another animal roared in the forest—a similar but much shriller bellow. Probably its mate. The bear gave them one last glance and went down on all fours, trotting off into the sunset.

Helen thought about their near lovemaking then, the incident that had been a prequel, so to speak, to this mind-boggling spectacle right out of a Disney wilderness movie. "Well, that was good for me. How about you?" she quipped.

At first, Rafe gaped at her. Then he burst out laughing and pulled her to his side in a warm embrace. "Oh, sweetie, someday we'll tell our grandkids about this." Immediately, he stiffened at his foolhardy words. "I didn't mean that," he quickly amended, "about grandkids, I mean. I just meant that—"

"I know exactly what you meant, Rafe," Helen said tiredly.

Maybe they weren't meant to be together after all.

Then again, maybe Rafe was all wet.

Yeah, she liked that idea.

Chapter Nineteen

By the following evening, everything was back to normal again. The cabin was relatively clean, and no one had been injured. Zeb said they should consider themselves lucky.

Helen sighed, putting aside her uneasy thoughts, and continued to read, "And the redskin's arrow went straight and true through the evil villain's heart, ending his miserable life forever." She put a slip of ribbon on the page to mark her place and closed the book, *The Last of the Mohicans*.

"More," Hector complained sleepily from across the table where he nestled in Rafe's lap.

"That's enough for today, sweetie," she said, putting the worn leather volume on the shelf, along with Zeb's three other precious books, the Bible, Edgar Allen Poe's *The Purloined Letter*, and Charles Dickens's *Oliver Twist*.

Rafe stood with the child in his arms and admonished gently, "Helen said no more tonight, and that's that."

Hector made a whimpering sound of protest and nuzzled Rafe's neck. Rafe laid the boy on his pallet near the fireplace, where he fell instantly asleep. Returning to the table across from Helen, he sipped the last of his coffee. Zeb continued to rock back and forth in Effie's chair, puffing on an unlit pipe—she'd managed to convert him from the revolting chewing tobacco—and the only sounds in the cabin were the *creak, creak, creak* of his rocker, and the occasional hiss and crackle of the fire.

"This isn't a very exciting nightlife for a hotshot lawyer," Helen said, wanting to break the silence.

Rafe yawned widely—it had been another grueling day digging for gold—and propped his elbows on the table, bracing his chin. He regarded her tenderly. "I like it."

"Did you watch a lot of TV when you were a kid?" she asked, forcing her mind in a different direction.

"Nah. I told you, my mother was a tyrant. She always worked, sometimes two jobs a day, and—"

"What kind of jobs?"

"Cleaning houses mostly. In Beverly Hills." He chuckled. "We got the neatest hand-me-down clothes," he recalled, wrinkling his nose at her. "Gucci loafers. Polo shirts. Girbaud jeans. Even a leather bomber jacket from Michael Douglas one time."

"Really?"

"Oh, yeah, we fit in swell at the local public schools. The other kids wore chic de Levi, and we sported designer duds. That went over *real* big."

"That's probably when you first learned to fight."

"Yep."

Her lips twitched with amusement. "Tell me more about your mother."

"She's about five-foot-zip. Wears polyester slacks—though all us kids have tried to break her of *that*—with sweatshirts. Her feet hurt from standing all day, so she's never without her thick-soled orthopedic shoes. She's a ball of energy, always has to be doing something. She yells a lot, but not in a mean way—"

"Maybe she had to yell. A sort of survival skill to be heard over all you children."

"Probably. Anyhow, my mother had a way of saying our names that could be heard blocks away. When she yelled, 'RA-FAY-ELL SAN-TEE-AGO!' I ran like hell or got my bottom whacked."

They exchanged a smile.

"And your father?"

His face tightened. "My father came and went as he pleased. Stayed long enough to give my mother another baby, then zipped off into the sunset. I think it's the only time I ever saw my mother cry . . . when my dad walked out. He's dead now, but I heard a few years back that the bastard had a wife and family in Mexico, too.'' He swallowed with some difficulty, then added flatly, ''He was a son of a bitch. We kids were glad when he left.''

Helen fought back tears. She wanted to reach across the table and take Rafe's hand, but somehow she knew he would take the gesture for pity. ''Tell me about your brothers and sisters.''

He rolled his shoulders in hopeless resignation. ''I'm the oldest. Juanita is next. She's thirty-three, a teacher in one of the project schools.'' Grimacing, he added, ''Juanita and I don't get along. She was always beating up on me, as a kid, and she still rags on me, as an adult. Anyhow, she's got three kids she's raising herself. Her husband got killed in a drive-by shooting five years ago.''

Before Helen had a chance to react to that horrifying news, Rafe went on, ''Antonio is next. Tony's a police detective upstate. He's thirty-two and single. Women think he looks like Antonio Banderas, and he bleeds that for all it's worth.''

''Next?''

''Inez is thirty, a police officer for L.A.P.D. Not the most popular job these days,'' he noted, obviously referring to the continuing bad press from the O. J. Simpson trial. ''She's single, and, like me, plans to stay that way.'' Helen tilted her head in inquiry, and he explained, ''She got stuck with lots of the babysitting, like I did.''

She frowned, beginning to get an image of Rafe's family that was contrary to what she'd always imagined. ''Hmmm. You give the impression of having been a rebel . . . a gang member . . . and yet your brothers and sisters have law-and-order careers.''

He shrugged. ''Some of us do, but we all went through some rocky times, too. My mother earned every one of her gray hairs.''

''Okay, that's three. You have five other siblings, right?''

He nodded. ''Luisa is twenty-eight and has five kids.

She's on welfare, although she helps my mother out on some cleaning jobs sometimes. LuLu—she hates that nickname, by the way—is divorced and lives at home.''

A flash of anger in Rafe's eyes warned Helen not to ask for more details about Luisa—for now.

"My mother and I have to help her pay her bills most months. Her husband left her with a pigload of debts. Plus, she has a baby with asthma. I'm hoping LuLu finds another husband soon so she'll get off my back. I don't suppose you know any wealthy, eligible bachelors who're in the market for a ready-made family?''

She knew he was only kidding, or was he? "Go on."

He stood and stretched, yawning again, then walked over to nudge Zeb awake.

"What? What?" Zeb flustered. "Are you done with yer story already?" he asked Helen.

She and Rafe laughed companionably as Zeb shuffled outside. With still another yawn, Rafe sat on the bed and began to unlace his boots while she threw a quilt over Hector and made sure he wasn't too close to the fire.

When she turned back to Rafe, he'd already removed his boots and socks and was starting on his shirt.

"So, finish with your family. You were down to Luisa."

He pulled a face at her. "Eduardo is next. He's, oh, about twenty-six. Eddie keeps changing jobs. Last I heard he was a firefighter. Before that, he drove a truck, worked for the post office, was a disc jockey, and dozens of other things. Even a—you won't believe this!—male centerfold." He raised an eyebrow at her. "He's trying to find himself."

"Is he married?"

"Nope, but he's been engaged to the same girl for some time. Her parents don't consider him very stable. He's not."

"Does he live at home?"

He shook his head. "He and my youngest brother, Ramon, who's twenty, share an apartment in Long Beach. Ramon, when he's not being a rabble rouser, attends UCLA."

She decided to save her questions about the rabble rousing for later. "You left two out."

"I didn't think you'd notice," he groaned. He was down to his T-shirt, which he quickly pulled over his head. He stood, about to unbutton his pants. "Helen, Helen, Helen," he admonished, "I hope you're not thinking of watching me get naked. After yesterday's near disaster, I'm not sure I could take any more temptation."

Disaster? He considers our making love a disaster? She cringed, ducking her head so he wouldn't see the hurt.

Rafe came up behind her and pinched her bottom, whispering against her ear, "Just teasing, Prissy."

When she looked back over her shoulder, he was already in bed with the quilt up to his waist.

"Finish," she ordered.

"Yes, ma'am." He saluted. "Jacinta is twenty-three, a nurse. J. C. thinks she knows everything. Really. She's the world's biggest know-it-all. Worse than me. She graduated from nursing school last year, and she plans to go to graduate school soon." His brow furrowed. "She might have already started by now. Wonder if she got the money."

Rafe's reminder of their return to the future jarred her. To her surprise, Helen realized that she hadn't thought about going home in a long time. How could that be?

"And the last one is Carmen. I skipped her out of order . . . deliberately." Rafe's voice softened when he said her name. "Carmen is twenty-two. She has the most beautiful smile in the world. I ought to know. It cost me eight thousand dollars in orthodontic bills."

Helen could tell that Rafe was especially close to this sister, despite his griping.

"Carmen is a dancer. As long as I can remember, practically from the crib, Carmen's been dancing. All kinds of dancing, but the worst was the tap dancing. Lord, oh, Lord! I threatened hundreds of time to hide those damn tap shoes. She would tap from the kitchen table to the refrigerator. She would tap to the bathroom. She would tap while taking out the garbage. Sometimes I still hearing that tap-tap-tapping in my dreams.''

She couldn't help giggling at that image. "So, is Carmen the one who taught you to dip?"

He jiggled his eyebrows at her. "Nah, that was Barbie Bimbolini. She taught me to dip, and a few other things."

"Liar," she hooted. "Geez, couldn't you be more original than *Bimbo*lini?"

He crinkled his nose at her. "Anyhow, Carmen doesn't tap dance much anymore. She's into modern dance, and she just made the L.A. Dance Company. She's touring Europe right now. Of course, she needed five thousand dollars for extra expenses, and guess who she came running to?"

"Oh, Rafe, your family sounds wonderful!"

"Huh?" Her compliment stunned him. "You must be nuts. I just told you the good stuff. They're a bunch of screwball, loud, interfering, demanding leeches. We had a motto in our house: take a breath, you lose a turn. Take my word for it, you wouldn't like them. Nope, you definitely wouldn't like them."

"Rafe, I already like them."

He gave her a level stare. "Then you *are* nuts."

"And I love you."

He closed his eyes and his lips moved silently. If she didn't know better, she'd think he was praying. If fact, she thought she heard him mention St. Augustine.

She decided to answer his prayers and not push him beyond his endurance. "I'm going outside to do some forms and meditate," she said.

"Stay near the house," he cautioned.

She turned in the doorway to peer back at him. Rafe was half-sitting against the headboard with both arms folded behind his neck, grinning. His body still carried bruises from his various beatings. His hands were calloused from hard work. She wanted more than anything to make love with the handsome rogue, to feel him inside her body again, to show him with kisses and caresses just how much he meant to her, to strengthen this tenuous bond that was growing day by day between them. *But I can't.*

"Go to sleep," she said. *Maybe tomorrow will be the day we hit a strike, and we can head home. Maybe then we can end this sexual torture you've imposed on us. Maybe then we can plan a future together.*

Together? Will we be together in the future? Helen wondered, suddenly alarmed. Rafe had never mentioned marriage, or living together, or commitment of any kind. In fact, over and over, he'd made it clear he'd never marry or have children.

That night, Helen had trouble meditating and doing her forms. No matter how hard she tried, she couldn't bring her mind to a state of harmony. Rafael Santiago was clouding her concentration.

"I'll give us two more weeks of prospecting. If we don't hit a strike by then, we'll go home," Rafe told her the next morning. "It's October ninth now. Our deadline will be October twenty-third. Okay?"

Startled by his sudden announcement, she asked, "Why? I mean, why are you giving up now?"

He shrugged. "Reality, sweetheart. We're in a race against the elements. Another two months and we risk being snowed in for the winter. Even Rich Bar will start to empty out soon when the winter exodus to the south begins."

Helen knew that the northern diggings pretty much closed down for the winter when the rainy season began, and that could be anywhere from late October to early December. Roads became quagmires. Streams flooded into virtual swamps. And at higher elevations, snow was a deadly threat.

"If I were the only one involved, I'd probably just stay till I struck a bonanza, or die trying," Rafe continued, "but I won't do that to you, honey."

"We *have* been here in the past for almost eight weeks already," she replied defensively. "Heck, we've been at Angel Valley alone for more than a month."

"And still no gold, no harness, no parachutes, and no immediate hopes for returning to the future," he pointed out before she could say so herself.

She followed Rafe down to the stream, explaining at length as they walked why his mercenary attitude toward life was filled with loopholes. "You know, Rafe, the worst thing about being in the rat race is, even when you win, you're just another rat."

Rafe gathered together his pick and shovel and several tin pans, trying to tune Helen out.

"Furthermore," Helen droned on, "you know what they say about lying down with dogs. You come up with fleas. Just extrapolate that to rats. If you run with rats, you eat a lot of vermin." She continued to rant on regardless of whether he answered her or not.

He scanned the area and decided to set up his equipment in a new spot today, where the stream widened slightly and had some interesting boulders on its banks.

He tried to ignore Helen's long-winded lecture on all his shortcomings and all her wonderful, superior philosophies on everything from money to family values to the meaning of life.

He glanced up when Helen wound down to silence. She was standing with her hands on her hips, tapping a foot impatiently at his failure to acknowledge her advice. Her flaming hair was tied back into a ponytail, topped by a wide-brimmed hat. She was wearing her camouflage pants laced into the high skydiving boots and the blasted green T-shirt tucked into her waistband.

Her enticing curves pulled at him like a sensual magnet. He thought seriously about tackling Helen on the spot and wiping that patronizing look off her face with about two thousand kisses.

"Well, did you hear what I said?" She tapped her foot like an Army major, reprimanding a lowly private.

He did *not* like her condescending tone or the blasted foot tapping.

As they entered the stream together, he decided to retaliate. Zeb and Hector were approaching, carrying more shovels and pans. Before they got too close to hear, Rafe said, "You know what's one of the first things I'm gonna buy when we get back to the future?"

"A BMW?"

"That's the second thing." He cuffed her gently on the chin. "First, I'm gonna buy me a Magic Marker, and I'm gonna connect the dots all over your sweet body."

"Dots?"

"Yep, those cute little freckles that cover your skin, starting right here." He put a fingertip on her right breast, just above the nipple.

"Oh." Her mouth parted on a sigh.

Man, oh, man, he loved the way she responded to his mere touch. And, even better, her foot was planted firmly on the bed of the stream. No tapping now.

"Then down to here." He traced the fingertip down to a point between her waist and belly button.

She made a kittenish sound deep in her throat. He really, really liked it when she made a small kittenish sound deep in her throat.

And still no foot tapping under the water.

"Over to here." His finger moved even lower, stopping just above the vee of her trousers. She sucked in her stomach reflexively. He didn't think she could move her foot if her life depended on it. *Damn, I'm good.*

"What're you doin'?" Hector asked, splashing up to them.

"Playing a game," Rafe choked out. *Damn, I'm in trouble.*

"Kin I play, too?" Hector begged. "Please, please, please?"

Rafe looked to Helen for assistance.

She made a motion of zippering her lips.

"Oh, hell!" Rafe let out a whoosh of air. "Listen, Hector, this was an adult game Helen and I were playing. I'll find a children's game to play with you later."

"Oh, all right," he said with childlike agreeability.

"Would you go get me that other shovel?" Rafe asked then.

Hector sloshed off to the other bank.

Helen taunted him then by swinging her hips as she walked by him.

And, damn it, he could swear both feet were tapping.

"These two weeks are gonna go by way too slow," he called after her.

"Do you think so?" She stood on the far bank, and she was tapping her foot to beat the band, grinning from ear to ear. Then she started whistling. Whistling!

"I'd better go start dinner," Helen said late that afternoon.

"Betcha heard my innards growlin'." Zeb chuckled from where he was shoveling pay dirt, which Rafe had loosened from the hard bedrock. Then he dumped the gravel into buckets for eventual panning.

They'd been working steadily, except for a short lunch break, for eight straight hours. Her arms were numb from the repetitive motion of swirling the pan of gravel and water. She had a blister on her palm. Her back might not ever straighten again. Her thigh muscles screamed from the unnatural crouching position she'd been in most of the day. Maybe she would just crawl up the incline to the cabin.

"You better take *el niño* with you," Rafe suggested as he leaned on his long-handled pickax, panting.

Hector's shoulders drooped with exhaustion, and he cast pleading eyes to her. Although he hadn't worked as hard or steadily as the rest of them, it was a long day for a little boy.

Helen tousled his overlong hair. "Maybe you could help me find some more carrots."

His eyes lit up with gratitude at the reprieve. Then her words sank in. "Carrots again! Yeech!"

They all laughed.

"Hey, even carrots sound good to me," Rafe chipped

in. "I'm as starved as Zeb. My stomach feels like it's shrunk in half."

He took off the wide-brimmed hat he used to shade his eyes and swiped a forearm across his forehead. Sweat dripped down his bristled face—he hadn't shaved that morning—and covered his bare skin with a sheen right down to the waistband of his low-slung Army trousers, held up by suspenders. Helen watched, fascinated, as one drop drizzled in a straight line from the middle of his collarbone, across his ridged abdomen, and right into the cavity of his navel.

"Helen," he warned.

Her eyes shot up with embarrassment.

He laughed. "Don't be embarrassed. I'd gawk, too, if you were standing in front of me with nothing but a pair of camouflage pants and a pair of suspenders. In fact, I think I saw a photo just like that in *Playboy* once. Girls of the Armed Forces, I think the series was called."

"You are—"

"Disgusting? Actually, honey, you wouldn't have to pose in the nude for *Playboy*. They'd welcome you just the way you are."

She looked down and saw that perspiration had caused her T-shirt to mold her breasts and abdomen like a film of green Saran Wrap. And her normally loose military pants were plastered to her hips and legs due to her treks back and forth across the stream.

Rafe winked at her, but she was too tired to rise to his bait, or think of a smart comeback. Luckily, he decided to drop the enticing subject of their mutual, very visible sexual attributes.

"God, I could go for a cold beer right now," Rafe told Zeb. "I can't believe it's so hot for October."

"Injun summer," Zeb explained, "but it could change overnight. You gotta appreciate the good days whilst you got 'em. Bad days are sure ta come." The old man looked at the clear sky with a worried frown.

*   *   *

After dinner, Rafe stumbled to the bed, where he lay propped against the headboard waiting for Helen's nightly ritual of reading. He couldn't have sat upright across the table from her if his life depended on it. His eyelids drooped with exhaustion.

"How much did we make today?" Rafe asked Zeb.

The old man took his pipe from his mouth and adjusted Hector on his lap. The boy was playing with a crude wooden horse Zeb had whittled from a piece of hardwood over the past few weeks.

"I'd say 'bout two pounds." Zeb calculated in his head. "There was some flakes and a few tiny nuggets today, along with the usual dust. Not a bad day."

At the going 1850 rate, that would amount to more than five hundred dollars, Rafe knew, or more than twelve thousand dollars in the future. Divided in half with Zeb, and then his half shared with Helen, it wasn't nearly enough. He needed to go back to the future with a minimum of one hundred thousand dollars to get himself out of debt and his family off his back. Only then would he be able to make any kind of plans for a future with Helen. He sighed at that last possibility, refusing to allow himself even to think about a future with Helen until he was sure he had something to offer.

"Did you say something?" Helen asked, sitting down at the table. Despite the dimness of the room, light from the lantern positioned next to her open book gave him a perfect view of her fresh-scrubbed face. Rafe liked looking at Helen.

Exposure to the sun had caused more freckles to erupt over her clear skin. He liked them. She'd bathed in the lagoon, after he and Hector and Zeb had done the same, and her clean hair sprung into damp, unmanageable corkscrews all over the place. He liked them, too.

She gazed at him with concern and repeated, "Did you say something?"

I love you, he mouthed silently, but aloud he said, swallowing over a lump in his throat, "I just wondered if you were going to read tonight."

Helen nodded, her lips parted with emotion, and he knew which of his words she was reacting to.

"Sí, sí, sí," Hector piped in. "You hafta finish the story."

"Before you start," Zeb said, coughing nervously, "there's somethin' I gotta tell you."

Rafe and Helen exchanged looks of foreboding.

"I'm gonna have to make a trip ta Rich Bar."

"What?" he and Helen exclaimed at once. "Why?"

"Well, I din't want ta alarm you, but that bear done more damage than we realized. Ain't enough flour ta last more'n a month and hardly any salt pork ta mention."

"We can make do." Helen began to panic.

Zeb shook his head. "It ain't the seasonin' I'm worried 'bout. You'll need salt ta preserve the game I bag fer the winter. When I get back, I gotta do some serious huntin'."

"I guess we could all go," Rafe said hesitantly, knowing it would cut seriously into the deadline he'd set with Helen. She glanced over at him as he spoke, and he saw that she realized the importance of the time element, too. "Maybe we could wait for two weeks. Then, Helen and I would continue on home from there."

Hector's wide eyes shot from one to the other of them, obviously wondering where he fit into all these plans.

Zeb patted the boy's shoulders and said, "Nope, I gotta go tomorrow. Can't take no chance of hittin' the bad weather. Hector will come with me, and you two'll stay here, ta hold down the fort, so ta speak."

"NO!" Rafe and Helen responded at once, their eyes locking in dismay.

Alone! In a secluded cabin! With my testosterone already blinking a zillion kilowatts! No way!

Before they could voice further protests, Zeb went on. "It's gotta be this way. They may still be lookin' fer you as that Angel Bandit. And, if they take you away, Rafe— no, no, no, don'tcha be thinkin' it ain't possible—then Helen here would be at the mercy of a few hundred wimmen-hungry miners what thinks she can do the corkscrew.''

''What's a corkscrew?'' Hector asked.

Zeb's chest rumbled with mirth. ''A dance,'' he lied.

''How long would you be gone?'' Helen asked, biting her bottom lip with concern. Her eyes were wide with horror.

Zeb tapped his pipe stem against his teeth. ''I figger four days goin' and four days comin' back. Add an extry day or two fer unexpected delays, and I'd say ten days at the most.''

''Ten days!''

''It's the best way, you'll see, onct you think on it. This way, you two kin continue ta work the claim, and mebbe you'll even hit a strike. It could happen.''

The only strike Rafe could imagine right now was a lightning bolt from heaven with a divine message from the Lord, via St. Augustine, delivered in a Bill Cosby voice out of the clouds, ''Celibacy, celibacy, celibacy.''

''One more thing,'' Zeb added. ''This'll give me one las' chance before winter ta check fer you and see if Pablo showed up. I know Mary said she'd contact you if he come, and I know she promised ta send that harness and those tent things up here, but you'll sleep easier knowin' what's happened so far, one way or another. An' I can report back on the miners' mood toward the two of you. Yep, it's the best way.''

Rafe and Helen groaned with surrender.

''Besides,'' Zeb concluded with a huge smile, ''you two younguns ain't had no time fer a proper honeymoon. Effie allus said a man and his woman needs the privacy ta frolic naked in the sunshine afore the cloudy days come.''

''Frolic?'' Helen sputtered.

Naked? Rafe thought.

''Oh, Lord!'' Helen exclaimed.

Oh, Lord! Rafe shuddered.

Rafe began to wonder if this whole time-travel adventure, and these upcoming ten days, were a divine test of some sort.

Yep! a voice in his head said.

Chapter Twenty

Just after dawn, Zeb and Hector prepared to leave. The old man gave them last-minute instructions. "You don't need ta cut no more firewood, Rafe. I chopped more'n enough after Effie died, workin' off my grief. We got wood ta last us two winters."

Rafe nodded. "Should I continue to let the horses graze during the day and put them in the barn at night?"

"Yep, but you best steer that F. Lee away from the wild clover. He does work up a good case of wind."

"Tell me about it." Rafe grimaced.

"And iffen it was me, I'd jist keep on workin' the same area of the stream. I have me a good feelin' 'bout that spot. It's got good color."

Before Rafe could respond, Zeb turned to Helen. "There should be 'nuf flour fer the two of you till I get back. Put out those fishin' lines the way I showed you, an' shur as shootin' you'll have trout ta fill in with the occasional salt pork. I went out early this mornin' and got you a string of rabbits. They's hanging in the root cellar."

"An' you can always dig up some more carrots. Maybe use 'em all up before we get back," Hector added hopefully.

Helen laughed and hunkered down to put her face eye level with the little boy, who'd become dear to them all. He gazed back at her with his huge chocolate eyes, and she pulled him into her arms, squeezing tight. "You behave now," she whispered.

Hector pulled away with discomfort at the open show of affection.

Rafe shook his hand, then in an undertone advised, "Take care of Zeb. He needs you."

Hector eyed Rafe questioningly. "He does?"

"Definitely."

Hector broke into a wide smile.

"Are you sure you took enough gold dust, Zeb?" Rafe worried.

"I got plenty. Don't want ta take no more or we'll have miners followin' me back ta jump our claim."

And they were off, with Zeb calling over his shoulder to Rafe, "I left one of my rifles. Those pistols of your'n won't be worth bat turd if that bear comes back."

"That's a reassuring thought," Helen said.

The rest of the day went surprisingly well. Rafe worked the claim alone all morning while she did her meditation routine, then tidied the cabin, weeded the garden, and washed some clothes. After a simple lunch of bread and coffee and leftover fish, Rafe went back to digging, and Helen swept up the dead ashes from the fireplace into a crock. She was saving them, according to Zeb's directions, for soap making on his return. In addition, another crock held ashes for the making of pearl ash or saleratus, a primitive form of baking soda.

Whistling contentedly, she cut up one of the rabbits for stew, combined with mushrooms, wild onions, parsley, and yes, the last of the carrots, and set it to cook slowly on a hook at the back of the fire. Then she added some flour, water, and a pinch of sugar to her sourdough mixture, which the bear luckily had missed, and kneaded out the dough on the table. Before long, she had two loaves baking in the hot coals.

Her "housework" done, Helen walked down to the stream to help Rafe. "How's it going?"

"Okay." He was sitting on the bank with his widespread legs planted up to the knees in the water. Every few seconds he leaned forward and added more water to his pan, then swirled and sloshed until only the heavy material remained at the bottom. "I probably got another few ounces today."

Helen filled another pan with gravel and sat beside him, following the familiar routine. At first, they just worked together in companionable silence.

Rafe finally spoke. "I'll bet your father is worried about you."

"I suppose so, assuming we're missing in the future."

He cocked his head inquiringly. "What do you mean?"

"Well, maybe we're living a separate, double life then and now, though I don't think so. Surely we'd sense that. Heck, we don't even know if time passes at the same rate then as now. Or if they've found our bodies. Or anything."

"Hmmm. I never thought of it that way." He pondered those different scenarios while picking out three wheat-sized flakes of gold from his pan and putting them in a sack behind him. "Helen . . ." he started, then stopped himself.

"What?"

"I was just wondering . . . uh, what about Elliott?"

"What about him?" She couldn't understand Rafe's sudden reticence, or his somber demeanor as he continued to twirl his pan. For a second, she was mesmerized, watching his hands, the long fingers moving expertly. They were really beautiful hands, despite the callouses and grime.

"Are you still going to marry him?"

Rafe's question jolted her. "Marry? Elliott? Rafe, I would never have been able to make love with you if I considered myself still committed to another man. No, I won't be marrying Elliott."

"Good."

Good? What did that mean? Helen's heart expanded with all kinds of possibilities. "Why do you ask?"

"No reason," Rafe said, then smiled at her—a warm, telling smile that kissed her senses.

"Tell me about your father and your childhood," Rafe urged. "I spilled my guts about my fun-house family. Don't I deserve a little payback?"

"My life was boring compared to yours. My mother came from a middle-class San Clemente family. Oh, wipe that gloating sneer off your face. I'm not rich, no matter what you think. My grandparents died right after she and my dad were married, so we lived in the family house."

"Acres and acres, I suppose."

"At least. Actually, it's on a rather small lot on a tree-lined street. A nice house, don't get me wrong, but not a mansion, by any means."

"That's comforting."

"Stop being so sarcastic."

"Okay. Continue. You lived on Leave-It-to-Beaver street in middle-class America and . . . ?"

"Behave." She slapped his arm. "My mother got cancer soon after I was born. It was a slow progressing type, but she was sickly most of the time. She died when I was eight."

Rafe set down his pan and put an arm around her shoulder, pulling her into the crook of his neck. He kissed the top of her head and said, "I'm sorry."

"That's okay. It was a long time ago," she said, drawing away eventually, although she loved the feel of his soothing embrace. He picked up his pan again. "Anyhow, I don't think my dad ever intended to be career military, but after Mom died, he seemed restless, without direction. I guess the military gave him order and meaning at a time when he had none. We lived on fourteen bases in seven different countries by the time I graduated from high school." She glanced at Rafe, whose face held tender compassion for her. "Hey, it wasn't that bad. Remember, we drove expensive cars and went on fancy vacations."

"Yeah," he said, probably remembering his earlier envy of that lifestyle. Then he forced a cheerful note in his voice. "Too bad I didn't know you then. I could have sent my brothers and sisters over to keep you company. In fact, you could have adopted them."

She grinned at the image. "I probably would have welcomed them with open arms. You, too. I would have shown your sisters my paper doll collection. And your brothers would have liked my dad's tin soldiers on a miniature battlefield in the library—''

"Library? You have a library? Hell, do you have a drawing room, too?"

She made a harrumphing sound.

"And how would you have entertained me?" he asked suggestively. "Would we have played doctor? Or spin the bottle? Or grope?"

"Grope?"

"I made that up," he admitted sheepishly. "Sounds good, though, doesn't it?"

She laughed. "You must have been a very naughty boy."

"I tried. So, why did you go to Stonewall and not some artsy, high-class private college?"

She braced herself for the mockery that was sure to follow when she answered, "Because my dad went there."

He raised both brows at her, and they *were* mocking.

"Well, I had no idea what I wanted to do," she said defensively. "It's not as if I was giving something up for my dad. And he never pushed me."

"Are you sure about that?"

"What are you implying?"

"Don't get yourself all steamed up, sweetheart. I just wonder if you weren't trying real hard to please your daddy."

She refused to answer.

"What about your art?"

"How do you know about my art?"

"I saw some paintings you had in an exhibit in Grant Hall. They were really good, Helen. Anyone with that kind of talent should use it. Even a crude, city jerk like me could see that."

"There's no future in being an artist, except for teaching. And I never wanted to teach."

"No future? Like in making money?" He scoffed. "That doesn't sound like you. It sounds like something that might

288

come out of the mouth of a . . . father?''

She exhaled loudly. "Well, I made a decision, and I'm living with it. So there."

"Do you still paint?"

"Rarely. I don't have time."

He studied her intently, seeing way too much.

"Let's change the subject."

"To what?"

"Us."

He stiffened and shifted away from her a little on the bank, putting a distance of several feet between them.

"Rafe . . ." She searched for the right words and could only come up with, "I love you."

"Uh huh. I love you, too, babe. So?" He was still staring at her suspiciously, as if he expected her to jump on him any minute and tear off his clothes.

She was tempted.

"What's going to happen to us when we go back?" Strangely, she never doubted that they'd return to the future. It was only a question of when and how.

Startled, Rafe asked, slowly, "What do you want to happen?"

"Now that's a non-answer if I ever heard one. Pure legalese. You know exactly what I mean. Do you see us having any kind of future together?"

"Yes." His answer came too quickly.

She arched a brow.

"Ah, Helen, I don't know. It depends on so many things. The gold—"

She cringed. What kind of future could they possibly have if it depended on money?

"—and your dreams—"

Babies.

"—and my family, and your father—"

"My father?"

"Honey, get real. Your dad isn't going to be happy about your breaking up with the colonel, but he's going to be over-the-wall livid at you consorting with a poor Hispanic lawyer.''

"Oh, that's totally uncalled for. My father is not prejudiced. And I am so sick of you putting yourself down and using the race card as a yardstick for everyone.''

He shrugged. "I'm just trying to prepare you for the opposition you'd get.''

"Rafe, you still haven't answered my question. What kind of future do you see for us? Forget all the obstacles. If you had your way, how would it be? Would we date? Live together? Or . . . ?'' She couldn't say the word. It was already too embarrassing that she was the one having to force the issue.

"Marry?'' Rafe gazed at her bleakly. "Damn! You're really pushing the big one today.''

She lifted her chin defiantly. "I just want to know where I stand.''

"You have the right, darlin','' he said tenderly, "but I don't have the answers for you now. I'll admit the thought of marriage scares me, big time, but I want to be with you. And, no, I don't want to date you, like a teenager.''

With a flash of humor, she tried to picture Rafe picking her up on a Saturday night to attend a movie. A drive-in, she'd bet.

"Stop smirking,'' Rafe grumbled.

"So, you don't want to date?''

"No. Would you consider living with me?'' The yearning in his eyes stopped her breath. She felt blessed to have him care so much. "I don't have a house, just an apartment. Of course, things will be different if we find some gold, but . . .'' He shrugged again. "Would you live with me?''

"Maybe.'' The prospect didn't thrill her. A temporary arrangement was not what she wanted from Rafe.

He sighed dejectedly. "Helen, we want different things.''

That was true. When she could speak over the lump in her throat, she asked softly, "Would having a baby with me be such an awful thing?''

He set his gold pan aside and leaned back on both elbows, studying her with sadness. "No. That's the worst part. It sounds more and more appealling."

Her blood churned wildly with elation. She dropped her pan in the water and began to move toward him.

He sat up and put out a halting hand. "Let me finish. I want you so bad that I find myself making bargains with myself. Maybe one baby wouldn't be so bad. Yeah, a child—our child—would be a different experience. If that's what it takes to have you, probably I'll do just about anything. That's the way I'm thinking. Is that the kind of father you'd want for your kid?"

She shook her head.

"And I know for damn sure what would happen after that. It wouldn't stop at one baby, Helen. You'd want more. To keep you happy, I'd agree, and before you know it, I'd be—"

"Trapped," she finished for him.

"Am I right?" he asked. "Am I painting the picture with all the right colors?"

"You're making a lot of assumptions about me. Rafe, let me hold your hand or touch you while we talk. This is too important to discuss with you keeping your distance."

"No way!" He laughed. "You touch me and it's all over. I'd agree to anything. *Anything!*"

She smiled and scooted over anyhow, lacing her fingers with his. He made a low, hissing sound, but didn't pull away.

"What makes you think I wouldn't want you enough to compromise?" she said.

"Compromise? When a woman says compromise, she usually means something different from a man. I'm a lawyer. I know these things."

She squeezed his hand. "If you'd be willing to have a baby to please me, why wouldn't I be willing to *not* have babies to please you? Love goes both ways, you know."

Rafe went still. "You wouldn't be happy."

"I wouldn't be happy without you, either."

"So what's the answer?"

"You're a lawyer. I'm a military leader. The answer's obvious."

He thought a moment. "Negotiate?"

"Yep."

"Sounds like a stalemate to me."

"No, it sounds like a beginning," she whispered, swaying closer.

"What are you doing?" he choked out.

"Negotiating."

"Uh uh. That's kissing. Negotiators don't kiss. Did you ever hear of Henry Kissinger kissing Brezhnev? Stop that! Remember my rules, Helen. No kissing. I distinctly said—"

"Shut up, Rafe." Her lips pressed against his lightly. "The first rule in negotiating is to forget the rules."

"That must be an ass-backwards Army rule," he muttered, dropping back to the ground and pulling her on top of him with a muffled curse of surrender. His legs were still in the water, up to his calves. "I've never seen *that* in a legal text. Kiss the negotiator. Nope."

"Shush," she coaxed against his mouth.

"Oh, God, oh, God, I've missed you." Rafe moaned, adjusting her body on top of his. Surrender was so damn sweet.

With one hand on the back of her waist and another at her nape, he kissed her deeply with all the pent-up passion of the past weeks. When he closed his eyes, he saw a kaleidoscope of bursting colors behind his lids.

He should resist.

He couldn't resist.

Rafe's lust-crazed brain fought hard to wipe out his conscience, but it lost. Just barely. He had a clear image of St. Augustine and God up there playing a moral tug of war with Satan. *Over him.*

The good guys won, by a hair.

He lifted Helen off him and over to the side. Nuzzling her neck, he asserted gently, "Not now, babe."

She whimpered.

And his racing brain revved into high gear. No checkered flags in sight.

Groaning, he leaned over her and put both hands on her forearms. Despite his restraint, she raised her head slightly, and her tongue darted out, licking his lips.

His favorite body part just about jumped out of his pants.

''Rafe.'' She sighed.

He was losing it fast. *Hey, God! Yo, Auggie! You better call in a herd of angels for backup.*

Springing up abruptly, Rafe dashed into the cold stream and sat down. The shock just about killed him. Then he lay back fully in the shallow stream, counting to ten under the water. When he came up, dripping wet and testosterone battered, he looked to the left. Helen sat on the bank, blithely panning gold as if she hadn't just set off an explosion in his body.

He splashed toward her and grabbed his pickax, planning to put some distance—and hard, mind-numbing work—between the two of them. That was when he noticed she wasn't as cool and calm as she pretended. Her breathing was uneven, and her hands trembled around the pan. Even worse, her nipples peaked noticeably under the T-shirt.

Helen was a deadly adversary.

He stomped away with his axe and shovel. That was when she did the worst thing of all. She started whistling.

He was sure the devil made her do it.

Despite Helen's calling him several times for dinner, Rafe worked until dusk. For his efforts, he managed to add about a pound of dust and flakes to his small cache. Not a bad day, but Helen, not gold, had been the inspiration for his obsessive efforts. When he finally set his tools aside for the day, he thought seriously about lying down on the spot and falling asleep. His body was numb with exhaustion—his goal, of course.

Just to be safe, he plodded wearily to the lagoon for a bath. On the way, he grabbed some clean clothes from Helen's makeshift clothesline. He entered the frigid water like a prisoner about to undergo water torture. "Br-r-r-r!" It was definitely torture. Any parts of his body that even considered rebellion gave up the fight with a shudder.

He could face Helen now, he thought, and marched up the incline to the cabin, carrying his dirty clothes. The minute he opened the door, he was catapulted back to step one.

Helen was sitting before the fire on a low stool with a basin of soapy water. She was shaving her legs with Zeb's straight edge. And she was wearing only her T-shirt and his black silk boxers.

Rafe said a silent Hail Mary and headed straight for the bed.

"Don't you want to eat first?"

He dropped down onto the bed, face first, with a groan. "I'll eat extra for breakfast," he mumbled into the quilt. Luckily, he fell asleep immediately.

The next morning, he awakened to the sound of driving rain. Instead of being upset, he gave a silent prayer of thanks. He would put in another grueling day, even in the rain. It would be muddy and miserable. There was no way he would get turned on by Helen under those conditions. Right?

Wrong!

Helen insisted on working with him. And neither pelting rain, nor icy stream, nor sliding mud could dim his pleasure in ogling her in a wet T-shirt.

He threw down his shovel after only an hour.

"Where are you going?" Helen asked.

"To sharpen Zeb's razor."

"Why?"

"To slit my throat."

He was sitting by the fire, nice and dry, reading Zeb's Bible, or trying to—he kept hearing a snickering in his head—when Helen came in carrying a dead rabbit from the root cellar. She was sopping wet, from plastered hair to squeaky boots. He put the Bible aside and rocked back and forth, watching her dry her hair and take off her boots and lift the hem of her T-shirt. He felt like a time bomb was ticking under his skin—tick, tick, tick.

"Why don't you do some meditating now?" he suggested.

"I meditated this morning."

"Well then, gargle or whistle or say something really irritating."

She grinned and licked a drop of rain off her upper lip.

"I'm sick of rabbit," he growled, shooting up suddenly from the rocking chair. "I think I'll go check those fishing lines of Zeb's."

"Coward," she called out after him.

An hour later, she followed him down to the stream where he was hunkered on the bank, shivering with cold.

"Come back to the cabin," she said, placing a hand on his shoulder. "I won't tease you anymore. I'll even sleep on Zeb's pallet tonight." When he said nothing, she asked, "Did you catch anything?"

"I don't know. I haven't checked yet," he admitted with a laugh.

"Oh, Rafe!" She sighed, dropping down beside him. She put an arm around his stiff shoulder. "I love you so much."

"Yeah, ain't love grand," he said wretchedly, then grinned at her. "You're killin' me, babe. You know that, don't you?"

She nodded, laying her head on his shoulder. "I'll make it easier for you from now on. I promise."

"Hah!" He shot her a skeptical glance. "You could begin by not parading around in that T-shirt anymore."

"Oh."

"I have visions of champagne breasts dancing through my head."

"I think that's supposed to be sugarplums."

"Whatever."

She shook her head at him. "Are you okay now? Why don't you come up and have some rabbit soup."

He grimaced. "I'm going to start hopping pretty soon."

"As long as you don't develop a cotton tail," she said as he stood and helped pull her to her feet.

"It's definitely not cotton."

"Oh, you!" She jabbed him playfully in the side with her elbow. She was just as sick as he was of rabbit, rabbit, rabbit. Looping her arm in his, she joked in a Bugs Bunny voice, "What's up, doc?"

"You know damn well what's up, darlin'."

It was a sweet, companionable moment. Helen wanted to cherish the feeling, the love that enveloped them. She wanted to tuck away the memory of that instant out of time so she could bring it back over and over to cherish in the dark days to come.

The dark time came way too quickly, despite the fact that the rain had stopped and the afternoon sun was peeking out from behind the clouds.

They had a visitor. Again. But this time Big Ben had brought his wife, Big Bertha, with him.

Helen and Rafe raced away, crossing the stream, and scrambled up a tree. Of course, neither of them had bothered to bring a gun with them. Huddled on a limb together—not that a tree would daunt those two beasts—they watched the animals approach the cabin. Without even knocking, Ben, the social clod, shoved at the door with a paw the size of a hubcap, pulling it off its leather hinges. Bertha waddled meekly behind him, growling something that probably translated to, "Way to go, cowboy!"

They heard loud slurping noises.

"Guess we don't have to worry about eating any more rabbit stew," Rafe commented dryly.

"Let's hope they don't crave *crème de la people* for dessert."

"Good thing I left my bag of gold back by the diggings," Rafe noted. "Otherwise, they'd probably eat that, too."

"It's just like you to think of money at a time like this."

"What do you want me to think about? Sex in a tree?"

She darted a quick scowl at him. "Surely you aren't still thinking about *that*."

"Honey, I'm always thinking about *that,* especially when

you've got your hand on my crotch.''

She glanced down quickly. "You rat! I do not." Her hand was resting on his thigh.

"Close enough."

For a long time—about fifteen minutes—the two bears lumbered around inside. When they heard the sound of splintering wood, Rafe joked, "Do you suppose they're making out on our bed?"

"At least someone's making good use of it."

It was Rafe, this time, who elbow-nudged her. "Behave, or I'll show you how Tarzan did it, hanging from a limb with Jane."

"I assume this is the X-rated version of Tarzan."

"Super-X."

"I'm glad you've still got your sense of humor."

"Is that what it is? Seems more like deathbed ramblings."

"I love you, Rafe."

"I love you too, Helen." A short silence ensued. "So, how about taking off your T-shirt? If I'm gonna die, my last wish is to feast on your breasts."

She reached for the hem of her shirt.

"Are you crazy?" he yelled. "I was only kidding."

A mighty roar rippled over the small valley as Big Ben stood on his hind legs, bellowing his rage to them. While they'd been chit-chatting, the two bears must have come out of the cabin.

Bertha was coming up out of the root cellar through the slanted wood door, which she'd already bashed in. Bertha apparently had no social graces, either. In one paw she carried the remaining two skinned rabbits Zeb had left for them. In the other, she clutched a slab of salt pork.

Ben stared at Bertha liked she was Linda Lovelace offering him a treat.

Casting one last glance at Helen and Rafe, Ben and Bertha loped off into the trees. With a sigh, Rafe said, "We are never, ever again going to leave that cabin without a gun."

Three hours later, after a massive clean-up effort, they assessed the damage. A broken table. Little food. Shredded blankets. Bear shit.

"Phew! It still smells like bear in here," Rafe complained.

"Rafe, you're going to have to go hunt some game." Helen was seriously alarmed about the lack of food now, especially since Zeb and Hector wouldn't be back for at least another seven days.

"Like what?"

"Rabbit. Deer. Elk. You know, wild game."

He laughed. "Helen, the only wild game I've ever caught was cockroaches. Of course, some of them were big as rabbits."

She tapped her foot with impatience.

"Helen, I don't even know what an elk looks like. Is that the animal that walks across the opening credits of *Northern Exposure*?"

"No, that's a moose."

"Geez! See what I mean?"

"You're a good shot. You shouldn't have any trouble."

"You're a good shot, too, Miss Equal Rights. Why don't you go shoot Bambi? I'll stay and dig for gold."

"Okay, but if I go hunting, you have to gut and skin whatever I kill."

"What? Oh, hell, I'll go hunting. But I'm not killing Bambi, I'll tell you that right now. A rabbit, I can handle— I think. Even an elk maybe. But no way am I going to look one of Santa's helpers in the eye and shoot."

"That's reindeer, you goof."

"Reindeer. Regular deer. It's the same family."

He grabbed a rifle off the mantle—luckily Big Ben hadn't eaten it—and stormed off, muttering something about how Daniel Boone had probably been nagged to death by some woman, too.

"My hero!" she said with a rueful laugh.

"I heard that," he said from outside.

Less than ten minutes had gone by when Helen heard a rifle shot. Then silence.

She stopped in the middle of sweeping up the remaining broken crockery. "What could he be shooting so soon?" she wondered aloud, then, "Oh, my God! Rafe must have shot himself."

She rushed out the door and across the yard, then came to a skidding stop. Her mouth dropped practically to the ground.

Rafe was dragging a ten-point buck across the stream, swearing some blue words, a few of which had her name attached to them. When she came up to him, he just glowered at her and continued to drag the dead deer—a bullet hole showed clean between its wide open eyes—up the incline toward the cabin.

"You actually shot a deer?"

"Yeah. Are you happy now? I shot Bambi."

"That's not Bambi. That's dinner."

He sliced her a blistering scowl. "I think I'm gonna puke."

"Oh, Rafe, don't be silly. Killing game for survival is a necessity. It's not like you did it for fun or anyth—"

"Fun? I'm gonna have nightmares the rest of my life about Bambi and reindeer—Oh, God, reindeer have horns, don't they?"

"Antlers, not horns," she corrected.

"I didn't shoot Bambi. This is even worse. I shot Rudolph. Look at his nose. It's red."

"That's blood."

"Wonderful! I really am going to upchuck now."

She patted Rafe on the back after he dumped the carcass near the front door. "Why don't you go wash up?"

"I'm going to bed," he announced. "Wake me when it's time to go home. This is the worst thing I've ever done in all my life. . . . well, the worst thing I've done in a long time."

She laughed. "Did I ever tell you that you're my hero?" she called after Rafe.

He stopped in the middle of the doorway, took a deep breath, then turned around. His blue eyes were wide and vulnerable, questioning.

"It's sort of like a lady sending her knight off to slay a dragon," she explained quickly, "but you slayed me a deer, instead." She smiled at him warmly. "My hero."

"Your hero, huh?" The grin that spread across his delicious mouth could have melted the hardest heart, and hers was as soft as butter for him already.

She nodded, unable to speak over the lump in her throat.

"Good," he said in a husky voice. "I'll collect my lady love's token later." He turned again to go into the cabin and threw over his shoulder, "And don't be thinking of offering me any scarf."

She knew exactly what he had in mind.

Chapter Twenty-One

Rafe didn't go to bed, after all. And he didn't jump Helen's bones, either. After three hours of helping her pull out deer guts, skin the carcass, then cut the animal into steaks and chops and roasts and other disgusting things, he'd lost that lovin' feelin'.

Helen knew how to place the carcass belly-up on a slope so the blood would drain away from the meat. She'd shown him how to open the chest cavity by splitting the sternum and taking out the bladder intact so it wouldn't contaminate the flesh. As if those were skills he ever expected to need back in L.A.! *Geez!*

"Where did you learn to do all this crap?" he asked, not impressed.

"Survival school. Didn't you learn this, too?"

"You must have gone to a different survival school than I did. My instructor was big on eating grasshoppers and slugs. He never mentioned butchering Rudolph."

"Would you quit with the Rudolph stuff?"

After a while, Rafe went back to the stream to prospect some more. It was only late afternoon. Although there was a decided chill in the air, he inhaled deeply of the fresh breeze.

The rain that morning had turned the stream bank muddy, but, nevertheless, he sat down and began to swirl a pan from the pile of gravel he'd dug earlier. The dull, repetitive motions gave him time to think, and a warm feeling of contentment passed over him as he reviewed the day's events.

Although he'd complained to Helen about having to hunt game, there was a satisfaction in having accomplished a goal and seeing the product of his efforts. It was probably a male pride kind of thing—man providing for his woman, putting food on the table, that sort of nonsense. Lawyers dealt with paperwork most times. Sure, it was a good feeling to win a case, and he prided himself on his record, but this was a totally different kind of rush.

He liked it.

Helen came out of the cabin, and he watched as she picked up a hoe and began to work Effie's old garden plot with a determined zest. Helen did everything with zest, even making love. *No, no, no, I'm not going to think about that now.* She began working the still-wet ground, and every time she stretched and chopped at the ground, he got a real good look at her backside.

And the beast inside him reared its head—again.

Helen bent over from the waist and picked up some . . . *Oh, Lord, more carrots! Great! Rudolph and carrots. A regular feast.*

And he imagined how it would be to make love with Helen from behind. Maybe even outdoors. Yep, he could stomp over there and say, "I am the man, you are my woman. I am the hunter, you are my prey. Get naked so I can boink you in a garden of mud."

He laughed aloud, but his mind was on a fast track. He had a clear vision of a bright sunny field and Helen on her hands and knees in front of him. Naked, of course. He would push her shoulders gently down to the crushed, fragrant flowers, and when he entered her, she would scream out his name . . .

"Rafe!"

He blinked.

Helen was walking toward him with a basket, yelling, "Rafe! Rafe! Guess what I found?"

His spirits lifted. "Gold?"

"Don't be silly. No, I found some turnips."

His spirits dropped.

"I'm going into the woods to see if I can find some more herbs and edible plants to add to our diet."

Well, next to making love to you on all fours in a field of flowers, edible weeds are right up there on my top ten.
"I don't know if that's a good idea, Helen, especially with the bears nearby."

"I won't go far, and I'll take a gun with me. Don't worry. I'll be just beyond the lagoon if you want me."

Oh, I want you all right.

"And if I can find some wild onions," Helen was continuing to babble on from across the stream, "we can have liver and onions for supper tonight."

He narrowed his eyes. She couldn't possibly have guessed what he'd been fantasizing about. Could she?

For four days, Rafe managed to resist Helen's allure. She didn't overtly try to tempt him, but he was a screaming mass of unfulfilled testosterone. Helen standing in a loose flannel shirt and baggy pants, asking him what he wanted for breakfast, "Venison or venison?" was enough to set him off.

Well, Zeb and Hector should be back in two or three more days. Surely he could hold out that long.

"So, are you going to help me get the honey?" Helen asked as he finished up his breakfast of bread and—*what else?*—venison. Helen had told him the day before about a beehive in a nearby tree. She had a plan—*Helen always had a plan*—for him smoking the bees out of the tree and her climbing the tree to get the honeycomb.

"It would taste really good on fresh-baked bread," she coaxed. "I have a little sourdough left."

Had he ever eaten fresh honey? He liked honey. Yep, he could taste it now. Drizzling on a piece of bread. Drizzling on . . . Oh, no, here I go again . . . on Helen's breasts. She's naked, of course. Maybe up in that tree getting the honeycomb. Yep, she climbed the tree, naked. And when she comes down with the waxy thing in her hands, there's honey drizzling down her chest, over her breasts, those luscious champagne breasts with their raspberry tips. And she says, "Rafe, darling, my hands are full. Could you lick off this sticky stuff?" And he, being naked, too, of course, and a real helpful gentleman, hoists her up against the tree trunk and uses his tongue to lap the delicious peaks. Some honey even drizzles down on his . . .

"Rafe, you're daydreaming again."

He grumbled something about spoilsports and turned away so she wouldn't see the evidence of his perpetual horniness. He wondered idly if lust could be terminal.

"Will you help me with the honey?"

"Okay."

Boy, was that a mistake!

They smoked the bees out of the tree with lit, pitch-filled, undried evergreen limbs, escaping with only one or two stings. Rafe kept an eye on the swarm, which hung around in the vicinity but didn't seem threatening. And Helen climbed the tree with ease, up about twenty feet.

She wasn't naked, but that didn't matter much to Rafe's overactive libido. Her straining breasts in the flannel shirt, her curvy bottom in the camouflage pants, were enough to set his blood humming. No, no, no. Forget humming. His blood was singing a full-blown opera.

Helen wrapped a big honeycomb in a piece of oilcloth she'd brought with her and threw it down to him. He laid it on the ground, waiting for her and watching the bees. She left a chunk of honeycomb for the bees so they wouldn't be too mad. Then, climbing down carefully, Helen set off one of those sudden erotic fantasies that he was prone to these days.

Helen living in the jungle. Swinging from the trees. Wearing only a skimpy leopard skin—fake, of course, for political correctness. He chuckled. *Were they Tarzan and Jane? Nah, that was too easy. She was Tarzette, and he was the famous Harvard anthropologist, come to study the beautiful woman living amongst the apes. They had some*

*unusual sexual practices, those apes did, and he wanted
firsthand knowledge of...*

"Rafe, would you stop that daydreaming and help me?"
Helen snapped. She was hanging by both hands from a limb
about ten feet off the ground. "Catch me," she demanded.

He grinned. Hey, she wasn't wearing a leopard skin, and
he wasn't carrying his Harvard notebook, but what the hell!
He moved in for the kill.

"Rafe . . . Ra-afe! What *are* you doing?"

"Checking for bee stings." He was unbuttoning her flannel shirt, spreading the fabric, exposing her chest, about
eye level. Rather mouth level. With a sigh, he took a hard
nipple between his lips and began to lick. It tasted sweeter
than honey.

Moaning, she arched her neck back between her upraised
arms, thrusting her breasts forward.

He fingered one breast and suckled at the other. Her
booted foot inadvertently rubbed against his erection, and
his knees almost buckled. A prickling sensation began at
the back of his neck, probably an approaching climax,
and . . .

Prickling?

"Son of a bitch!" he exclaimed, realizing that some bees
were setting up camp on the back of his neck. Quickly, he
told Helen to jump. He caught her, and they were out of
there, grabbing their booty. When they were back at the
cabin, laughing over their escapade, Helen examined his
neck and found only a few stings. Nothing serious.

Another close call!

That afternoon, he worked steadily. He even found several nuggets the size of marbles, so he was feeling opti-
mistic.

Belting out an old Jerry Reed country music ballad, he
sang, "She Got the Gold Mine, I Got the Shaft." It didn't
matter that he couldn't carry a tune. Singing set a rhythm
to his work.

Life was good. He was starting to get a little more gold—

they had about a thousand dollars worth so far, not a lot, but a start—he was in love, soon he and Helen would be back in the future, they could make love like Energizer bunnies until his battery—or something else—wore itself out.

Yep, life was good.

St. Augustine must be real proud of him. He was handling celibacy better than he'd ever expected. Maybe in another life he'd been a monk.

He smiled.

Until he got a gander at Helen.

She was walking up from the lagoon, where she'd apparently just taken a bath. Wearing only a T-shirt and his black silk boxers—she'd taken a real shine to his underwear—she stopped momentarily to dry her hair with a linen towel. When she bent forward and shook out the drying curls, fluffing them with her fingers, the hem of the shorts rode up. And he got a clear view of her tatoo.

He lost it then. He really, really lost it.

He cradled his head in his trembling hands. Craving inflamed his senses and turned his blood molten. His muscles engorged and throbbed.

"To hell with the condoms," he raged. Throwing down his pan, he sloshed through the water, overcome with his need for Helen. A man could only take so much. If temptation was good for the soul, he'd been a saint. But every man has his limits.

Helen was already at the cabin when he caught up with her. "Rafe, what's wrong?" she asked with concern, dropping her towel.

"Not a damn thing," he said huskily, lifting her by her waist up against the log wall. His lips came down hard on hers, and his arousal grew, hurtling him toward a mind-blowing meltdown.

She took his face in both hands and forced him back a bit, trying to understand. "Rafe, what . . . Oh, my God, don't do *that*!" He was tonguing her ear with a feverish rhythm. "What's going on here? What changed your mind?" she choked out disjointedly.

"You, baby. You changed my mind." He ripped out the words.

Meanwhile, his frantic hands were busy sliding off her shorts and palming her bare buttocks. As he began to unzip his pants, he murmured, "I love your ass."

"Rafe, stop a minute and think. What about birth control?"

"I'm comin' in bareback, babe. Damn the consequences." He released his erection with a cry and surged into her before she had a chance to question him further.

This was going to be the quickest "quickie" in history if he didn't slow down soon.

Helen was confused by Rafe's about-face. And extremely aroused. Her inner folds shifted to accommodate his size and rippled around him in reflexive welcome.

"Helen." He said her name as if she were a dream come true. His heavy-lidded eyes were wild and luminous with his need for her. "Help me," he pleaded in a guttural voice. "Love me."

"I do," she whispered, placing a caressing palm against his face.

Locking her legs around his waist, Helen urged Rafe to begin the strokes that would give them both relief.

"Oh, hell! Oh, damn. O-o-oh . . . I . . . can't . . . I . . ." He grew even larger inside her. Still unmoving, he threw back his head, arching his neck with anguish. His eyes were squeezed tight, and sweat beaded his forehead.

She would have begun the movements herself, but her lower body was pinned to the wall, impaled, by Rafe's heavier weight.

"Rafe, look at me."

At first, he refused to open his eyes. Perhaps he couldn't. When he finally did, his blue eyes appeared unfocused, pleading.

"Move, damn it! Now!"

"I can't," he gritted out. "Just wait."

"No," she cried out, and reached a hand between their bodies, skimming her own silky curls, damp with arousal.

307

Then she took the base of his hard sex between her fingertips.

He let out a keening groan and jerked, as if burned, and pulled out, then instinctively eased back in, one excruciating millimeter at a time. The friction was so intense, she screamed. Or maybe it was Rafe.

She moved her hands up to his shoulders and let Rafe take over then as he allowed his passion to rule the play. Cupping her buttocks, he drove into her with increasingly shorter and harder strokes. He buried his face in her neck and nipped at her soft flesh. She felt his heartbeat thud against hers.

"NOW!" Rafe yelled and slammed into her one last time. His big body shuddered against hers as he released his seed. "HEL-EN!"

Blood drained from her head, and tingles of exquisite pleasure swept her skin, catapulting her in huge spirals upward and upward, culminating in a series of convulsions so fierce she shook.

They both fell to the ground, unable to stand on their seemingly boneless legs any longer. Their mingled breathing was harsh and loud in the still air.

She was lying on the ground at his side, her face pressed against the red flannel covering his chest. His arms were thrown over his head, and his bare legs were parted as far as they would go in the slacks that pooled at his ankles.

At first, Helen thought Rafe had passed out, but his lungs heaved too hard for him to be unconscious. Then she realized his chest wasn't pumping from deep panting. The lout was laughing.

Humiliation washed over her as she saw herself the way he must. A frustrated thirty-four-year-old woman who practically attacked him at the least sign of sexual interest. Heck, she couldn't even remember what had prompted this lovemaking. She didn't think she'd begged him to take her, but she might have, her frustration level had been that high the past few days.

Rafe continued to laugh silently, his eyes closed.

"You jerk!" She gave him a shove of disgust and started to sit up.

"What was that for?" he inquired, opening his eyes lazily.

At the same time, he looped an arm around her shoulder and pulled her back down and on top of him.

She braced her arms on the ground beside his head and glared down at the laughing scoundrel who wrapped both arms around her waist, locking her in place. "Because you're laughing at me."

He nuzzled her neck. "Oh, babe, I'm not laughing at you. I'm laughing at me. Think about it. I just set the world record for E-T-E."

"E-T-E?"

"Yeah. Time from erection-to-ejaculation—E-T-E. Believe me, sweetheart, it's not a contest guys aim to win." His mouth curved into a smile so loving she would forgive him anything, even laughing at her. "Besides, if that wasn't bad enough, I can't remember the last time, if ever, I made love with my pants around my ankles. I lacked finesse, Helen," he concluded, as if that were the greatest crime in the world. "I'm pitiful."

She smiled then. Pitiful was not a word she'd ever use to describe Rafe. "Who needs finesse? Wham-bam is okay now and then."

"Now *you* are the one laughing at *me*. Helen, I'd really kind of like to make love this time in a bed. I'm getting too old for caves and wall-bangers and the hard ground. Do you suppose you could move off me, real easy, without turning me into a eunuch?"

She giggled. "I aim to please." She stood and quickly donned the black boxers on the ground.

Rafe got to his feet with a groan and zipped up his slacks. Before she had a chance to step away, he pulled her into his arms, his expression growing serious. "I love you, Helen," he murmured as he lowered his lips to hers.

"I love you, too," she said against his mouth.

Their kiss was short, but tender and filled with all the

emotion they'd had no time to demonstrate in their first tumultuous coming together.

Later, when Helen prepared to crawl into bed with Rafe, he said, "I have to warn you ahead of time. I have lots of fantasies about you, and I'm planning to indulge every one of them."

Her eyes shot up.

"Does that frighten you?"

She thought a moment, then shook her head.

He opened his arms for her then, and Helen flew into the bed, relishing the feel of his bare skin against hers.

His face turned serious then as he moved over her, taking most of his weight on his elbows, which framed her face. "I haven't been a religious guy for a long time, but I thank God for you, Helen. You're like a gift He's given me, despite all the problems I've thrown His way."

"What a nice thing to say!" She put one hand on the nape of his neck, pulling him closer. The other caressed his face, delicately. "Since you've got religion, I suppose that means you'll have to make an honest woman of me."

"Oh ho! Aren't you the bold one now? Proposing to a man."

She turned her face to the side. It had been presumptuous of her.

He put a forefinger on her chin and tipped her face back. "Helen, will you marry me?"

Tears brimmed her eyes. "Yes."

"The first time we run into a preacher, or a padre?"

She nodded, then frowned. "Here or in the future?"

"Both."

They exchanged a smile of pure love, and Helen did feel blessed then.

Rafe stared down at Helen, amazed at all the new feelings of warmth that filled him almost to overflowing. He brushed his lips across hers, and she sighed.

"I love you so much," he whispered. "I never loved anyone before. I didn't know it could feel so . . . so . . ."

"Wonderful?"

"That, and so much more."

Her brow furrowed. "But, Rafe, I don't want us to be blinded by all these emotions. We still have problems to—"

"Shhh," he said, stopping her words with a kiss. "We're going to work out our problems. I've told you before, there must be some divine reason for our being in this crazy time warp."

"You really are getting religion, aren't you?" She laughed.

"Not *that* much religion." He rubbed his hairy chest across her breasts in emphasis.

She inhaled sharply at the delicious torture, and he grinned.

"Let me get the last of this serious business off my chest—"

"I like what you do with your chest," she purred.

"Stop interrupting me," he said, nibbling at her bottom lip with his teeth. "What happened before can be excused as a momentary lapse of judgment, but—"

"It felt like more than a lapse to me," she said with feigned indignation.

"You are really asking for trouble, aren't you? But I'm not going to let you put me off. Our lovemaking outside happened in a heated rush, without thinking. I know what I'm doing now, though, and I'm taking the gamble willingly."

"And if there's a baby?"

His stomach flip-flopped with queasiness. "Then we'll have a baby."

She blinked back the tears that misted her brown eyes— gorgeous, adoring brown eyes. "But you'd rather not?"

"I don't know what I want anymore. Yes, I do. I want you. And whatever else comes with the package, well . . ." He shrugged. "I just don't want you to worry. Okay?"

She nodded.

"Now, soldier, let's start with fantasy number one," he

311

said, changing the mood abruptly. "I'm the officer, and you're my new recruit. You must obey my every command. Is that clear?"

"Yes, sir!" She tried but failed to suppress a giggle. "Should I salute?"

"The officer salutes first. You know that," he reprimanded, then raised himself slightly, looking down. "Yep, I'm saluting."

She arched her back, lifting her breasts to abrade his chest.

"I like your method of saluting, too," he rasped out, pressing her down to the bed with his lowering mouth. He kissed her forehead tenderly, swept her cheek with his lips, then blew against the pulsing hollow at the curve of her throat. She was eager for more, but he wanted this time to be a slow celebration of love. "Easy, babe, easy."

Helen balked, glaring at Rafe. She didn't want to go easy. She wanted him, all of him. No cool restraint. No fighting his feelings. Framing his face with both hands, she pulled him to her lips.

His first kiss was so slow it took her breath away. The second started with his tongue tracing the parted fullness of her lips, then dipping in to explore the erotic recesses of her mouth. She felt that kiss inside her fluttery belly and swelling breasts. With a moan, she gave herself up to the devouring kisses that followed, alternately soft and sweet, then deep and sinfully hot.

When he dragged his lips from hers, struggling for breath, she choked out, "Some military drill! What was that called?"

"Plundering." He smiled against her neck and moved south. Rolling to the side, he examined her body with his hungry eyes, not touching, just looking. "Hmmm. I think it's time for some reconnaissance."

"An exploratory survey of the enemy's territory?"

"Uh huh. Oh, I see bunkers ahead that look . . . interesting. Beware those two sentinels on the top." He kissed first one, then the other taut nipple.

"Do you always kiss the sentinels?" she gasped out.

"It's a new military strategy," he said thickly, wetting her with his tongue, then blowing her dry with his searing breath.

"Ah," she sighed, then, "A-a-ah" as he continued to explore her "bunkers" with lips and teeth and teasing tongue. While he fondled one breast and took another deep in his mouth, suckling, she shivered with the wildfire that overwhelmed her.

"Uh oh, I see a sand trap up ahead." His mouth left her breasts, which ached for more attention, and moved to her navel. He studied her navel with his fingertips and pointed tongue.

"Did you find the enemy?" she asked shakily, finding it increasingly harder to play games when blood roared in her ears and her senses reeled with yearning.

He shook his head. "It was a mirage . . . an *alluring* mirage. But look, that forest up ahead could hold hidden perils." He moved between her parted legs, kneeling. His erection stood out like a beautiful symbol of his love for her.

"What perils?" she said breathlessly, feeling the incredibly tantalizing brush of his fingertips over her soft curls. Did that groan just come from her, or him?

"Warm lagoons. Perhaps quicksand," he said in a voice raw with passion as he dipped his fingertips into her slick need. She should feel embarrassed. Instead, she spread her legs wider for his exploring fingers.

"Do you know that you have freckles in the most scandalous places?"

She cringed. "I hate my freckles."

"I love your freckles," he said and kissed one of them that was, indeed, in a scandalous place.

"Channels," he added then. "We have to look for treacherous channels." He ran long fingers along her satiny folds to demonstrate.

"I want you," she whimpered, reaching out her arms to pull him forward.

He forced her back down with a hand on her chest and a gentle kiss. "No, there's more. Hidden caves, perhaps?" He slid one finger, then another inside her.

She began to writhe from side to side, begging unintelligibly, "Now . . . please . . . oh, oh . . . yes, I like that . . . please . . . RAFE! No, I don't want to wait . . . I want . . . RAFE!"

"One minute, darlin'," he said in a shaky voice. "I see something. Could be dangerous." He slipped his fingers from inside her, and she cried out in protest. "Shhh," he cautioned. "Don't you want to know what it is?" he asked, lowering his head to look at her more closely.

"No," she snapped.

"Now, honey. Patience. Remember the Army survival code."

She said something vulgar about the survival code.

He chuckled, then looped his arms under her knees, raising them and exploring the creases with caresses that were tickling and surprisingly erotic. He abandoned that play momentarily and looked down once again. "As I was saying, sweetheart, I think I've discovered an ammunition dump."

"A dump," she sputtered.

"Ammunition dump. See this here . . . Aha, a bullet."

She looked down and shuddered.

"Do you think it's live?" he asked with mock seriousness.

"I think it's about to explode," she said waspishly. "Enough of the military strategy and games. I want . . ." Her words trailed off in a shiver as Rafe tested her with his tongue, then took the sensitized flesh between his lips.

"Definitely deadly," he said against her throbbing center.

"No!" she cried out as the first tremors of her impending climax rippled over her. Liquid pleasure oozed from her. "I want you to come with me."

He gave her one last flick of his tongue, then knelt upright. His eyes were glazed with passion, his lips wet and parted. Guiding her hand to his steely erection, he hissed with raw sensuality, "Take me then."

She did.

The instant he filled her, she climaxed around his shaft, weeping with frustration. "Too soon, too soon."

"No, it was perfect, *cara mía*. Perfect. I love you, I love you, I love you," he said with each agonizing stroke.

When she was keening with mindless yearning, he reared back on his knees, the velvety tip of him barely inside her body. "And does the enemy yield?" he whispered in a plea cloaked with double meanings.

"She surrenders . . . everything," Helen said, and raised her hips for his final plunge. Rafe's ragged outcry blanketed her cries.

When they finally lay sated in each other's arms, murmuring sweet love words, Rafe asked, "Did you like my fantasy?"

Helen thought, how like a man, always needing his ego to be bolstered, even when a woman had shown her appreciation in all the important ways.

"I loved it."

"Good." A decidedly mischievous tone marked his voice.

"Good?" *What was he up to now?*

"Yep. 'Cause you get to reciprocate." He jiggled his brows at her.

"Reciprocate?"

"Is there an echo in here?"

She cuffed him on the shoulder. "Explain."

"Well, it's only fair . . ."

She slanted a suspicious glance at him. The rogue!

". . . It's only fair that you show me your secret fantasy." He winked. "Man, oh, man, I can't wait."

Chapter Twenty-Two

"I don't have any sexual fantasies," she said primly.

"Liar." He laughed.

"Well, maybe one. Just a little fantasy."

"A little one? There's such a thing as a little sexual fantasy?" He arched a brow.

"Meditating."

He groaned.

"I knew you'd think it was silly."

"No, no, no. I'm game." *God, she wants to have yoga sex.* "Are you sure you wouldn't like to try the Lone Ranger? I'd let you be Tonto."

"And what would you be—the masked guy, or the horse?"

"Hmmm. I'm not sure."

"Nope, no diverting me here, Rafe. This is *my* fantasy," Helen insisted.

So, he built up the fire and, according to her directive, he was the one who sat cross-legged in the lotus position before the roaring flames.

"Try to find your center."

"No problem, babe." He peered downward, watching his "center" come to life, although it was really interfering with, rather than heightening, his inner peace.

"Concentrate," Helen demanded for the twentieth time.

"Oh, yeah, I'm concentrating, all right. Come here, sweetie, and let me show you my concentration."

"Behave."

He did, for about a second, until she sat on his lap, right

on top of his "center," and blew to hell any chance he ever had of concentrating. Even so, she proceeded to give him all kinds of advice on how to let his mind float out of his body.

And she was serious, too.

"Rafe, get your hands off my tush. You're supposed to have them on the floor, palms up, loose and relaxed. And don't move."

"When do we get to the good part?"

"This *is* the good part."

"Oh." *Boy, does she have a lot to learn!* He played along with her, though, and was amazed to find that he could sit perfectly still for a long time—five minutes—with the woman he loved impaled on his erection. It was probably a record of some kind. He'd have to check his brother Eduardo's *Penthouse Book of World Records* when he got home.

But he couldn't think about that now. Helen had moved to step two of her fantasy. Every time she *ooohm*ed, he felt the most incredible vibrations in all his essential hot spots. *Maybe her fantasies aren't so far off base, after all. Maybe I'm the one who's got a lot to learn. Hmmm.*

Rafe's conjectures soon proved true when, to his absolute astonishment, he learned how to control the movement of his favorite organ just by focusing. It was like driving a car with a remote control.

And Helen developed a neat trick of squeezing him from inside in something she called a Kegel excercise—Helen could use technical terms like that even in the midst of hot sex, that's the kind of marvel she was.

Yep, Helen's fantasy was turning out to be a surprise. Of course, he liked his own fantasies better, but he didn't tell her that, either. He was too busy experiencing an explosive climax.

They rested then—*thank God!*—and ate leftover venison and raw turnips. They sat at the table, bundled in blankets, murmuring softly. The air had turned very chilly.

"I'm so damn sick of venison," he complained. "What

317

I wouldn't give for chocolate chip cookies! Or a cheddar and chicken burrito. Or barbecued ribs. Or a thin-crust pizza with pepperoni and sausage and mushrooms and onions."

She smiled and made a tsking noise. "You don't really eat like that, do you?"

"Of course, I do."

"Those are all empty calories."

"Yep." He wrinkled his nose at her. "Bootie calories."

"Huh?"

"They go right to your butt."

"Well, you don't have to worry about that. You have a very nice . . . butt."

He grinned. "Thank you, honey, and likewise. I'll let you check it out later."

They both laughed then.

In a little while, Helen stared at him shyly, hesitating.

"What?"

"I never knew people laughed when they made love," she confessed.

He tilted his head at her. "Sex is fun. Why would that surprise you?"

She blushed.

"Oh, Prissy, I'm going to make you laugh so much." And he wasn't referring to tickling her funny bone.

Rafe took Helen's hand across the table then, and they talked of inconsequential things. Usually, he didn't like to chitchat after sex. He just wanted to fall asleep, or go home. Everything about sex with Helen was different.

Was it love that made the difference?

Shaking his head at that disarming cliché, he rose and pulled on a pair of pants and boots. He needed to go outside for a nature call and to get some more firewood.

A few moments later, Helen was straightening out the bed linens when she heard Rafe yell, "Helen, come here! Quick! You won't believe this."

Helen glanced toward the door, alarmed by the rising pitch of Rafe's voice. She wrapped a blanket tightly around her shoulders and rushed outside.

It was snowing. Hard. A regular blizzard.

And Rafe stood with his arms outstretched joyously in the moonlight, his tongue catching snowflakes. Apparently he didn't see much snow in L.A.

"Isn't this great!" he said eagerly, letting snowflakes settle in his hair and on his chest and bare shoulders, oblivious to the cold. He reminded her of a little boy.

She leaned against the doorframe, feasting on the glorious sight. She wished she could freeze the scene for all time. "I'm going to paint this picture when I get back to the future," she told him softly.

"Yeah. What're you gonna call it?"

" 'The Man I Love.' "

"Too unoriginal. It's got to be something like 'Snow in the Sierras,' or 'Wild Man in Angel Valley.' "

"I like my title better."

"Okay," he said agreeably, and opened his arms to her.

She stepped toward him and opened her blanket, enveloping them both in its warmth. When he'd heated both their bodies with his kisses and roving hands, she showed him how to make snow angels, in the nude—*yes, she was losing her mind*—and Rafe showed her how to have snow sex—*yes, they were both losing their minds*.

The next day, they awakened, burrowed under the quilts, to find even more snow had fallen—ten more inches—and it was still coming down. They looked at each other, coming to the same conclusions.

"Zeb and Hector aren't coming back soon."

"We're going to be snowed in."

They exchanged a smile. The gods were smiling on them, it seemed.

After a breakfast of bread and honey—Rafe kept complaining about the wax—he showed her another fantasy. It involved honey. She'd never realized what a versatile food honey was.

Later, Rafe dressed warmly and went out to care for the animals and gather up his tools and bag of gold dust, bringing them up to the cabin. As he went out the door, he commented dryly, "Too bad you won't be able to dig up any more carrots with all this snow."

"We can still have liver and onions," she called after him.

"Hah! If you make me eat liver and onions, I'll make you have foot sex."

For a long time after he was gone, she pondered his words. *Foot sex?* He was teasing, of course.

That afternoon, Rafe suggested they try another one of her fantasies.

"I don't have any more. Really."

"Invent one then."

Flushing pink from her scalp to her curled toes—she was still nude under a blanket wrapped toga-style around her body—she offered hesitantly, "Well, there is the rocking chair."

They both glanced at Zeb's armless rocker, then at each other.

Rafe broke into a slow, lazy grin. "Helen, Helen, Helen. You are a very quick learner."

For a week, they were marooned in the cabin, going out only to take care of bodily functions, feed the horses, and bring in firewood. They weren't bored. They made love and talked and read books aloud and made love and shared secrets and ate enough venison to grow hooves and indulged Rafe's numerous—*really numerous*—fantasies and her burgeoning ones, and they planned for their future.

Of course, their idyllic interlude had to end eventually. It did, with a bang.

Big Ben came knocking, and knocking, and knocking.

They both dressed and Rafe got the rifle off the wall, checking the ammunition.

"You're going to kill him?" she cried in panic.

He considered her grimly. "He might go after the horses. Or us."

"But what about Bertha, his wife?"

Rafe cast her a incredulous look. "Bears don't get married."

"How do you know?"

"Give me a break, Helen. Do you really think I want to kill some animal weighing as much as a Mack truck?"

She shook her head slowly. "Be careful." Grabbing their two pistols, she started to follow him.

"What do you think you're doing?"

"I'm coming to help."

"No way! Those pistols would be like a cap gun to a bear."

"I'm coming," she asserted.

By now, Ben was on the other side of the cabin, near the garden, sniffing the ground, presumably hunting for carrots. Then, still sniffing, he moved to the stream bank. The snowfall had stopped days ago, and the sun was warm, but a foot of snow still lay on the ground.

"Shoot in the air. I don't want to waste my ammunition," Rafe advised her. "We might be able to scare him away."

"BAM!" Helen shot just above the beast's head.

At first, the animal just turned his huge head toward them, almost in puzzlement. Saliva drooled from its mouth, and yellow teeth the size of sharpened piano keys stood out in deadly detail. Just to show off, he reared up on his hind legs to his full height, about ten feet, and growled loud enough to wake the dead.

"I thought bears hibernated in the winter," she said fearfully.

"It's not really winter yet. Besides, he likely wanted a midnight snack. Us."

"Very funny. Maybe you could turn this into one of your sexual fantasies."

"Maybe," he said grimly and raised his rifle, taking careful aim.

"Try for the shoulder. A bear's heart is located in the shoulder area. What you want to do is break through the

321

shoulder so the bullet will enter the heart or lungs and anchor there.''

Rafe grunted. ''You are a real font of information.''

''This isn't the time for sarcasm, sweetheart. Shoot!''

Rafe pulled the trigger, but, in just that instant, Ben heard his mate calling from the distant woods and he lurched to the side. Rafe only winged his ear.

The bear lost its balance, though, and hit a small oak tree. Bellowing his rage, Ben righted himself and took the trunk of the young sapling in his wide mouth, shaking and snarling until he'd pulled it from the ground, roots and all. He was probably practicing, imagining it was their necks.

''God!'' Rafe exclaimed, taking aim again, this time with Helen's second pistol. He hit the beast moving toward them on all fours right through the top of his shoulder. Blood showed immediately on the mangy fur. ''Did I hit the right spot?''

''I don't know. Possibly a little too high.''

Ben reared up again, his vicious eyes centered on them, but his ears perked to the persistent cry of his mate in the forest. Bertha could be calling for help, or perhaps she was just worried about her man. In any case, Ben let out a mighty roar, which clearly said, ''Later, dudes!'' and loped off in the snow.

At first, Helen and Rafe just gaped at each other, then they exhaled at the same time, neither realizing they'd been holding their breath. Rafe hugged her, and they walked over to the area where the bear had pulled the tree from the ground. The snow around it had been pounded down by the animal's massive weight, and loose limbs and dirt littered the white snow.

Rafe tried to pick up the tree and found it too heavy. Deep teeth marks marred its bark. They glanced at each other in mutual horror at what they'd just escaped.

Releasing her hand, Rafe walked to the other side of the fallen tree to examine the hole where the tree had stood. With a quick intake of air, he dropped to his knees and closed his eyes, almost like he was praying.

"What is it?" she cried, alarmed at the pallor of his face. Rushing forward, she knelt down beside him. Rafe's face was buried in his trembling hands. Maybe this was a delayed reaction to the danger they'd just escaped. "Honey, it's over now," she soothed.

Rafe raised his head and sheer bliss spread across his face. "No, Helen, it's just beginning." He pointed to the cavity in the ground, and she saw at least a dozen huge nuggets, and the reddish earth was loaded with a yellowish dust. Still more nuggets and dust clung to the long roots of the fallen tree. Rafe pumped his fist in the air in the victory sign.

Gold! Rafe had finally hit his bonanza.

He pulled her in his arms. He danced her around the snow. He kissed her and hugged her and shouted his joy.

"We can go home now, honey," Rafe exclaimed jubilantly. "All my troubles are over now."

Helen should have been happy. For some reason, she started to weep.

The next afternoon, they were in the root cellar, stacking the last of the gold they'd gathered from the hole and its immediate surroundings, when they heard a shout echoing over the little valley.

"HEL-LO-O-O-O!"

"Zeb!" they both said at the same time.

"I can't wait to tell Zeb about our strike," Rafe said with boyish zeal.

Helen scanned the cloth bags lining the walls—close to 150 pounds of gold nuggets and dust. Rafe had told her over and over since yesterday that their bonanza was worth almost forty thousand dollars by 1850 rates and a cool million in the 1996 exchange.

She was excited over their windfall, too, but nowhere near as much as Rafe. Helen couldn't help thinking that Rafe was headed for a major disappointment. Although he constantly criticized her for nagging, she said nothing now, not wanting to rain on his parade.

Smiling, Rafe laced his fingers with hers and pulled her up the steps. When they got to the other side of the cabin, Zeb and Hector were just emerging into the valley from the steep path up the mountain. They were followed by a milk cow, whose moos were being drowned out by the cackling of some chickens in a small crate tied to the back of Zeb's mule. The new additions must have cost a mint and been a chore getting up the mountain.

"Hector is back," Rafe said, casting her a significant look. Of course, she was happy that Hector had returned with Zeb, but his return meant that Pablo must not have arrived in Rich Bar yet. Therefore, no parachutes.

But that concern was put aside for now in the joyous rush of the reunion. Between hugs and clasping hands and everyone talking at once, Rafe got out that they'd hit pay-dirt, thanks to the bears, and Zeb gave them bits and pieces of gossip from Rich Bar. Hector took the horses off to the barn to unsaddle and stable them, then ran in a hundred different directions, wanting to explore all his favorite trees and birds' nests and other childhood delights.

"Don't go too far," Rafe warned. "The bears may still be close by."

"I'll go out and get those grizzlies tomorrow," Zeb said confidently. "Can't have them consarned varmints tramblin' through a homestead, 'specially with a young'un about."

Helen wanted to protest, but Rafe put a cautioning hand on her arm. After all, this was another time and culture, and they had no right interfering. Especially since they'd be leaving soon.

A short time later, they drank tin cups of fresh brewed coffee with slices of her newly baked bread, slathered with honey. Zeb had brought fresh supplies with him, including coffee beans. Hector took his honey bread outside, wanting to check on the fish lines. Rafe faced Helen across the table and Zeb moved to his rocking chair.

Swiping a fingertip over the top of the honeycomb, Rafe dipped it in his mouth, making sure she saw the gesture.

When he winked at her, she knew he was remembering the same thing she was. And it wasn't bees.

The lout! A lovable lout, but a lout just the same. She made a face at him, and he just grinned.

Meanwhile, Zeb let out a loud sigh of contentment, glad to be home. And his rocking chair went *creak, creak, creak.* With each *creak,* the grin on Rafe's face grew wider and wider.

"Don'tcha just love the sound of a rocker?" Rafe mused. "It brings to mind so many . . . memories."

"Stop it," she hissed.

"Me? What am I doing?"

Zeb looked from one to the other of them. Then he clapped his knee and hooted with laughter. "Well, I'm mighty pleased ta see you two been workin' those bed ropes. I jist knew you two would settle yer little spat quick-like iffen me and Hector gave you some time ta frolic a bit," Zeb whooped.

"You're right there, too, Zeb. Helen surely does love her . . . frolicking." He dazzled her with one of his sweet smiles. "Ain't that right, honey?"

"That's enough!" She slammed her hand on the table and stood, almost knocking her bench over. "I'm going to start dinner." She flashed Rafe a meaningful glare. "And we're having liver and onions. With carrots on the side."

"Um um!" Zeb said, rubbing his stomach with anticipation.

Rafe looked a little green.

She turned her back on them then, pulling out the iron kettle to begin dinner.

"Tarnation, boy, what you doin' with yer feet on the table? My Effie woulda whacked me with a broom iffen I ever done that."

Helen didn't want to look, but she couldn't help herself. Rafe had taken off his boots and pushed the bench up against the wall. Leaning back, his legs were crossed at the ankle, propped on the table, and he was wiggling his toes in their wool socks. "Liver and onions, didja say, honey-

bunch?'' He gave his big toe an extra jiggle in warning.
Foot sex!
''Better close your mouth, babe. You might catch a fly.''

Dinner that night turned out to be trout, which Hector
brought up from one of the fishing lines, small browned
potatoes, which Zeb had purchased in Rich Bar for an exorbitant price (not that they couldn't afford it now), and a
sweet custard made with eggs and milk and raisins from
their new extended family. Zeb sheepishly explained,
''Growin' boys need their milk, and I had a yen fer fresh
eggs.''

''Where in the world did you find a cow? And chickens?''

''There wuz this down-'n-out family from the states what
needed some gold ta go home. Good thing you struck gold
whilst I was gone, though, 'cause I jist 'bout spent my
whole poke.''

She patted his hand indulgently.

Zeb picked up a sleepy Hector and laid him lovingly on
the blankets before the fire.

''Tell me some more 'bout how you shot that buck. And
the bear . . . Give me the whole story agin,'' Zeb exhorted.
''Spec'ly the gold. I love ta hear you talk on yer first
glimpse of the gold.''

Rafe had already told Zeb three times, but Helen could
see that he liked to talk about his adventures. Even the deer
slaying had lost some of its repugnance for him in the re-
telling.

When Rafe finished, she sat next to him on the bench
and he pulled her close, with an arm resting loosely over
one shoulder. Zeb's eyes teared a bit, watching them.

''Give us the gossip from Rich Bar,'' Helen encouraged
then.

''Well, I already gave you the *Godey's Lady Magazine*s
what Mary sent,'' he told Helen. ''She said that Yank feller
over on Smith's Bar gave 'em ta her, and she don't have

no use fer such fripperies. She'd druther read them dime novels of hers.''

She smiled. "Are she and Yank a couple now?"

"Lordy, no. She gave 'im a black eye las' Sabbath when he tried ta kiss 'er.''

They all laughed.

"And what other news?" Helen prodded.

"Well, I brought a copy of the *Sacramento Transcript*. Plenty of news in there. Of course, everyone's celebratin' statehood.''

"California just became a state?" Rafe asked in awe.

A chill ran over Helen, realizing that such an historical event was taking place around them. Rafe's wide eyes told her he shared her feelings.''

"Yessirree. We's the thirty-first state ta join the union,'' Zeb went on. He lit up the pipe with some fragrant tobacco he'd been given by Yank. "Anyways, President Fillmore signed the bill on the ninth of September, but word din't reach San Francisco till October eighteenth, when the steamer *Oregon* brought the good tidings. There's celebratin' goin' on from one end of the state ta the other. Lordy, lordy, I never seed so much corn liquor drunk in all my born days.''

Next he told them about all the strikes reported during the past month or so. An eighteen-pound nugget was found at Sullivans Creek, a twenty-five-pound one just up the river from Downieville, and a fourteen-pound one at Carson Hill. The latter was just lying on the ground waiting to be picked up. Zeb said prospectors from a hundred miles around were rushing to these sites to join in the bonanzas.

Rafe frowned. "It's important, then, that word doesn't get out concerning this strike here in Angel Valley."

"Do tell," Zeb said, puffing away. "I'm far enough away here that those greedy buggers will stay away fer some time. But the least whiff of gold and they'll be on this sweet spot like dogs on a bone.'' Zeb chuckled softly. "You won't believe the tale being passed around 'bout Carson Hill. Seems a miner died and they was burying the poor soul, but the preacher what come to do the service wuz a mite wordy. The story goes that some of the miners got restless listenin' ta the preacher go on an' they began ta sift the dirt in their hands as prospectors are wont ta do. Well, lo and behold, one of the gentlemen yells, 'Color!' Seems there wuz gold in the hole they dug fer the coffin.''

"Oh, Zeb, you're making this up." Helen chortled with disbelief.

Zeb crossed his heart with a forefinger. "I swear ta God. 'Course the men couldn't bury the corpse till they dug the hole some more. It wuz two days afore the final restin' took place."

Rafe squeezed her shoulder with shared enjoyment of Zeb's story, and his eyes flashed with humor.

Zeb's expression changed suddenly. Jumping up, he put his pipe on the mantle. "Well, tarnation, I can't believe I din't tell you the most important news of all. I brought you a present." He rushed outside, and they heard him shuffling in the saddlebags that he'd left beside the door.

She and Rafe gasped when they recognized the objects Zeb handed them ceremoniously. He cackled with merriment.

The harness and parachutes.

"Where did you get them?" Rafe asked, fondling the fabric, which was dirty but intact.

"I thought Pablo hadn't come to Rich Bar since Hector came back with you," she said. "I was afraid to ask."

Zeb's face turned stormy. "Oh, Pablo wuz there, all right. The bastard! Excuse my cussin', Helen, but any man what denies his own kin is lower 'n a toadstool."

"He didn't believe that Hector was his nephew?" Rafe asked.

"No, it weren't that. He said he don't have no time ta care fer no snot-nosed young'un. He and that Sancho wuz schemin' fer some easy way ta get rich, robbin' good folks, no doubt."

"Poor Hector," Helen said, peering down at the sleeping child. "He has no one now."

"Well, now, I beg ta differ. Hector has me, and we certainly ain't poor no more."

They all felt a glow of happiness then at the way fate had conspired to bring them together to this mutually beneficial end. Without Hector there to keep Zeb company, and Zeb there to care for the child, she would have felt guilty leaving Angel Valley.

When all the new events finally settled in, Helen watched Rafe, who was studying his coffee cup with equal pensiveness. Sensing her scrutiny, he looked up. There was both happiness and regret in his blue eyes. She felt the same way.

"What do you say we go home, babe?" he said in a husky, emotion-choked voice.

She nodded, too overcome to speak.

Home.

Chapter Twenty-Three

Three days later, Helen and Rafe were prepared to leave Angel Valley, never to return.

Their saddlebags and clothing were packed with seventy-five pounds of gold nuggets and some dust. They would carry only nuggets on their bodies on their journey to the future—visions of gold dust flying through space were enough to turn Rafe white with horror—but they required the less-conspicuous flakes for spending money until they got back to the landing site.

"Make sure you don't show any nuggets to anyone you pass. Nuggets 're a sure sign of a strike. Me and Hector don't want our purty l'il valley swarmin' with unwanted visitors."

Since Zeb's return, they'd worked feverishly to close over the hole near the stream, and stored most of the wealth in a specially devised hiding place under the barn. "I ain't doin' no more prospectin'," Zeb had declared adamantly. "This is more'n enough ta las' me a lifetime. Me and Hector's gonna become farmers." Zeb's split would be worth almost $20,000 at the 1850 standard.

Rafe had divided their half of the cache with Helen, despite her objections. She'd sewn pockets throughout the interior of their clothing to hold most of the nuggets. Rafe had a particular affection for one ten-pound nugget, which he'd kept as part of his share. Helen felt jealous sometimes, watching him caress the blasted rock. How he was ever going to carry it while skydiving, she had no idea, but he assured her he would.

Finally, it was time to go.

She tried not to cry, but the tears came in buckets.

"Don't you be worryin' none 'bout me," Zeb said, hugging her tightly. "I got Hector now."

"But you'll be lonely here." She was sobbing.

Zeb's rheumy old eyes twinkled. "Were you and yer man lonely whilst you were alone here?"

Helen blushed as Rafe came up beside her, drawing her to his side with a comforting squeeze. His eyes were clouded with emotion, too.

"Besides," Zeb went on, "there's this Injun woman up north aways that I bin eyin' fer some time. Mebbe . . . well, mebbe . . ." He ducked his head bashfully.

"Well, aren't you the crafty one!" Rafe laughed, leaning forward to shake his hand. Then, on second thought, he drew Zeb into a friendly bear hug.

More tears spilled down Helen's face.

The whole time, Hector hung onto Zeb's thigh for dear life, probably fearful that she and Rafe would take him away from the only real home he'd ever had. Helen kissed Hector good-bye, although she'd done so a half dozen times already. Then Rafe hauled the boy up into his arms and murmured something in his ear. Hector nodded and looked lovingly toward Zeb.

They mounted their horses.

"Will you write?" Zeb asked.

She stared at Rafe, unsure how to answer.

"We can't," Rafe said. "I wish we could. I can't explain, Zeb, but it would be impossible where we're going."

Zeb walked up, close to their horses, and confided, "I understand. Actually, I know who you really are."

"You do?" Had they somehow let something slip in the weeks they'd lived with Zeb? She glanced at Rafe.

Rafe grimaced with uncertainty.

"Yessirree" Zeb whispered. "Yer angels. Delivered by God ta help an old man who wuz ready fer the whiskey jim-jams. The good Lord sent you two ta save me and give me a new reason fer livin'." His eyes scanned his beautiful valley and landed upon Hector, who chased a squirrel across the yard, already having put the pain of departure aside with youthful resilience.

"Angels?" she and Rafe exclaimed together, then exchanged a warm smile.

It was as good an explanation as any.

They rode off in silence, both contemplating all that had happened to them in the space of only eleven weeks. The good things far outweighed the bad, in Helen's opinion. It was going to be harder than she'd ever imagined to leave the past.

They traveled leisurely through the hills of California, heading southward. Autumn was painting the rich forests and vast plains with its winter palette of rust and gold and burnt umber. The air turned brisk.

They spent their days riding, their conversation soft, skirting the important decisions to be made ahead. At night, they camped out in their tent under the stars, turning to each other with a wild hunger, as if reassuring each other with their bodies and throaty love words that the future would take care of the problems they were unable to solve themselves.

On the fourth day, they arrived in Rich Bar. The winter exodus had already commenced, with miners by the thousands heading for the dryer lowlands. So they felt safe staying one night with Mary at the Indiana House, renewing their friendship. They told no one about their good fortune, not even Mary, fearing for Zeb and Hector's safety.

But Helen had another secret, too, and she wondered how long she could delay telling Rafe what had been troubling her for days.

She was pregnant.

This should have been a happy time for her. It was what she'd always wanted—a baby. And a child formed of the love she shared with this glorious man . . . Well, it was the answer to all her dreams.

But not Rafe's.

She kept putting off her disclosure, wanting to hold on to the priceless bond between them a little bit longer. The instant she told him, she knew their relationship would change. She didn't doubt his love for her. He wouldn't abandon her. But she didn't know whether his love was strong enough to withstand this test. And, more important, she didn't want to burden him with her dream.

"And even though the town is jist 'bout deserted, we got us a padre, and Papa's hired a Mexican band to play here for the next two weeks," Mary rambled on. "Don't that beat all? A town what won't let furriners get a mining permit puts out the welcome sign for a Spanish priest and a Mex band?"

Helen jolted back to attention. They all sat at a table in the Indiana House dining room, where Mary had taken them before even showing them to a room.

Then the words sank in.

"*Padre!*" Rafe exclaimed, casting Helen a significant look.

"*Padre!*" Helen echoed breathlessly.

"We can get married," Rafe whispered and dragged her close to his side, kissing the top of her head. They sat side by side on a bench. "Thank God, I can make you an honest woman now." He pinched her bottom playfully for emphasis. "I wouldn't want to be jumping off a cliff with *that* sin on my soul."

Swatting his hand away, she hissed, "Behave! Mary's watching." Helen smiled affectionately at Rafe then, even though mixed sentiments of elation and guilt engulfed her. Elation because she would be marrying the man she loved; guilt because she was, in fact, not quite an honest woman.

Should she tell him about the baby now?

Should she wait?

"Did you see that prospector outside with eight blasted kids running all over the place?" Rafe was asking Mary.

Helen stiffened.

"That's the new postmaster," Mary informed him.

"God! It looked like a regular baby factory." Rafe shivered with distaste.

Helen decided her news could wait.

On the thirtieth of October, 1850, Helen Anne Prescott married Rafael Joseph Santiago in a canvas tent chapel in Rich Bar, California. Their only witnesses were the padre and a perplexed Mary and Yank, who didn't comprehend why they wanted to remarry.

Rafe tucked the marriage document into the jacket of the black suit Yank had sold him from his general store. Mary had lent Helen her mother's cream-colored gown, which was of some silky material that shimmered with gold threads. It was edged with green and gold embroidery. In Rafe's opinion, there was never a more beautiful bride in all the world.

"You're mine now," he murmured huskily as they followed behind Yank and Mary and the padre, heading toward the wedding party. He couldn't believe he'd actually gotten married, or that he was so happy about it.

"I was yours before the wedding, Rafe."

"But it's official now."

"I doubt whether it will be legal in the twentieth century."

"We'll get married again. See how eager I am to please?"

"I noticed," she said suspiciously. "What do you want?"

"Well, I was wondering if we could skip the food and drinks and dancing and move on to the good stuff."

"Like what?"

He whispered a few explicit "for instances" in her ear.

"RA-AFE!"

"God, my mother's going to love you."

They had, in fact, left the party early, begging exhaustion from all their travels and the necessity of an early start in the morning.

They'd fooled no one.

Helen had blushed repeatedly at Rafe's blatant efforts to seduce her in the midst of all the Indiana House guests. It had been a lovely party, which served the dual purpose of a welcoming event for the new postmaster. In fact, the celebration still carried on. He heard the band playing through the open bedroom windows.

Not that Rafe recalled many details of the day. He had no clue as to what he'd eaten or drunk or whom he'd spoken with, although he remembered vividly a slow dance with Helen.

She had shocked everyone by dipping *him*.

He needed her so much. It was frightening just how important she'd become to him.

Once they'd gotten upstairs, he'd made speedy work of removing his clothes and hers and showing her too quickly on the rag carpet just inside the bedroom door how great his need for her was. Lying in the bed now, naked and sated, he wanted her again.

There was just enough light from the full moon and a dozen lit candles for him to see his new wife. *Wife!* He rolled the word on his tongue and said it aloud softly, "Wife."

He saw her lips twitch with a suppressed smile. The witch was teasing him.

He wrapped a long strand of her hair around a finger and inhaled the rose scent of the soap she'd used to shampoo with earlier. Actually, he was the one who'd washed her hair and combed it dry, taking great delight in all the little aspects of readying her for their wedding.

"Are you sniffing my hair again?" she said, pretending to be half-asleep.

"Yes, is there somewhere else you'd rather I . . . sniff?"

She giggled and kept her eyes squeezed shut. "You are so . . ."

"Disgusting?"

"Adorable."

"Adorable? Adorable? Men don't want to be adorable,"

he growled, sniffing her breasts, which also smelled like roses. *I think I'll take a couple of bars of that soap back with me.* "Men want to be sexy and handsome and virile and—"

"Stop fishing for compliments, you lech." She peeked at him through slitted eyelids and reached for the sheet to cover herself.

"No way!" he laughed, flipping the linens to the end of the bed. "I'm not done sniffing yet." In the course of his nasal excursion, he noticed some bruising on her forearms. His fingermarks. "Damn, did I hurt you?" he asked, leaning over to kiss each of the bluish prints.

"Do carpet burns on my tush count as hurting?" she said drolly.

He chucked her under the chin. "They'll look good with your tattoo."

"Hah! I don't see you getting any wool fibers on your behind."

"O-o-oh! Is that an invitation?"

"Oh, you!" She lifted her face and kissed his lips tenderly. The expression on her face turned more serious. "I love you so much, Rafe. No matter what happens, always know that, I love you, and I'll never stop."

Blood drained from his head with foreboding. "Why do you say it like that? What do you think will happen?"

"Nothing. It's my wedding day, and we have so many important things ahead of us. The jump, for one thing. We can't know for sure what will happen, and I just wanted you to know . . ."

He relaxed, but then he declared adamantly, "We're going to be together in the future."

"You don't have to convince me. I married you, didn't I?"

"Yeah, you did." His voice came out raw and raspy with emotion. Then he grinned. "So, do you think sex will be boring now that we're married?"

She snickered. "So far it's been rather . . . quick. Hard to judge. Maybe you'd better . . ."

"Practice?" He moved over on top of her, spreading her thighs with his knees. "Oh, babe, I thought you'd never ask."

Slowly and deliberately, he kissed her lips and shoulders and breasts and belly and inner thighs. Her wrists and palms. Even the soles of her feet. Over and over, he worshipped her—*his wife*—and between gentle kisses, he whispered love words. Some of them romantic, others dark and erotic. English and Spanish.

She moaned and whimpered and returned his throaty endearments.

"I love you, Rafe. I love you, I love you, I love you."

"You are *mi corozón,* my heart. I will love you till the end of time."

He twined his fingers with hers and admired the candlelight flickering over the matching gold bands they wore. He'd secretly purchased them from Yank. Surprisingly, these gold rings meant more to him than all the gold he hoped to carry back to the future. They *were* his future.

When he eased into her, braced on his elbows, he felt her ripple around him. He closed his eyes against the sweet burn and shuddered, almost weeping with the joy she brought him.

"I can feel your love flowing into me," she purred with his first stroke.

"And yours comes back to me," he answered as he withdrew and her hips lifted in pursuit.

With each thrust, he held himself rigid inside her until the ripples started again. Then he stopped. "Tell me."

"I love you."

He started again. Then stopped. "Tell me."

"I love you."

"Again."

"I love you."

Over and over, he controlled her, setting the pace, urging the love words he needed to hear.

They were magicians that night, creating enchantment in a room that seemed worlds apart, separated by time and distance from the rest of humanity. Only they existed. Rising higher and higher under the magic spell, they climbed to new plateaus of sexuality. His arousal was the magic wand, her sheath the charm, but the sorcery was in the love that permeated them.

When he finally thrust his release into her body, she pulled his face down, taking his cry into her mouth. And her body clasped him hotly as they both spun and spun and spun. Splintering into perfect ecstasy.

For one split second, they were given a vision of eternity. And harmony.

After dawn the next morning, their horses were saddled, ready to leave Rich Bar. And Helen couldn't find Rafe.

They'd already eaten breakfast in the dining room. Then Rafe had gone out with Yank while she finished packing.

"Do you have any idea where Rafe is?" Helen approached Mary now as she scrubbed the dining tables.

"Yank said something about taking Rafe to see a grove of redwood trees."

"Trees? Rafe wanted to see trees? Now?" she exclaimed.

Mary laughed. "Yep. I thought it was mighty peculiar, too."

They walked out onto the porch together and saw Rafe and Yank walking toward them, though a considerable distance away.

The postmaster's wife, Julie, strolled up then, balancing an infant in one arm and a toddler in the other. Helen offered to hold the baby while Julie engaged Mary in a conversation about curtains.

Helen closed her eyes and savored the precious scent of baby skin and talcum powder. With a sigh, she cuddled the gurgling baby onto her shoulder.

"Well, I guess that's what happens when you marry them. They just dawdle around."

Helen turned at the sound of Rafe's teasing voice and saw him flinch at the spectacle of her holding the baby.

He was not pleased.

"Let's get this show on the road," he grumbled, walking away from her and over to his horse.

Her eyes widened with hurt at his harsh tone. But then she gave the baby a soft kiss before handing her back to her mother. Making a face at Rafe's back, she said, "Hey, you're the one who went off tree watching."

"Nag, nag, nag." He was observing her again, but lovingly now that she no longer cradled the infant in her arms.

"I love you, too, you dope."

"You can't get on my good side with sweet talk, babe."

"Wanna bet."

Yank and Mary burst out laughing behind them.

"Ain't marriage grand?" Rafe remarked rhetorically.

"Yes!" they all said.

Helen had been somber and weepy ever since they'd left Rich Bar three days ago. Ever since he'd snapped at her. But, hell, it had been such a shock seeing her holding that baby, her eyes misty with longing. She'd looked so . . . so right with a baby.

Damn! Damn! Damn! He had to make things better with Helen. "Honey, do you want to stop for the night?" It was only late afternoon, but they'd been riding since early morning. Her face looked white and drawn. She nodded.

Rafe dismounted in a small clearing, much like the one where they'd camped with their three captors more than eleven weeks ago—it seemed like aeons. He reached out his arms for her, and she slipped off her horse.

When she made to move out of his embrace, he closed his arms around her waist. Tipping up her chin, he asked, "Helen, what's wrong? You've been moody for days. If it's about Rich Bar, well, I'm sorry if I bit your head off. It was the sight of you with that baby—"

"Forget it!" she clipped out and pushed out of his hold, leading her horse toward the stream.

He stared after her in confusion. "What the hell's wrong with you? You're behaving like a woman with a bad case of . . ." A sudden thought occurred to him, and he brightened. ". . . PMS."

She inhaled sharply and glared at him.

"Are you getting your period?" he asked. He couldn't keep the hope out of his voice.

"You don't have to be so happy about it."

"Helen, I'm not exactly happy—"

"Liar!"

He scowled with exasperation. "I'm not exactly happy," he repeated, "but you and I need time to iron out our problems. Maybe later babies will be a viable option. This is the best way. Really. You'll see."

"Sometimes you are so dull-headed," she sputtered. "Viable option? We're not talking legal briefs here. We're talking human life. And you, my friend, had a vasectomy. I'm assuming that reproduction won't be a *viable option* in the future."

He grimaced, knowing this was his cue. He at least had to make the offer. "I could always have the operation reversed."

She laughed, and it wasn't a pleasant sound. "I wish you could have seen your face when you said that. Green. Green as Kermit the Frog." She shot him another glare. "You frog!"

He caught up with her and grabbed her by the shoulders, forcing her to face him. Tears brimmed in her eyes, and her lips quivered.

His stomach lurched. *I don't want to hurt her.* "Helen, don't do this now. We've just found each other. We have time to resolve all these things. Just don't force this issue now."

Tears spilled out of her eyes and streamed down her face. He felt like crying himself.

"You're right." She sobbed, wrapping her arms around his neck. "I'm just being silly. We have lots of time."

Rafe wasn't so sure, though. That night, they slept in each other's arms, but they didn't make love. He didn't want to initiate anything that would result in a pregnancy at this late date. And Helen knew that he didn't want to make a baby with her.

Not now. Not yet. *Oh, hell!*

He had to plan for their future. At least he'd taken one step in that direction. While still in Rich Bar he'd asked Yank where he might find a young redwood tree. Rafe wasn't sure that carrying the gold nuggets back to the future on his body was going to work. So, he'd sought insurance. Some place in the past that would endure into the future. He'd thought and thought, trying to come up with some hiding place that would last into the future, but be free from pilfering hands.

A redwood tree.

Yank had watched with interest as Rafe climbed the young tree and placed an object in the crook of two limbs—his favorite ten-pound nugget. Luckily, Yank hadn't asked any questions, and he'd promised not to go back after they'd gone. Yank undoubtedly thought Rafe was batty, but, for some reason, Rafe trusted him.

It had been a stupid thing to do, he supposed, leaving a ten-pound nugget in the past where someone might find it. Although he couldn't imagine too many people would go climbing redwood trees.

Yep, it had probably been a stupid thing he'd done.

It had *not* been a stupid thing.

Rafe came to that conclusion the next day when they approached the landing site and ran into bandits. Not Ignacio and Pablo and Sancho. Ignacio was dead, and the other two yahoos were reportedly off to Mexico to join up with Joaquin Murietta.

No, this was Rafe's nemesis—the Angel Bandit—and his notorious sidekick, Elena, along with a half-dozen mean-looking scoundrels. Within minutes, his ancestor relieved them of every blessed piece of gold they'd worked so hard to gather. It was a good thing he'd already put his crucifix and wedding band in his boot, and Helen had done likewise with her ring, or the bandits would have taken those, too.

They'd made them remove their clothing and torn off all the concealed pockets. Luckily, Elena took Helen into the bushes for a private strip search, but not out of consideration. Elena didn't want Helen's nude body to attract her lover, the Angel Bandit.

There was no question this dude was Rafe's ancestor. Possibly his grandfather many times removed. Except for the cruel cast to his features, they were the spitting image of each other, right down to the blue eyes—an anomaly in Mexicans.

"You can't do this," Rafe protested. "You're my . . . my grandfather."

"Are you loco?" the Angel Bandit asked. "I am only thirty-four years old. How old are you, *señor*?"

Rafe snorted with disgust. "The same. What's your name, by the way? I can't call you Angel."

"Why not?" Turning his sultry eyes on Helen and surveying her body with appreciation, he asked her, "Do you not think I look angelic, my pretty one?"

His mistress, Elena, clouted him on the back with a tambourine, shrieking, "I weel cut off your balls, Gabriel, if you even look at that *puta*."

At the same time Helen ripped out, "Get a life!"

Both women glanced at each other with understanding. They turned up their lips in one of those "Men! The slimeballs!" expressions of contempt.

All the time they'd been talking, the Angel Bandit's gang aimed deadly weapons at Rafe and Helen. These were no nincompoop outlaws. These men were vicious and competent.

Rafe took a deep breath for patience and tried again. "Listen, Gabriel, (*Was it a coincidence that they both had angel names?*) you've got to see the resemblance between us."

The bandit peered closer. "*Sí,* you do have my mother's blue eyes. The people in our village called her a witch."

"Lucia Sanchez was a bitch," Elena commented snidely.

"*Sí, sí,* she was that. A witch and a bitch. But that ees not for you to say."

"See, see," Rafe interrupted, "my mother's maiden name was Sanchez, too. That proves you're my grandfather. So, give me back my gold."

"Thees gold ees mine, *Señor* Santiago. The only question here ees whether I let you live or die. I want to know why you have been impersonating me. My reputation ees suffering badly."

"How did you learn the secret of my corkscrewing trick?" Elena demanded of Helen. The hardened prostitute didn't look at all like Helen, except for her obviously dyed red hair. "And what ees thees gargling and forms?"

Helen started to laugh. At first, Rafe thought she was going off the deep end, but then he realized the ludicrousness of the situation. They'd come full circle, back to a scruffy group of nitwits and a comedy of misidentification and miscommunication.

"They are both *loco*," Gabriel said, backing away.

In the end, after an hour of arguing and exchanging insults, the Angel Bandit and his mistress, Elena, rode off into the hills with their band of desperadoes, generously leaving Rafe and Helen alive, for "the sake of family." *"Hasta la vista!"* they yelled as they departed.

Rafe and Helen were left wearing their camouflage BDUs, but nothing they'd gathered in their travels to the past remained with them. No guns. No horses. No gold.

Surprisingly, Rafe wasn't devastated by their loss. It was probably fated to end this way from the beginning. And he had Helen; that was the most important thing.

"Well, babe, are you ready to go home?"

She nodded.

"We're going to have to go down without jumpsuits," he said as they spread the parachutes out on the ground and inspected them for rips.

They could have waited another day, but neither of them wanted to put off the inevitable. Rafe donned the harness and repacked chute. Walking to the edge of the cliff, they took one last glimpse back, trying to assimilate all they'd seen and done.

"I'll never forget Ignacio and Sancho and Pablo," he said. "They were the catalysts into our adventure."

"And Sacramento City. Remember your gambling success and our unusual ante?"

He grinned. "After that, we rode to Marysville and met up with Henry. We'll have to look up his name in a history book when we get back. Maybe he became a famous writer."

Her lips curved up at that thought. "I will never, ever, forget the cave," she whispered.

His eyes held hers. That went without saying. Then he turned the mood. "But I taught you to dip. That's something. Do you think we'll go dancing a lot when we get back?"

She shrugged. "If you want. Will you go horseback riding?"

"NO! Do you want me to get bow-legged?" Chuckling, he put an arm around her shoulder and squeezed her close. "Most of all, there were Mary and Zeb and Hector."

Her lips parted on a sigh of agreement. "And the cabin. Our time alone at the cabin."

For one long second, they gazed at each other, remembering.

Finally, he swallowed hard. "It's time. Hop on, babe."

Helen jumped up, locking her legs around his waist, her arms around his neck. "I love you, Rafe," she said against his ear.

"I love you, too, babe," he said and stepped off the edge of the cliff.

Within seconds, their parachute bloomed out above them, like a celestial cloud.

Chapter Twenty-Four

Disoriented, Rafe lay perfectly still for several moments, eyes closed, trying to figure out what the hell had happened.

He'd been in an airplane preparing for a skydive when Prissy Prescott had ripped her harness and veered close to the exit. He'd lunged forward to rescue her—that's the kind of guy he was, a flaming hero—and they'd both fallen into space.

Holy Hell!

He was alive; so they must have landed all right.

But why did he feel so fuzzy? And what was that whirring noise in his head? Probably the headache he'd had earlier was blooming into the mother of all migraines.

He couldn't think anymore. Too many questions. Later.

But what about Prissy? Had she survived?

He forced his eyes open. Everything was black. *Oh, shit! See what happens to heroes? I'm blind. Please God, not that.*

He flailed about with his hands, and discovered he was covered with the parachute material. He wasn't blind, after all. He would have giggled if he was a giggling kind of guy.

Thank you, God!

He tossed the fabric off, over his shoulders. That's when he realized he was lying on top of his commanding officer, Prissy Prescott, who was spread-eagled, flat on her back on the ground.

She didn't look too happy.

But, whoa, something didn't seem right about this scenario. It was almost as if it had been played out before. Nagging, senseless images flickered into his mind—Mexican bandits, gold miners, a secluded cabin, Helen . . . Oh, my God! Helen and him, *naked,* doing The Deed. He'd like to freeze-frame that image, but his head throbbed when he tried to hold a thought. Maybe he'd suffered brain damage from lack of oxygen.

You're losin' it, buddy. First, blindness. Now, retardation. Slow down and think.

Helen moaned and put a hand to her forehead as if she, too, had a headache.

"Are you okay?" he asked, raising himself slightly on outstretched arms.

"No, I'm not okay, you imbecile. You are going to be court-martialed for this, soldier."

Huh? This is the second time she said that to me.

"Hey, I just saved your life," he said with affront.

I've said that to her before, I know I have.

"Saved my life? Captain, you caused me to fall out of that freakin' airplane," she raged irrationally, her face turning a decided shade of purple.

"Tsk, tsk. Watch your language, *Major.*"

"Oh . . . oh . . ." she stammered heatedly, no doubt searching for the right adjective to describe him. "You're going to be in the stockade for a year. I'm going to sue you for assault. I'm making it my personal mission to see that you pay for this debacle for the rest of your worthless life."

She absolutely, positively, has said those exact words to me before. In fact, this whole dialogue took place before, verbatim. Is there an echo in my head? Or am I going nuts?

Ignoring his uncomfortable thoughts, he asked, grinning down at her, "Is that all?" He'd just realized that a certain part of his body hadn't understood that the *uplifting* thrill of free-falling was over, and it was time for some *downlifting.*

Helen's mouth forced a delicious little "o" of surprise as she made the same discovery. Her windblown hair looked like she'd been pulled through a keyhole, backward, and freckles stood out like tobacco juice on her pale skin. But she was damned near irresistible, in Rafe's estimation. She frowned and darted a suspicious glare at him. Was she having the same feelings that something strange was going on?

He adjusted his hips against hers and whispered, "There's something I've always wanted to do, Helen. From the first time we met."

"So you said before."

"I did?" He leaned down, preparing to kiss her.

"I wouldn't, if I were you, Captain," a stern voice said behind him. "Unless you want to be seeing bars for the next year or two."

Rafe rolled off Helen and into a sitting position. He was staring at enough brass to fill the Pentagon, not to mention a dozen soldiers with weapons raised.

"Why aren't they Mexican bandits?" Helen murmured, sitting up beside him.

"What?"

He and Helen blinked their mutual confusion at each other.

"What are you talking about?" he asked.

She shook her head as if to clear it. "I don't know. It just popped into my head."

"Helen! Oh, thank God you're all right," one of the brass shouted. The ranks parted for the general—her father—who reached out a hand and drew her to her feet, hugging her in relief.

"Daddy," she cried, burying her face in his chest for a moment before she remembered herself. Within seconds, she pulled on her military mask. Until another high military mucky-muck showed up—this one younger, about forty. Helen ran into his arms and they embraced, like lost lovers. It must be the colonel . . . her fiancé.

A raging, totally-uncalled-for jealousy swept over Rafe as he observed the trio march off to a waiting helicopter.

The chopper must have made the whirring noise he'd heard in his head.

"What happened, honey?" he heard her boyfriend ask as he kissed her cheek.

How dare he kiss Helen? She's my wife. Rafe's mind came to a screeching halt. *Wife? Wife?* Yep, he was suffering brain damage.

"I don't know, Elliott. Everything happened so fast. It's starting to come back to me, but it's so . . . so confusing." She glanced back at Rafe over her shoulder then, and their eyes connected and held, questioningly.

Her father put an arm around her shoulder, drawing her away. "We'll talk later. The important thing is you survived." Helen and her fiancé climbed into the waiting chopper with some other officers, while General Prescott said a few words to another general standing by. They both gazed at Rafe, and their expressions were not congenial.

Almost instantly, the craft was airborne and he was left alone. Well, not quite alone. The other general and a squad of goons were looking at him as a likely target.

"Young man, you have a lot of explaining to do," the general said in a you-are-dogmeat kind of voice. He motioned for several military vehicles to come forward, and Rafe was hustled to his feet.

I am in deep shit. And I don't even know why.

That evening, after being interrogated in a conference room back at military headquarters, he was finally released. His memory was back, totally, and he was madder than a bull, threatening to sue every screwball officer on the base, and to go to the newspapers with the story of his treatment, or both.

For five hours, they'd harassed him with their questions.

"Why did you push Major Prescott out of the airplane?"

"Have you ever been treated for psychological disorders?"

"Do you understand the meaning of 'behavior unbecoming to an officer?' "

"Have you ever spied for a foreign government?"

On and on, the stupid questions had gone. Oh, they'd covered their asses in some regards. They'd had him examined by military doctors to make sure he was physically unharmed by the incident. And they'd fed him some gross Army food, and allowed him to use the toilet facilities. If they hadn't, he'd have sued them for that, too.

It was when he'd stripped in the base hospital for the checkup that he'd seen the items in his boot. The usual knife and the crucifix, but two more items, too—a wedding band and a piece of aged paper that said he and Helen Prescott had married on October 30, 1850.

Everything came back to him in a flash then. That was when his memory returned, and along with it, his anger over his treatment.

He'd demanded to see Helen, her father, probably the president of the United States, too. He'd turned into a raving maniac. No wonder they'd called in the psychiatrists then and begun asking him whether he'd ever suffered delusions and all that psycho mumbo jumbo.

He was dressed in his civilian clothes now, preparing to go home—Uncle Sam had decided to release him from this year's National Guard duty for service beyond the call and all that crap—when General Prescott walked into the room.

The general saluted. Rafe and the military types in the holding room returned the salute. "At ease," the general said, then asked the others to leave the room.

Stepping forward, Prissy's father walked toward him, extending a hand. Reluctantly, Rafe shook it.

"Captain Santiago, my daughter tells me I have a lot to thank you for."

What kind of bullshit is this now? More Army mind manipulation? "Where's Helen? I want to talk to her. Now!" Rafe paced the room, anxious to be off this looney-bin base.

Her father laid his hat on the table and ran a hand through his close-clipped gray hair. He was a good-looking man with Helen's eyes, Rafe noted idly. And her temper

. . . the general was clearly displeased by his churlish tone. "Major Prescott has gone home with her fiancé," he informed Rafe. "She's been relieved of duty for the time being . . . to recuperate."

"Recuperate? Is Helen hurt?" he asked.

The general's head shot up at his distress, and his cool demeanor slipped, but only for a second. "Helen is fine physically, but she was distraught when her memory started to come back. She made it clear to me . . . well, actually to a lot of people—" he smiled in remembrance—"that you were her rescuer. Actually, I think she called you her hero."

"Helen said that?" Rafe's spirits lifted for the first time that day.

"Yes, but, as I said, she was distraught."

"I want to see her."

"That's impossible. I just wanted to thank you for saving my daughter. She's left the base, and I think it would be best for everyone if you didn't try to contact her in the future. Just know that we are all thankful for a job well done. I'll be recommending you for a medal."

"I don't want any damned medal," he stormed, ignoring the general's stiffening body. "I want Helen, and I'm going to have her."

"No, Captain Santiago, you are not." On those words, the general left the room, and Rafe was free to go home.

Home? Where the hell is home now?

The next day, Rafe sat in his office, a desperate man.

The press was hounding him with rumors of his being some kind of Rambo military hero. A publisher had called to offer him a book deal. Larry King wanted him on CNN. His mother and his family clamored for attention. Clients were bugged that he didn't return their calls. Lorenzo was near tears with anxiety.

Worst of all, he'd been unable to contact Helen last night or all day today. And she hadn't called him, either. Her private residence, as well as her father's home in San Clemente, had unlisted numbers. Military headquarters wouldn't reveal private information. He'd asked his sister Inez and his brother Antonio to use their police contacts, but they hadn't come through for him yet.

"Are you sure she didn't call while I was in court?" he asked Lorenzo for the fiftieth time.

"No, sir. I gave you the list of all your calls."

"Stop shaking. I'm not going to bite your head off."

"Yes, sir." Lorenzo's teeth were chattering so loud he could barely speak.

I guess I did yell at him a little, he chastised himself. *I'm just so damned upset.*

Actually, his office was running better than he'd expected.

His secretary, Phyllis Manno, who had been out on maternity leave, had come back today to help them make some sense out of the shambles Lorenzo had made.

"A disaster . . . a disaster," she kept muttering as she waded through the piles of paperwork. She was only here for the day, so he'd have to hire a temp for the next month. Lorenzo had been told to contact the agency last week. But he couldn't think about that now.

Although Rafe's time travel—Lord, he couldn't believe he'd actually traveled in time—had taken about three months in the past, only one day had been lost in the present. That, on top of the two days he'd already spent at the military base before that, meant he'd only been away from the office for three days.

Incredible!

The phone rang, and he picked it up before Lorenzo or Phyllis could answer. "Hello." *Please, God, let it be Helen.*

"Rafe, is that you? Geez, didn't Lorenzo give you my message? I've been calling all day."

He let out a sigh of disappointment. It was his brother, Ramon.

"What now?"

"I'm in jail."

"Damn! Where?"

"Mexico. A little village in the hills. These local *policía* are nuts, Rafe. You gotta get me outta here."

"Okay, slow down. What did you do?"

"I didn't do nothin'. I was just helpin' the migrant workers unionize, and—"

"Damn it, Ramon, I warned you about this before. When will you ever—" He stopped talking when he heard a rough voice barking out orders, followed by Ramon arguing, then a cracking sound, like a punch or hard slap.

"Ramon . . . Ramon, are you there?" Rafe spoke into the phone, panicking now.

For a long time there was only silence, then Ramon's voice came on again, weaker this time. "I need your help. Real bad."

"Tell me where you are and what the charges are." Ramon spat out the information quickly.

"It's three o'clock. I'll hop the first plane I can get."

"Hurry."

"I will. Take it easy, Ramon. Don't say anything. Just tell them you'll talk when your lawyer gets there."

The phone went dead before he got a response.

Rafe glanced up to see Lorenzo and Phyllis staring at him with concern.

"Ramon again?" Phyllis asked.

He nodded. His youngest brother was always getting into trouble. Ramon's ideals clashed with harsh reality. Rafe should just let him sit in jail for a few weeks to teach him a lesson, but Mexican jails were no place for an education. They could spell death for an inexperienced boy of twenty.

"Call my mother and explain, will you, Phyllis?" he said, choking back his worry.

She nodded and took notes as he belted out the things he needed for his trip. His mind spun with all the details to be handled through his Mexican contacts. He had to withdraw a sizable amount of money from the bank for bribes. That was the way lawyering was still done in some parts of Mexico. Plane reservations. Passports. Ramon's birth certificate proving American citizenship.

Then he thought of Helen, and groaned.

"Lorenzo, I should be back here with Ramon by tomorrow night at the latest. It's important to me that you take all my messages. Keep changing the tapes on the answering machine, not like the last time when you forget and the tape ran out. Especially—are you listening carefully?—I'm waiting for a call from Helen Prescott. If she calls, you tell her I had to go to Mexico. Tell her to leave her number and I'll get back to her as soon as possible. Can you remember that?"

"*Sí.*"

He started to add, "And tell Helen I love her," but decided that was not a job he wanted Lorenzo to handle.

There were at least fifty phone calls to be returned as a result of his three-day absence—clients, friends, family— but he had no time now. He asked Phyllis to cancel his court docket for the next day.

The door opened abruptly, and his sister Inez rushed in, without knocking. "I heard about Ramon. I'm going with you."

"Absolutely not!"

He tried shoving her to the side, but she wouldn't budge. In fact, she shoved back. Inez was of medium height, with coal-black hair and dark, glittering eyes. A petite fireball.

"I've already made my reservation on the same flight as yours. So, listen up, brother. I'm going, whether you want me or not."

"It's too dangerous."

She told him something vulgar he could do to himself, and Phyllis and Lorenzo cringed in the background. Inhaling deeply, she wagged a forefinger at him. "I'm a cop. He's my brother, too. I'm going."

"You were supposed to be checking on Helen's telephone number for me," he accused. "How come everyone expects me to jump when they ask for a favor, but when I want something, it never gets done?"

"Ramon is more important than locating one of your bimbos."

"Watch your mouth, little sister. That's my wife you're talking about."

Everyone in the room gasped. "Well, well. You can tell me all about this remarkable woman on the plane, bro. Besides, my partner is getting the information for you. It'll be here when you get back."

With a shrug of surrender, he gave in, and Inez flashed him one of those million-dollar smiles of hers. The kind that had men banging at her door in herds. He wasn't impressed; he knew how much it had cost.

He had one last call to make. Going into his private office, he called Eduardo and gave him specific directions on how to reach a certain redwood tree and bring back a precious item he'd hidden there, wrapped in oilcloth. That done, he tried Antonio to see if he'd gotten Helen's number, but all he reached was his brother's answering machine.

Within an hour of Ramon's call, Rafe was out the door and headed for the airport with his nagging sister badgering him the whole way. Five hours later, he sat beside his brother in a drab Mexico prison cell. They were both under arrest.

Inez was holed up in the local hotel running up his American Express bill. He hoped a few of the bills would be for telephone calls to bail them out.

And all he could think was, *Helen, where are you? I miss you, babe.*

Helen had been drugged for two days.

She'd been frantic when her memory returned and she'd learned that Rafe was being detained for interrogation, as if he'd done something wrong. "I want Rafe. I want Rafe," she'd kept screaming. Only when her father had promised to get Rafe released had she sat down and stopped shrieking.

"That soldier was responsible for almost killing you,"

her father had seethed. "I'll see him court-martialed."

"Helen, your father's right," Elliott had added. "He didn't follow correct military procedure."

Both men had flinched when Helen told them what they could do with their "correct military procedure."

After setting her father and all the other brass straight, Helen had been examined by the base physician, who learned that she was pregnant. That had created a new flurry of arguments.

First, she'd had to explain to Elliott that, of course, it wasn't his child. They hadn't had sex in months. He'd been on assignment overseas much of the time.

After apologizing for her "infidelity," which was difficult to do without disclosing details about the time travel, Helen had called off the wedding. Elliott had been surprisingly good about the whole thing, wanting to know what he could do to help her. Elliott was a good man.

Her father hadn't been so understanding. Not about her breaking the engagement. Not about her involvement with "that rogue lawyer." Not about her pregnancy. Not about her plans to leave the military. In fact, nothing she'd said set well with him.

Helen hadn't cared. Rafe was the most important thing.

When Helen had begun raging at her father again, demanding to be taken to Rafe, her father had signaled the doctor and they'd given her a sedative, one that was safe for pregnant women. She hadn't awakened for two days.

Now, a week later, Helen was finding it impossible to make contact with Rafe. Oh, it wasn't that she couldn't locate him. She had his office number in L.A., which she'd called repeatedly. Most times, she just got Rafe's answering machine, but sometimes Lorenzo answered. "He is still in Mexico, Miss Prescott. That's all I know. Would you like to leave a message?"

Helen had a feeling that Lorenzo wasn't writing any of her messages down, or that they weren't being transmitted to Rafe. Why else wouldn't he call her?

* * *

"I know why he hasn't called you," her father told her three weeks later.

"You do?" Helen looked up hopefully. She'd been kneeling on the floor, sorting through boxes that had been sent to her father's house. They represented all the belongings she'd accumulated over twelve years in the military. She stood now, waiting.

"Honey, I don't want you hurt," he said softly. "Really, I just want you to put this man behind you. You're too good for him."

"Tell me," she said icily.

He handed her a newspaper clipping from a Mexican-American newspaper out of L.A. It was a photo of Rafe. A different Rafe than the one she knew. Dressed in a business suit. The power lawyer. He was boarding an airplane. A gorgeous, dark-haired woman stood next to him. He had his arm looped over her shoulder, protecting her from the cameras.

Her heart froze in that instant and she couldn't breathe. "What . . . what does the caption say?"

Her father cleared his throat. "It's dated the day after your skydiving accident. The article says that Rafael Santiago, well-known Hispanic attorney from Los Angeles, is off for a trip to Mexico. And it mentions that he is a hero from a recent military operation and is being considered for a medal."

The words didn't matter. It was the picture of the couple that tore at her heart.

He hadn't loved her, after all. To him, their lovemaking had been an interlude, a brief affair. Even the marriage had been a sham.

She handed the clipping back to her father. She almost hated him for bringing this news. With a control she'd cultivated over the years, she refused to give in to tears. Later, she would assimilate this betrayal, but not now. Not in front of her father.

"And that's not all, Helen."

She flinched. She wasn't sure she could take any more.

He showed her another clipping, this from a tabloid. A young man identified as Eduardo Santiago was holding a huge gold nugget that he claimed his brother had found in a redwood tree the day he'd been involved in a skydiving accident in the California mountains.

So, Rafe hid his precious nugget, after all. And he found time to go to Rich Bar to his gold, but no time for me.

Her father held out his arms to comfort her, but she ducked away. "Not now, Daddy. Maybe later I'll forgive you for this. But not now."

"Helen!" he called out as she walked stiffly from the room. "Where are you going?"

"To begin a new life for myself," she whispered, slipping the gold band off her finger.

In early December, three months from the time of the ill-fated skydiving accident, Helen was putting up Christmas decorations in the townhouse she'd purchased for herself outside Sacramento. Not exactly the little house with the white picket fence she'd always dreamed of, but she was happy with her new life. Well, not exactly happy, but content.

After her father's disclosures, Helen had cried for days on end in the seclusion of her apartment. Then the anger had set in. How dare Rafe do this to her? The jerk! Soon after that, she'd grown determined. She had a baby to consider, and Rafe wasn't good enough for her—just as her father had said.

She was painting again, taking it one day at a time, and moving on with her life. Oh, she wouldn't deny that Rafe was on her mind still, but she was getting better about the crying bouts.

"Where do you want this one?" Elliott asked, holding up an angel ornament near the tree. It was from a box of heirloom decorations handed down from her mother.

An angel! She started to tell Elliott to put it away, but stopped. "Anywhere. In the back. I never liked that one much."

"Oh." He looked at her with concern. Laying the box aside, he stepped up, taking her by the forearms. "Are you having second thoughts about the wedding, darling? New Year's Eve is almost a month away. There's still time to cancel if you're not sure."

She shook her head. "No, but I'm troubled that you're getting the short end of the stick. I care for you deeply, Elliott, but you know I'm not in love with you. I'm doing this for my own selfish reasons . . . for the baby." She put a palm protectively over her still-flat stomach.

"I love you enough for both of us, sweetheart, and I'm convinced you'll grow to love me, too." He hugged her warmly, and Helen almost wept with yearning for another man's arms. Why couldn't she feel the same passion for Elliott that she had for Rafe? Why? It just wasn't fair.

Elliott pulled away slightly and worried his bottom lip with his teeth. "Will you tell the father—Rafe—about the baby?"

"Someday. Not now."

He frowned.

"You disagree?"

"He has a right to know."

She nodded. "Even if I wanted to, I haven't had any luck locating him."

"You haven't tried in two months," he pointed out, then added, "Have you?"

"No, I haven't." She kissed him lightly on the lips, seeing his jealousy. "And I do love you, Elliott. Someday, I hope to be 'in love' with you, as well."

"C'mon, let's finish decorating this tree," he said in a choked-up voice, squeezing her to his side.

But all Helen could see was the blasted angel peeking out from the boughs at the back of the tree.

Three months after surviving an amazing skydiving accident, Rafael Santiago survived imprisonment in a Mexican jail. The latter had been the scarier event.

Twenty pounds thinner, bearded and long-haired, Rafe

walked out to the waiting car, driven by his sister Inez. Ramon hurried to catch up.

"I don't see why you're so mad at me," his brother said. "Everything turned out okay. We're free. Big deal!"

Rafe turned slowly, set his briefcase on the ground, and punched his youngest brother in the jaw. Ramon fell to the ground with a thud.

"That woman has driven you crazy," Ramon yelled after him.

"No, you and my family have driven me crazy," he raged, slipping behind the wheel and shoving Inez over to the passenger side. As they pulled away from the curb with Ramon barely making it into the back seat, he demanded, "Where's the telephone number?"

"Now? You want it now?" she asked incredulously.

"I want it right now," he gritted out.

She rummaged in her purse, where he noticed at least a dozen American Express receipts, and finally handed him a scrap of paper. "Here. She's living outside Sacramento now. Bought a townhouse."

Before she had a chance to say more, Rafe swerved the car over to a skidding halt at the side of the road. A phone booth stood there like a miraculous shrine. He jerked his phone card from his wallet, praying it would work.

"I told you, Inez. He's nuts. I been listening to him talk about this chick twenty-four hours a day for three whole months."

"Screw you, Ramon," Rafe said and jumped from the car.

Rafe's hands trembled as he dialed.

It stopped on the third ring. "Hello."

"Helen?" He felt as if his heart was lodged in his throat. "Is that you, babe?"

There was a gasp, followed by a throbbing silence.

Then he heard the dial tone.

At first, he just stared at the phone, blinking with confusion. Then he stomped back to the car and turned angrily on Inez. "What the hell is going on?"

Inez and Ramon exchanged significant looks. Apparently, they'd been talking while he was at the phone. "Tell me," he yelled, and Inez jumped.

"She's getting married."

Chapter Twenty-Five

Helen was not at all surprised to hear a pounding on her door at midnight. Nor was she surprised to look through the security peephole and see Rafael Santiago standing on her doorstep.

But she was shocked when he stepped inside—an angry, pacing animal who looked as if he'd as soon tear her limb from limb as crush her in his embrace. She ducked the arms that reached out for her. And he did, indeed, growl.

"Rafe, what happened to you?" She wasn't talking about his hurtful absence from her life for three long months. His hair reached down to the shoulders of a rumpled, dark business suit. A months' old beard covered his face. He'd lost a lot of weight.

Despite all that, he looked wonderful to her. He was still Rafe. And she knew in that instant that growing to love Elliott was going to take a long, long time. Because learning not to love Rafe was going to take a long, long time.

Quickly, she put the sofa between them, fearing her crumbling defenses. She had to be strong. Elliott had wanted to stay after Rafe's call, but she'd declined the offer. This was something she had to handle herself.

He just stared at her, alternately hungry and ferociously furious, and paced, taking in all the aspects of her new home. Touching objects. Watching her.

The room was dim and cozy from the single lit lamp. Too intimate a setting for what she had to say. She flicked on the Christmas tree and the blinking colored lights went into full action.

Rafe blinked as if disoriented. "For a second—" he swallowed hard—"for a second, the colored lights reminded me of Zeb's colored-bottle windows. When the sunlight came through. Like a stained-glass window."

He remembers the time travel, too.

Shaking his head as if to rid it of unwelcome thoughts, he turned his steady, questioning gaze on her. Hurt and longing lay naked in the depths of his burning eyes.

He's hurt? How dare he be hurt? I'm the one who was crushed here. She had to pull herself together. Glancing down, picking nervously at the nubby fabric on her sofa, she asked, "Have you been ill, Rafe? I had heard you were in Mexico. I assumed you were vacationing. Especially after reading about your gold nugget."

He made a snorting noise of disgust. "You assume too damn much." He threw the words at her, like stones, then added with a tired sigh, "You always did." He shot her a look of searing condemnation.

He's condemning me? "Let's cut to the chase here, Rafe. It's midnight. I'm tired. You look like you could use a blood transfusion. I haven't heard from you for three months. Where the hell have you been?"

"Prison."

She staggered under that unexpected answer, thankful for the support of the sofa.

"Why?"

"My brother, Ramon, screwed up, and landed us—" he waved a hand dismissively—"it doesn't matter why. You and I have more important things to discuss." Suddenly, all the anger left his face and he held his arms out for her. "Come here, Helen. I missed you so much."

A whimpering sound of distress escaped her lips before she pressed them firmly.

When he saw that she wasn't coming to him, an icy shield came over Rafe's vulnerable eyes, and he sank into a chair. "So, it's true. You really are going to marry Colonel Sanders."

She didn't bother to correct the name. "Yes, Elliott and

I are going to be married. On New Year's Eve.''

"Why?"

"Why? What kind of question is that?"

"Do you love him?"

She should have said yes, but the word lodged in her tight throat. "You have no right to interrogate me."

"I have every right."

Angry herself now, she went to the desk and pulled out two newspaper clippings. She threw them in his lap. "You lost the right with these."

He studied the two articles. At the picture of his brother holding up the gold nugget, Rafe cursed under his breath, "Stupid idiot," but at the picture of him with the woman, he just shook his head in confusion. "So?" he snapped.

"So? I'll tell you 'so.' You couldn't wait to get back and get your precious gold, could you? No concern for me, or my safety, or all the . . . all the love you claimed to have for me." Helen had to stop and inhale deeply. Her voice was unsteady with emotion. "And the other . . . Well, you two-timing bastard . . . you couldn't wait to find another piece of tail, could you? That's all I was to you. A little diversion."

"Are you done?" he seethed, standing and heading toward her with feral intent. "That woman you're calling a piece of tail is my sister Inez."

She gasped. "It is?"

"Yeah, babe, it is. And Inez would strangle you for the insult. However, I get first dibs."

He moved closer.

She eased herself around the sofa toward the hall, turning on a light behind her.

"You thought I wanted another woman, Prissy? How could you? I told you I would love you forever."

She put the back of her hand to her mouth to muffle a cry.

He moved several steps closer.

She moved several steps backward.

"What about the gold? It's always money with you,

Rafe. More important than anything. Even . . ."

"Even you? Is that what you think?"

She nodded. "Why didn't you call?" she asked weakly.

"I couldn't. Why didn't you wait for me?"

"Things changed."

"What things?"

"Rafe, please, don't make this harder than it already is. I was hurt, at first, by your betrayal, but—"

"Betrayal? You thought I'd betrayed you?"

He'd backed her against the wall with an arm braced on either side of her head. His face was lowering toward hers. So close. She yearned to lean up into the impending kiss. She couldn't. Instead she moaned.

"I love it when you moan for me," he said huskily, placing his lips a hairbreadth from hers. "Does the colonel make you moan, Prissy?"

"Yes."

"Liar." He breathed against her mouth and brushed his lips across hers. A whispery caress. Not really a kiss. *Hah!* He made a low hissing sound, and cupped her face with his hands, devouring her with his hard kisses.

Her determination shattered under the onslaught of the passion that always flared between them. Between each devouring kiss, he kept murmuring, "Helen." One word, that's all.

Her rubbery legs gave way and Rafe chuckled against her neck, putting his arms around her waist and holding her against his aroused body. The whole time, he traced a path of searing kissing from her lips to her ears and neck and back again.

Helen surrendered to Rafe's raw sensuality. She couldn't help herself. Only Rafe could make her forget everything. Soon they would be engaging in sex on the hall floor, two steps away from her studio on the one side and the nursery on the other.

The nursery!

Alarm bells went off in Helen's dizzy brain and clanged

a halting message to her overcharged senses. *The baby. I have to think about the baby.*

She tore her mouth out from under Rafe's kiss and shoved against his chest. "No!"

"No?" Rafe asked dully. He raked his fingers through his long hair with agitation. "Why?"

"Because . . . because we have to talk." She stepped to the side, putting some distance between them.

He said something really vulgar about talking and moved closer, trailing a forefinger over lips that felt swollen from his kisses, and throbbing for more.

"Because I'm going to marry another man." She swatted his finger away and edged farther along the wall, hitting a door jamb.

"No, you are not. You're already married to me."

"Yes, I am, Rafe. And our marriage isn't legal."

"You love me. It doesn't matter what you say. Your body just told me that."

"It was just . . ." Her words died off as she saw his eyes fix on something over her shoulder. Too late, she realized that her studio was visible through the doorway, cast in shadows from the hallway light and a full moon shining through the many windows.

"You're painting again?" he asked with surprise, and, before she could stop him, he stepped into the room and switched on the overhead lights. A dozen paintings in various stages of completion stood on easels and stacked around the room. All of them depicted scenes of their travels together, most of them set in Angel Valley with the cabin in the background.

She groaned.

"They're good, Helen," he said, smiling at her with pride as he examined each of them in detail.

She leaned against the wall, not sure how much more she could take.

Rafe chuckled when he saw her depiction of Ben and Bertha. He grew serious at the image of him and Zeb standing in the stream prospecting for gold, highlighted by the magnificent mountains. He cast her a sidelong glance of awareness when he came to one painting—him standing in the snow, wearing only trousers and suspenders, his arms raised joyously to the skies. "Can I have this one?" he requested softly.

"No!" she cried, too quickly. It was her favorite painting.

His one brow rose inquiringly.

"It's not done yet," she prevaricated.

"Then this one?" He pointed to one of a man and woman standing before a primitive cabin. All of her paintings had a blurry, impressionistic character. The figures would be recognizable only to her and Rafe.

"All right."

He tucked the painting under one arm and walked toward her, taking her hand. "I'm beat, Helen. I haven't slept in two days. I came here directly from the airport. My mother's probably catatonic with worry. I'll come back tomorrow. We'll settle things then." He was leading her toward the front door, an arm looped intimately over her shoulder, her head resting on his chest.

NO! She couldn't see him again. Another emotional encounter like this would devastate her. Might even hurt the baby.

She halted near the doorway and faced him, resolved to end their relationship in the only way possible.

"Rafe, I'm pregnant."

He jerked back as if she'd punched him in the stomach. His face whitened with horror. "A baby?"

She nodded.

"You and Elliott are having a baby?" he lashed out. "Oh, God, what a fool I've been. Here I thought this was all about love and caring, but, no, it all boils down to this obsession you have with kids."

Helen reeled under Rafe's misconception. She hadn't meant to imply that the baby's father was Elliott. She'd been about to explain. "You bastard!"

"You bitch! How could you?"

"Me? Me?" she sputtered.

"You are always so almighty condescending about my greed for gold. Well, take a good look at yourself sometime. Oh, you had a great time pulling my strings, didn't you? Making me feel guilty because I didn't ooze fatherhood dreams. Damn it, how could you jump into another man's bed? So soon?" Rafe's mouth was tight and grim now, his eyes slicing her like blue daggers.

"You misunderstand—"

"Misunderstand? What did I misunderstand? Are you or are you not pregnant?"

"I am but—"

"Were you raped?"

"No, but—"

"Do you want this baby?"

"With all my heart."

He lifted his hands in a hopeless gesture of defeat, then masked his expression with insolent pride. "Well, that's that, then. Thank God it's not mine, because I sure as hell don't want any brats. And certainly not yours."

She flinched. "Rafe, let me explain—"

He extended a hand to stop her approach. "No. I shouldn't have come. It's over, like you wanted. We were doomed from the beginning." Opening the door, he stumbled out, then turned and said in a soft whisper of regret, "Be happy, babe."

A week later, Helen sat miserable and distraught by the telephone. Rafe hadn't come back again, and he refused to accept her calls.

His angry words about not wanting children had hurt Helen the most. Because she knew they were true. They proved more than anything that her marriage to Elliott would be the best thing for her and the baby. Still, she had to tell Rafe the truth. But if she told him now, he'd feel obligated to marry her, and she loved him too much to ruin his life that way.

Christmas carols played on the radio. Her home was decorated brightly for the holidays. The season of cheer. Hah! She did nothing but cry. Something had to be done soon, or as Elliott and her father had warned, the baby's health would suffer.

The doorbell rang, and Helen jumped. She did that a lot lately. Not that she thought Rafe would return, but she subconsciously hoped.

She opened the door, and her eyes widened with astonishment. A Hispanic woman of about fifty with graying dark hair stood gazing up at her. She wore a Los Angeles Lakers sweatshirt, polyester slacks, and orthopedic shoes.

Rafe's mother.

Oh, God!

"Can I come in? I am Rafael's mother. My daughter Luisa is parking the car. She will be here shortly."

Helen watched dumbly as Mrs. Santiago passed into the hallway, then entered the living room. Luisa soon came scurrying after her, making a swift introduction and apologizing for their arrival without calling first.

After bringing them some coffee and Christmas cookies on a tray that she set on the coffee table, and after fifteen minutes of uncomfortable small talk about the weather and her home, which Mrs. Santiago liked very much, Helen said to the younger woman, "You're LuLu, aren't you? Rafe said you have five children. Where are they now?"

"Out in the car," Luisa said. "Mama's gonna take them to the mall this afternoon while I go to my classes at the community college. I'm studying to be a nurse's aide."

"In the car? But it's cold out there. Bring them in."

So, Helen soon had five children crowded around her kitchen table eating cookies and milk, and Rafe's mother and sister sitting in her living room chit-chatting about trivialities.

Mrs. Santiago soon got down to business, though. "Why are you making my Rafael so unhappy?"

"Me?" she squeaked out.

"*Sí.* He won't eat. He won't answer his telephone. He punched Ramon."

368

"Mrs. Santiago, I don't think you understand. I'm engaged to marry another man on—"

"Engaged? How can that be?" She and her daughter exchanged puzzled frowns. When Mrs. Santiago turned back to her, she said, "But Rafael said you were married to him."

Helen cradled her face in her two hands.

"Did you marry him?" Luisa asked. "Rafael never lies. I do not understand."

"Yes, we were married, but it wasn't legal."

Mrs. Santiago tilted her head. "Rafael said you were married by a priest."

"Well, a padre did marry us, but—"

"A padre is a priest, and that makes it legal in God's eyes." She took both of Helen's hands in hers as if welcoming her to the family. "*Mi hija* . . . my daughter."

Helen closed her eyes. How could she explain an unexplainable situation?

Meanwhile the five children, ranging in age from two to eight, were leapfrogging down her hallways. Their screeching laughter filled the house. Helen could barely think. She began to understand Rafe's feeling of being crushed by his family.

After an hour of arguing fruitlessly over her involvement, or lack of involvement, with Rafe, Mrs. Santiago and her brood left. At the doorway, Rafe's mother patted her hand. "Don't you be worrying none. Rafael loves you. You love him."

"But I don't love—"

"Shhh. A mother knows."

Helen closed the door and went to bed for the rest of the day.

The next day, Helen opened her door to the persistent ringing of the doorbell, and her mouth dropped to the floor. She had another visitor. Rather, two visitors. Leaning against either doorjamb were two Hispanic men. One looked like Antonio Banderas with a long ponytail, wearing a leather jacket and dark sunglasses. The other, younger one, wore faded, very tight blue jeans with a pristine white T-shirt, sporting the logo, "Firemen Have Big Hoses."

Oh, God! Antonio and Eduardo Santiago.

"We came for the Christmas cookies," Tony said, strutting in without an invitation. "Mama says you bake a mean cookie."

"And I like milk," Eddie said, wiggling his eyebrows at her.

They both took after Rafe. Tall, dark, and exceedingly, dangerously handsome.

"So, when are you going to put Rafe out of his misery?" Antonio asked later, as he sprawled in an easy chair, his long legs stretched out and crossed at the ankles. He did resemble Antonio Banderas. Women must go nuts over him. "He's driving everyone loco. He won't even dance with Carmen, and he always dances with Carmen at Christmas."

"Dance?" She blinked with bafflement. *I'm in Bedlam, and my roommates are two studmuffins.*

"Yeah, didn't he tell you? Rafe's usually so blinkin' serious, but—"

"Rafe? Serious? Are you kidding me? The guy who jokes while falling out of an airplane? The guy who claims he can have tongue hard-ons? The guy who teases till he drops? The guy who can ride a horse with a blister on his butt and laugh? The guy who thinks he's the happy gunslinger? The guy who—"

"A tongue hard-on?" Tony and Eddie exclaimed at the same time. Then they both burst out laughing.

Eddie was standing near her Christmas tree, playing with the ornaments. Wasn't he the firefighter, the one Rafe said had once posed as a centerfold? Yep, he was the one, she decided, looking at his tight buns.

When they finally stopped laughing, Tony commented, "Damn, I haven't laughed so hard since Carmen talked all of us into being the Village People in a talent show."

"Yeah, but you got to be a sexy construction worker. I had to be an Indian," Eddie grumbled.

Helen wondered which one Rafe had been, but before she could ask, Tony continued talking to his brother, "And how 'bout the time Carmen talked Rafe into being her tap dance partner at the church Christmas recital?" At Helen's raised brows, he explained, "He was sixteen, and Carmen was about five. Her partner got the measles, and Rafe got recruited. Every Christmas since then, Carmen makes him tap dance with her at the church recital. It's a tradition."

Yep, I'm in Bedlam. And visions of Rafe tap dancing are pushing me over the edge.

"That Carmen could talk a dog into doing the hula. Hell, I remember the time she taught me to moon walk."

"You can moon walk?" Tony said. "I didn't know that. Show me."

"NO!" Helen cried, and they both looked at her. Her nerves were shot. *Good Lord! First tap dancing. Then moon walking. Next, it would be dipping.* More softly, she said, "Did you guys come here for some particular reason? Other than my cookies?"

"Yes. You've got to get back together with Rafe. He's really hurting," Tony said.

"Man, I've never seen him care so much for a woman, and it's obvious you've got the hots for him, too," Eddie added.

"I do not," she protested.

"You are so crude, Eddie," Tony criticized his brother. "Hots? Geez, didn't I teach you any finesse?"

"Hah! You wouldn't know finesse if it hit you in that ugly face."

"Ugly? You're just jealous because women mistake me for Antonio Banderas. Don't you think I look like Antonio Banderas?" The latter question was addressed to Helen.

"A little," she said, and a headache the size of Tony's ego bloomed behind her eyeballs.

Eventually, she walked them to the door, getting more harangues on why she should be with Rafe. She heard Eddie comment to Tony as they walked to their car, "What the hell's a tongue hard-on?"

"Damned if I know. But you can be sure I'm gonna ask our big brother. He's been holding out on us."

"Oh, brother!" Helen mumbled, and went to bed for the day.

The next morning she went Christmas shopping, early, just in case any more of Rafe's family showed up. She didn't get home until late afternoon. As she parked her car, she glanced up and groaned. Four Hispanic women were sitting on her doorstep, chattering to beat the band. She wondered how any of them could get a word in edgewise. Three children were racing across the lawn and stopped abruptly in front of her. "Where's the cookies, *Tía* Helen?" one of them asked.

Tía? Doesn't that mean ¿aunt? Oh, my goodness!

She assumed these three kids belonged to Juanita, Rafe's oldest sister. There were only eight nieces and nephews total.

This time she served wine and Christmas cookies to the adults—she would have to bake another batch—and cookies and diet soda to the kids—she was out of milk. She listened to Rafe's four sisters tell her in a chaotic hodgepodge of Spanish and English why she should knock some sense into their brother and take him back.

"Take him back? I never had him," she said, but no one paid any attention to her. They were too busy spouting their own opinions.

"*Carámba!* You should have seen him when I picked him up at the prison," Inez related, rolling her eyes. She was the L.A. policewoman, the person in the newspaper clipping with Rafe. "He didn't ask about Mama, or his office, or anything. All he wanted to know was, 'Where's the telephone number?' He had everyone in the world searching for your phone number and address. I wouldn't be surprised if he called the FBI. Of course, that was before they locked him up. Then they wouldn't let him talk to anybody."

"Well, I think Rafe is ill," Jacinta interrupted. Jacinta,

Helen remembered, was a nurse and had just started graduate school.

"Ill? Rafe? What do you mean?"

Everyone turned at the anxiety in Helen's voice, and they smiled knowingly. She flushed and tried to backtrack. "I mean, he was thin when I saw him, but not ill." *He didn't kiss like a man on his death bed, that's for sure.*

"Oh, not that kind of ill," Jacinta said, waving a hand in the air. "He's heartsick. No, no, don't look at me like that. People can make themselves physically ill when their hearts are broken. It's a scientific fact."

Oh, Lord!

"Well, I don't care about that. I want to know how I can plan the church Christmas party if Rafe won't dance with me." Carmen—the youngest, the dancer, Rafe's favorite—tossed her mane of curly black hair over a shoulder and cast an accusing eye at Helen, as if Rafe's refusal to dance was the biggest tragedy in the world.

Helen had to smile. Carmen was a spoiled brat, and adorable. "Listen, I've enjoyed talking to all of you, but there's been a big misunderstanding. I'm being married in three weeks, and—" she inhaled for courage—"and I'm pregnant."

A loud silence followed her words.

"Please understand, I've always wanted children, and Rafe doesn't want any children, and it was always a big problem between us," she rambled. "So, I guess you understand why—"

"Rafe doesn't know what he wants," Juanita scoffed.

"I think he would have twenty children with you if you would take him back," Inez added. "He would even love another man's child. Yes, he would."

"Beg him and he will do anything for you," Carmen advised.

Juanita took her time before answering, "Having children isn't everything, you know, but—"

Her three sisters groaned.

"Juanita, you think you know everything," Carmen

whined. "Don't give us a lecture."

"—but this is something you and Rafe can work out if you love each other," Jacinta went on, ignoring her sisters. "I'm sure after you are married, Rafe will come to his senses."

Helen gritted her teeth. "That will never happen. Rafe had a vasectomy." *I don't believe I just said that to four virtual strangers. I need an aspirin. I need sleep. I need sanity.*

Everyone stared at her as if she'd just said Rafe had grown two heads.

"Oh, my God! Mama will have a heart attack," Juanita said, making the sign of the cross over her chest.

"You can't tell her," Helen insisted.

It was as if she was invisible. They talked right over her.

"Vasectomies can be reversed," Jacinta said, and her sisters asked her to explain. On and on the four women went until Helen began to think Rafe had the right idea about his family being a big pain in the behind.

When they finally left, helping her clean up the empty wine bottles and offering to send her some of their own Christmas goodies to replenish her stock, Helen sank into bed with a cup of herbal tea.

She refused to answer the doorbell the next day. There was only one more family member left, and Helen didn't need to peek through the peephole to know that her visitor—a younger, more sensitive version of Rafe—was Ramon. His eyes were a luminous blue, tearful with misery.

"Helen? Are you in there? I can hear your Christmas music. Your car is parked out front. Please, I have to talk to you."

Helen pressed her forehead against the door. She really, really couldn't handle any more stress.

"It's all my fault that you and Rafe broke up. Please, you gotta take him back. He won't even talk to me. He punched me. He's making Mama cry."

He waited for her response. When she didn't answer or

open the door, he continued, "Man, he loves you. Doesn't that count for something?"

Again, the poignant silence. Helen bit her lip to stifle a sob.

"I had to listen to him talk about you for three months in that damn jail. Sometimes I thought I'd puke if I heard the name Helen again. He's got it real bad. Don't you even care?"

Tears were streaming down Helen's face.

Finally, she heard Ramon walk away, muttering, "Women!"

That day, Helen collapsed in bed, not even trying to find the blessed numbness of sleep. She loved Rafe's family. Despite all his griping about his clinging mother and siblings, when they saw him in pain, they all united to help him. That was what families were all about. She hoped he would see that someday.

Helen would love to be enfolded in the warmth of his family, but there were two people she had to consider here, two people she loved very much. Rafe and her baby.

No matter what everyone said, Rafe did not want children. It would make him miserable in the end to be saddled with a baby.

And what kind of life would it be for a child with a father who had not wanted him or her?

Helen placed her hand over her stomach, and her baby moved for the first time, as if reassuring her that she was making the right decision.

But it was so hard.

Chapter Twenty-Six

"I'm a gold-plated fool."

Rafe made the declaration aloud on December fifteenth, more than a week after his confrontation with Helen.

"I'm a thick-headed, gold-plated fool," he immediately amended, because only a thick-headed jackass would take so long to come to his senses.

Hmmm. A gold-plated fool. That gives me an idea.

He headed for the shower with a determined step, ready to set his life to order.

Hallelujah! a voice in his head said.

Why had it taken him until now to realize that he and Helen had been given a special gift in their time-travel experience? A celestial nudge had sent them to the past to discover the meaning of love. What he needed now was a celestial kick in the ass for his stupidity in almost losing it.

Hallelujah! the voice said again.

For days, he'd walked around like a zombie, feeling sorry for himself, barely living. He'd gone to work, carried out his legal practice like a robot, and come home to an empty apartment, refusing to talk to anyone—even his mother who kept leaving messages on his answering machine. All her little sermons harped on the same topic; "Rafa-el San-ti-ago, you are going to hell for having that vistorectomy operation. You better go to confession. Do you hear me, Rafael?"

Rafe couldn't dwell on the explanation he'd have to give his mother now. He looked at the wedding band on his finger. He had a mission, and its name was Helen.

Damn, he loved her, and she loved him. He knew that, no matter what she said. So what did anything else matter?

He didn't even care about her being pregnant with another man's child. Well, actually, he cared, but he could live with it. The baby would be Helen's child, and he would love him, or her, like his own.

The important thing was that he was miserable without Helen. He couldn't face a life without her. He was sure—at least, he hoped—she was miserable, too.

How could he have been so dumb?

He called her right away, before he lost his nerve, but got no answer. The same thing occurred throughout the day, and the next morning. He even drove over, but there was no response to his repeated knocks on the door.

A neighbor came out and informed him that Helen had moved out temporarily, and her mail was being forwarded. Rafe's eyes narrowed with resolve. She couldn't hide from him. He'd set Antonio and Inez to work sniffing out her whereabouts. In the meantime, the U.S. mail would forward any messages. Or packages, if he paid the forwarding postage in advance.

Rafe grinned. He had some serious shopping to do.

Helen was staying at her father's home in San Clemente until the wedding. Her father and Elliott had been right to talk her into moving. The visits from Rafe's family had distressed her terribly, turned her into a virtual basket case. She needed some calm before she started her new life, both as a wife and mother.

Then the packages started to arrive.

The first day, she got a small parcel, forwarded from her address. It had no return address. Opening it hesitantly, she found a Rolex box. A Post-It was attached with only one word, "Remember."

Rafe.

But why would he send her a Rolex watch? She flipped

the lid, but didn't find a watch. Inside was a black felt-tipped marker.

And she remembered Rafe saying that one of the first things he would buy on their return to the future was a marker. To connect the "dots" across her body. A sexual fantasy.

She tried to be angry, but she had to smile at his creativity. No romantic roses or boxes of candy from this rogue. He knew just how to shake her heart.

The next day, she got a letter. It contained a copy of a receipt from the House of Transcendentalism. Oh, my heavens! Rafe had signed up for meditation classes.

That made her smile, too, because she knew how wretched he would be.

The third day, another parcel came. This one contained a book. *A book?* Rafe had sent her a coffee-table edition of Alberto Vargas paintings. A Post-It note stuck out of one page on which he'd written, "See what I mean?" Helen blushed when she saw the gorgeous, redheaded nude pinup Rafe had circled.

Is that really the way he sees me? My goodness!

The fourth day, a florist delivered a houseplant, with no card attached. It was an *Anthurium,* better known as "little boy plant." Her father walked by just as the delivery boy left, and he remarked, with a shiver of distaste, "Who sent you the plant? God, I've always hated those things—looks like a bunch of hard red tongues."

Indeed!

The fifth day, she thought Rafe had given up. No such luck. It was just that the package was so small and had been buried under a pile of mail. When she peeled back the expensive foil paper, she saw Tiffany imprinted on the box.

Tiffany? What could Rafe possibly afford at Tiffany's?

She soon found out. Inside was a silverplated corkscrew, and a notecard. "You still owe me." The only signature was a smiley face.

The rascal!

The following day, a mailer came with a cassette tape. Helen didn't want to play it. In fact, she set it aside while she prepared dinner and wrapped Christmas presents and went out to a movie with Elliott. But she thought about it. Too much. And, in the end, she played it while she sat in bed that night. When she pressed the button on the small cassette player, Rafe's voice came out, deep and masculine. She trembled as she listened.

"Helen, I love you," he said. "Please don't turn this off. Just listen to me. We love each other, you can't deny that. Your being pregnant isn't a problem for me . . . anymore. Really. I'll love your baby like it's my own. But I don't want to tell you all this stuff on a tape. I want to tell you in person. In the meantime—don't laugh—I have a song to sing for you. Your favorite." Then he launched into an off-key version of "Wind Beneath My Wings."

Helen cried over that gift. A lot.

She stayed in her room the next day when the mailman came, but her father handed her a stack of correspondence when she came down stairs, including one envelope with no return address. She opened it tentatively, and began to weep openly.

"Honey, what is it?" her father asked, but Helen couldn't tell him. How could she explain what a wonderful, hopeless dolt Rafe was? And why he was so wrong for her.

The letter contained a medical form. A reverse vasectomy had been performed on Rafe yesterday. His Post-It this time said, "Well, I did it. I went under the knife today. *Again!* The doctor doesn't guarantee the procedure will work. No promises. I love you. Rafe." Then there was a P.S., "Ouch!"

"Helen," her father said, puzzled by her anguish over Rafe. He'd been trying to talk to her for weeks. "Are you sure this marriage to Elliott is the right thing?"

She gaped at him in astonishment.

"Maybe . . . well, maybe, if you love Rafe," he practically choked on his name, ". . . well, maybe that's who you should be with. I know I've pushed you sometimes in the past, sweetie, but, really, just follow your heart."

She couldn't believe her ears. Her father actually encouraging her to consider Rafe?

"Thank you, Daddy, for caring. But, really, for many reasons, marrying Elliott is the best thing."

Helen's wedding was going to take place in three days, and Rafe was frantic. None of his plans had worked out. Even when he'd located Helen and called on the phone, her father had informed him in a surprisingly gentle voice that Helen wouldn't talk to him. "Perhaps," General Prescott advised, "it's time for you to give up."

"Would you?" Rafe asked.

"Hell, no!"

"Same here, then. Hell, no!"

He thought he heard General Prescott laugh and mutter, "Good luck" before he hung up, but he was probably mistaken.

Okay, three more days. Time to call in some markers with his family. And make some big plans.

It was a gamble, but he was betting that he would win.

He had to.

Helen was standing at the altar of a small chapel outside Sacramento three days later, wearing her mother's ivory satin wedding gown and a simple veil on her head. Elliott was at her side, handsome in his dress blues, along with her father, a few witnesses, and friends.

Everyone had tried to talk her out of the wedding, urging a postponement because of her distraught state, but she was determined to put some closure on her past life with Rafe.

It was the only way.

The minister was halfway through the ceremony when he got to the part, "Does anyone know just cause why this marriage should not take place?"

"I do," a husky voice boomed from the back of the church.

Her heart dropped to her toes. *Oh, no! He wouldn't.*

She turned.

He would.

"Holy Hell!" Elliott said at her side. She had to agree when she turned.

The minister frowned his disapproval at Elliott's swearing in church, then cried out. "You can't bring horses in here."

"Are those real guns?" Elliott's eight-year-old nephew, Darren, exclaimed. "Wow! This wedding is cool!"

"Oh, my God! I think that's Antonio Banderas back there. Hurry! Get the camera," Helen's cousin Mary Kay gushed.

"He looks like a Mexican desperado," her Aunt Irene said, almost swooning with shock.

"Damned if he didn't do it," her father said admiringly.

She shot her father an inquiring, suspicious glare.

Rafe did look like a desperado. And so did his brothers, Antonio and Eduardo and Ramon, all dressed in nineteenth-century clothing, with ammunition belts crossed over their chests, revolvers in their hip holsters, and sexy, wide-brimmed hats tilted cockily over their faces. And, unbelievably, all riding horses up the aisle of the church.

"Young man, what's the meaning of this?" the minister shouted. "What reason do you have for disrupting this marriage?"

"She's my wife."

"Wh-what?" the minister stammered, and everyone in the church gasped.

Her father gazed at Rafe oddly. "Is this true?"

"Absolutely." Rafe held out a piece of parchment for her father to peruse. His thumb was probably planted over the date.

Her father turned on her then. "Helen?"

"Oh, Daddy, it's not legal. Yes, we were married, but—"

She had no opportunity to finish, because Rafe leaned down and swooped her up into the saddle in front of him, imprisoning her with his arms.

"You can't do this." Elliott rushed forward.

Antonio aimed a revolver at Elliott, muttering, "I could lose my job for this, Rafe. You owe me big time."

Elliott backed away. "Helen, I'll call the police. Don't worry."

"No, don't call the police," she told him in a panic. "I'll straighten this out." Then, she raised pleading eyes to her father. "Daddy?"

He nodded at her silent supplication. "We won't do anything until we hear from you."

Rafe ordered Tony, Eddie, and Ramon to stay behind and hold everyone off until they escaped. Then his horse galloped out of the church and down the steps. Some spectators were standing outside—wedding groupies. One of them said, "I've heard of some weird marriages before, but this one takes the cake!"

Helen kicked and squirmed and demanded that Rafe put her down. "Let me go," she shrieked.

"Not on your life, babe." He laughed, then groaned as she elbowed him in the ribs.

He rode the horse only to the end of the church parking lot, where he quickly dismounted with her. To her outrage, he tied her up with rope and gagged her before shoving her in the back of a Jeep Cherokee. She was going to kill him for this.

She heard Rafe talk to Tony then. Apparently, Eddie and Ramon were still in the church. Rafe told Tony to return the horses and go reassure General Prescott.

Just before he left, she heard Tony say, "Well, big brother, the oars are in the water, and you're headed upstream. Let's see if you sink or float."

Rafe said something about being an Olympic-class swimmer.

Then they were off.

Rafe drove for more than an hour, carrying on a continuous one-way conversation with her.

"Don't be mad, Helen. This was the only way."

Imgfhh!

"I love you, honey. We'll work everything out."

Yrrflift!

"My mother says I'll go to hell if I don't marry you, and I know you wouldn't want that."

Flckye!

And most outrageous, "Do you have to pee? I hear pregnant women have to pee a lot. I'll stop along the highway if you want."

Hhmmflfhbgt!

"I checked out some history books last week. Did you know that there were two outlaws named Pablo and Sancho who supposedly rode with Joaquin Murietta?"

Brrgdll!

"And Rich Bar was just like we saw it. And, honey, there really was an Indiana Girl and Yank and Curtis Bancroft. I'll show you some of the books later. After our honeymoon."

Arrrggghhh!

Finally they stopped, and Rafe helped her out, releasing her ropes and gag with apologies for having had to restrain her.

"That's a really nice gown, sweetheart. Your mother's? Will you be wearing it for our wedding?"

She sliced him a scorching glare as she stood on wobbly legs and looked around at the secluded cabin. Then she punched him in the stomach.

"Ooomph! I deserved that, honey. Do you want to do that again?"

She did.

"Ooomph! Feel better now?"

She did.

While he carried in numerous boxes of supplies, she stormed toward the cabin. "Planning on staying for a while?" she snarled.

"Yep," he said and made a big point of showing her the car keys, which he then tossed in a wide arc into the thick forest.

"Are you totally insane?" she raged, beating at his chest. "We'll never find them now."

"I know. But, not to worry! Tony knows where we are. This cabin belongs to his boss. He'll pick us up in three days."

"Three days!" she sputtered.

"Uh huh," he said, toting in the last of the boxes. "Consider it our honeymoon." Then he winked. *He winked.* "It will take me at least three days to teach you something I learned in that Mexican prison."

"I don't want to know."

"There was this guy in the next cell who knew a whole lot of good stuff, and, boy, did he like to talk."

"I don't want to know." Helen folded her arms over her chest. Somewhere along the way she'd lost her veil. Her hair was half in an upsweep and half straggling down her face. She saw at least three runs in her stockings. And she *did* have to pee. She was not in a good mood.

"C'mon, Helen. Don'tcha want to know what he taught me?" Rafe prodded with a big grin. "It's the art of . . ." He paused dramatically.

"What?"

"Corkscrewing."

Helen refused to talk to him all day.

While she was in the shower, he hid her clothes. All of them. Now she had only a blanket to keep her warm. And him. She declined his latter offer with a silent, contemptuous lift of her chin.

She ate the tortilla he made for their dinner, but wouldn't react to his ongoing monologue on love. And it was really good.

He threatened to sing to her, "Wind Beneath My Wings," and she put her hands over her ears. He liked that because it made her blanket slip.

So, he decided to tell her exactly how corkscrewing was done, in explicit detail. She didn't say a word, but he could tell she was interested.

After that, she declined his offer of a glass of wine. So he chugged down a beer, and she sipped at a lemonade.

It was time for his "Hail Mary pass." His long shot. His last chance. Going to the closet, he took out several burlap sacks and placed them on the table in the center of the room. Then he started to take off his clothes.

Helen was sitting in a wingback chair near the fireplace. She pretended she didn't notice when he took off his boots.

"God, my feet hurt. How do cowboys wear these high-heeled boots all the time without getting fallen arches?"

No response.

"I don't suppose you'd massage my feet."

She scowled.

"Maybe later." He chuckled.

Next he took off his shirt and saw her eyes widen. *Good.* He stretched and rubbed his face with a palm. "Do you think I should shave, hon?"

She cast him a double scowl.

Good.

He undid the buckle on his belt, and she stood abruptly. The blanket slipped again.

Good.

Loosening the top button of his jeans, he said, "Where do you want to live, Helen? After we get married again, I mean. My practice is in L.A., but if you want to live in Sacramento or anywhere else, let me know." He pulled the zipper down and her eyes followed its path.

Good.

"I'll even live in a little house with a white picket fence if you want. Buy a lawn mower. And a barbecue grill. We can even get a birdhouse. Yeah, a birdhouse would be great." Rafe gave himself a mental pat on the back. He was on a roll.

Her mouth formed a little "o" of incredulity. He wasn't sure if she was reacting to his words or his pants sliding to the floor. He wasn't wearing any underwear. That was a good, last-minute touch in his opinion.

Her eyes about bugged out.

Good.

He walked over to the table, nude, and opened one of

the sacks. "As for the baby, well, I don't care if it's a boy or a girl, but if it's a girl, I want to call her Angel."

She made a choking sound.

Good.

"If it's a boy, you'll probably want to call him Zeb or—"

"No son of mine is going to be named Zebediah," she said, then bit her lip, realizing she'd inadvertently spoken to him.

Good. "Well, we could always call him our little desperado. Hmmm. I like that. Desperado Santiago."

"Get real!"

"What's wrong with that? If people can name their kids Storm or Rock or Ridge, why not Desperado?"

She cut him a Prissy scowl. He was making headway.

"Or . . ." Rafe turned serious, finding it really difficult to make this concession, "you can call him Elliott if you want."

Tears filled her eyes. "Oh, Rafe."

Hey, "Oh, Rafe," was good. Real good. Later, they would discuss visiting arrangements for Elliott, but he wasn't feeling *that* magnanimous today.

"Put some clothes on," she snapped.

"Why? Do I make you nervous?"

"No."

"I need to have my clothes off to show you something."

"I've already seen it."

"Not this way, babe," he laughed. Then he dipped a hand into the sack and came out with a heaping scoop of gold dust. With a dramatic gesture, he sprinkled it over himself.

"Are you crazy?"

"Crazy for you." Scoop after scoop, he sprinkled over his body, even his hair.

"That must be worth a mint. Stop it. What's the point?"

He threw a handful of the gold dust toward her, and it landed on her hair and shoulders. He stopped momentarily, dazzled by the beauty of her fiery hair and creamy shoulders covered with the sparkling dust.

He forced himself to speak above a croak. "The point is, sweetheart, that money, or BMWs, or fancy vacations, or bachelorhood—none of those things—mean anything without you. Someone famous once said that a life lived just to satisfy yourself never satisfies anyone. It was probably St. Augustine; he's been the plague of my life lately." He threw out his hands helplessly. "So, to hell with the gold." He gazed at her with open longing, then smiled. "How about opening that blanket and letting me share the gold with you?"

Her lips twitched with a grin. "You're impossible."

"Do it," he coaxed in a raspy voice.

She raised her chin, resisting.

"I love you."

"Would you really live in a house with a white picket fence?" she asked, taking a step—a tiny step—toward him.

"Babe, I'd live in an igloo with a white picket fence and penguins for pets if that would make you happy." He clenched his fists to keep from grabbing her. *Don't push her. Take it easy. Let her make the move.*

"And the baby," she said shakily. "You could love another man's child?" She widened her eyes to keep the tears from overflowing and moved a step closer.

"I would love *your* child, Helen."

One tear slipped out and crept slowly down her cheek. He wanted to reach out and catch it on his finger, or mouth, but he was afraid he'd scare her off.

"You would hate my body when it grew big and ugly with another man's child."

"Sweetheart, I would love your body, no matter what."

"I'm already changing," she confessed, her teary eyes trying to communicate something important to him.

He frowned, unable to get the hidden message. "Show me," he said huskily.

She dropped the blanket, and her eyes closed with her innate modesty. Someday, he'd like to cure her of that self-consciousness, but he was too busy now trying to keep his hands off Helen's enticing body.

"You're beautiful," he whispered, "and the changes are so small only a lover . . . a man who loves you . . . could see them."

She opened her eyes, questioning.

"Your breasts are fuller. God, I want to hold them." Instead, he sprinkled gold dust over them. The flakes settled on the upper mounds, the puffy aureoles and the taut nipples.

She moaned and looked down. "I'm beautiful," she sighed with surprise.

"That's what I always said, babe." Then he sprinkled gold dust over her stomach. The only evidence of her pregnancy was a slight swelling. Some of the flakes settled on her hips and in her belly button. Even on her red curls, turning them into golden flames.

Every atom in his body yearned for her. He wanted an end to their problems, a healing of the pain, and, more than anything, he wanted their bodies united in lovemaking to seal the future.

She giggled. "This is the most outrageous thing you've ever done."

"No. No, it's not, babe. The most outrageous thing I've ever done is almost lose you."

She whimpered. "I'm not sure."

"I'll make you sure. Don't be afraid, honey. Please." He was stalking her magnificent body, taking handful after handful of gold dust from the sacks and covering her with it. Her tattoo got extra attention. A gold butterfly. He liked it.

Then she was scooping out the gold dust, too, tossing it at him. It was a playful game, but somber, each circling the other with smoldering, tentative eyes. The feel of the dust sweeping his body was like a sensuous caress.

Finally, he could stand no more. He held his arms out for her. "Let me make love to you, Helen. Let me make love to my wife. Because that's what you are to me. Regardless of the legalities. Before God, we're man and wife."

"That's what your mother said."

"Oh, no! Now you're going to quote my mother." He was still holding his arms open for her. Moving up to her, he put his hands on her forearms, trying to pull her into his embrace. She had gold dust on her lips. He wondered how gold dust would taste and lowered his head.

She pressed her hands against his shoulders. "Wait."

He groaned. "I've been waiting so long."

"I have to tell you something."

The stiffness of her body told him it was something important. He tilted his head, waiting.

"You said you would love another man's child . . ."

"Yes?"

She licked her lips nervously. "And if it were your child?" Her eyes probed to his very soul.

He blinked at her, not understanding. When he did, finally, conflicting emotions churned within him.

My baby!

Then, *She was going to give my baby to another man!*

His hesitation wounded her. He saw that in her shocked eyes before she spun away.

He fought a silent battle in his head. A part of him wanted to forgive and forget. Another wanted to yell at her for her deceit. He chose the former, and yanked her back against his chest, burying his face in her neck. Then, wrapping one arm around her waist from behind, he laid the palm of the other hand against her tummy. "I love you, *and* my child."

He swung her into the circle of his arms then and carried her to the bed. Laying her on the comforter, he kissed her gently, then kissed her savagely. She gave herself freely to his kisses, her surrender a silent affirmation of the life she chose to share with him.

Their first coming together was tender and slow. His grainy endearments. Her breathless whispers. When he entered her silky sheath on a hissing inhale, they both gazed at each other, stunned by the power of their joining. Love seemed to surround them in every touch and stroke and mindless, soul-searing kiss. They rose and rose to each higher crescendo, then splintered together to the skies.

Only later, after their first fierce coming together, when they lay sated and murmuring softly, did Helen remember Rafe's promise.

"What promise?" he asked, nuzzling her breast.

"A corkscrewing lesson."

He laughed and rolled over on his back, taking her on top of him. "The trick is in the twist of the hips, and the Kegels, of course."

"Of course," she said, teasing, as she eased herself on top of him. Very slowly. "Like this?" she asked sweetly.

Rafe made a gurgling sound of assent.

Then she noticed something and flicked a piece of gold dust off his eyelash. "You rat! This isn't gold dust. It's dime-store glitter."

He grinned and put his hands on her hips, holding her in place.

She punched his chest, which was heaving with amusement, at her expense. "You didn't throw away your gold, did you?"

"Now, honey, I may be a fool, but I'm not a gold-plated fool."

With a lot of convincing, she agreed.

Epilogue

In a place far, far away, St. Augustine turned to the Celestial Majesty, who was leaning back on His throne, legs propped on a cloud.

"We did good, didn't we?" the former reprobate beamed.

"Yep!" God said, but not in a boastful way. Boasting was not God-like. Still, He added, with a little chuckle, "Another one for our side!"

St. Augustine started to give his boss a high-five, but stopped himself (the grace of humility still came hard for him). Instead, he handed God a clipboard, and He made a huge check mark with a golden marker. God had a thing about clipboards.

"Who's next?" God said, rubbing his hands with anticipation. "Has anyone seen that fourth Wiseman? The one who got lost on the way to Bethlehem?"

SANDRA HILL

HOT & HEAVY

As Lieutenant Ian MacLean prepares for his special ops mission in Northern Iraq, he sees no reason the insertion should not go down as planned. He leads a team of highly trained Navy SEALs, the toughest, buffest fighting men in the world. As a 34-year-old bachelor he has nothing to lose. He has the brains, guts, and brawn to out-maneuver, out-gun and just plain run circles around any enemy.

Madrene Olgadottir comes from a time a thousand years before Ian was born, and she has no idea she's landed in the future. After giving him a tongue lashing that makes a drill sergeant sound like a kindergarten teacher, she lets him know she has her own special way of dealing with over-confident males…

SANDRA HILL

A TALE OF

TWO VIKINGS

Toste and Vagn Ivarsson are identical Viking twins. They came squalling into this world together, rode their first horses at the age of seven, their first maids during their thirteenth summer, and rode off on longships as untried fourteen-year-old warriors. And now they are about to face Valhalla together. Or maybe something even more tragic: being separated. For even the most virile Viking must eventually leave his best buddy behind and do battle with that most fearsome of all opponents—the love of his life.

TRULY, MADLY VIKING

SANDRA HILL

His boat off-course, somehow thrust into the twenty-first century, Jorund Ericsson has cause to question his surroundings. And though the befuddled Viking thinks he's found heaven when he spies the lovely doctor, she simply thinks him crazy. Jorund realizes what has truly driven him to the edge is her enticing figure.

He sails into Maggie's life, claiming to be a Viking from the tenth century, which makes her smile. But it isn't laughter that causes her stomach to flutter when the Hercules look-alike claims her lips. And soon he has her believing his story, though questioning her own sanity. Then the psychologist realizes there is another possibility: Neither of them is truly mad—but both are truly, madly in love.

___52387-6 $6.99 US/$8.99 CAN

Dorchester Publishing Co., Inc.
P.O. Box 6640
Wayne, PA 19087-8640

MISSING MAGIC
KAREN WHIDDON

Heir to the kingdom of Rune, Cenrick sees it as his responsibility to seek out the truth. There are disturbing reports of a great evil befalling his people. The solution lies in the world of mortals, in a quest that may mean his very soul—and his heart.

Lately, Dee Bishop's life is going to hell in a handbasket. But that hardly necessitates surrender. And when she is told of a conspiracy that threatens a reality she's never fathomed, she swears to set things right. Looking into this dark stranger's eyes, she can imagine nothing worse than a life without magic.

Metal and mysticism, technology or sorcery: two worlds in conflict. The dangers are greater than they'd ever imagined. But so are the rewards.

A Connecticut Fashionista in King Arthur's Court

MARIANNE MANCUSI

Once upon a time, there lived a fashion editor named Kat, who certainly was not the typical damsel in distress. But when a gypsy curse sent her back in time to the days of King Arthur, she found she'd need every ounce of her 21st-century wits to navigate the legend. After all, just surviving without changing history or scuffing your Manolos takes some doing!

Luckily, she's got her very own knight in shining armor, Lancelot du Lac, on her side…even though she's not quite sure she wants him there. After all, shouldn't he be off romancing Queen Guenevere or something? Will Kat manage to stay out of trouble long enough to get back to her world? And what will Lancelot's forbidden love mean for the kingdom of Camelot?

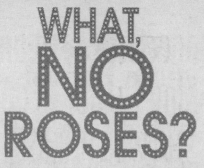